STA

Please return / renew by date shown.
You can renew it at:
norlink.norfolk
or by telephone
Please have your library card & PIN ready

D0715556

25 FEB 2015

John Sweeney is a reporter for BBC *Panorama* who became a YouTube sensation when he lost his temper with a senior member of the Church of Scientology. Before joining the BBC in 2001, Sweeney worked for twelve years at the *Observer*, where he covered wars and revolutions and unrest in more than sixty countries, from Algeria, Bosnia and Chechnya to Zimbabwe.

Over the course of his career John has won two Royal Television Society prizes, an Emmy, a Sony Gold award, the *What the Papers Say* Journalist of the Year Prize, an Amnesty International prize and the Paul Foot Award.

He is the author of eight books, including most recently *North Korea Undercover – Inside The World's Most Secret State*. His hobby is falling off his bike on the way back from the pub.

Elephant Moon is his first novel.

ALSO BY JOHN SWEENEY
NON-FICTION

North Korea Undercover – Inside The World's Most Secret State
The Church of Fear – Inside The Weird World of Scientology
Big Daddy – Lukashenka, The Tyrant of Belarus
Wayne Rooney: Boots of Gold
Purple Homicide
Trading With The Enemy: Britain's Arming of Iraq
The Life and Evil Times of Nicolae Ceausescu

ELEPHANT MOON

John Sweeney

SILVERTAIL BOOKS • *London*

First published in Great Britain in 2012 by Silvertail Books Ltd
This edition published in 2014 by Silvertail Books
www.silvertailbooks.com
Copyright © John Sweeney 2012
1
The right of John Sweeney to be identified as the author
of this work has been asserted by him in accordance
with the Copyright, Design and Patents Act 1988
A catalogue record of this book is available from the British Library
All rights reserved. No part of this publication may be
reproduced, transmitted, or stored in a retrieval system,
in any form or by any means, without permission
in writing from Silvertail Books or the copyright holder
Typeset in Ehrhardt Monotype by Joanna Macgregor
Printed in the UK by CPI Group (UK) Ltd, Croydon, CR0 4YY
ISBN 978-1-909269-10-1

To the refugees who fled Burma in 1942 and the elephant men and their elephants, who did their best to save them.

The elephant is nature's great masterpiece...the only harmless great thing.
John Donne

Man and the higher animals have the same senses, intuitions, and sensations, similar passions, affections, and emotions, even the more complex ones such as jealousy, suspicion, emulation, gratitude, and magnanimity; they practise deceit and are revengeful.
Charles Darwin

PROLOGUE

1 May 1940, Rangoon

MISTER Stripes the tiger, stuffed, mounted and plunging through the club wall, mocked Grace with his eye of green glass. Overhead, a ceiling fan shuffled the heat.

'The Japanese can't fly. They have a defect in the tube,' Colonel Handscombe surveyed the others around the bridge table, holding on to his secret knowledge for as long as possible, 'of the inner ear.'

Looking away from her fan of cards out through the windows of the Pegu Club Grace glimpsed a gardener watering a green chequer-board of lawn, exquisitely cross-mown and surrounded by rose bushes, blooms, a herbaceous border. It could have been Lymington, were it not for a vulture by the cess-pit pecking out the guts of a white-bellied rat.

'One heart.'

'Also, they are myopic.'

'Two hearts.'

'And their balance is defective.'

'Three clubs,' said Grace, not rising to the bait.

'So why worry about them? Eh?'

'My dentist is Japanese,' said Miss Furroughs, timid, pink-cheeked, a little white mouse of a rebel.

Grace felt imprisoned by the walls of the room. Outside the club was an unknown city which she ached to explore, to see and hear all she could, ponies trotting by, the Rangoon Electric Trams, wheels biting rail, monkeys yelping and honking, the whole exquisitely alien world.

Back home, the blossom would be out. It was 1 May 1940, and England was fighting for its very life. But here, in this backwater of the Empire, there was no war, only starch and protocol and sticky heat. What was so dreary to Grace was the pettiness of British life in Burma. Was it one of the Russians – Chekhov? Tolstoy? – who'd remarked 'nothing worse than a provincial celebrity'. Whichever Ivan said that had probably met someone very much like the colonel: handsome-ish, tall, in his mid-forties, with a fine jaw, a sweep of grey hair, the pitiless grey eyes of a lounge predator and mediocre to the core. Grace had gathered he did something 'hush-hush' at Government House in Rangoon. Whatever it was, she found it hard to imagine a circumstance in which he could further the war effort. Yet the others appeared to think he was a catch.

More fool them.

Miss Furroughs sipped her sherry and said, 'Three no trumps.' Damn. That meant Colonel Handscombe would be dummy, so they'd be in for yet more monologues on the Japanese menace or eugenics or the price of fish.

'Your dentist is almost certainly spying for Nippon,' said the colonel. The cards fell on the table, a light patter of applause.

'I speak as I find, Colonel,' said Miss Furroughs.

'You know what they're all talking about in the bazaar now, don't you? When the Japanese will strike.'

'I have no idea about the military side of things, but Mr Magaguchi is a gentleman and quite the best dentist I have ever had. Nothing wrong with his balance,' said the headmistress, relishing her rebellion.

'The Japs can't fly,' repeated the colonel, his logic as circular as the sweep of the fan.

'But they can fix teeth,' the headmistress snapped back, so fast that Grace found herself gurgling out loud. She tried to hide her fit of giggles by faking a cough, but she somehow choked. Helpless, acrid-throated, she mouthed 'water'. The colonel called out: 'Boy!'

No one stirred.

'Boy!' Handscombe barked, louder this time.

An Indian servant, snow-white hair, his hands a-tremor, appeared bearing a mahogany tray and poured water from a cut-glass decanter into a tumbler filled almost to the rim with ice, decorated with a sprig of mint and a dwarf strawberry. Grace drank deeply, nodded her thanks, recovered her poise and only then did the servant bow and depart.

'I rather think that gentleman hasn't been a boy for a while,' she said.

'Boy,' repeated the colonel.

Pig, thought Grace.

What about Miss Furroughs? She had trapped Grace into this dreadful game, so she was not beyond deviousness. A stern old-fashioned mouse, Grace was damn sure the way the headmistress was running the school was of no real use to the half-caste orphan girls, the human stain of Empire, who were supposed to live and flourish there. On the other hand, every now and then the eyes of the old lady would twinkle and she would say something fierce and sparky. Tiny, barely five feet, she seemed unafraid to squeak her mind. Grace sensed Miss Furroughs' *tendresse* for Colonel Handscombe, yet the headmistress was more than happy to indicate when she did not agree with him, and Grace could not but admire her for that.

The colonel began to bang on about why the three big clubs in Rangoon – the Pegu, the Gymkhana and the Boat – had to 'maintain standards'. He sluiced back his gin and Indian tonic, dug out an ebony case from his white linen jacket, offered cigarettes around, lit up a Lucky Strike and puffed out a cirrus of smoke.

'This pressure for us to give everything on a plate to the Burmese, let alone the Indians and the Chinese, has to be resisted. We can't wear our shoes in their pagodas. Fine. They can't wear their native costumes in our clubs. They don't want to come to our clubs anyway. But if they do, all we ask is for them to wear a suit and tie if they're a chap or a proper dress if they're a girl. What could be fairer than that, eh?'

Play dribbled on for a few more hands until Grace sensed that someone had entered the room behind her back.

'Mrs Peckham!' The colonel clapped his hands, a sea lion at the zoo reacting to the arrival of a bucket of fresh mackerel. Miss Furroughs's face turned vinegar-sour. The newcomer, a brunette in her mid-thirties, significantly younger than the headmistress, was the original fourth hand for bridge. Grace shot up, offering to withdraw.

'No, no, no, I couldn't possibly deprive you of the pleasure, Miss–' returned Mrs Peckham, her voice silken, eyes weighing up Grace coolly, the youngest woman in the Pegu lounge by a decade or more.

'Collins,' said Grace. 'Miss Collins. But I really must give way. I have enjoyed myself enormously.'

'You are most welcome to stay, Miss Collins,' said Miss Furroughs. It sounded like an order.

'Yes, do stay,' said the fourth, whose name Grace had forgotten. She added: 'Mrs Peckham's *husband* is in the Royal Navy and he's at sea.'

Colonel Handscombe blew his nose into his handkerchief while Mrs Peckham smiled woodenly, a medieval saint pierced by a red-hot poker.

'I am most awfully sorry,' said Grace, breaking the spell of unpleasantness, 'but my father always used to say that too much pleasure is bad for the digestion. So, do take my seat Mrs Peckham, goodbye and thank you very much once again.'

Backing out of the bridge room, she nodded at Mister Stripes up on the wall, whose glass eye stared on, unperturbed. She turned and picked up speed, flew down the stairs and skipped across the lawn, out of the club and onto the street, bent-double, cackling with glee. The morning mists had gone so there was still an hour or two left to walk around before the suffocating heat of the middle of the day made any exertion horrible, and Grace set out to indulge herself in the sights, sounds and smells within Rangoon from which the walls of the club sought to protect her.

In tight white bodices and longyis, two Burmese women floated towards Grace, clouds painted on porcelain. Drifting towards the great river, she passed high walls hiding lush gardens, and was hailed by bicycle rickshaws tingling their bells. No thank you.

A rich Chinese businessman piloting a brand new Mercedes with fusspot care slowed to offer her a lift. No thank you. A Sikh taxi-driver driving an antique Ford crawled beside her, imploring her.

'Oh, leave me alone.' Shaking her head, Grace walked on. From their entreaties, her decision to walk in the heat of the day appeared eccentric, no, peculiar, for a European lady. She didn't give a tuppenny damn.

A screeching cut the air. Rounding the corner came an ox-cart, the racket made by wheels spinning in wooden axles without benefit of oil, carrying a grand piano half-cloaked by a grey blanket, thick bandy mahogany legs peeping out from under the cloth. The driver, hidden by a straw hat, brushed a whip against the left-hand side of the lead ox and the cart turned down a lane towards a white-picketed house underneath a flame tree.

One hundred yards on, to the west, the stupa of the great Shwedagon temple rose up above the city, sunlight, blisteringly bright, bouncing off its golden spire, a cathedral to an alien God.

A pony, pitifully thin, plodded by, pulling a sweeper's cart, trawling a host of flies and a great stink past branches sagging with blossom, air-bursts of jasmine and magnolia. For Grace, that moment fixed the smell of British Rangoon in her mind's nose: perfumed blooms, stinking dung. Pye-dogs yapped at her from behind a ten-foot-high fortress made of cactus and bamboo. Startled, a little jumpy, she hurried on.

Grace heard what she thought was the sound of a ship's engine, a mechanical rhythm, rising and falling. She saw statues of half-lion, half-men, red-eyed and gilded, tongues lolling, guarding a shrine housing a Buddha, his mouth adorned with ruby-red lipstick, spirals of incense rising in the air, the prayer wheels whizzing away. The sound Grace had supposed came from a ship's engine was really a dozen or so of the faithful, humming a chant.

An ancient Hpoongyi – a monk, shaven-headed, clothed in saffron – leaned against a stick and bowed with ornate politeness, but a younger monk hurried by, staring at her and, as he passed, spat on the ground by her sandals. Grace was astonished and hurt.

The old monk called after the pupil in Burmese querulously and, in perfect English, said 'Good morning, Miss.' He bowed again: 'I am sorry for the rudeness of my pupil. He is young and foolish.'

'Why is he so angry with me?' Grace said. 'Because I am a female?'

'No. Because you are British. They think the British are like a house-guest who has overstayed his welcome.'

'And what do you think, sir?' she asked.

'That one should not be rude to a guest.' The old monk smiled, and bowed deeply for a third time, and shuffled slowly off.

Beyond the Buddhist temple were wooden godowns, warehouses for rice, tea and rubber, a mosque for the Mussulmans, mostly from the Indian minority, a teak sawmill buzzing furiously, a Chinese temple, and shacks where you could buy a ball of rice and a cup of sweet green tea for a few annas, a fraction of the ten rupees for high tea at the Strand Hotel. A few yards back from the river's edge lay a chaos of stalls, where hawkers sold monkeys gnawing at the bars of their cages, fishwives offered stinking cuts of river dolphin, mudfish and the huge-headed trevally. By sacks of saffron, turmeric and ironwood, traders stood chatting, smoking cheroots.

The meat ponged to high heaven, dripped blood and was covered by a fizzing blanket of flies. What kind of animal carcass, Grace wondered, had these strips of flesh come from? Snake? Monkey? Elephant?

Close to a stall noisy with squawking chickens, tethered upside down, a Burmese woman was selling a curl of amber imprisoning a tiny bee. The woman said something incomprehensible and a young Burman, passing by, stopped to translate. Earnest, fresh-faced, slight, he sported a careworn black suit in the western style, wire-frame glasses and was holding a book in his hairless right hand. His hair was slicked back and oiled. The Burman translated the amber seller's price into beautifully enunciated but slightly old-fashioned, Victorian English. It was impossibly high – two month's wages at the school – and Grace both wanted it very much and knew that she could not afford it.

The Burman addressed Grace solemnly: 'She says: "My Honoured Lady, you must buy the bee. It is fifty million years old, as old and beautiful as you are young and beautiful."' Blushing, Grace handed over a fistful of rupees to the amber seller, knowing that she could now barely afford to eat for months. The woman fastened the bee around her neck with a leather string. School dinners, grim as they were, would ensure she would not starve.

Turning to thank her translator, she wondered whether he might be able to help her answer some of the questions that teemed in her mind. He bowed slightly as Grace reached out, accidentally touching him, stroking his face. Startled, he dropped his book. Grace, quicker than him, bent to pick it up, turned it over to examine the front cover. On it, a swastika.

'*Mein Kampf?*'

'Heil Hitler,' he replied.

'Are you enjoying it?'

'Yes. It is the future of the world.'

'Have you tried *Pride and Prejudice?* Same themes, but not half as tiresome. Heil bloody Hitler, indeed.'

The Burman scuttled off pretty damn fast, almost knocking over a butcher carrying a roasted pig on a long skewer. The amber seller eyed Grace coldly, as if to say: 'Why fall out over a book?'

Alarmed that she might have stumbled on a Nazi Fifth Column, but also wary that she might be making too much of a trivial incident, Grace paid a visit to Government House, a fairy-tale castle in pink and white stone, the citadel of British rule. People called it St Pancras. An Indian servant in turban and silk cummerbund showed her to a waiting room, decorated by a pencil-thin lizard clamped to the wall above two black-and-white photographs, one of a fat Beefeater, the other of a thin king, Edward VIII, the last but one. To this corner of the Empire, news ambled on flat feet.

After an ocean of time, an extraordinarily tall Englishman entered, sporting a white shirt and knee-length white shorts, making him looking even more ridiculous than nature had intended. At the sight of the lone female, the half-baby-giraffe, half-man gulped, announced in a gravelly voice that his name was Mr Peach, and gulped again. He had a floppily cut head of very dark hair and, if you squinted in poor light, might just pass as handsome-ish. But he behaved as though she might bite him at any second, fear mixed with hopeless longing. In her driest, most matter-of-fact tone, she explained meeting the Burman in the market down by the river.

'*Mein Kampf*, you say?'

'Yes.'

'Oh dear. Would you care for a cup of tea?'

Even as the outlying marches of the British Empire were being threatened by the Axis Powers, some things would not change.

She would rather run away, but she was damned thirsty and a tiny bit intrigued. She nodded in a bored sort of way. He rang a bell and when a servant appeared ordered tea for two and some cake, if they had any, if it would be no trouble.

'Can you describe this chap?' asked Mr Peach.

'A Burmese man, around average height, wearing a black suit, very worn, and a white shirt. Glasses. Oiled hair.' He jotted down the details in a small navy blue notebook.

'Any distinguishing features?'

'None.'

'Oh.' He stared at her and gulped again and then gazed out of the window.

'I'm terribly sorry. It's not a very good description.'

'Name?'

'I didn't catch his name.'

'No. Your name, Miss. Your address and place of work, if any.'

While he wrote her details down, he coiled and uncoiled his fabulously long legs and she suspected that he was trying very hard not to glance at the top of her blouse, and failing. He finished writing. Another pause, painfully long. Grace was about to get up to leave when the tall man spoke.

'He's almost certainly a member of the Black Dragon Society. These chaps are Burmese nationalists who side with Nazi Germany and the Japs. They're not proper Nazis. I don't think they'd know the difference between the SS and the Boy Scouts. They just want to see the back of us. Many of them have sworn an oath: "I will free Burma heart and soul without flinching from my duty even if my bones are crushed and my skin flayed."'

'Fanatics?'

'I'm afraid so. Usually the hard core dress in local costume, sarongs and the like. They smoke cheroots, not Lucky Strikes, their women are encouraged to boycott western clothes. In their hair they wear scarlet dak blossoms or stars of jasmine.'

'That sounds beautiful.'

'It is.'

The tea arrived but no cake. 'Shall I be mother? We'll log your chap. He stands out in that he was wearing a western suit. One of them pretending to be one of us. That makes him interesting. He might pop up somewhere else.'

'I just thought I should tell someone.'

'Yes.'

The pencil-lizard skittered a foot or two across the wall, and then froze.

'Mr Peach, may I ask you a question?'

'Yes, of course.'

'Why is there a "western dress only" rule in the clubs?'

'Back in Queen Victoria's day, when we conquered Burma and chased away their king, our chaps sauntered around holy temples in boots. A great insult. As time has gone on, the Burmese have insisted that if we visit their temples we must take our shoes off. Tit-for-tat, they can't come to our temples – the clubs, the Pegu and the Gymkhana and the Boat Club – without wearing western suits and frocks. Burmese nationalists have taken to wearing their native dress as a political statement. It's war by dressing up. Some say the rule against native dress is a not very subtle way of saying "No Burmese welcome".'

'What do you think, Mr Peach?'

'Personally?'

'Yes.'

'It's a not very subtle way of saying "No Burmese welcome".'

'May I ask another question?'

'Yes.'

'Can the Japanese fly?'

'They don't have wings.'

'No, I mean I was told that the Japanese have a defect in their inner ear, which means they can't fly planes.'

'Balls. Who told you that?'

'A gentleman in the Pegu Club.'

'A moron.'

'A Colonel Handscombe.'

'Ah.'

'Ah?'

'Colonel Handscombe.' He looked away, then turned his gaze back to her and said flatly: 'He's my boss.'

Mr Peach looked so sheepish, she couldn't stop herself bursting out laughing.

Another long pause. 'The Japanese *can* fly. They bombed Nanking, killing thousands. They've pretty much bombed every nationalist-held aerodrome in China.' He paused. 'As it happens, I'm trying to learn Japanese at the moment.'

'Why ?'

'To pass the time.' A reply so transparently nonsensical that she could not help being a little intrigued.

'No one learns Japanese to pass the time, Mr Peach.'

He said something in a soft lilt, strange tones rising and falling, and then translated:

'One fallen flower returning to the branch?
'Oh no! '
'A pale butterfly.'

Grace asked, 'Poetry?'

'They call it a haiku.'

'That's beautiful.'

'Colonel Handscombe is, well, he–'

'Is a crashing bore on the subject of the Japanese.'

'Yes,' Mr Peach said. 'But a bore is not necessarily wrong.' In his earnest deliberation on the matter, she perceived a deep sense of fair play, both exasperating and quietly admirable. She raised one eyebrow a fraction, signalling mild disagreement.

'He – we – should be worried about the current lot in power in Tokyo. They're pretty ghastly, frankly, and are in bed with Hitler. But the people, the culture are quite different. And the language has a rare beauty, an economy of expression. What did you make of the Pegu?' he asked.

'The liveliest thing in it is the tiger.'

'The tiger's stuffed.'

'Yes, Mr Peach, I noticed.'

The heavy melancholy lifted, his solemn, older-than-his-years expression changed, his face breaking into a tentative grin. He made to add something, then hesitated.

'Go on, Mr Peach.'

'I'd rather you didn't tell anyone this, Miss Collins, and in particular Colonel Handscombe.'

'No, I absolutely won't.'

'But I rather think these Burmese chaps might have a point. Not being on the same side as the Nazis and the Japanese military, obviously, but if you're the Burmese, you might not be very impressed with the British Empire.'

The fan wafted the cloying air this way and that. Grace waited for an explanation.

'In 1886,' Mr Peach said, 'we deposed King Thibaw, forcing him into exile. They have not forgotten that they used to be the masters of their own land.'

Fishing out his notebook, he flicked through a few pages: 'Listen to King Thibaw's lament to his late father, King Mindon: "*The golden-footed lord of the white elephant, master of a thousand gold umbrellas, owner of the Royal peacocks, lord of the sea and of the world, whose face was like the sun, always smoked the Esoof cheroot while meditating on his treatment of the bull-faced, earth-swallowing English*".'

The notebook snapped shut.

'The poor king was reduced to advertising cheroots. These are a proud people. The Burmese didn't ask to be ruled by us. We invaded, deposed their king. They resent our presence here very much. But it's worse than that. I'm sorry- I hope I am not boring you?'

'Not at all, Mr Peach. I was driven to distraction in the Pegu Club. You are not boring me in the slightest. Do carry on.'

People, men in particular, told her that she was an excellent listener. There was something, they said, about her beauty – the freshness of it, the lack of artifice – that brought forth confidences. Or was it just that men liked staring at her and had to fill in the awkward silences somehow?

'We say we are on a civilising mission, but there are about eight thousand Europeans in Rangoon, the lords and ladies of all Burma. With a tiny number of exceptions, the Burmese have been excluded from all our clubs, gymkhanas, social events. There is a pretence of power being handed over to the Burmese politicians, but everything that matters is still handled by the Governor, from Government House, from here. I have a friend, a professor, an Englishman, who speaks the most beautiful classical Burmese, knows more about this country than any Englishman alive, married to a Burmese lady of real charm and accomplishment, who studied at the Sorbonne. And because he is married to a Burmese who chooses to wear national dress, my professor friend and his wife are not welcome in all the grand European clubs in Rangoon. To be accepted, they have to wear *our* clothes in *their* capital. A deliberate humiliation. The point is, Miss Collins, the Burmese hate us and they want us out of their country. That's why the chap you met was carrying *Mein Kampf.* To the Burmese, my enemy's enemy is my friend.'

'Oh dear.'

'They don't realise that my enemy's enemy can also be my enemy.'

He gulped again, a sign that he had something more on his mind.

'Please do carry on, Mr Peach.'

'What I have to say is in confidence.'

'Trust me.'

'Can I?'

'Yes.'

'It does not paint our way of doing things in a good light, I'm afraid.'

'Carry on.'

'Very well. You're most kind. Last year a British officer, Lieutenant Fortescue, ginned up to his eyeballs, drove from the Gymkhana Club to hurry back to his regiment. He raced through a red light, crashing into a car carrying two Burmese ladies. They went flying, rolled into a ditch and were badly hurt. The older lady, a Chinese Burman, suffered a fractured skull, her niece broke her pelvis, rupturing her bladder. The case came before a young magistrate and he applied the law, finding Fortescue guilty, jailing him. There was an almighty row. People said that British officers shouldn't be jailed because of a silly accident, and the Burmese can't drive anyway. The officer appealed against his sentence. Everybody and his dog turned up for the appeal. The newspapers, a whole gang of officers from this chap's regiment, their girlfriends, their aunties. The senior appeal judge for Lower Burma took about five minutes before he freed him. I'm quoting from memory, but the appeal judge said: "I see no reason why an officer, whether he happens to be a British officer or a Burman holding the King-Emperor's Commission, for a piece of isolated negligence, however gross, ought to be deprived of a useful career in the public service by serving a term of rigorous imprisonment".'

'I see,' said Grace.

'Really? I fail to understand why an army officer guilty of gross criminal negligence should expect to get away with it just because he's British.'

'No, sorry, that's wrong.'

'The judge made the point that he would apply his interpretation of the law equally, whether the culprit be a British or a Burman officer.'

'That does seem fair.'

'There is no Burman officer in any regiment of the army.'

'Ah. So, in reality, that's not fair at all.'

'No. In reality, the opposite of fair. After the appeal, Fortescue was treated like a hero and the junior magistrate was transferred out of his job and shunned. When he goes to the clubs, especially the Pegu, everyone falls silent until he leaves.'

'Oh.'

'I am that junior magistrate.'

'I am very sorry to hear that, Mr Peach.'

He stared out of the window, lost in his own reflections. After a while, she stirred and he studied her again, and gulped.

'I must be going, I'm afraid,' said Grace.

'Yes. Thank you very much for coming and thank you for the information.'

A Sikh guard bowed to her deeply as she left the pink and white castle and walked out on to the street. Grace wondered what kind of empire it was, if its very own guardians no longer believed in it?

The first letter inviting her to take afternoon tea with him arrived the following morning.

Stone spelt wealth in Burma, plain bricks meant some money and the poor made do with wood. The old schoolhouse at Bishop Strachan's was brick, the rest – classrooms, offices, a three-storey dormitory for the girls and the little chapel – were made of teak on low wooden stilts, the buildings forming three sides of a square. The orphanage had been set up by a pious Victorian, a good man in a crowd of hypocrites, to give girls abandoned by their Burmese or Indian mothers and, of course, their adulterous British or American fathers, something of an education.

To Grace the school was a dead end, not remotely useful to the girls, not seriously of benefit for the war effort, badly paid – for the first time in her life money was becoming an issue because her father had lost 'rather a lot on bonds and shares' invested in Europe – and irrelevant for the future of these unwanted children.

After the school day was over, she set out for the headmistress's office and tapped on her door.

'Come! Miss Collins? What a pleasant surprise? How can I help?'

'Miss Furroughs, I just wanted to have a word with you about…' Grace's courage started to sink, bow first. '…I just thought that… well…'

'Go on, Miss Collins.'

'…the syllabus, Miss Furroughs. It seems a little…'

'…a little what?'

'Old-fashioned. We are teaching the girls the correct way to curtsey, how to address a bishop, how to write a sonnet, how to memorise the six wives of Henry VIII: "divorced, beheaded, died…"'

'Are you suggesting we change the curriculum, Miss Collins?'

'Well, I thought that it might be useful to teach the girls something, perhaps, a little more modern, a little more practical, a little more about, say, Burma.'

'Burma?'

'Burma.

The old woman's face turned to flint.

'How long have you been at Bishop Strachan's, Miss Collins?'

'Two months.'

'Well, Miss Collins, I have been here two decades, since 1920, to be exact. And I would not dream of changing the syllabus. We teach the girls how to behave in polite society, as if they were in Regent Street. That is how we have struggled along in the past. And this is how we will continue in the future. Thank you, for your observations, Miss Collins, but if you forgive me I have some administrative work to attend to.'

Cast down, Grace retreated to her room, little more than a closet, housing a single bed, a chair and a side-table, a wash-basin and a long shelf, on it a few novels, a silver hairbrush and a black and white photograph of her mother in an ebony frame, a woman of rare beauty whom Grace had never known. On the side-table beside her chair was a stack of the girls' exercise books.

Running a hand through her hair, limp in the suffocating air, she began going through their homework, here and there tut-tutting at bad spelling or ticking a sweetly-written sentence. Marking the books seemed to Grace, in the great scheme of things, pointless. By her side was a copy of the *Rangoon Times*. Yet more news of the Nazis rolling up the map of Europe, of ships sunk, of battles for places she'd never heard of, lost. Time oozed by, but suddenly it was pitch black outside.

Kneeling in front of her bed, she prayed for victory, for her father, for the children she was teaching – God Help Them. She switched off the light, stepped out of her clothes and, naked, clambered underneath her mosquito net into bed.

The slow wet heat of Burma lay on her, as thick and prickly as a woollen blanket. She lay sleepless, writhing this way and that, guilty that she was playing no part in the great battle being fought and lost in Europe. Grace wanted desperately to do her bit yet her absent father had managed to place her out of harm's way in this over-baked, stinking backwater. Good people were dying and she was doing nothing of consequence to help them, to defeat the evil that was swallowing up the world.

Nearby a pye-dog yelped and, much further off, a train sloughed through the night.

The slow rhythm of teaching helped soothe Grace. Geography had always been her best subject and she had a knack for making it interesting. She shunned the map of Europe, it being full of traps. But she explained, as best as she could, how the earth formed and the seas rose and fell and the ice came and went and why volcanoes boiled up and rain fell down. They listened and absorbed. In other lessons, *Romeo and Juliet* still had a power to move young hearts, and her classes lapped up the Tudors and Stuarts, grew fascinated by the chopping off of heads, wooed by Keats, dulled by geometry – eeyuck – laughed out loud at Voltaire, and listened, rapt, to the stories of the giants of medicine, astronomy and exploration. Occasionally – or, especially during maths - the girls tempted her off the syllabus and asked questions of affecting simplicity: *what is England like? Can you eat snow? Have you met the King?*

'It rains all the time', 'yes' and 'not yet' were by no means good enough, and she lost herself utterly, talking about the colours of an English autumn, or recounting a snowball fight in Sussex or the mild affection the British had for a King who, the complete opposite of Mr Hitler, could barely speak a sentence without the most dreadful stammer but, unlike Mr Hitler, sought to talk politely about other people. The school bell clanged, breaking her reverie. Thirty young faces, smiling to themselves. They had tricked her away from the hypotenuse and the cosine, yet again, and she burst out laughing: 'you naughty terrors!' It became the catchphrase they used against her, to be sung out by the girls whenever they suspected they had the edge on her, which was more often than not.

Kneeling by her bed one morning, during the daily ritual of washing herself with a jug of water, a moment of realisation – she'd fallen in love with this hopeless school teaching dead lessons to black-balled children in the back end of beyond. Teaching her forgotten orphans, abandoned and denied by their parents, was part of it, part of the war against ignorance and hate. Marking essays, ticking the correct use of the apostrophe, taking off marks for poor punctuation, was her part in the fight against the men who marched in step; semi-colons and sonnets against tanks and Stukas.

True, Grace disliked how 'the cream' – pretty rancid cream, in her book - of European society in Rangoon treated the children at close hand: sly looks as the school crocodile of half-castes passed by, the dearth of invitations for the children to meet with other Christian schools, how the girls from Bishop Strachan's were placed at the back of the side aisle for services at the Anglican cathedral. But the children were a blessing, sometimes troubled but more often smart, loving and lively, and she relished the delicious irony of implanting in them everything she herself had been taught by the hand-maidens of

British rule: every grace, every nuance of fine breeding, the superstructure, she had begun to suspect, of a cardboard empire.

The more Grace loved teaching, the more she had in common with Miss Furroughs, the less starchy her headmistress became towards her. The flint began to soften.

On a glorious Friday evening in 1941, after Easter but before the monsoon broke, Miss Furroughs popped her head around Grace's door after school and invited her around to the headmistress's study for just a small glass of sherry. They drank till two in the morning, emptying two and a half bottles, hooting with glee at the folly and foibles of British rule in Burma, of teaching, of men. From that time on, Grace woke up every morning with something she had never had before – a purpose in life – to give 'her children' the very best possible education they could enjoy as the world hurtled to hell in a dung-cart.

Time-tables, earthquakes, *Macbeth*, igneous, metamorphic and she never could remember, French irregular verbs, *A Midsummer Night's Dream,* amo, amas, amat. School life treacled by.

One evening, as the grim year of 1941 was drawing to a close, Grace was taken to see *The Road to Zanzibar* at the New Excelsior Cinema in Rangoon by Mr Peach. Grace had no idea why she had said yes to Mr Peach's pleading: boredom at refusing him for the thousandth time, she supposed. Or a failure to come up with ever more incredible excuses as to why she couldn't spare the time. Bing Crosby's tunes were catchy, Bob Hopes's jokes – 'I'm so nervous my bed is still shaking... It's a snake' – dire but somehow annoyingly cheering, Mr Peach's palm on her bare knee soft, wet and not so terrible that she had to remove it. The moment the film was over and the credits started to roll, he grasped her hand, blustering: 'Don't call me Mr Peach. Herbert... Bertie...'

'I shall do no such thing. Mr Peach, I really must be going...'

'How about a drink? Champagne?' And, almost without hope: 'Cocoa?'

Blurting out some nonsense, she made her excuses to Mr Peach, the word 'Bertie' never crossing her lips. The aisle leading to the exit was clogged with customers, moving absurdly slowly, as if from a well-attended funeral. A champion hurdler at school, she took off, skittering over the banks of seats, astonishingly fast. He tried to make chase, but his long giraffe-like limbs got entangled in the flip-back seats, generating ribald remarks from people in the queue, and she was out of the door and into the night before he had got to Row K. Tucking herself into a cycle rickshaw, she laughed gaily at the absurdity, but also the sweetness, of a date with Mr Peach. The rickshaw raced to the school, where she knew Miss Furroughs would be bent over a Jane Austen or one of the Bronte sisters, endlessly re-reading, and draining yet another small bottle of dry sherry.

Instead, the headmistress was sitting in her armchair, staring through her fingers clumsily masking her face.

'My God, what's happened?'

No answer, only a muted sobbing.

'Miss Furroughs, please tell me, what on earth has happened?'

'Haven't you heard?' She stared at Grace, her eyes red-raw.

'No. I was at the cinema. *The Road to Zanzibar.*'

'The wireless... the Japanese have bombed Pearl Harbour. The BBC are reporting that the Americans and the British have no choice but to go to war against Japan. This war is spreading all over the world.'

Head bent, her delivery broken, staccato. 'The last war, that was supposed to be the war to end all wars. That was why they all died. I had a lover, you know. I was twenty-five, not then a spinster, when I met him. He was forty, unmarried, a chaplain, Church of England. Such a good man. We met in Dorset, fossicking, at Easter in 1917. Had to return to his regiment in Flanders. On his next leave, we were planning to get married. We even booked the church. Killed at Passchendaele. He died so all this nonsense would never happen again. And now it is happening all over again. So he died for nothing.'

Without expression, she repeated her last few words.

Grace leant down to stroke her grey hair.

'I think Mr Gandhi is right,' said the headmistress. At the Pegu Club, over bridge, such talk was High Treason. 'War is wrong, it's just stupid and wrong.'

She began to sob, unbearably. To drown her crying, Grace found herself talking, opening herself up as Miss Furroughs had.

'I never knew my mother,' said Grace. 'She died in childbirth. Father was – is – high-up in Whitehall, something in the Treasury. He sends cheques and short letters on my birthdays, loving me coldly, from afar. I was brought up by a succession of nannies, then placed in a small boarding school on the South Downs. I hated it. The winds swept through the dorm. Icicles in the lavatory in winter. I was achingly lonely. Shortly after the war started, Father used his clout and got me on a ship bound for Canada. I had just turned eighteen. I had never been at sea before and was as sick as a pig. I just wanted to die. The only place where I could fight the sea-sickness was out on deck but it was bitterly cold so I was wrapped up, dressed up like the Michelin Man in duffel coat and jumpers. The cold cut you to the bone but better that, than the stink of people being sick on D Deck.

'One night, very late, I was shivering so much I was about to turn in, when, underfoot, I felt a shudder. Deep, bass notes coming up through the soles of my feet, transmitted up my legs, then my spine, drumming into my brain. I hurried inside and began climbing down to my deck but had only gone one flight when the ship's lights flickered, on and off, then died. Blackness. It was utterly terrifying. I turned around and began to feel my way up. The ship started to list. Climbing up that stairwell must have only taken a few seconds but it felt like years. I had to put my whole weight behind opening the door and then I almost fell out on deck, the sea at a crazy angle, the whitecaps and troughs almost above me, the salt-spray whipping into my face. Star shells lit up the night, fireworks. A destroyer zig-zagging towards us, a great white surf foaming as her bow sliced through the waves.

'*Boom! Boom!* Depth charges mushroomed ahead, sending great fountains of water into the air, soaking me. A klaxon hooted and a man's voice, so calm, as if he was reading the football scores, came over the Tannoy: "All hands on deck. Abandon ship."

'More people were coming out on deck. An old man in pyjamas asked me, "Have you seen Mabel?" Ropes dangled down. A lifeboat swinging on davits, an Indian seaman grabbing me, pushing me into a boat which rose up then fell down with the rise and crash of the waves. At school, they had drummed into us all that stuff about the British stiff upper lip. Well, that turned out to be nonsense. The British, some at least, weren't selfless, but selfish, disgracefully so.'

The old lady was still sobbing mechanically.

'I had never been so cold as in that lifeboat. A lurching, freezing darkness, hour after hour of it. When the moon came out we hoped for rescue. Instead, a great explosion. A tanker, half a mile away, had been hit. Small black figures, silhouetted by orange fire, crawled over the tanker's rails and leapt. The sea was burning. They were boiled alive. I will never forget the screams. Long after the tanker had gone, the oil on the surface continued to blaze, making night, day. From the lifeboat, we could hear a few survivors cry for help. We tried to row towards them. A big wave lifted the lifeboat and I could see them, bobbing up and down. The destroyer reappeared and surged past us, curving left, then swerving right. We shouted for them to stop. It did not slow down. It did not stop. The seaman next to me explained: "If she slows down to pick up those men from the tanker, even for ten seconds, she'll be a sitting duck for the U-boats. So they don't stop, ever. And everyone knows that."

'And then a man's voice, as clear as a bell over the slap of the waves, "Taxi! Taxi!" For a dying man, a good joke.'

The old lady spoke for the first time in what seemed like hours: 'Yes. That was brave of him.'

'One felt so proud,' said Grace. 'By the time we managed to row to the men in the sea it was dawn. We called out: "Hello! Anyone there? Anyone alive?" No answer. The sea was covered with bodies, and not one of them was alive.'

The headmistress exhaled a long, deep sigh.

'So, Miss Furroughs, I am very sorry for your loss. But the people who died in the boiling sea? And that chap who called out, "Taxi! Taxi!" They didn't want this war. I fear Mr Gandhi is wrong. Putting our hands up and surrendering to Mr Hitler and now the Japanese is not the proper thing to do. I'm afraid that we're going to have to fight, and fight like tigers.'

The only sound was the tick of the clock in the headmistress's study. Grace ran her fingers through the old lady's hair, mothering the woman old enough to be her mother. She hummed to herself the Bing number from *The Road to Zanzibar,* 'You Lucky People, You'.

Try as she might, she could not get it out of her head.

Part One

RED SUN RISING

CHAPTER ONE

December 1941, Rangoon

The Saturday after Pearl Harbour was the date of the annual pre-Christmas treat, part of the fixed calendar of the school year. A party of thirty girls would go to the Rangoon Zoological Gardens to admire the tigers, laugh at the monkeys, hiss at the snakes, and then have cakes or ice cream for tea. One year before, not to have taken the girls to the zoo just before Christmas would have seemed peculiar, but the mood in Rangoon was becoming uglier by the day. The evening before the trip to the zoo, Grace tried to raise her anxiety with the headmistress.

'Miss Furroughs, I'm just wondering about the trip to the zoo. Do you think it's a good idea to go?'

'The girls are looking forward to it, Miss Collins.'

'But I'm a little worried. The city has become unstable.'

'The girls are looking forward to it, Miss Collins.' The old lady returned to *Wuthering Heights,* the matter closed.

The daughter of a Burmese woman and an American oilman, long gone back to Texas, led the crocodile. Seventeen, but both looking and behaving older than her age and almost but not quite European in appearance, Emily was one of the stars of the school, noted for her ability to recite Miss Furroughs' favourite poets – Keats, Wordsworth but above all Tennyson – from memory. In the old days, just six months ago, Emily's pale cream skin would have been held to have been an advantage, but no more. If the Japanese did invade Burma, half-caste Emily was not European enough to be evacuated to India, but not Burmese enough to submerge into the local population. And that held true for all of the children at Bishop Strachan's. Even a few yards out of the school gates, Grace noted, more and more young Burmese were staring at the party in a way no-one could consider friendly.

The walk between the school and the zoo was only a mile long, but at one point they had to pass the street market by the river, where Grace had bought her bee trapped in amber. Even in December, Rangoon was fantastically warm, around 80 degrees Fahrenheit. Whatever the time of year, Miss Furroughs was a stickler that the girls must wear their uniforms of maroon cardigans and white dresses at all times. Grace thought that rule ridiculous, and allowed the girls the option of leaving their cardigans behind. The girls had set off in high spirits and as they passed an enormous Indian policeman doing traffic duty at a crossroads, he tipped his white solar topee at them – they all knew it was for Miss Collins' benefit – causing a wave of chatter and giggles.

Scrawled in fresh red paint on any available surface, fences, walls, anywhere, were slogans in the otherworldly wriggles of Burmese script, their meaning beyond Grace's grasp. Soon the crocodile passed the same red paint, this time in plain English: 'Free Burma', 'Strike for Your Independence', 'Down with the British' and 'Asia for the Asiatics'.

Casting her mind back to the Burman with his copy of *Mein Kampf* Grace shuddered at what might happen if – or was it when? – the Japanese walked through the front door of Bishop Strachan's. They called the British rulers the 'Heaven Born', so high and mighty they were, so far removed from the lot of the ordinary Burmese. The Heaven Born were snobbish and cruel about mixed-race children. They did their best to ignore them. But they would not harm them. About the intentions of the Japanese towards the living consequences of British Imperial lust, she could only feel dread.

Half-way along the market, the crocodile stopped dead. Grace jogged to the front to find Emily weeping, her white dress and face spattered by gobbets of red. Grace stammered: 'B-b-blood?'

'Betel juice, Miss.'

'Oh, bless.'

'Miss, I stopped the crocodile. I don't want the other girls to see.'

Taking out a handkerchief from her handbag, Grace dabbed Emily's face. 'Who did this, Emily?'

The girl motioned to a group of young Burmese men in sarongs, who were staring at them, blankly. Arching her heels, she turned towards the men: 'Excuse me, which one of you spat at my pupil?'

The shortest of the Burmese walked up to Grace, coming within an inch or two of her face, and spat, phlegm and betel juice dripping down her left cheek, just below her eye. It was quite the most disgusting indignity Grace had ever experienced. She wiped the spit off her own face with her bare hand.

'How dare you! How dare you spit at my pupil, who has done no harm to you?'

Three of the men stood in front of her, blocking her path. The fourth and fifth circled around her back. No figure of authority was in sight. Calves trembling, heart thumping against rib-cage, in a voice as imperious as she could muster, she said: 'Emily, would you please run back to the police officer at the crossroads and tell him to come here immediately. Immediately, Emily, if you please.'

The girl ran off, back down the crocodile. The men shuffled closer towards Grace, encircling her.

On the far side of the street a European couple, holding hands, were walking towards a black saloon. The hard white light at noon was blinding. But she knew him from somewhere.

'Colonel Handscombe!'

Head jerking in recognition, he ducked into the car and was behind the wheel in seconds. The woman opened the passenger door, dived in and the car was accelerating away before Grace could finish her sentence. As it passed her she saw the two of them laughing at some huge private joke, and then the saloon turned a corner, fast, and was gone. But not before she had recognised the woman. Someone had mentioned her name just the other day, saying that her husband was on the *HMS Repulse*, steaming for Singapore. Ah, yes, Mrs Peckham.

The Burmese grew closer. Standing at a distance behind the knot of men threatening her, but somehow part of them, was an onlooker. Threadbare western suit, smooth face, oiled hair, glasses, carrying a book in his hand. The man closest to her made a move to fetch something behind his back. Grace caught a glimpse of an ebony handle – a knife?

'Now, look here, you chaps,' said Grace, her voice squeaking, high-pitched, 'you may hate the British Empire and all that. Good for you. If you think I go "Ra-ra" every time I see a British soldier you'd be wrong. But these girls and I are not the bull-faced, earth-swallowing British army, we have done nothing wrong and frankly for you to go round spitting at us half-castes disgraces Burma. Old King Thibaw would be ashamed of you. You may well be the future of Burma, the new rulers of this land.'

The market-goers had seemed indifferent to the confrontation but as Grace found her voice some began listening to the blonde Englishwoman berating the Burmese youths. Many would not have understood a word she said, but about the tone of her voice, about a lone woman taking a stand, there was something urgent and brave.

'People may well be on your side for a time, and they will welcome anyone who can help them see the backs of the British. But if you take power by force you run the danger of staying in power by force – better men than you will ever be have fallen in that trap – and eventually, in ten, twenty, fifty years' time the people will hate you. You may well be Lords of Burma but everyone will know what you are.'

Her right hand slowly raised, the index finger pointing at them in condemnation: 'Nothing more than thugs and crooks who stay in power by thuggery and crookedness. If that is the future, then God save Burma. But right now every single man, woman and child in this market-place is watching you, watching what you do to us. So, how are you going to begin this "Burma for the Burmans" of yours? By spitting at half-caste orphans? By knifing their school marm? Is this the new Burma? Is this the best you can do?'

She stopped, conscious only of her fear and the hammering of her heartbeat against her ribs and the hatred in the eyes of the gang fixed on her. The market's constant hubbub fell silent. No one moved. No one spoke. From the river beyond came the sound of a tugboat hooting. Nearby, chickens squawked and a pig snorted irritably.

From nowhere, a tiny Burmese woman – the stall-holder who had sold her the bee – appeared next to her, slipping her arm in Grace's. She snarled something in Burmese at the gang. Grace had no idea what her friend had said, but it did not sound complimentary.

The gang melted away. Just before the reader in the threadbare suit disappeared, he studied her again, spat on the ground and treated her to a smile of royal sourness.

The Indian policeman came running, followed by Emily, but by then the men had vanished. Grace offered Emily her cardigan to wear, to cover up the red stains on her blouse. Emily put it on without saying a word, out of character for a girl with near-perfect manners.

'Emily, I...' Grace stumbled, her mind feeble with anxiety. 'I'm so sorry.' In truth she could think of no words to ease the fact that the girl had been spat at because she was a half-breed, a by-product of the British Empire. From that moment on, Grace detected an aloofness on the part of Emily that she found unsettling.

Grace's friend who had sold her the bee had vanished before she had time to thank her properly. But Grace understood her swift disappearance was not impolite. A Burmese woman who stuck up for a European in public in these times could get into trouble.

They carried on walking in the stifling heat. A sign on the front gate of the zoo announced that because of the emergency it was closed. They returned in silence, Grace regretting that she had not persevered with her objections to this foolish trip. Her weakness with Miss Furroughs meant the girls – Emily especially – had suffered pointless humiliation.

When told about the spitting gang, Miss Furroughs dropped her head onto her chest and said nothing for a time, wringing her hands together. Sitting upright, she asked: 'How is Emily coping with it?'

'Not very well, Miss Furroughs. On the walk back from the zoo, she seemed withdrawn. It was very disturbing. I cannot forget the look of the man who spat at me, as if I wasn't human. For Emily, it must have been far worse.'

The headmistress nodded and said, 'Poor Emily' and repeated herself.

'We shouldn't have...' but Grace left the sentence unfinished. The headmistress sat in her chair, staring ahead of her, her eyes unfocused.

Retreating to the empty staff room, Grace tuned the school wireless to pick up the BBC. Whistles, mush, then the atmospheric static gave way to 'Lilliburllero'. The announcer, back in the studio in London, she imagined, sitting in a black dinner jacket, poised to read out the bulletin. 'This is the BBC News from London.'

A crackle, then the plummy voice told of the loss of the *Prince of Wales* and the *Repulse,* torpedoed by Japanese bombers off Singapore, hundreds of sailors believed to have gone down with their ships, missing, presumed dead.

Kneeling, she said a prayer for the sailors and poor, cuckolded Peckham, RN: 'Our Father, Who art in heaven.' As the words tumbled out, she tried not to think of those other sailors in the Atlantic, screaming as they drowned in the burning oil.

A walk in the cool of the evening brought Grace down to the river towards her favourite Buddhist pagoda, the one she had mistaken for a ship's engine. Two saffron-clad monks hissed at her. Returning to the school by another route, she saw a line of Indian policemen armed with lathis – bamboo sticks topped and tailed with brass metal blunts – facing an angry crowd of Burmese.

Doubling back, she bumped into a living tree, which apologised profusely and started gulping.

'Mr Peach.'

'Sorry. Awfully sorry.'

'I should have looked where I was going.'

'You should be careful around here, Miss Collins. The Mussulman areas are safe. Anywhere near a minaret, within earshot of the muezzin's call, the people will look after you. But in the Burmese Buddhist parts of town, I am afraid to say' – he gulped again – 'it's not safe any more.'

His mouth opened and closed and his eyes darted around a point somewhere above Grace's head. He wanted to say something more to her, but could he get it out by sunset?

'Yes, Mr Peach?' Something about him brought out a streak of cruelty in her. Did she enjoy playing with him, watching him suffer? Yes, she thought, she did.

Nothing sensible came from him, just his mouth sucking in and blowing out air.

'Well, Mr Peach. I must be on my way.'

'Miss Collins? Why did you run away from me?'

Ah, finally, he'd managed to get it out.

'A joke.'

'You don't hate me, then?'

'Of course not. Don't be silly.'

'Well, I must… I ought to let you know what's going on. The situation here is Rangoon is not good. Our chaps have yet to hold the Japanese. We keep on falling back. Everywhere. I shouldn't tell you this,' he lowered his voice until it was just on the edge of hearing 'but I'm now doing intelligence stuff. Last week the only early warning radar kit in Burma was flown back to India. The RAF is next to leave, to save the planes for the battle for India. They're making plans to evacuate the Europeans from Lower Burma, but not to tell the "useless mouths".'

'What?' gasped Grace.

'They call them the "useless mouths". Refugees, people who can't fight. The Indian civilians chiefly, and the mixed races. Like the girls at your school.'

'Mr Peach!' She cried out his name so loudly that a British police sergeant turned his head and fixed them with a stare. Lowering her voice, she tried again: 'You're not for one second suggesting that the British Empire is secretly planning to abandon Burma?'

Jaw firm, mouth no longer opening and closing like a goldfish, he made no sound at all, but, almost imperceptibly, nodded his head.

The next morning, over breakfast, Grace told the headmistress about the two great battleships, now lying at the bottom of the sea.

'Mrs Peckham's husband?'

'I don't know,' said Grace. 'Very few survived.'

Silence between them.

'Miss Furroughs,' Grace continued, 'people are talking about evacuating Rangoon. They are saying that the military situation is gloomy, that the necessity of defending Britain means that there aren't enough soldiers and tanks and planes for the Far East. I believe that, for the safety of the children, we should consider planning to evacuate the school from Rangoon and arrange to travel to the safety of India.'

There, at last, she'd said it. The headmistress, pouring out jasmine tea, jerked the teapot spout against her cup, spilling its contents over the tablecloth. She wiped up the mess with a napkin.

'This nonsense is just because of that silly spitting incident, isn't it? You just can't stand Rangoon any more. Not fashionable enough, I suppose?'

'No, Miss Furroughs, that's not it. I have heard certain information from someone close to the Government, that there is a plan – that the Government is planning to abandon Burma.'

'Nonsense. Abandon Burma? Poppycock. I won't hear a word more on this subject. Good day, Miss Collins,' and she scurried out.

Two days before Christmas, Grace was kneeling in the school gardens, picking some fresh flowers for the dinner table, when the corner of her eye caught a sparkle far above. Thin silver arrows glinted in the late morning sun and from them tiny flashes of light began falling towards earth. The ground bounced up and smacked her hard in the face. Soil plugged her mouth and throat and nose, her eyes, burning, jammed shut. A thing scissored by close to her right ear, spinning fast, hissing.

Flowers, sunlight, normality, gone; in their place dust and snot and screams. A screech of tyres, a dull thump, a horn blaring; half-human voices, crying out, bawling, gibbering with terror.

Blinded by the dirt in her eyes, retching, clearing out the muck from her throat, Grace needed water, desperately, and began to crawl forward, her fingers prospecting the earth in front of her. Her left index finger snagged against something. Feeling its shape with her fingers, a crazily twisting curl of metal, razor sharp, an inch long, still hot to the touch, as if from an oven. With wonder, she realised that they – the airmen high above in their silver machines – had intended this, that there could be no other explanation for the riot of noise and dust and this horrible piece of ragged-edged shrapnel.

They mean to kill us.

The dust began to settle, her eyes to open, to see some fuzzy dirt-brown fog instead of a hot darkness. Coughing up snot and dirt, the back of her throat unbearably sore, Grace staggered upright and started to limp towards the school buildings. As she did so, she reflected that at least she would not have to put up with any more claptrap from Colonel Handscombe. The Japs could fly, that had been proven.

Racing to the cellar of the old school-house, she swung the door open. The space was dank, empty of life. She backed out, astonished, and over the buzzing in her ears she heard them. The sound grew, defining itself, clear and loud:

'Yea, though I walk in death's dark vale,
Yet will I fear no ill;
For Thou art with me; and Thy rod
And staff me comfort...'

The ground juddered as a fresh stick of bombs fell, maybe two hundred yards away. Running up the steps, she found the whole school kneeling at their pews inside the wooden chapel.

'Miss Furroughs!' Grace screamed over the psalm. 'Miss Furroughs, the chapel is not safe. The children must go to the cellar of the old schoolhouse. One bomb will kill us all.'

The singing faltered.

'For Christ's sake, Miss Furroughs, the chapel isn't safe!'

'Miss Collins, how dare you swear in the House of the Lord!'

'And how dare you risk their lives? The children must go to the cellar, Miss Furroughs. *Now*. The chapel is made of wood. It's not safe.'

The headmistress's face came alive and she spoke: 'Hurry to the cellar, children.'

Emily found Grace.

'Miss, the two boys. I don't know where they are.'

'Oh, Lord.' Two boys, little Michael, aged five, and Joseph, ten, twice Michael's size but with half the wits, had somehow been adopted by a school for girls. They called Joseph a Mongol but she hated the word. Michael and Joseph were also half-caste orphans – no one knew who the parents were – and helpless. At five, Michael was street-smart but Joseph had the body of a ten-year-old boy and the mind of a toddler. Yet he would never do anyone any harm, ever, and he had a strange gift of sensing moods: most often happiness but also fear. When scared, he ground his teeth, the prelude to a kind of shivering fit that the girls found deeply upsetting.

And both had vanished.

'Where did you look?'

'Everywhere.'

'Did you check the boys' lavatory on the third floor?'

'No, Miss. I'm not allowed...' but Grace was already running out into the yard and up the flights of the dorm. She pushed open the heavy door to the boys' lavatory. Not so far away, someone started screaming, a piercing, animal noise. She pushed open the door to one cubicle. No-one there. She pushed opened the second door, and there they were, lying on the floor, hands over their ears, Joseph grinding his teeth. Grace clapped her hands around both of them, said, 'Come on you two, let's pop down to the cellar,' and the three of them pelted downstairs.

A third stick of bombs clattered down, blasting every window in the school, but by then the two boys and the teacher were safe in the cellar.

Re-emerging from the inner gloom with a lit kerosene lamp, Miss Furroughs hissed: 'You should not have blasphemed in the chapel, Miss Collins. I fear that you are setting an entirely wrong example to the children.'

'Miss Furroughs–'

'Swearing in chapel is the very worst example to set to the students.'

'But the chapel is not safe during an air raid. They could have all been killed.'

'That is entirely beside the point.'

This was not just unfair, but maddening. 'I have no wish to work at a school with dead students because of the folly of the headmistress.'

'Then you should look for a new post somewhere else.'

'Thank you very much for saving the boys, Miss,' interrupted Emily.

'What? Where were they?' snapped Miss Furroughs.

'Hiding in the boys' lavatory on the third floor,' Emily carried on, coolly. 'Miss Collins found them and rescued them, Miss. While you were looking for the lamp, Miss.'

'Did you?' she asked Grace.

'Yes, Miss Furroughs, I did.'

The headmistress shivered and turned away, her lip trembling. The faces of the children stared up at them, at a world of adults gone mad.

Four thousand people were killed in Rangoon that day but, somehow, the school and everyone in it stayed safe.

On Christmas Eve morning Grace hand-delivered her letter of resignation. Miss Furroughs opened up the envelope in her presence, read the note, and tore it up.

'Ruby seems to be getting more obstreperous by the day. Have a word with her, Miss Collins, or I am afraid that I will set her detention.'

Grace made to speak to defend the good name of Ruby Goldberg, half-Burmese, half-Bronx grifter, but thought better of it, and closed the door behind her.

On Christmas morning, the children pounced on their presents. It seemed pitiful stuff to Grace – cheap bangles, hand-me-down frocks, a few books for the passionate readers – but the girls were genuinely grateful. The boys got hand-carved wooden rifles. When the bombers returned, just as Christmas lunch was about to be served, they ran out into the playground and started firing their toy guns at the Japanese airmen. Grace shooed them, and everybody else, Miss Furroughs too, into the cellar.

Cold and dank, it felt like a tomb. They shuddered as a fresh stick of bombs thump-thumped down on the defenceless city. From the crack between door and cellar floor a dagger's blade of sunlight sliced through the dark, lighting up socks and shoes fidgeting in the dark. The thump-thumps grew nearer, showering dust over the little feet. Grace found herself singing the opening line of 'Once in David's Royal City' but stumbled over the words as the explosions thudded closer to home, her voice quavering, drying up.

In the prickly silence, a child started to sob.

But then came: *'stood a lowly cattle shed...'* Ruby sang like a night-club artiste down on her luck, haunting, sexual and brimful of soul. Soon the whole school was belting out the carol, drowning out the hateful clatter of war.

When they finished, the cellar clapped and cheered and whistled, Ruby's voice powering through a fresh and terrifyingly close bomb-burst: *'Silent Night, Holy Night...'* Her audience gasped at the cheek of it, some laughing out loud, then the children took courage and sang their ironic taunt at the bombers above:

'All is calm, all is bright,
Round yon virgin mother,
Holy Infant so tender and mild,
Sleep in heavenly peace,
Sleep in heavenly peace.'

And still the school survived, untouched.

The Christmas Day air raid pricked the headmistress's inertia. That night, Miss Furroughs mumbled to Grace that it might be a good idea, on mature reflection, for the school to plan to leave Rangoon and travel by ship to Calcutta for a while. But the half-caste orphans were not a high priority in the colonial scheme of things – on the contrary, the children were an awkwardness, an embarrassment, somehow never quite worthy of active consideration – and no orders were made for their embarkation. Had Miss Furroughs pressed the matter, something might have happened. But she did not. In the past, the headmistress had been quick, sometimes unpleasantly so, to express her anger or irritation at the most trivial failing of Grace or the children, let alone any shortcoming by the colonial Government, the diocesan officers or even the

Lord Bishop of Burma. In her prime, Miss Furroughs had been afraid of no one and nothing. But in these days she seemed overwrought. Money might have solved the problem. Bishop Strachan's school had precious little, and the better-heeled Anglicans were steadily disappearing by ship or plane.

New Year came and went. Day after day passed without word from the Government for the arrangement of their safe passage to India. One morning, Grace came down to breakfast to find the front page of the *Rangoon Times* folded on her place, proclaiming the official message, that everyone should 'Stay put' – keep on working and let the British soldiers do their job, stop the Japanese and all things would be well. Miss Furroughs entered and nodded at the paper.

'Stay put?' asked Grace, incredulous. 'No one will fall for that.'

'Nonsense. Colonel Handscombe told me at the Club that he is going to stay and fight, at the last ditch.'

'Bully for the colonel. Was he on his own?'

'What do you mean by that?'

'Nothing, Miss Furroughs.' Grace hadn't told her that she'd seen the colonel and Mrs Peckham holding hands. It would not have been proper. And given that Commander Peckham of *HMS Repulse* had since officially been listed as missing, presumed dead, Mrs Peckham was now a widow, free to be courted by whoever she chose. That was how it was in war.

'Whatever Colonel Handscombe does in his ditch,' Grace continued, 'does not mean the school should be there with him. The children are no longer safe in Rangoon.'

'No, Miss Collins, that conflicts...' The headmistress stopped mid-sentence, as if she doubted her own mind.

'We *must* leave for India,' countered Grace.

'But that's not the official advice! We shall stay until the order,' again, Miss Furroughs halted abruptly, her pattern of speech maddening, indecisive, 'for evacuation.' Her voice tailed off, her last words uttered so meekly that Grace had to strain to hear them 'But not before.'

Locking herself in her study, Mrs Furroughs read and sipped dry sherry, distracted, unsure, inert.

The news was always grim, grimmer than before. The Japanese made their way up the Malayan peninsula towards Rangoon methodically, village after village, river after river. Not just the richer Indians but the poor ones too started to leave Burma. Grace's anxiety grew but Miss Furroughs had a way of sensing when she was about to raise the subject of the school leaving for India, or booking tickets on one of the ships, and blocking her.

Singapore fell, the Empire disgraced. In the days that followed, the part-time staff at the school - Burmese, Indian and Chinese teachers, cleaners, cooks – said their goodbyes and left, with the exception of the ancient school caretaker, Allu, a Mohammedan, originally from Bengal. One evening, before dinner, Grace had to run to the night market to buy some fresh vegetables and fruit for the children, because the last cook had gone.

While there, the electricity was cut – no one knew why – and the market was plunged into almost total darkness, people whistling and laughing nervously as they struggled to feel their way along. A feeble glow-worm of light came from the flickering candles at a small Buddhist shrine at one end of the market; here and there starlight penetrated through gaps in the canvas awnings above the stalls. When an unseen chicken squawked in its cage by Grace's feet it sounded so freakishly loud she jumped in her skin, called out and her voice was recognised by Mary, an Anglo-Burmese nurse at the hospital and an old friend. In the murk, Mary told Grace the gossip gathered from the wounded soldiers in her ward. Her latest patients included a tiny handful of the troops who had escaped from the great defeat at Singapore by sailing to Indonesia and then being flown up to Rangoon. On the way their transport plane had been shot up by the Japanese and three of them had ended up badly burnt, with little chance of survival. Medical supplies were fast running out, and all the boys' talk was of defeat.

'They're so bitter about their general, Percival – he's the one with the awful buck teeth,' said Mary, her face three-quarters invisible in the darkness. 'They say he was just petrified, that, in the face of the Japanese attack, he turned to stone. They should have been digging trenches and securing supplies and fighting. Instead the officers insisted on endless roll-calls, parades up and down the streets and the troops painting the stones in the barracks white. One sergeant who came back from the front line filthy – he'd had to hide in a storm drain from Zeroes – was put on a charge for being improperly dressed.'

'Madness,' said Grace.

'The morale of the British troops was rock bottom but with the Indian soldiers, it was worse, a lot of talk of how they should follow Gandhi, that the

British should "Quit India".'

Mary's voice lowered to a whisper: 'There's been nothing about this on the BBC but my chaps say that after the surrender, thousands of the Indian troops went over to the Japs. The Japs have promised to free India. They call themselves the Indian National Army, the INA, but my chaps call 'em Jiffs, Japanese Indian Fighting Forces. They say there are thousands of these Jiffs.'

Grace fell silent. If the Indian troops abandoned the British it would be a catastrophe.

'What are your plans, Grace?'

'The whole school should go to India. We need to go now but getting it organised is difficult. And you, Mary?'

'The day after tomorrow they're flying out all the European nurses and the injured they're happy to move,' she paused delicately, but Grace caught the inflection, which implied there were other patients who weren't going anywhere, whom they had pretty much given up on, 'but that will leave the hospital horribly understaffed. There will be about two hundred patients and only seven nurses.'

'What are you going to do?'

'I've decided to stay on, to look after my chaps.'

'That's very brave of you, Mary.'

'Don't be silly. Anyway, must dash. Got to get back to my boys, do some bedtime reading, keep them from getting into trouble.'

Trouble? Grace had visited Mary's burns ward: a long line of beds, crowded together, gauze bandages over blackened skin, whimpers of pain, softly muted.

'Good luck, Mary,' and her friend disappeared into the night. A half-caste, Mary would not have been welcome if she had turned up at the posher clubs in Rangoon. And when the Japanese arrived at the hospital, and found Mary and her boys, what then?

Still no word of when they were going to leave Rangoon. That night, after school dinner – a miserable affair of rice and beans, somehow both under-cooked but yet burnt to a cinder by Grace – she was determined to raise the subject of leaving yet again. The second she opened her mouth, Miss Furroughs skittered along the school corridor and slammed the door of her study behind her.

The air raids grew more frequent. One night the untouchables who had emptied out the thunder-boxes of the British sahibs and memsahibs, the Indian money-lenders and the Chinese merchants, taking away the night soil of the town for generations, vanished. The imperial city was rotting from within.

One lunchtime in late February Grace abandoned her class and went to Government House. A manservant in a maroon sarong showed her straight past Sikh sentries, up a brick staircase, into a vast, empty hall, boasting oil paintings of past Governors on one side and a panoramic view of the city and the river curling in a great bend beyond. Clouds of black smoke were rising from the refinery.

'Hello, darling, how the devil are you?'

To say that Mr Peach was pleased to see her was something of an understatement.

'What about a kiss?'

Mr Peach, she realised, was drunk.

'Mr Peach, that is no way to talk to a guest.'

'Sorry, love, sorry. Only we're all going to hell. Bloody army blew up a bridge on the bloody Sittang River, leaving two thirds of a bloody division on the Jap side. Indian soldiers can't bloody swim. The British ones can swim but they'd like to have a general who knows how to fight. The one in charge has a hole in his arse, an anal fistula is how I have to explain it to Whitehall. Top secret, but he pongs, literally, so no one can go near him without throwing up. No wonder we're losing. And leaving.'

His gulping stammer had gone.

'Leaving?'

'Top Secret. Sssh.'

'What?'

'Sssh. You are lovely, you know. Give us a kiss...'

'Mr Peach...'

'Here. Watch this.' He lobbed a red billiard ball at an oil of a grand old Victorian gentleman. It gouged a hole the shape of an egg in the canvas, the frame falling to the floor with a tinkle of broken glass.

'Know who he bloody was? Bloody Sir Augustus Rivers Thompson. Chief Commissioner or Lord High Everything Else. Can't leave this lot for the Japanese to smash up. So let's do it instead.' He offered her the pink.

'Come on, darling, you have a go...'

'Mr Peach, I demand that you sober up. I have come on behalf of Bishop Strachan's school. We need to know what is going on.'

Something imploring in Grace's voice got down through the great well of alcohol to his brain– that, and some innate sense of decency.

'I'm sorry.' He collapsed into a leather armchair and said in a different, much quieter voice, 'I'm sorry. The order for the final evacuation of all government staff in Rangoon was made this morning at six, effective immediately. To be promulgated tomorrow morning at six, by me. I'm the last man in. And out. Governor's gone, Government's gone. We've burnt the code books, burnt the files, bar one, opened the prisons, the leper colonies and even the bloody loony bins. Last passenger ship leaves tonight.'

Oh, no, no, no, thought Grace. She felt a sickening realisation that her very worst fears were about to come true. The school had left it far, far too late. Miss Furroughs had been so weak, so horribly indecisive. Trapped in Rangoon, the children would suffer far worse than men spitting at them.

'Rangoon is finished,' Mr Peach continued. 'The Japanese may be here tomorrow. Or next week. But soon. Get out now. If you can go by sea, do it. The road is good to Mandalay, then it's just a track, then there isn't a road, at all. After that, it's a bloody long walk.'

She made ready to go.

'Before the war,' Mr Peach interrupted himself with a long, noxious belch, 'we didn't build a bloody road between Burma and India lest all the bloody Indians came teeming in. So there isn't one. Oops! We've spent the last hundred years fretting about the bloody Russians threatening the north-west frontier through Afghanistan into India, never thinking that the bloody Japs might walk through the north-east frontier from Burma. How unintelligent is that, eh?'

In the distance, the muffled bark of an explosion. Grace's ears were attuned to the sound of bombs by now, but this was different, in a lower register. Artillery?

'And do you know what is really scaring the pants off the red-hats? Sssh,' he pressed a finger to his lips. 'How many Indian troops were bagged at Singapore?'

'I'm afraid...'

'...forty thousand. And how many of our loyal Indian soldiers have become Jiffs?'

Silence.

'Thirty thousand.'

She stared at him.

'Three quarters. Where is the leader of the Jiffs, the so-called Indian National Army, one Subhas Chandra Bose? They call him the Netaji, that's Hindi for Fuhrer. Where's Hitler's Indian, eh? We don't bloody know. Special Branch lost him. Bloody useless.'

Eyes closed, he started to sway like a tall tree in a great storm. Grace thought he might pass out. Suddenly, his eyes opened wide.

'Another top secret, for you. Some of the Jiffs have found out that Japs aren't such nice chaps, after all. They ran away from the Japs, landed up here, and Colonel Handscombe had them tortured, beaten on the soles of their feet because "I'm teaching these bloody traitors a lesson they won't forget." I told him to stop it. He carried on. I told him I knew an American newspaper correspondent who'd print his name as a torturer unless he stopped it, and then he stopped it. So I got to talk to the chaps, sepoys - Indian soldiers – ordered to surrender at Singapore, who turned Jiff and then ran away from the Japs. Forty-four of them, so that makes me something of an expert. I've interviewed more ex-Jiffs than any other official in the British Empire. These chaps aren't traitors. They want the British out of India. But with the Japs they smelt a rat. One Jiff told me that a Jap general said to them all: "Let the Japanese be the father. Indians, Burmese and Chinese will live like a family. However, if the Indian child is thin and needs more milk, we will give him more milk." Bugger that, thought my chap, and he was off. So I wrote a report on what the runaway Jiffs have to say. My report says we've lost Burma. And if we don't do something about the Jiffs, we're going to lose India too, and then the Japs and Jerry will join up in Delhi and we're all goners. The solution? Announce pretty damn quick that we will be handing India over to its people as soon as the war is over and make the point, loud and strong, that neither Hitler nor Hirohito have shown much respect for any other nation apart from their own, so if anyone thinks that the Nazis or the Japs are serious about independence,' he hiccoughed again, 'they're talking out of their arse.'

He picked up a thin buff folder and waved it at her.

'And the response from on high? Nothing. Zero, if you'll pardon the pun.'

An enormous blast rattled the windows as a dust cloud rose a quarter of a mile away, over what used to be the army's central barracks. They were leaving nothing behind.

'No reply,' continued Mr Peach. 'Why not? Got me thinking. I'd burnt all the other bloody files. And the code books. When I'd burnt everything, well almost everything, I started on the cellar. First, the bubbly. Then the white wine. Then the red. Bit tiddley, tiddly-pom-tiddly-pom. Where was I? Ah, yes, sssh, top secret, just before I popped the Peach report on Jiffs into the boiler I thought I would have a look at it. I'm in charge, after all. And why hadn't anyone replied to it? After all, it had called for us to quit India. That should have caused an almighty palaver, Winston screaming bloody murder, etc, etc. Instead, nothing. Why was that, eh?'

'I have no idea,' Grace said.

'Colonel Handscombe decided not to send it up, that's why. He made a note in the file that Peach's report was "too defeatist". And now all lines are down to the outside world. So I've written a report no one's read and, in the meantime, the danger is that more and more chaps will join the Jiffs, and we'll end up not only losing Burma and India but the whole bloody world. And is anyone listening? No. Has anyone in London got an idea of how dangerous the Jiffs are to the Allies? No. Or that they could be turned round, if we promised them independence? No. And where is Colonel Handscombe, that noble last-ditcher?'

Like a clockwork soldier, Peach rotated three hundred and sixty degrees, his eyes scanning the horizon. Of the colonel, no sign.

'So, may I summarise? Total balls-up. Eh, gorgeous?'

A red ball took out another mutton-chopped nabob. 'Are you sure you don't want a go? How about High Commissioner Charles Umpherton Aitchinson? Come on, darling.' He belched again, a revolting noise. Grace had had enough.

'I love you,' Mr Peach shouted, beseeching, swaying. 'Do you love me?'

'Mr Peach, you're a damned fool.'

Grace started to back out. Hearing a crash, she turned and saw that he'd fallen plumb down and was now slumped over a leather chaise longue, dead to the world. The manservant who first had led her to Mr Peach started to walk slowly towards him.

She ran down the echoing steps of the seat of British rule in Burma, dashed past the guards and was out on the street. A white-bellied rat scuttled down the steps, passed her and the last she saw of it was its long reptilian tail vanishing into a drain. Even the rats were giving up on the British Empire.

A cycle rickshaw took her past the front of a mansion owned by a wealthy Chinese merchant, a Catholic, famous in Rangoon for his gleaming Rolls Royce. The house was being ransacked, with Burmese looters running out with upholstered chairs and mahogany side tables balanced on their heads. The front gate was open and she could see the main hallway, barren apart from a picture of the Sacred Heart. None of the looters had fancied it.

Back at the school, Grace ordered everyone to go to the dormitories and pack for India. She pounded on the door of Miss Furroughs' study and told her about the order for evacuation. The headmistress was a picture of wretchedness, her eyes bloodshot.

'What is it, Miss Furroughs?'

'I went to the Club, to hear what Colonel Handscombe was planning to do. They told me that he had flown to Calcutta three days ago. Along with Mrs Peckham.' The headmistress snuffled. 'They are engaged to be married, and her husband not dead a month.'

Grace cut through the self-absorption of the older woman. 'Colonel Handscombe is a pig. Good riddance to him. The school must leave Rangoon immediately. Now.'

'Yes, Miss Collins, I am sorry. I fear I have been a complete fool.'

'But, we are leaving–?'

Grace was interrupted by the harsh growling of an engine.

'Yes. I've asked Allu–'

An antique green single-decker bus chuntered into the school yard, Allu behind the wheel, *Hants & Dorset Motor Bus Company* still clearly visible on its sides where it had been ineffectually over-painted. The bus had spent the prime of its life in the New Forest, running between Lymington and Southampton, before being shipped out to Burma, a gift to Anglicans in the colony from the Bishop of Winchester. The exhaust snorted a cloud of half-burnt oil and the engine uttered a metallic death rattle. His Grace, clearly, hadn't been much of a mechanic.

Grace stepped outside. 'Will this wreck get us to the docks, Allu?'

'Well, Miss, it might. Three miles. But not much further.'

Grace could have sworn she smelt alcohol – the local hooch – on Allu's breath, but what to do about it? Nothing, for the moment. When everyone had boarded and their bags stowed, Miss Furroughs was missing. Fully engaged with removing excess baggage from the bus, Grace sent Emily, the headmistress's favourite, who found her in the school chapel, kneeling in a pew, lost in prayer. The schoolgirl coughed, to alert the old lady to her presence.

'Please, Miss,' said Emily, 'Miss Collins says the bus is ready and we must go. Please, Miss.'

Eyes closed, fingers steepled in prayer, the headmistress made no move. Emily turned and walked down the aisle, down the steps and onto the bus. 'Please Miss Collins, Miss Furroughs won't come. I told her the bus is ready to go, but she didn't hear me.'

'Damn!' She snapped at one girl who had smuggled the school's umbrella stand on the bus – 'no, we're not taking that, you clot!' – and ran off to the chapel. Grace opened the thick wooden door, dipped her hand in the water stoop out of habit and crossed herself, quickly. Sunlight poured through the stained-glass windows, bathing the headmistress in blood and gold. As Grace walked up the aisle, the deep bass of artillery rattled the windows. That was the loudest she'd heard, ever. The war was getting closer. She knelt down, beside the headmistress, two pews down from the altar. Another series of booms from the big guns, disturbing the motes of dust spiralling in the sunlight. Grace said a prayer for a safe journey for the children, then spoke, her voice harsh in the quiet of the chapel: 'Miss Furroughs, we must leave. We need to secure places on the ship. It's our last chance.'

'Go without me.'

The young teacher shook her head. 'I can't do that. I can't look after sixty children on my own. For their sake, you've got to come, Miss Furroughs.'

'I'm sorry, Miss Collins, I'm so sorry,' the headmistress wept and unsteadily rose to her feet. Grace felt an overwhelming sense of pity for the older woman. She had lived a good life, taught and educated two, three generations of children at Bishop Strachan's, but now her entire world was collapsing. All the simple certainties of the British Empire, of everyday life in Rangoon, of everything that Bishop Strachan's stood for were dying. Grace placed her arms around the headmistress's shoulders and led her towards the bus.

Allu revved the engine, put it into gear, let slip the clutch and 'Hants & Dorset' slouched through the school gates.

As they drove towards the docks, the headmistress leaned close to Grace, gesturing at Allu. 'You don't think he's one of those Jiffs, do you?'

Grace said no, she did not, and stared out of the window at a city emptying of people.

CHAPTER TWO

Half a mile from the port gates, the smell of disaster lay everywhere. Dock cranes hung like gibbets against a darkening sky. Blankets of smoke, thick, coal-black, billowed from a dozen burning oil tanks. The bus drew on towards the docks, the children silent. Allu pulled Hants & Dorset to a halt and the children poured out, adding to a vast, swirling crowd. The atmosphere was vile, people punching wildly so that they could get a yard nearer the dock gates.

A black Rolls Royce edged through the crowd, turned and reversed down a wooden jetty a few feet from its end. The Rolls stopped and a uniformed chauffeur emerged and opened the passenger door. A fat white man in a claret suit, white-bearded, ruddy-faced, an out-of-season Santa Claus, got out and walked back towards land as the chauffeur pushed the Rolls over the edge of the jetty into the muddy brown slop of the Rangoon river.

The fat man didn't look back but placed himself in the middle of a small army of servants carrying suitcases on their heads. As they barged through the crowd, splitting the party from Bishop Strachan's into two, he shouted: 'Get these black bitches out of my way.'

Pushing through the mob, Miss Furroughs caught up with him and slapped him hard on the cheek.

'How dare you insult my children. We are not savages, sir, and I'll ask you to remember that.' He touched his face, glared at her, and then pushed on towards the ship. The girls, for the first time since they'd left the school, smiled amongst themselves.

Grace ran to a ticket booth, its grille closed, and darted round the back. Sitting on a chair, smoking a cheroot, was a Burman. She told her story – ten-a-penny on that day – but the shipping clerk took pity on Grace and promised to see what he could do. While they waited, Grace overheard Ruby entertaining the other children with a sotto voce impression of Miss Furroughs: 'You horrible little man. We are not savages, sir.' In the ordinary way, she might have given detention to Ruby for mocking the headmistress. Not that day.

Grace had always tried hard not to show it, but she adored Ruby. She should have been ugly with her beaky nose and heavy features, but Ruby's brown-black eyes danced with mischief and character. Ruby was as thick as thieves with Emily, the great classical beauty of the orphanage, and there were times when Grace envied the friendship between the two girls who were only a few years younger than her.

Half an hour later, the clerk returned.

'Yes?' said Grace, desperate for good news.

He would not look her in the eye.

'No booking for Bishop Strachan's.'

'Is there any chance?'

'No chance of booking. No spare places on the ship for two European ladies, never mind sixty-two half-Burmese children. The ship is too, too crowded. No room to sit. Japs maybe bomb ship. No good, lady, no good.'

'Is there nothing you can do?'

'My brother-in-law, he is engineer on the ship. Maybe, for a thousand rupees, he can help you lady, and the other lady. But the children?' He stared at the ground, and shrugged.

'Why?' asked Grace, pushing him.

'They are half-castes.'

They clambered back on the bus and Allu drove to the railway station. Humanity as far as the eye could see blocked the main street approaching the station. Grace got out of the bus, climbed up and stood on the engine cowling – not very lady-like – and saw hundreds of people pressing against a thin line of Indian policeman threshing the crowd with staves, beating them back. Beyond them, a locomotive puffing steam, a train overflowing with faces – people on the roof, legs hanging off the sides – but motionless. No one going anywhere.

Hants & Dorset wheezed in reverse, away from the station, and then took the road north, heading three hundred and something miles to Mandalay. Grace thought that the engine must give up the ghost in the next few miles or so.

At a crossroads the traffic was controlled by a European man who did a perfect impression of a policeman's hand signals – blocking a line of traffic with an imperious flat palm, waving vehicles through with extravagant, scimitar sweeps of his other arm – the impression of authority enhanced by a white solar topee on his head. Other than the topee, he was stark naked. One of the lunatics Mr Peach had spoken of was relishing a taste of freedom. Many of the girls had been weeping but at the sight of the man in the topee, they stood up in their seats and stared and giggled. Grace frowned at them, feebly, dutifully. That made him all the funnier. The bus moved on and the girls settled down and Ruby stood up and silently re-enacted the naked traffic policeman's hand gestures – one palm flat, blocking, one arm waving on – and a fresh wave of hilarity swept over the bus. It was a lovely moment, and, better, they were on the road.

'Discipline is going out of the window. We cannot allow standards to drop,' said Miss Furroughs.

'It's not just standards that are dropping, Miss Furroughs,' said Grace, trying to turn her laughter into a hiccoughing fit.

At the edge of Rangoon, paddy-fields quilted the landscape. The traffic slowed to sludge, the beginning of a monstrous traffic jam that threatened to last all the way to Mandalay. Stuck in the jam, the school bus was a target for hawkers and beggars of every description.

Molly saw them first.

'Miss,' she said urgently. 'Miss, look! Look!'

Five lepers clawed up at the windows of the bus. Faces without form, stumps fingerless. Allu was uncertain, hesitant. Miss Furroughs barked at him: 'Drive on! Damn you sir, drive on.'

The children gazed at the lepers, aghast. Joseph, the Mongol boy, started to grind his teeth and cry out. Grace ran down the length of the bus to comfort him and as she did so, there was a sudden lurch as Allu found a break in the traffic, and Hants & Dorset accelerated away.

The lepers were by no means the most distressing thing they encountered on the road north to Mandalay. By mid-afternoon, they had joined an enormous queue of lorries, ox-carts, and a sea of people, Indians, Chinese, Anglo-Burmese half-castes and a sprinkling of the Heaven Born, travelling in limousines and sedans. Grace got down and walked up the queue, north, towards Mandalay for a spell, simply to get some exercise. Two planes screamed past. Red, white and blue roundels – the RAF – but, to her astonishment, they opened fire, machine-guns stuttering into the traffic jam, blowing up a petrol lorry in a great cascade of orange half a mile ahead.

Grace remembered what Mr Peach had told her, that they'd sent back the radar kit to India. The poor airmen had no clear idea where the Japanese might be, had no way of telling who were enemy and who were refugees, so they were fighting blind. And that, back on the road, meant breathing in the stink of burnt flesh from half a mile distant.

'The Japanese?' asked Miss Furroughs. Grace hesitated, then shook her head.

'Oh, sweet Lord, what a terrible time,' said the headmistress.

'No one knows where the Japs are,' Grace mumbled.

They swept past broken bodies lying in blood-treacle, survivors stone-faced, the injured mewing in pain. In the back of one wreck – a lorry, once – she saw a tail of chalky rubble leading to an off-white football, lying on a mat of charred black goo. With utter horror, Grace realised what exactly she was looking at: the chalky stuff had been someone's backbone and the football a skull, the black the remains of skin, blood, vitals. And of all this had been a horrible own goal. The invisibility of the enemy made them all the more terrible.

At the end of the first day they planned to pass the night in a house owned by a planter, a friend of Miss Furroughs. The shadows were lengthening as the bus turned off the main road into a kind of heaven: peacocks strutting across a lawn, gorgeous flowers, blue delphiniums, scarlet poinsettia, snowy bauhinia, purple wisteria and yellow laburnum tumbling out of a rockery, a fishpond set in crazy paving. Hants & Dorset pulled up under the deep coolness of a cedar tree. Allu switched off the engine, slipped on the hand-brake and the girls piled out, to stretch and yawn and run on the grass. Grace turned to Miss Furroughs: 'Heavens, we could be in Surrey.'

Of the planter, of anyone, no sign. The headmistress tapped on the door knocker. No one stirred. Allu tooted the horn once, lightly. No response. He leant on it, and the horn blasted across the lawn, igniting the peacocks in a paroxysm of squawks. Still, nothing. The children dozed on the grass. At length, Grace walked around the back and pushed open the door to the kitchen. Empty rooms decorated with oil paintings of stags at bay in the Highlands and stuffed pheasants in glass cases led to a large open space, lined with books and paintings, with a view of the plantation beyond. It would have been one of the most beautiful rooms she had ever been in, were it not for the white-haired planter, his face a violent green-black, his feet turning a fraction, to and fro, to and fro, as he swayed from the upstairs balcony, dangling from a rope.

On hearing the explanation for the silence, the headmistress plunged her head in her hands. Nothing was said to the children, but they seemed to sense the gloom of the adults. They got back on the bus, Allu intending to drive through the night. Later, Grace realised that it would have been wiser to stay at the suicide's house, grim as it was, but the proprieties of peace-time still ruled their minds. They tortured themselves by trying to sleep on the bus.

Allu zig-zagged on the unlit road once too often and ended up in a ditch, on the edge of paddy-fields.

They might be able to sort it out in the morning but it seemed as good a place as any to stop, they thought, until the mosquitoes found them.

While the bus struggled to sleep, Grace sought out Allu and smelt his breath. It stank of moonshine. 'Allu, you cannot drive the bus and drink. You are our only hope.' She found his knapsack and rummaged through it, pulling out a bottle, half-full, of hooch.

'Miss, I am so very sorry. But without the drink I have no courage to drive.'

'Oh, Allu...'

He grabbed hold of the bottle – he was a strong, wiry little man, despite his age – and lobbed it into the dark, setting off the frogs in the ditch to a new riot of belching.

In the morning, Grace had to beg for petrol from the retreating army. She had none of the right chits or signatures but it turned out that it was simple enough. All she had to do was stand by the side of a road, a blonde Englishwoman holding an empty fuel can upside down. Once the driver of an army lorry saw her, he would stop. The soldiers would clamber out, cracking jokes, offering petrol, making a quick brew of tea, playing bang-bang with the boys and flirting with the older girls, while Miss Furroughs clucked around like a perturbed mother hen.

By noon, molten heat fell from the sky. The bus clattered on, sending up a cloud of dust, creamy particles that plumed everywhere, up noses, into eyes, past lips pressed tight shut. Impossible to drive a yard without every single window on Hants & Dorset that could open being open; impossible to breathe in a bus cloaked in its own fog of dust.

The things they saw: the face of a buffalo, brutal, staring out of the dust, missed by Allu by a chance few inches; waving puddles of mirages, of water promised but never produced; saffron-robed monks, staring at the bus; an old mad man, gibbering to himself, half-way up a pipal tree.

To keep fear at bay, they sang hymns until throats grew sore and mouths dry, 'Now Thank We All Our God' and 'The Day Thou Gavest, Lord, Is Ended'. When the bus overtook an army convoy, they belted out 'Onward Christian Soldiers'. The Fourteenth Army was a hodge-podge of all the nations of the Empire – Mussulmans, Sikhs, askari from the East Coast of Africa, West Africans, Hindus, Parsees, Buddhists, the soldiers, blue-black, brown, yellow and only occasionally pinkish-white – but they would wave at the singing bus as it stuttered past, savouring a moment of surreal innocence, before returning to their real world of retreat without end, of killing, and being killed.

Once a day, but every day, as dusk approached, Miss Furroughs let the girls have one song that wouldn't improve their souls. Their favourite, much to her feigned annoyance, was 'Somewhere Over The Rainbow'.

Just Hollywood trickiness, exploiting homesickness yet bottled up in that song, was something real too – their longing for a true home, for any place where they could feel safe – and Grace was never able to listen to 'Hants & Dorset' croaking out 'Over the Rainbow' without her eyes brimming.

They drove further and further from Rangoon, becoming more and more exhausted and crabby with each other as the journey seemed without end, past Gyobingank and Prome, Magwe and Taungdwingyi, into the Yenangyaung oilfield. The sun was falling and the ghostly nodding donkeys, the oil drills silhouetted by fading light, were a symbol of Burma's curse – because without the oil, the Japanese might have thought the country not worth the candle. As they drove on, the road became more clogged up with the walking refugees. They were nearly all Indians, only a few Chinese and Anglo-Burmans. The Burmese proper, of course, had little cause to run as they saw the invading army as liberators. Time was when the Indians, especially the money-lenders, had lorded it over the Burmese. These days the boot was on the other foot, and, at night especially, Burmese thugs robbed and killed the Indian refugees, hacking off the hands and feet of stragglers, showing no pity.

For those who could walk, the road was the least dangerous place for the refugees, and on they trudged.

The luckiest refugees sat on top of carts, pulled by ponies or by their menfolk, wielding an umbrella from the sun. A few travelled in hand-pulled rickshaws, like lords of creation, but most walked, clutching prize possessions – buckets, pots, blankets – under their arms or yoked on a stick across their shoulders. One man pushed a bicycle with only one wheel. The condition of the walking refugees grew worse, the shade of almost every other tree sheltering an emaciated form, the green verges by the road littered with yellow pats of diarrhoea.

Cholera.

Nothing they could do to help but gaze at lives draining away, as they drove on and on.

A road sign, to Mandalay: thirty miles. Eyes locking on to the sign, staring down the length of the bus and out of the back windows, Grace saw, advancing on them, from behind, fast, a superior cloud of dust. Soon she could pick out four motor-cycle outriders and behind them a gleaming black Rolls Royce, its radiator so highly polished it mirrored the sun.

An Indian refugee, gaunt, stick-limbed, saw the motorcade coming towards them too, and stepped out into the middle of the road, carrying a bundle containing a dirty white object in his coal-black hands, aloft.

The motorcade kept pace but angled towards the far side of the road, kicking up dust, sweeping past the refugee with his bundle high in the air. The object, Grace realised, was a baby, long dead.

The Rolls overtook the school bus and Grace recognised the wife of the Governor of Burma cupping her hands, her attention taken by a uniformed aide-de-camp sitting by her side lighting her cigarette. The far side wheels of the Rolls left the asphalt and bit into the rough ground at the edge of the road, and the grand party experienced a gentle bump, delaying the lighting of the cigarette for a second or two, and they turned a corner and were gone.

How many dying refugees had Grace seen on the road? Thousands. She stood up in her seat to look back at the refugee with the bundle, but the bend in the road shut off her view. Collapsing in her seat with a jolt, she wondered, could a God of mercy order man's affairs in this way? No, He could not.

For her, at that precise moment, her faith in God and her belief, long drummed into her, that the British had an especial right to rule over other people, died.

Mandalay, when Hants & Dorset lumbered through the city gates, was a paradise, the old citadel of the Burmese kings still full of colour and life and market-sellers, unscarred by war. They were billeted in the eerie grandeur – stained-glass windows, mysterious compass and arch designs – of a Masonic Hall high up on a conical hill, overlooking the roofs of the city.

One evening, just before lights out, Grace discovered the two boys in the cellar of the hall, trying on strange hats and aprons. Half-laughing, she scolded the boys for their cheek and told them not to play with the Masonic stuff again. They left good-humouredly, but Grace suspected that they were hiding something from her.

They grew too comfortable in the Masonic hall.

On Good Friday, 1942, the school held a simple service, Grace going through the motions of prayer, her mind elsewhere. When the service was over, she caught up with Miss Furroughs in the garden overlooking the gilded palace of Mandalay.

'We need to leave here, Miss.'

'Oh, no, not that again. Can't you...'

'We need to leave Mandalay. The Japanese are on the march, again.'

'No. It's not necessary. We'll stay...we'll leave when there is an order. But...so...there's nothing we can...' Half-finished thoughts, barked out, the headmistress aggressively indecisive.

'The monsoon will be here in May, then getting to India will be all but impossible. We've got to leave now,' Grace insisted.

'How do you suggest?'

'The bus as far as it can go. Then walk...'

'The bus is old, it won't get very far. And the children cannot walk.'

'I know the bus is old. But it hasn't let us down so far.'

'We could fly. People are heading for Myitkyina.' She was referring to the last aerodrome in British hands in Burma, to the east, close to the border with China.

'Miss, have you forgotten what happened at Rangoon docks? No room for half-castes. Will sixty-two half-caste orphans really get seats on an aeroplane? I don't think so. It's better that we drive as far as we can, west, and walk out of Burma.'

'Miss Collins, these matters are not, are not...–' The maddening half-sentence, ending in thin air.

The Japanese suffered no such indecision.

At noon on Good Friday, without warning, without benefit of air-raid sirens, the bombs started to fall on Mandalay, a city built of wood, of shacks and glorious gilt pagodas and royal palaces. The hall stood half-way up a hill, several hundred yards out of the city, giving them a hawk's eye view of the destruction.

They saw too much.

A steady breeze from the west, from the Irrawaddy, cascaded sparks, then fires, igniting market stalls, knots of trees, houses, temples, churches, schools. First whole streets – and every living thing in them – and acre after acre of Mandalay were roaring an angry, raging orange. People washing their pots stood up, heard a whoosh of moving heat, and their lungs caught fire. Shopkeepers dithered, not knowing down which corridor of fire they had to run, and, in seconds, turned to ash and fat. Eucalyptus trees exploded before the rip-tide of heat, spitting out leaping tongues of flaming sap. Fur on fire, monkeys leapt from tree to tree, spreading the heat above the roof tops. At street level buffalo bellowed, stampeding, crushing a confusion of people running the wrong way, towards the flames. Survivors manhandled victims with fried skin to the hospital, only to discover that it was an inferno. A stick of bombs fell on the railway station goods yard, igniting the wagons of a fuel train, and the fire storm consumed the city.

The children watched the city burn, listless, mute. There was nothing they could do. Grace fussed over the two boys, cuddling Joseph, who at the first sound of the bombs began grinding his teeth. Soon, even he stopped and stared at the horrors unfolding below them.

It was around three o'clock when the alarm was sounded. One of the girls had seen a tiny figure making her way down the last of the steps carved into the hillside, which led from the Masonic Hall to the heart of Mandalay. Most of the path was hidden from them, zig-zagging down the far side of the hill, but the last stretch was in plain view of the whole school. Grace called out to her, as loud as her lungs would allow: 'Miss Furroughs, Miss Furroughs come back!'

Her shouting was lost in the cacophony of a city burning.

The headmistress moved slowly, deliberately, taking one step at a time. She did not turn back. She paid no heed as the sky grew dark, a pre-natural sunset. Miss Furroughs was three hundred, maybe four hundred yards down the hill. All Grace had to do was to get to her feet and run down and stop her. She was a much fitter woman and she could well have caught up with her. But for some reason Grace found it impossible to move. She stared and stared, immobile, mouthing: 'no, Miss, no,' again and again. The old lady was still in view, now five hundred yards from the hall, her path less steep, beginning to level out on to the plain where the city lay when the saw-teeth of engines sounded high in the sky, bombers coming in low for a fresh attack. The children ran for the safety of the Hall's basement, half buried into the side of the hill. Grace shooed them in, and looked back, once. The last Grace saw of the headmistress was her white blouse and black skirt being swallowed up by the smoke.

CHAPTER THREE

Towards dusk, the air acrid from the still burning city, Molly spotted him first. 'An Indian soldier, Miss, on a motor-bicycle. Asking for someone in charge.'

An officer of some kind, face strikingly pale, tall, painfully slim, eyes of light green, a beaked nose. Hanging from his shoulder a leather satchel – a despatch rider? Taking Grace to one side he started to describe what he had witnessed: 'A refined lady, middle aged, very correctly dressed, white blouse, dark skirt, short, with white hair. Miss…'

'She's,..' The urge to panic was animal and strong, but the quickest of glances told her that Emily and Ruby were staring at them. Grace tilted her face closer to his ear: '...dead. Isn't she?'

The officer nodded. 'I am most terribly sorry, Miss.'

'She meant to kill herself, didn't she?'

'I do not know. We saw her go out onto King's Street, just after four, in the middle of a bombing raid, when the flames were at their strongest. And then she was killed. But it was Queen Elizabeth who said: "I would not open windows into men's souls." We don't know what was in her soul. I am very sorry for your trouble, Miss.'

He spoke Oxford English, exquisitely.

'I would not open windows into men's souls. Yes, that is right.'

The most powerful emotion for Grace was one she was ashamed to admit to anyone, and certainly not to the young Indian officer. Relief that she no longer had to beg Miss Furroughs to make decisions, relief that, with the headmistress gone, they could press on to India as fast as possible, relief that she had a better chance of saving the children on her own. Had the old lady realised that she was slowing them down, that her indecision and helplessness at the thought of leaving Burma was becoming a danger to the children? Was that why she had walked into fire?

Eyes smarting, she pushed past the officer, out of the cellar. Below stood the burnt city, mile after mile of charred black, here and there wisps of smoke rising from still smouldering fires, and she wept in shame that she had done nothing to save her friend.

The officer had come to her side.

'I am sorry for your loss, Miss.'

'Sir...'

'Jemadar Ahmed Rehman, at your service.'

Grace told him her name.

'Miss Collins–'

'Call me Grace, please.'

'–Miss Grace, the children cannot stay here,' he said flatly. 'The Japanese will be here in days.' The Jemadar started to speak, soldier's stuff, talking for talking's sake, giving her time to adjust. She wiped her eyes with the edge of her sleeve and listened.

'The bombers will return. Mandalay is on the Burma Road – it's the main, no, probably the only supply route for the Allies to get arms and ammunition through to China. If the Japs cut the Burma Road, they weaken the ability of China to fight, and that will free more Japanese soldiers, so they can conquer India. They will keep on bombing Mandalay until everything is burnt. And soon, the Japanese army will come here, too. The front is one hundred miles away, but the Japanese keep on overtaking us. They did so at Moulmein, Rangoon, the oil fields at Yenangyaung. Mandalay will be next. It may take them a month or they could be here in two days. But no one is safe in Mandalay.'

'We must go to India as quickly as possible,' Grace said firmly. That simple statement of the obvious, without having to defer to Miss Furroughs, without qualification, without anxious introspection, carried with it its own pleasure – and instantly stirred her guilt again, that she had not stopped the old lady from walking into the flames.

'Tomorrow, Miss Grace. There is no time to lose.'

'Tomorrow, yes. But the route, east or west...'

'Drive west, as far as we can. Then walk to India.'

'East? The aerodrome at Myitkyina?'

'When they get round to it, the Japanese will bomb it to smithereens.'

'West, then. We'll need petrol, food, water. Can you help?'

'I shall try.'

The Jemadar vanished but, shortly after dusk, a lorry rumbled up the track that passed the rear of the Masonic temple. In the back of the lorry were crates of tinned food, boxes of biscuits and jars of jam, jerrycans of petrol for the bus and water. By the light of a kerosene lamp she spied an enormous strawberry sponge cake, resting on a crystal glass cake-stand.

'Where did you get that?'

'Miss, it was baked for Generalissimo Chiang Kai-shek and his wife by the best pastry chef in the whole of Burma. But it has been decided that it is to be diverted for refugee use.'

'Did you steal it?'

'It has been decided that it is to be diverted for refugee use.'

'Did you steal it?'

'You have no idea how much trouble I had to go to get it.'

She could not help herself from giggling.

'Do you want me to take it back?'

'No, Jemadar, I don't. We shall have it for dessert.'

He bowed, comically low, and set out about transferring the provisions.

Unaware of the cake, the children tucked into the rations provided by the Jemadar, tins of bully beef, sardines, jam, condensed milk.

She popped outside and caught the two boys, Michael and Joseph, playing on the steps of the Masonic Hall with a revolver.

'Bang-bang, you're dead, Miss,' said Michael.

'Where in heaven's name did you get that? Give it to me, Michael. Give it to me right now.'

'It's the Jem's, Miss. He gave it to us to play with.'

'Well he should have done no such thing and he is clearly out of his mind.' Horrified, she confiscated the weapon and marched out to the back of the hall, where she found him taking boxes from the back of the lorry and stowing them in Hants & Dorset.

'Does this object belong to you, Jemadar?' She held the revolver by the bottom of the handle, with evident disgust.

'Ah, yes, that's mine, Miss Grace. Thank you for finding it. I knew I'd left it somewhere.'

'Jemadar, what on earth do you think you are doing? The boys told me you gave it to them.'

'Oh, did they?' He replaced the revolver in his holster, bent down and shoved a wooden box full of tins of strawberry jam into the belly of Hants & Dorset.

'Why on earth let them play with a deadly weapon?'

Standing up, his sea-green eyes mocked her. 'Ah, that was because they were playing with this...'

Tucked into his officer's belt was a Masonic dagger, decorated with an arch and compass emblazoned in ivory on its onyx handle, which he pulled out and waved in the air, its blade flashing murderously in the reddening light.

'So, Miss Grace, the same question. Why let them play with a deadly weapon?'

'I had no idea.'

'On a technical note, a dagger is dangerous at all times, but a revolver, when you have taken all the bullets out, is not. I gave them my revolver, minus the bullets, to distract from the loss of the knife, which I took from them. I explained they could only play with my gun for half an hour and they had to give it back to me in exactly the same condition – I stressed the word *exactly* – I had given it to them. Is the knife yours?'

Blushing, she shook her head. 'Of course not. It must belong to the Freemasons. I don't want the damned thing, you silly man.'

'You are very kind.' He replaced the knife in his belt and walked past to the lorry and took out a box of sardines, marked *Made in Japan*, in his arms. In the distance she caught sight of Emily, staring towards them. The moment Emily realised that Grace was looking at her, she turned her back and walked away.

Amongst the children, the boys' nickname for their hero, The Jem, stuck.

'Girls and boys,' Grace called the attention of the whole school, 'Miss Furroughs has gone ahead to the border to help organise things. But she has sent us this cake to send us on our way.' Cheers and claps as the Jemadar brought in the cake.

'You'd better take your dagger to divide up the cake.' The Jemadar offered her the knife.

'Once and for all, it's *not* my dagger.'

'Really?'

'Oh, you're impossible.'

'Cut the cake and keep it. It might come in handy.' The children didn't get more than a sliver each, but it tasted like angel food. When no one was looking, Grace wiped the dagger clean on her dress, wrapped it up in a dish-cloth and slipped it into her handbag.

The Jem disappeared, to return the lorry, but came back on his motorbike an hour later.

'It has been decided that I am to be diverted for refugee use,' he said.

'How did you do that?'

'Piece of cake,' he said, and unrolled his hammock, tied it to two columns of the Masonic Hall, climbed in and feigned sleep.

They almost didn't make it out of Mandalay.

They started off late, the children irascible and mewing about having to get up so early. Joseph wanted to play with the Jemadar's pistol and Grace snapped at him to behave, which made him cry.

Long after dawn, with the early morning mists gone, the bus pulled up at the eastern end of the Ava Bridge. Red iron girders hurdled across a mile of the Irrawaddy, the greatest river in all Burma. A military policeman, nervous, edgy, barred their way, blowing his whistle, gesturing at the bus to turn round, yelling: 'Go back, go back.' The Jem ignored the policeman and gunned his BSA motor-bicycle around the road-block. More British troops, green hackles on their berets, emerged from the shade, rifles at the ready, blocking his path. Allu pulled the bus up in front of a wooden barrier.

The tallest of the soldiers marched swiftly up to the bus and leapt on board, angling his neck so that it didn't bash against the roof of the bus.

'What the bloody hell is going on? We're blowing this bridge in three minutes and you must go back.'

'Mr Peach!'

'Oh, Miss Collins, it's you!'

'Mr Peach, you escaped Rangoon.'

'Yes, just. It's Lieutenant Peach, actually. Emergency commission in the field. But, but, but… you must go back. We're going to dynamite the bridge any second.'

'Mr Peach – sorry, Lieutenant Peach – we're terribly sorry but this is our only chance.' The children watched, fascinated, at how in the presence of

Miss Collins the warrior bearing of the astonishingly tall officer began to melt.

'If we can't cross the river by the bridge,' Grace continued, 'we will have to abandon the bus and walk and that will be a disaster, especially for the young ones.' She looked around her, and the girls shrunk, goggle eyed, helpless.

'But I've got to dynamite the bridge in three minutes.'

'Couldn't you just have a word with your commanding officer. Just to let us through, and then blow the bridge? Could I speak to the commanding officer, Mr Peach?'

The gangly lieutenant shook his head. He gazed at the children – sixty-odd, nearly all girls apart from two little boys, and one of them a little backward at that. Scowling at them all, he glared at Miss Collins, said: 'Bugger this,' more to himself than anyone else, backed down the steps of the bus, turned to his men, and lifted up a flat palm and roared his command.

'Hold! Hold the firing sequence. Hold the demolition.'

At once, cries of 'Hold!' echoed and re-echoed down the line of troops to the solitary Royal Engineer, poised to fire the detonators. A red flag came down and a yellow flag snapped high in the air by the command post, a second yellow some way down the bridge, a third by the engineer hovering over his fuses, a fourth three quarters towards the far bank, and finally a fifth on the far, western bank a mile away. Almost instantly a field phone jangled in the command post in the shade of a banyan tree. Lieutenant Peach scurried to answer the call.

Silence as everyone – soldiers, orphans, Allu, Miss Collins and the Jem – strained to listen in to the lieutenant's side of the conversation.

'Sorry, sir, but we've got to hold... Yes, sir, on my authority, sir, that we hold and let them pass... No, sir, you cannot order me to proceed. I am the senior officer here... Yes, sir, I know you are a brigadier... but with respect, sir, you are on the west bank of the river and I am the officer in charge of the east bank... I'm giving the order that we hold the demolition until these VIPs have passed. They are the daughter of an earl, yes, and the party includes relatives of the Marchioness of Dufferin and Ava.'

Ruby looked at Emily, an enormous 'What?' written on their faces.

'They can speed across the bridge in ten minutes, maybe less. Yes, their vehicle will make it, sir...'

Peach turned to squint at Hants & Dorset, its ancient engine wheezing in the heat. '...virtually brand new... Yes, sir, the moment they've crossed the bridge, sir, we'll blow it sky high. On my head be it, sir.'

He put down the field phone and walked towards the bus. 'Go. Go now. And if that museum piece of a bus breaks down on the bridge, I will be shot. *Go*.'

Grace got up from her seat, hurried down the steps, lifted her hands around Lieutenant Peach's neck, dragged his mouth down towards her height and stood on tip-toe and kissed him on the lips. Wolf-whistles from the other British soldiers as the lieutenant's face turned salmon-pink, then post-box red. The sergeant-major, a squat barrel of a man, roared for the troops to stand to attention 'for the VIPs', and thirty men snapped into brigade ground salutes.

'Good luck, Lieutenant Peach,' said Grace and she ran back to the bus and Allu did his best to coax some life out of old Hants & Dorset. Grumbling into motion, belching smoke, it lurched off towards the bridge, with the Jem, after a crisp salute for Lieutenant Peach, following on behind. Ruby began 'We'll Meet Again...' which the children took up, all the while frantically waving goodbye to the soldiers, who were sternly saluting and grinning their heads off at the same time.

Sergeant-major Eric Barr came over and stood next to the officer.

'That old fuss-pot is going to have me shot when he sees our VIPs,' said Lieutenant Peach.

'Well, sir, he can fook off, sir.'

The sergeant-major was King's Own Yorkshire Light Infantry, from Barnsley.

'The brig won't send 'em back over the bridge again, sir. Any road, we may be losing every bloody battle and on our way out of Burma, but we've got standards, sir. If we're not going to help the likes of 'em poor bastards, sir, what are we doing here?'

'Well put, Sergeant-major.'

Lieutenant Peach sighed as the bus rattled across the bridge. The sergeant-major coughed, officiously, as if he was about to make a formal announcement, a toast-master at a banquet.

'Yes, Sergeant-major?'

'Sir, when we first heard that you were going to be our new officer, sir, we all thought you were an arse, sir. We'd all heard about you jailing that officer. But we heard wrong, sir. The men would like you to know you're not an arse, sir.'

'Not an arse,' said Lieutenant Peach, frowning. And then, after some thought, 'Very good, Sergeant-major.'

The lieutenant stared after the bus clattering along the bridge's span: 'Let's hope they don't get strafed while they're crossing the river. God speed, little bus.'

But the luck of Bishop Strachan's held, for a time.

Hants & Dorset rumbled off the far end of the bridge, coughing and chugging past a group of staff officers, whose gallantry withered once they saw the VIPs they had gathered to salute with their own eyes. Elbows held at perfect angles hung downwards; moustaches drooped; shoulders slumped. A vein on the brigadier's temple throbbed and he marched to the field phone, a martinet bent on revenge. 'Get me that idiot, Lieutenant Peach. I'm going to bust him down to Private... ' But no one stopped the bus.

Ruby turned to Emily: 'Good morning. I'm not sure that we've been properly introduced. I am the grand-niece of the Marchioness of Dufferin and Ava... '

Emily's giggles were interrupted by a *boom*.

A mushroom of smoke and dust and water rose up into the air and slowly fell in on itself, revealing a tangle of metal knitting lying higgledy-piggledy in the river, and two spans of the bridge gone.

The signalman on the west bank of the Irrawaddy saluted the brigadier. 'Sorry, sir, you wanted Lieutenant Peach?'

'Yes, I bloody do,' said the brigadier.

'Phone line is dead, sir,' said the signalman. Behind the back of the brigadier, he replaced the receiver in its cradle and permitted himself a ghost of a smile.

Ten miles, twenty, thirty, one hundred. Past Shwebo, Ye-u, Pyingaing, always to the west, past an army camp, hidden from the sky, littered with the junk of war, empty wooden crates of ammo, a fifty-five-pounder with a broken axle, brown tents thronging with British and Indian soldiers resting in the shade of a giant banyan tree. The Jem overtook, fast, on his motorbike and disappeared around a bend. He drove on a few miles and then pulled over, hiding from the sun in the cool of a fig tree. Arms resting on the handlebars, he closed his eyes and waited. The sounds of Burma – the itchy crackle of insects, the moo of an ox, a weird hiccoughing, repeated endlessly, hard to place, maybe a bird - and then an engine, growling and whining, and, in a higher register:

'Daisy, Daisy,
Give me your answer do,
I'm half crazy,
All for the love of you...'

This singing bus, he thought, will be the death of me.

For some magical reason the engine of Hants & Dorset kept going. Every thirty miles or so, they had to top up the radiator with fresh water. At one stop, the wheels got stuck in sand, as soft and treacherous as the dunes at West Wittering, where Grace had swam when she was at school. They feared they would have to abandon her, because the bus by now had become a friend– and a female one at that– and walk. The Jem disappeared on his motor-bicycle and returned with a Honey tank on his tail. The school decamped off the bus while the tank men fixed a chain to the chassis of Hants & Dorset, Allu looking on, nervously. The tank's tracks bit deep through the sand onto harder, packed earth beneath and soon the bus was on the road again.

Theirs was a race against the Japanese, and the monsoon. When the rains came, the dusty cart-tracks along which the bus could struggle, just, would be turned into sludge and mud, becoming impassable. But for the time being the landscape was parched, the earth bone dry, the bus stirring up a great wash of fine red dust high in the air, making it a comically easy target for Japanese fighters overhead to spot them and descend for a kill. But still, somehow, they drove on, unhurt.

At a road junction, they spotted a small fuel depot. Allu pulled up and Grace got down to beg for a few more gallons of fuel. The clerk in charge was Indian, the lord and master of a hut with palm fronds for a roof and no walls. He refused Grace's chit for more fuel and handed it back.

'The details are not correct, Miss. You must go back to Mandalay and get it counter-signed by the appropriate authorities.'

'Sir, we cannot do that. They have blown up the bridge. We saw it happen with our own eyes. And Mandalay is burnt to a cinder. We cannot go back.'

'The paperwork is not correct, Miss.'

'For God's sake, don't you know there is a war on?'

'The chit must be counter-signed by the correct authorities,' he insisted.

She sighed deeply.

'The paperwork is not correct, Miss.'

No response. Her shoulders heaved, tears welled up and ran down her cheeks. Out of the corner of her eye she saw Emily stare at her from her seat on the bus, her face revealing that she was, to put it mildly, unconvinced by her teacher's performance. Likewise, the little man was not to be moved. The moment she stopped, he repeated in a voice as unfeeling as an abacus: 'The paperwork is not correct, Miss.'

The Jem, as usual, was nowhere to be seen. He had been scouting ahead, making sure the road was clear, searching out stores, shops, anywhere still open and working where they could pick up extra food and water. The splutter of his returning motorbike lifted her. When he arrived, she whispered the problem into his ear. Smiling, he said: 'Boorishness, too, has its geniuses,' and went into battle.

The Jem sat down opposite the depot clerk, studied her chit, delved into his leather satchel – she'd never seen him without it, not even when asleep in his hammock - and extracted the largest rubber stamp Grace had ever seen. He brought the stamp down with a bang, counter-signed the chit with an expansive scrolling signature, turned it over and stamped it three more times and counter-signed.

A bead of sweat formed on the clerk's upper lip.

The Jem turned the chit over again, back to the first sheet: stamp, stamp, stamp. Again, he counter-signed, then handed it over to the clerk.

The clerk said impassively: 'Everything is now in order. You may have the fuel.' Sitting with her face in her hands, Grace studied the Jem through her fingers. The clerk walked off to help Allu fill up the bus.

'I swear you are a sorcerer, Jemadar.'

'I don't have a white rabbit, Miss Collins. At least, not yet.'

She read the chit upside down and felt a twinge of unease.

'The name you've signed. That's not Ahmed Rehman, that's not your name.'

'Ah, yes. "When fighting for truth and justice," wrote Balzac, "it's never a good idea to wear one's best trousers".'

'Sometimes, I wonder about you.'

'In what way?'

'You might be a Jiff– you know, "Asia for the Asiatics" and all that.'

He frowned, momentarily.

Emboldened by his unease, she challenged him directly. 'So, are you a Jiff, Jemadar?'

'A Jiff, Miss Collins? Perhaps we Indians are a little smarter than that. I no longer think that the British have a God-given right to rule the lesser breeds without the law, as Mr Kipling thought. One day India will be free of the British, although I suspect we may still play cricket and drink tea and sit around and chat when there is work to be done. But are the Japanese our friends? Perhaps it is the case of better the devil you know.'

'And do you think every Briton is a devil?'

'Well, yes, I do rather. I know one in particular I cannot but serve, never mind what hell she may take me to.'

'Your eyes are of the deepest green, Jem,' she said, 'just like the stuffed tiger in the Pegu Club. But do I trust them?' She marched back towards the bus, holding a smile within herself.

'Grace...' the Jem called out, but the moment between them was lost. He gunned his motorbike and was off. Soon, all that she could make of him was an exclamation mark of dust rising in the air, one, two, miles ahead, shimmering in the heat.

The immense flatness of the Irrawaddy Plain, here and there interrupted by stubs of rock, capped by Buddhist stupas, gleaming in the harsh sun, gave way as they drove west to a more undulating landscape, and soon they were travelling through a frozen green sea of sharp ridges, high peaks and low ravines, the road circling and wheeling and doubling back on itself.

Half-dozing in the front seat immediately behind Allu, Grace opened her eyes as she sensed Hants & Dorset chugging to a halt. A white pole lay across the road, figures moving in the deep shade of a banyan tree. Three or four British soldiers brewing up, a kettle whistling. A checkpoint, of sorts. In no great hurry a corporal walked up to them, perched on the first step of the bus and took in the rows of children, many asleep, quiet.

'Afternoon, Miss. We're supposed to check everyone's papers, Miss, but then we're supposed to be doing lots of things. This lot looks pretty harmless to me. Refugees?' She nodded. 'Can you vouch that you're not concealing the enemy?'

'Yes, Corporal.'

'Good, thought so. On your way, then.'

'Who are you looking for?' It was the very first checkpoint they had come across.

'Deserters, suspicious people without papers, Jiffs–' said the corporal.

'I see. Have you seen our Jemadar? He's on a motorbike?'

'Nope. No one on a motorbike the whole afternoon.'

'And the Japanese?'

'One hundred miles away, according to our latest intelligence. That means they're playing cards round the next bend. Good luck.'

Allu put Hants & Dorset into first gear and the ancient green bus moved out of the shade onto the road, driving on and on, its wheels still kicking up a great quantity of dust; the flow of air through the open windows providing the children with some measure of relief from the heat. They passed small knots of Indian refugees, straggling along the road, fewer in number, now, but no less exhausted.

She heard the familiar pop-pop-pop of his motorbike, overtaking the bus. The children waved, calling out: 'Hello, Jem!'

How could that have happened? Before the checkpoint he had been miles ahead of them, and somehow he had fallen behind. The old bus must have overtaken him when she had been sleeping.

Through cathedrals of green they drove on, past rice paddies and teak forests and tidy European bungalows with white picket fences, empty, and wooden houses on stilts, thatched by sheaves of palm, where the Burmese watched them pass by in silence, like standing stones.

The violent white of day, making black silhouettes of the shade, began to dim. To the west, a dark bottle green, the road immediately ahead a golden brown. They passed a farmer, following an ox ploughing up an old rice paddy, turned a bend and drove on and on...

As the sun died behind the hills, Hants & Dorset eased to a full stop. The children got out, stretched their legs, scrubbed their faces in a mountain stream tumbling down rocks on the far side of the road. Grace busied herself, feeding them, playing with the boys, making sure that she had a word here and there with the more anxious-looking girls.

Night fell with the suddenness of an axe. Only then did she hear his motorbike, the sound of its engine making her all but purr with pleasure, and the realisation of that both terrified and excited her, very much.

He parked the bike at the back of the bus, lit a cigarette and waited for her to join him. There was something supremely arrogant about the way he did that, she thought, and smiled to herself.

'Tell me about that English lieutenant, the one who looks like a giraffe,' he asked.

'Oh, Lieutenant Peach.' Moonshine bathed them in silvery-grey, eerie and surreal, ghouls poised to frighten a ghost train. Looking at him along her eyes, she said: 'There is nothing to tell, Jem.'

'My name is Ahmed.'

'I prefer Jem. It is more proper.'

'Proper?'

'Proper.'

'I think there is something between you and Lieutenant Peach, you know. You kissed him. I dared to steal a Generalissimo's cake to impress you' – Grace's eyes widened – 'but I would never have dreamt of holding up the demolition of the biggest bridge in Burma. Not with the Japanese Imperial Army a few miles off. He dared risk the whole of Upper Burma to impress you.'

'I'm sure he didn't.'

'He loves you. If he didn't love you, he would never have risked disobeying orders.'

'I don't know about that. I find Mr Peach rather plucky, sir, but my heart belongs to another.'

'And who would that be?' The Jem's green eyes grew more tigerish.

'That would be telling, Jem, that would be telling.'

'That bee around your neck. How old is it?'

'Fifty million years old.'

'I would give my life to be that bee.'

She bade him goodnight, brushing against his arm, and began walking back towards the bus.

'Stop.'

'Jem, no… ' The kiss was urgent and longed-for. This was no time to fall in love – but what can you do other than stop time itself?

Allu rose before sunrise, said his prayers, and sat behind the wheel. The engine wheezed into life, causing a pack of vultures to thwack the air as they wheeled off. Away from the rising sun, mile after dusty mile, through walls of morning mist still hanging in the river valleys, desperate to put as much distance between them and the invisible enemy. Twice, Allu began to nod off before she jabbed him in the back and the old driver shook his head, dabbed his eyes with water from a flask and drove on. The mist thickened, lifted, thinned and fell heavier than before, sometimes clear for half a mile, at others a thick grey treacle flowing against the windscreen. A jolt, the haze of sleep pierced by tyres squealing, Allu wrestling with the wheel, his right leg pumping the brakes, uselessly.

Brakes don't work on thin air.

The bus lurched not forwards, but *down*. Through the open door at the front Grace gazed down at the rags of mist. They melted away revealing a dry river bed one hundred feet below. Molly, sitting next to her, squeezed her hand. 'I'm scared, Miss.' Grace wanted to say, 'So am I, Molly,' but instead she said: 'I'm sure the Jemadar will sort it out.' He was nowhere to be seen.

The bus creaked, its weight working loose a rock which fell with a clatter. The mist came back, and knowing the drop was there without being able to see it was all the more frightening.

'Pop-pop-pop.' The racket of the Jem's exhaust was the most soothing sound in the entire world.

Across the chasm his face came into view. 'Good morning, Miss Collins. Did you sleep well?'

'Very well, Jemadar. Thank you.'

'Have you had breakfast?'

'Oh, for God's sake, Jem, stop prattling on and get us out of here. Please!'

A dazzling smile. He picked up a big stone, the size of a brick, and went to the back of the bus. Warning the children not to worry, he smashed a window, removed the shards of glass with his gloved hands, and then helped the children squiggle out. As the bus emptied, the weight shifted forward and the bus tilted an inch down. Everyone froze.

Molly started to pray, out loud. 'Our Father, Who Art in Heaven…'

They heard the singing first, a wonderful low bass, an unreal sound from another world. Goggle-eyed, the children watched as soldiers of the King's African Rifles rounded the bend and marched towards them. The Jem grinned. 'You are in luck, Miss Collins. We won't keep you hanging around for much longer.'

The African askari tied ropes to the back of the bus, holding it down, allowing the rest of the children and finally Grace to wriggle out of the rear window. It was a tight fit, no easy way of pulling off an exit that could be deemed lady-like. Her etiquette teacher had overlooked the problem of leaving a bus over-hanging an abyss by the back window while wearing a frock in front of two hundred African soldiers. She extracted herself with as much dignity as she could and treated the Jem to her grandest scowl. Bowing, he said. 'Are you always in such a bad mood before breakfast, Miss Collins?'

Like a dog shaking dry its fur after a swim, she shook her head, but had to turn away from him to hide her smile.

One of the askari, Private Tomasi, coal-black, almost a boy, thin and very light, looped one end of a long rope around his shoulder and tied it off. After squeezing through the back window of the bus, he crept down the aisle to the front step, the bus tilting its nose as he went forward. He swung around above the drop, gripped the bumper, heaved himself up and rested his feet on it, his body leaning forward against the bonnet. Another askari threw him the end of a second rope, which he caught in one hand while he held on to the bonnet with the other, and then he tied the rope end round a metal ring fixed to the chassis. A third rope was thrown and that, too, was tied to the ring at the front of the bus. That done, he swung back through the open door of the bus in one smooth arc and popped out the back, as neatly as a circus trick. The askari fixed block and tackles to an enormous, overhanging branch of a teak tree, and three dozen of them tugged on the pulleys and the tackles creaked horribly but the front of the bus was hoisted an inch in the air. Another inch, and a third, and slowly the bus came to a level and they swung it back onto the road like a toy and Emily cried out, 'Three cheers for the King's African Rifles, pip pip!' and the girls hurrahed, and Allu fired up the engine and the bus spluttered back into life and everyone climbed back on and Ruby stood up in her seat and sang the first lines of sultry 'Summertime'.

'Ruby Goldberg, where on earth did you learn that?' asked Grace, incredulous.

'That would be a secret, Miss,' said Ruby.

At high noon, as they were passing a large army camp, hundreds of soldiers milling around, tents, lorries, guns, even a few tanks, backed up underneath the trees, Hants & Dorset gave out a pathetic woof, like the last bark of an elderly dog, and stopped. Allu stood up, took a straw mat from beneath his seat, stepped out of the bus, unrolled the mat, lay down and within seconds was fast asleep.

As places to break down in Burma, in the borderland between the great river plains and the highland jungle, the army camp was perfect: food and water, and a whole squad of mechanics given an exciting new challenge: how to bring back to life a dead bus engine. Observing the soldiers pouring tea for the children or attacking the innards of the bus, boredom, Grace realised, was the great enemy of soldiers everywhere, boredom while they waited for someone in authority to order them to the front line. Or to the next camp, and more boredom. They relished any excuse to do something different, to entertain the children, to fix an ancient engine, and, of course, to chat up the schoolteacher.

But of the Jem, no sign. It was weird, Grace thought. When they were in trouble, he would appear immediately. But if something happened and he was not needed, then he disappeared.

It took the mechanics two hours of sweat and tinkering before old Hants & Dorset groaned and gibbered into life, its exhaust pipe sending up a thick black smoke cloud. The senior mechanic, a Welshman, revved the engine as he told Grace, 'We've done the best we can. I'd give the old thing another ten miles and then it's going to die forever. Where are you off to?'

'India.'

'Well, pray for a miracle.'

Pressing his foot down hard on the accelerator, the engine growled, frighteningly loud. At that Allu stirred from his sleep, rubbed his eyes, stood up, rolled up his mat and waited for the mechanic to get down from behind the wheel. As he did so, Grace heard the distinctive pop-pop-pop of the Jemadar's motorbike.

He must have been waiting in the shade of some trees, a quarter of mile back, for hours. The bike neared the bus and dawdled to a stop. The children called out to him: 'Where have you been, Jem?' and he was about to reply when two things happened simultaneously. Allu let in the clutch and Hants & Dorset lurched forward and the mechanic started yelling at the Jemadar. The noise of the accelerating bus and the shouts of the children as they waved goodbye to their new friends was loud, but not so loud as to hide the Welshman's fury: 'Traitor! Traitor! I saw you in Singapore! You...'

The rest was lost. Grace twisted in her seat as the Jem accelerated past the bus, zooming through the dust, sashaying past a water buffalo standing in the middle of the road, dangerously fast.

No sign of his tell-tale two-wheel cloud of dust for the rest of the day.

Shortly before dusk, Allu pulled up by the side of the road for the night and explained to Grace that the following day they should reach the Chindwin, so it made sense to try and get a good night's rest.

Fat chance of that. Restless, she begged for the comfort of sleep, but in vain. The very dead of night, the crickets whirring and buzzing in the undergrowth, and a new sound, a motorbike being wheeled, its engine cut, towards them. Framed against a red half-moon rising, he came to a stop.

'So. The mechanic...' Ice in her throat. 'He recognised you. What did you do at Singapore?'

A stillness between them; his silence, an admission of guilt.

'Traitor? Jiff?' The words, hissed.

'Yes.'

Fury, sudden, irresistible, rose within her, her voice a high-pitched shriek: 'How dare you! You're a bloody Jiff! How could I have been so stupid! You appear from nowhere, always on your own, never with any soldiers or senior officers. You never stop at any of the army bases. You didn't speak to any of the soldiers at the bridge.'

She slapped him hard on the face. 'You used us.'

'Yes, I used the children.'

'And you used me. And what are you going to do now, Jiff? Because I swear to you that the very first British soldier I meet, I will condemn you out of hand.'

'Listen to me, Grace.'

'Why the hell should I trust a Jiff, a traitor?'

'Because... because I cannot be a traitor,' the Jemadar told Grace, 'to a foreign power, to an Empire that is occupying my country, imprisoning its leaders, holding its people captive. I am no traitor.' The passion died from his voice. 'But, at the same time... '

'But what, traitor?' said Grace.

'Can I trust you?'

'How dare you!' Grace repeated. She made to slap him, but he gripped her wrist with bewildering force, drawing her towards him.

Near them, something crackled in the undergrowth.

'What's that?' he whispered. Further off, an owl hooted to its mate. Under the red moon, his eyes on fire. He talked and talked until the moon hid behind a heft of clouds. In the near-darkness, her fingers traced the length of his jaw to just below the ear, down his neck, touching his shoulder-blade, and unbuttoned his shirt. They lay down on the grass. Bending over him, she untied her hair, and it fell down on to his naked chest, making a cave of dark gold.

The listener, unseen by the two lovers, locked in silent ecstasy, moved away.

Far, far way, almost on the edge of hearing, a wild dog howled at its own echo.

CHAPTER FOUR

The sun was dipping in the sky but there were two hours of daylight left, as SS *Birkenhead* nudged into the soft mud of the east bank of the Chindwin. Steam-powered, a side-wheeler, built when Queen Victoria was still in her pomp at the Laird yard on the Mersey, dismantled, shipped to Rangoon and re-built, her steam boiler an antique more than half a century ago before she first slogged up the great river, yet still her brass rivets held true. Teak deck, rebuilt in 1923 after a fire that all but did for her, a dirty canvas awning stretched over her 60-feet length, her flat bottom patched and patched again. The crewman, a Chin, with a tiny silver crucifix on a cord around his neck, went to tug the lanyard for her steam whistle out of custom, but checked himself and glanced astern towards the skipper, his foot resting on the teak tiller. The skipper pulled on his cheroot, blew out a cloud of smoke and shook his head.

These days, the less noise you made, the better.

Tumbling down from the foothills of Thibet, the young Chindwin was icy-blue and clear, but here, halfway between the Himalayas and the sea, the river thickened and slouched through jungle. The middle of the stream flowed a deep bottle-green, but by the bank the water moved, if anywhere, the wrong way – upstream – in lazy brown coils. The crewman clutched a mooring rope in one hand and slipped into the murk, waist-deep. He clambered up the bank and secured the ferry by looping the rope round a fat banyan trunk and tying it off. A gangplank of old bamboo poles, knotted together, fell across the gap between ferry and bank. And then the SS *Birkenhead* set down to wait.

A grumble of artillery, from not so far away, echoed off the hills that rose up from both banks of the river. The noise started a herd of water buffalo.

They plunged in and began the long swim for the far bank, a thin line of dark green, shimmering in the heat three-quarters of a mile away. High above the far bank, to the west, ridge after ridge of green hills climbed so high they lost themselves in broiling thundercloud.

Three British army Bedford lorries trailing field guns jerked along the mud track towards the ferry, from the north. The skipper spat out his cheroot and grimaced, the crewman fed the boiler with a fresh shovel of coal. The lorries halted short of the ferry and a dozen soldiers clambered out.

Jaws, slack-muscled, slobbered open; eyes red-raw, grimy, vacant; tics fluttered exhaustion: the faces of these men mouthed defeat. Shirts starched salt-white on their fronts, wet-black at the armpits and down backbones, dripped rivulets of sweat. Water-bags clacked against their hips, empty.

A sergeant, his elfin face almost beautiful, his blond hair cut short, jumped down from the cab of the leading lorry. The driver of the second lorry approached him, saying 'Christ, Sarge, are you sure about this?' Physically much heftier, the driver – a big gunner – was somehow wary of the sergeant. His voice was appealing as he said: 'Are you sure we shouldn't have tried to get through?'

'Yes, I am bloody sure, thank you very much, Fatty Arbuckle,' shouted the sergeant. 'The Japs are ahead of us. They're blocking us from the north.'

'But the captain would have pressed on. He would have stopped and fought the bastards and tried to get through, to join the others.'

'Yes, and that's why he's got a bloody hole in his face, Fatty, and now he's dead and I'm in charge.' The sergeant's name was Edgar Gregory – Eddie. 'Rangoon's gone, Mandalay's gone and we're bloody next. We're leaving. We're dumping the guns and we're dumping the ammo. We can't take the guns where we're going and we can't take *them*.' He gestured to the last of the three lorries, saying, 'If anybody agrees with Fatty, you can join them.'

In the back of that lorry, six soldiers lay nursed by a green-black cloud. Something called the flies to lift, hover and then return to their feast.

The King-Emperor's soldiers were throwing away everything they could not carry in the retreat, the longest retreat in the long history of the Empire. And they could not carry their dead. A breath of wind lifted the air and they smelt the tell-tale stink of honey and shit. The heat was baking the corpses.

None of the soldiers demurred. The big gunner dropped his head and walked slowly back towards his lorry, climbed into the cab and slammed the door behind him.

Gregory studied a map, shaking his head, and rapped out orders.

From the back of the first lorry, they took a wooden chest carrying explosive charges, Finchy larking, saying it was 'enough to blow up London Bridge', and manoeuvred it along the bamboo gangplank, which sagged perilously with the weight, then heaved it on board the ferry.

They ran to the back of the second lorry and carried three wounded on stretchers down to the bank and onto the SS *Birkenhead.* In their frenzy, the soldiers dropped the first stretcher clumsily onto the deck with a jolt. The injured man cried out – an unbearable sound, like that of a dog whose paw has been severed in an iron trap.

'Shut it. Stop that bloody screaming,' ordered the sergeant viciously and, in an instant, the noise turned to a feeble whimper. The two other injured held their tongues, too far gone or too afraid of Gregory to moan.

The lorry engines started up and all three, with their gun tenders, reversed into the Chindwin, the drivers opening the doors of their cabs and dropping down into the river to doggy-paddle back to the bank and safety. The water at the river's edge wasn't that deep and the first two lorries and tenders came to rest, barely half-submerged. The Japs would haul the guns back out easily, they were smart enough. Good luck to them, thought Gregory. He wasn't going to waste time hanging around in this dump. The Japs could be here in five minutes' time. Maybe longer. He knew they weren't that close when the captain had bought it, but it would be stupid to be caught by them now.

The third lorry – the one carrying the dead – fell into a deeper, sunken pool, the blinding glare of the afternoon sun glancing off the swirling water as it coiled in and out of the flatbed of the lorry. With no ceremony, corpses started to float off, downstream. One of the soldiers stopped on the bank, his arms laden with boxes containing tins of food, and nodded his head at the black shapes floating past.

'Sarge?'

Gregory cut him off. 'There's nothing we can do for them.'

The soldier ran on to the ferry, put down his load and walked, downstream, to the bow, looking out over the dead, and made the sign of the cross.

The Chin crewman hurried along the gangplank to the bank, untied the mooring rope from the tree trunk, slid down into the river and, chest-high in the water, walked beyond the stern and braced the pull of the river's current, listless close to the bank, against his shoulders. The SS *Birkenhead* was ready to leave.

The last few soldiers were hurrying onto the gangplank when a motorbike ridden by an Indian army Jemadar skidded to a halt. The Jem switched off the bike's engine, banged back the motorbike on to its rest and, still sitting astride his motorbike, shouted in English: 'You cannot leave! Women, children, are coming. You must wait.'

The Jemadar had an air about him, a natural authority. And that meant trouble for Sergeant Gregory. The other British soldiers on the ferry shuffled towards the commotion, causing the old paddle boat to tilt a little towards the bank.

Gregory, sitting on the side of the SS *Birkenhead* facing the bank, rifle resting in his hands, yelled up at the Jemadar: 'Shut your mouth, you black bastard.'

The sun, now steadily falling in the west, cast the ferry's shadow on the eastern bank. The Jemadar had to squint into the low sun to see his adversary's rank: three stripes.

'You must wait,' repeated the Jemadar, an officer of the British Indian Army – the most junior rank imaginable, lower than a second lieutenant but still an officer – and both men knew the sergeant had insulted his authority and the very foundation of the great military system to which they both belonged. But these were dark times.

The bus coughed and spluttered towards the river, and halted in a depression, a few dozen yards beneath a bluff overlooking the bank. Grace bade the children wait while she scampered up to the bluff and took in the scene fifty feet below her; in the heat of their argument, the Jemadar and the sergeant were blind to the presence of the witness above, watching them.

'You must wait.' The Jemadar got off his motorbike and made towards the gangplank. The sergeant shouldered the rifle and lined up on the young officer. The Jemadar stopped, took his revolver out of its holster, holding it close to his body, the snout pointing not at the sergeant but upstream, parallel to the river's flow. From the river, the crewman with the mooring rope around his shoulders looked back at the skipper, who stayed by the tiller, watching, making no move.

'You must wait,' said the Jemadar. 'That is an order.'

Grace determined to go down to the ferry and sort out the problem, to explain their desperate position. At that edge in time came a cry, from the bus.

'Miss, it's Joseph,' implored Emily. 'Miss, he's having one of his fits.'

Only Grace could handle this. Perched on the bluff, she stood stock-still. All she had to do was to return to the bus, to soothe the little boy, to kiss his forehead, and stroke his hair and at once he would begin to calm down. But there was something about the atmosphere by the ferry, the abandoned guns half-sunk in the water, the desperation of these particular British soldiers, and, worst of all, the flat tone of the blond sergeant, that chilled her being.

'You must wait,' said the Jemadar.

'Miss, please come, he's grinding his teeth!' cried Emily.

'We're leaving, nigger,' said the sergeant. 'Goodbye.'

Torn between the need to care for the boy and the urgency of going down to the river bank, she could not move.

'Miss, please come, *please*!'

The Jemadar jumped up on to the gangplank, his revolver in his hand still pointed upstream. He was three-quarters along it when a shot rang out. A flock of white egrets, pecking the river-bank mud, rose up into the sky. Red spurts arced from the Jemadar's neck but he stayed upright on the gangplank for an ocean of time, so long that Grace began to wonder whether he was only lightly injured. High in the trees, a rage of monkeys screeched at each other.

A thick gurgle of blood and air – a terrible, haunting, disgusting sound, of life leaving him – answered her question, and his legs crumpled. He fell face-down into the river.

'Oh no, oh no.' The body of the only man she had ever loved was floating downstream, the muddy water staining a darker red.

The gangplank was pulled back into the ferry, the crewman swung himself aboard the stern, and the SS *Birkenhead* surged from the bank and hiss-clanked off, towards the safety of the far bank, one hundred yards, two hundred, three hundred, going downstream.

As the ferry pulled away, across the water, Grace heard a snatch of 'Oranges and Lemons' being whistled.

Her eyes moved to the corpse, still floating face-down in the water, circling on itself and carried by a faster current downstream, away from her. She steeled herself to look away, up to the hills, and then she stared again. From that distance, the Jem could be mistaken for a log.

'Miss, please.'

It was Emily, by her side.

'Joseph's having a terrible fit. What's happened, Miss? You look… What's happened?'

'The ferry's gone and the Jem…'

'Miss? What's happened to the Jem?'

'He's dead.'

'Oh, no! What happened, Miss?'

Duty, loyalty to some terrible sense of responsibility, stopped her from telling the truth. That, and the confusion of grief.

'An accident, Emily,' she lied.

Finding Joseph on the bus, shivering and gibbering, she smothered him with kisses and the fit eased and she rocked him in her arms.

Word of the Jem's accident spread. A dozen girls started to cry.

'Children, children, please. It's going to be all right. We're all going to be all right. I promise you.'

They studied her, disbelieving.

'Children, it's going to be all right.' She could not weep; everything inside her had stopped.

As the ferry moved downstream it came into view from behind the bluff. Their only means of crossing the river was departing.

An instant later, there was a rasp against the air. Flying low over the tree-tops came two fighters, their fuselages and wings marked with the sign of the rising sun, their aero-engines making a high-pitched whine.

Zeroes.

They darted along the river, racing upstream, machine-guns opening up, causing jets of water to spurt as they closed on the paddle-steamer. It rumbled on, still making headway across the impossibly broad river. The fighters disappeared from sight, upriver, but their engine noise remained in earshot and soon they were back. And now they swept in low and fast, for a second strafing run, and this time the twin tracks of machine-gun fire found the explosives by the boiler, midships, and she went up, hurtling steam and red-hot gas and shrapnel of brass and iron high into the sky. Screams pierced the river valley and the bowl of hills above. The ancient ferry slewed around, shuddered, and, broken-backed, began to sink midships first, giving off a cloud of vapour as the river water swirled into the shattered boiler.

The watchers on the bus saw the ferry sink. No one on board could have survived.

Panic consumed Grace. She stood up, yelling: 'Children, run, get off the bus, the planes will come back. Run!'

Trapped with Joseph, right at the back of the bus, Grace grew frantic as girls crowded the aisle fussing over their things, reaching up to pull down bags from the rack overhead, bending down to pick up stuff from underneath the seats.

'Don't take anything! Run! Run! Run! The Japanese planes are coming back. Run!'

Only then did they move, running away from the bus, spreading out in a wave, heading for a stand of teak trees. The children were mostly ten, eleven, twelve years of age, but they had seen enough of war to know that shade was the place to hide from the enemy from above.

The last few children were still dithering on the bus. Grace physically pushed them down the aisle, roaring: 'Run! Come on – run!'

Pushing Joseph ahead of her, he tumbled awkwardly off the step, landing in a heap, squealing like a young pig. She leapt after him and picked him up, heavy as he was, and ran for the trees.

Allu was still behind the wheel. The old driver turned the starter and the bus engine coughed into life. He let in the clutch but the wheels would not bite on the soft sand. Still the wheels span, kicking up dust and sand, locked in stasis.

The sky was empty. But not for long. There was a thin, dry keening on the edge of hearing, barely discernible over the rumble of the bus engine, and then in a knife-slash of sound they came, axes hacking into wood, sods of earth and scoops of sand jumping five feet high as the machine-gun bullets found the bus and smashed windows, ripped great holes in the engine and shredded poor Allu, leaving him resting on the wheel, a muddle of bone and blood.

The sun died. To the west, the mountains, invisible in the heat of the day, took form, rising, immense, dark. A bat, silhouetted by wine-dark clouds, flittered off across the Chindwin, making no sound.

As slow and fat as dollops of treacle, a few droplets of rain spattered down. The downpour gathered force and then it really began to rain, sloshing the earth underfoot, the ground becoming a shallow, choppy ocean of mud and bog, the air thick with stair-rods of water. The children in their thin white cotton frocks and shorts and shirts were drenched. A rivulet formed underneath their feet and suddenly it was a raging stream, dividing off a small knot of the older girls sheltering under a stand of forest canopy apart from the main group. The world turned greenly dark, the force of the rain making it hard to see, to breathe. Grace hugged Joseph and Molly closer to her and felt them gibber with cold. Joseph's teeth started to chatter. He mumbled, 'Miss, I'm hungry.' His skin, to the touch, was almost icy.

Malaria.

They had no quinine. Taking off her cardigan, she wrapped it round the boy. Instantly, it was soaked. Out in the open, by the bus, the whole sky was a wall of water, but even under the trees the fall of rain was relentless, seeking out every last dryness and soaking it, goose-pimpling skin. The children could not spend the night out in the rain, but Grace had no idea how to construct a shelter. The Jem, of course, would have known.

When the Zeroes had struck, the bus did not burst into flames. Its wreck was the only shelter for miles, but none of the children would go near it while the thing behind the wheel stayed where it was.

'Molly, could you hold Joseph's hand? I just need to get something from the bus.' The little girl gripped the boy's hand so solemnly that, despite everything, the gesture would have caused Grace to smile had she been capable of feeling or demonstrating any emotion at all. The stream that hadn't been there half an hour ago was three feet wide as it splurged down towards the Chindwin. She skipped over that and emerged from beneath the trees. The full power of the rain in the open was brutal, pounding her head. Once up the steps and in the bus, any comfort from escaping the wet was knocked flat by the stink of death. The bus was suffused with a green dimness, but she could make out the memory of a kind brown face. The flies fizzed and fluttered over the congealing gore. Her hands swept the air. The flies rose, circled and spun, settling back on the dead man's flesh.

Someone spoke – every consonant and vowel articulated perfectly, as if the person was asking a guest whether he would like more tea: 'Do you mind terribly,' – she realised, weirdly, it was she who was talking – 'if I try and move you?'

No reply.

'Oh, Jesus Christ.' And suddenly she could sob. After a while, she could sense that she was not alone. Behind her, on the lower steps of the bus, stood Emily and Ruby.

'Can we help, Miss?' asked Ruby.

'Oh, Ruby, Emily – thank you, girls, thank you.'

Only then could she bear to do it.

Her fingers gripped his left arm. Not warm, but not yet cold. A fierce tug and the top half of the body sagged towards her. A harder tug and he – *it* – somehow jammed, the legs trapped in the gloom beneath the wheel. Reaching out, she curled her left hand beneath his armpit and pulled with all her strength. He would not budge. Crouching down, her hands groped in the darkness to feel what was trapping him – an ankle, twisted, caught between the pedals. Emily and Ruby pulled on his arms, while Grace wrenched the ankle clear and suddenly the dead man was free and they were all tumbling down the steps. With Grace by the mess that used to be his head and the two girls by his legs, they lifted him clear of the bus and staggered, sloshing through the porridge of mud underfoot, away from the children underneath the trees, down towards the great river. There, Ruby missed her footing and landed on her back, down in the muck, her frock, once white, a filthy parody of femininity. She stood up and they dragged him towards a spot where a gushing stream plunged down a decline to the river, its level rising fast.

'Oh Lord,' prayed Grace to a God Who, for her, no longer existed, 'bless Allu, our devoted driver, who never let us down.'

The body slithered down into a depression. Within seconds, it had gone.

'May he rest in peace. May Allah be with him.'

They slithered back to the dripping trees and gathered a crocodile of children, swinging them over the stream and into the shelter of the bus. Joseph, his hand as cold as snow, mumbled: 'I'm hungry.' Momentarily blinded by the rain, she saw the Jem standing at the entrance to the Masonic Hall, the first time they had met; flourishing the dagger he'd taken from the boys; kick-starting his motorbike; calling out, as they hung above the abyss, 'Good morning, Miss Collins. Did you sleep well?' Tilting into the river, blood gurgling from his neck.

A sound dragged her back to the green coffin, to Joseph shivering and mumbling, to the long line of children snaking towards the bus – a girl's voice. Straining eyes and ears over the steady thrumming of the rain, she picked out Ruby, in her sodden, filthy frock at the head of the crocodile, singing:

'Into each life some rain must fall,
But too much is falling in mine.'

'You would have got a detention for singing that back in Rangoon.' Ruby looked up, startled, but Grace added, 'so it is a good job we're in the middle of the jungle, you naughty terror,' and teacher and pupil started to laugh. A feeble joke, while only despair made sense, but that made it bite all the more. Bent double, Grace's ribs ached with laughter. They boarded the bus, ignoring the dark mess where the driver had sat. She rubbed down Joseph with a dry towel and he warmed up a little and picked up on their laughter and started to chirrup along with them, and soon, through exhaustion, flashed frail grins. For people used to one hundred degrees of heat, it was shockingly cold. Rain trickled through bullet-holes and broken windows, but the bus was drier than outside. The mass of children generated some warmth, and that eased the mood, too. Grace picked up a kerosene lamp and shook it. Not much oil left. Once lit, the bus was suffused with a glow-worm of light, etching shadow against shadow, while outside the rain pummelled down. It was almost cosy. Joseph settled down in a bed of blankets, nuzzling his thumb, his skin still clammy to her touch. Behind him sat Emily, moon-faced, staring out at nothing.

Taking out the Masonic dagger the Jem had given her, Grace went out in the rain and returned with an armload of thick, wide leaves, which she used to shore up the worst of the leaks. Hacking into the undergrowth drenched her, again. She dried herself a little, but it was feeding time.

In the rack above the seats only four boxes of food were left. When they were used up, they would starve. Just as she was about to serve out the rations she felt something between her legs, high up on her inner thigh. Returning to her seat at the front of the bus, she crouched down for some privacy and used the kerosene lamp to see three leeches, bloated with blood, nestling against her skin. Her eyes closed. A few months ago, she would have screamed her head off at this disgusting violation of her body. But Grace had become a different woman. Taking Allu's bag down from the rack, she fished in it until she found his matches and cheroots. She struck a match, lit up a cheroot, sucked on the smoke hungrily, to make the red glow at the tip hotter and stronger – Ruby cried out: 'I didn't know you smoked, Miss' – then she crouched down again and rammed the glowing end against the first of the leeches. It curled away from the heat, then, with a squish, fell from her skin, leaving a raw, bloody spot. Each time a leech fell to the floor, she stamped on it with her heel.

'God help me when we run out of matches.'

Doling out the rations, she walked down the aisle of the bus. Between two children: one tin of sardines – made in Japan – one packet of biscuits and a dollop of jam each. When she handed over the tin and the biscuits to Ruby, the girl cupped her hands and said, po-faced: 'Please, Miss, more.'

'For God's sake, Ruby, there isn't any more. Just eat it and shut up.'

None of the children had ever heard Miss Collins snap like that before. Ruby's cheery features crumpled.

'I'm so sorry, Ruby, but there isn't any more, I'm afraid.'

'What are we going to do when the food runs out, Miss?' asked Emily.

'Something will turn up, Emily. We will be all right.' She returned to her seat, wolfed down her meal and wondered at the hollow nonsense of what she had just said.

When Miss Furroughs had been in charge, every evening had ended with a prayer. For Grace, who no longer believed in God, prayer smacked of hypocrisy. She searched in her bag and found a battered copy of the novel, Moonfleet. By the light of the kerosene light, she started reading: *'The village of Moonfleet lies half a mile from the sea on the right or west bank of the Fleet stream.'*

One by one the children dropped off to sleep. Grace read on and on.

The world seemed still, the bus quiet apart from the rustle of sleeping children, and the unceasing drone of the rain without. Grace shut the book and, yawning, was about to close her eyes in a sleep of dazed grief when Emily, still awake, got up from her seat and sat down next to her. Despite the wretched circumstances, Grace realised that Emily was poised to become a young woman of astonishing beauty. She was fragile, though a quality that worried the teacher, like porcelain so precious you dare not touch it, lest it might break.

'Miss, there is something I need to know.' Her voice was so soft Grace could barely make out what she was saying.

'Yes, Emily, what is it?'

'Miss Furroughs, Miss. You said she had gone ahead, didn't you? No one would go ahead here. It's just jungle. There's nothing here. Nothing. What really happened to her?'

Grace pressed her fingers together, an unconscious mimicry of prayer.

'I told a white lie. I did it to protect the little ones, Emily. I'm going to tell you the truth, but I want you to promise me to keep it a secret. Can you do that for me?'

'Yes, Miss.'

'She walked out into the middle of the street in Mandalay during the air raid.'

'She... she killed herself, Miss?'

'No, Emily, or, I don't know. I don't know what she was thinking, so therefore you can't call it suicide. You cannot make a window into other people's souls – that's how the Jem put it.'

'He's gone too.'

A numbness consumed Grace. The rain pattered down, without ceasing. No moon. In the distance, a monkey hollered to its mate, a weird, alien sound.

'Miss, what's going to happen to us?'

'We are going to India, Emily. All of us. There will be bacon and eggs, jam sandwiches and tea. As much tea as you could ever drink.'

'Is that another lie, Miss?'

And she was gone.

Joseph had malaria. They had no way of treating it. He was the weakest in the whole party. She was no doctor, no expert on the tropics – God, no! – but there was something plainly grim about this dank river valley. The leeches were the least of the dangers. They had enough food for two days, maybe three if they stretched things out, and then they would begin to starve. They could use the bus for shelter at night, but not during the day, lest the Japanese planes return. They had no means of transport, no means of escape, no way of crossing the river. It was too wide for them to swim across. They had no one to help them. Allu dead, Miss Furroughs gone, the Jemadar murdered. If they stayed here long, many more children would fall sick and then they would start to die.

If the Japanese came, and put them to the sword... Well, that might be a mercy. Shuffling her limbs until exhaustion overcame discomfort, she dreamt of a man shouting for a taxi in the middle of a burning city, while she played bridge, the cards dealt by a man with no hands.

Part Two

THE NUMBER ONE ELEPHANT COMPANY

CHAPTER FIVE

Spring 1942, Upper Burma

Through a shifting fog, myths drifted through the trees. Shapes, grey on grey, stirred, fell still, moved again. Grace's eyes fluttered open. She saw only the bus, cocooned in the early morning mists. The rain had stopped in the night.

There was nothing else. The ghosts in the mist, gone. Closing her eyes, she ached to return to the comfort of sleep. She'd slept awkwardly, her neck cricked.

A vast grey wall, as high as a battleship, passed in front of her nose.

'Oh my giddy Aunt.'

The biggest living creature she had seen, ever, halted close to the bus, its trunk snuffling around a clump of bamboo, two massive tusks standing out proud. A fat round eye, some kind of goo running down from it, studied Grace as, with the laziest of pulls, the trunk uprooted the bamboo and bashed it against a tree, causing lumps of mud to fall off. The bamboo was dipped in a puddle like a maiden aunt dunking a biscuit in a cup of tea. But the smell was nothing like that of a maiden aunt. The air was drenched in a rich, moist, cabbagey pong.

'Miss! Miss! Elephants!' shrieked Molly, her voice electric with excitement.

The mist rose, a little, for two hundred yards or so, down to the Chindwin, and Grace could see that the bus was being passed by ten, twenty, thirty elephants, each one commanded by a Burmese elephant man, sitting high up on the animals' necks. The elephants plodded towards the great river, ears flapping, trunks and tails swishing the air, haunches swaying now this way, now that.

To Grace's mind, the swaying motion suggested that the elephants were tipsy, enormous drunks on their way home from a fancy dress ball, a fantasy both silly and utterly delightful. A calf, tripping along in the wake of its massive mother, emerged from the swirling low mist, passed the bus and, having sniffed the presence of flowing water, could not bear to dally. Skin covered in a threadbare coat of brown-red down, trunk raised aloft as if summoning a waiter, he pounded towards the Chindwin as fast as his very little legs could carry him.

'Look at the baby one, Miss!' shouted Molly and the bus erupted, an explosion of joy. On his backside he slid down the muddy slope into the water, making a fat splash.

'There's more babies! Oh, Miss, they're so sweet,' cried Ruby. Seven more calves hurtled across the open space, tobogganed down the mud bank into the water and, while mothers and aunties stood guard, there began a riot of squirting and squishing and squeaky trumpeting.

'Elfunt, elfunt,' cried Joseph.

'Miss!' It was Molly, the best watch-girl in the world. 'It's a man, with a dog.'

Sure enough, from the green curtain of jungle emerged a man with a dog. The man wore British Army uniform, had dark hair, turning to silver, was tall, lean; the dog a cocker spaniel, chocolate-coloured, who paused to sniff the air pompously, then caught up with his master. The pair of them looked as though they could have been out for a stroll on the South Downs. Another figure emerged behind them, an old Burmese gentleman in a sarong.

Leaping out of the bus, Grace ran towards the elephant men.

Another clump-clump of big guns, the sound muffling in the hills, making it hard to judge the distance between them and the artillery. Not far enough.

'The Japanese!' She barked the word, bubbling with fear.

'Good morning,' he replied, a little warily.

'They're only a few miles away.'

'Is that a bus? What's a bus doing in my jungle?'

'Have you got a boat?' demanded Grace. 'The Japanese sank the ferry. The river's too wide. The children can't swim it. Have you got a boat?'

He peered at the occupants of the bus. 'Schoolchildren?' He seemed astonished – no, worse, affronted - by the presence of the bus, the children and Grace, as if he'd caught them trespassing in 'his' jungle.

'The children can't swim this river. Have you got a boat?'

'What?'

'We left Rangoon six weeks ago. We...'

'What? Why didn't you evacuate sooner? What on earth do you think you are doing?'

Thrown, Grace turned away, hiding her face. 'We should have left Rangoon sooner. It was a mistake.'

'A bloody awful mistake, if I may so, and one for which your children have yet to endure the full consequences. I suppose you're hanging around expecting a bloody taxi, eh?'

The word 'taxi' hit her like a punch in the solar plexus. All her restraint, all her self-control vanished. Bent double, suddenly her chest racked with great gasping sobs: 'I begged her to leave, but she just wouldn't. I'm so... it's...'

The words tumbled out of her, incoherent, more than a little mad.

'The taxi thing...something happened to me... she just wouldn't listen... torpedoed in the Atlantic... but you must not abandon us, the children, now, we've come too far.'

He half-turned away from her, presenting his shoulder to her face. 'You realise we can't take you to India.'

'You can't take us?' She was incredulous.

'I'm afraid not.'

'But otherwise...'

A cone of sunlight punched through the mist and Grace was bathed in a pool of amber translucence, an actress spot-lit at the theatre. To him, she was one of the most ridiculously beautiful women he had ever met – a tumble of blonde hair, sky-blue eyes, a body exactly engineered to male desire, all curves and angles - and without doubt the most beautiful Englishwoman on this, the eastern and very much the wrong bank of the Chindwin. No competition, really. But off her rocker. Ga-ga. A madwoman, lacking only the twigs in her hair. No idea what she was doing up here, miles north of the main refugee tracks. Nor could he make head nor tail from her babbling, bursting into tears at the mention of the word taxi. Mad as a hatter she might be, but still, here she was. And the girls in the bus, staring out of the windows. Two boys as well.

Half-castes, by the look of them. Never mind that: there were far too many to look after, let alone feed.

'If you don't help us, the children will die.'

'How many children, er...'

'Miss Collins, Grace Collins. Sixty-two.'

'Adults?'

'Just me left.'

'You've had a rough time?'

'Our headmistress, Miss Furroughs, died in the Mandalay fire. Yesterday our bus was shot up by Zeroes. They killed our driver, Allu, and the Jemadar. I haven't told the children, but it wasn't an accident. He was murdered by a British sergeant, one of us.'

The man kicked a clump of mud with his boot. 'Have you any food?'

'Very little, I'm afraid. We've all but run out. A few tins of fish, some packets of biscuits, they're on the bus. Enough for two days, perhaps three. The children each have their own water bottle, but that's it.'

'If we take you, it will imperil the whole operation. We need to hand you over to the appropriate authorities.'

'What's your name?'

'Sorry. Sam Metcalf, formerly of the Burma Teak Corporation. Now a colonel, of sorts.'

'Show me the appropriate authorities and we'll happily go with them.' She scoured the horizon. Saw jungle, elephants, orphans in a wreck of a bus. If the appropriate authorities were around, they were well hidden.

'Hmpf.' It was more an elephant's snort than a word in the English language. He started to look around, searching for someone.

'Havildar Singh? Havildar Singh! Ah, there you are. Bloody Sikhs, always hiding.' An enormous Havildar – in rank the equivalent of a British sergeant – fierce in beard and turban, emerged from the trees, and the two men started to discuss something in Urdu. Lost in talk, they walked towards the elephants, now down by the river bank. The Sikh scowled, protesting forcibly.

Sam slapped him down, and the two men started shouting at each other, trading vicious-sounding insults. They fell so deep in argument that they did not see the smallest elephant calf get closer and closer to them. He lowered his trunk, raised it and fired, soaking Sam and Havildar Singh.

As the two men retreated from the jets of water, the children, still rooted to the bus, began to murmur. It was a sound Grace felt that she had not heard from them in a very long time: laughter.

But she could not allow herself to join in. The anxiety written on the face of the two men as they had talked down by the river terrified her. Not speaking more than a few words of Urdu, she couldn't hope to understand the row between Sam and the Havildar, but she was certain they were talking about the children and it did not look good.

'Well? Are you going to abandon us?' Grace's tone was brutal. 'We'll slow you down, won't we?' Gesturing to the Havildar, she added: 'Is that what he said?'

Beauty she might be, thought Sam, but she had the makings of an almighty pain in the backside.

'Do you speak Urdu, Miss Collins?'

'No.'

'No. And no, the Havildar did not say that. *I* said that, word for word. He said we've got no choice but to take you, at least to when we hook up with the main track of refugees. I was about to call him an old softie when we got soaked. So you owe him an apology.'

She looked directly into the Havildar's eyes and said: 'I apologise.'

The big Sikh nodded his head and wiped his moustache with the back of his arm. He had an air of steely gentleness about him. But – she couldn't see clearly – there was something wrong with his hands.

'We are very sorry to put you to any inconvenience,' said Grace, the words coming out more haughtily than she intended.

'Look, Miss...' Sam struggled to retain his calm.

'But we would be grateful if you could put us in the true picture.'

'I would be delighted to, Miss Collins.'

One of the elephants trumpeted irritably down by the river, and Grace could have sworn that Sam nodded, as if in conversation with it.

'In plain English?'

'In plain English.'

'Your party is a walking disaster for us. Elephants can't carry much more than they need to eat. A big tusker may get through six hundred pounds of green fodder, mainly elephant grass and bamboo shoots, a day. That's the weight of three big men. The harder you march them, the more you load them, the lamer, the slower you get. And you can't jeopardise fifty-two elephants by hanging around for the fifty-third. If we were to take you, we'd have to carry the children, more often than not. Our supplies would be split between sixty-three extra mouths. It would slow us down so that the Japanese would be on our tails in a trice. Disaster.'

Grace flinched at the word. 'So you are going to abandon us?'

He ignored her.

'The Japanese command the air. On the ground, they are ahead of us, to the north, and behind us, to the south. They are pressing in from the east, and their main force is probably no more than thirty miles away from us, if that. One advantage is that their grand objective is due north, Imphal, and we are slightly off at a dog-leg here. But their scouts will be very much closer and are probably watching us right now. We've got one hundred elephant men and forty Chin guards with us, but if the Japs find us, we will be in trouble. We will cross the river, but so can they. They can build bamboo rafts in half a day and they will come after us. Elephants in this war, well, this corner of the war anyway, are worth their weight in gold, so they are going to chase us all the way to India, if we ever get there. They will try to kill us and capture the elephants alive and get them back. They now control all the metalled roads and main tracks in this part of Burma, so the only possible escape route for us is due west, over five mountain ranges, to the safety of Assam. The mountains are six, seven thousand feet high. And that's out of the question for elephant. On the other side of the river is country I have never been in and the best map we have is a quarter inch to the mile. Remember the Little St Bernard pass that Hannibal took the Carthaginian army through over the Alps in order to give the Romans the fright of their bloody lives? That way,' he gestured to the west, 'is higher. No one's taken elephants that high, ever. We have forty-five elephants and eight calves, and now, thanks to you buggers, sixty-three extra mouths to feed, but we don't have enough food for our elephant men now, let alone for the month that it might take all of us.'

'So?'

'We shoot the elephants, turn back, brandish the white flag and surrender.'

A fresh wave of mist came down from the hills, blanketing the river valley.

'Are you going to do that?' Grace asked.

Sam scowled fiercely. 'Not on your nelly. We are not abandoning you and your children and we're not surrendering, nor are we handing over my elephants to the Emperor of Japan. Not while I'm alive and kicking anyway. So we're heading west.'

'You're going to do the impossible.'

'No. *All* of us are going to do the impossible. It's going to be a race between them and us, and it's a race we are going to win.'

'But you said it was impossible.'

'Stop arguing.'

Eyes tight shut, she breathed out so deeply her body shuddered. 'Thank you very much, Colonel. Thank you very much indeed.'

'Don't thank me too soon. We'll get you across the river and take you along with us for a day or so, but the moment we meet up with the main party of refugees, we will be saying goodbye. You will be quite safe from the Japs then. Understood?'

'Understood.'

'And there's one more bloody problem.'

'What's that?'

'Ministry of Agriculture rules.' He removed a scruffy piece of paper from his breast pocket, on which was typed the heading: *Importation of livestock from the Crown Colony of Burma to India, May 1942* and one line below that: *Elephant: 43*. Underneath, he added in pencil: *OL: 63*.

'OL: 63?' asked Grace.

'Other Livestock. You and the brats.'

She treated him with the ghost of a smile.

'Once we cross the Chindwin, we've effectively left Burma and we're in a kind of no-man's land. India is somewhere over that way,' he nodded towards the west, 'but if I don't keep a tally, some damn fool sitting in an office may try and refuse us entry. Still, we've got a river to cross. I warn you we're all going to get splashed a bit. Elephants do love a bath.'

'The children won't mind, I'm sure.'

'I need to plan the crossing, so we don't mislay the freight.'

Grace was puzzled. 'Freight?'

'The bloody children. We'll start crossing in ten minutes or so, then hike until sundown. The more miles we get between us and the Japanese, the better.'

'Shouldn't we cross the river immediately? With the Japanese so close?'

'You're on elephant time now. The elephants are not going to swim across that river until they've checked it out. No power on earth can change that. We'll move in ten minutes. Or something like that. First problem is that I need to talk to your lot about elephants. I don't want anyone squashed. Messy.'

Making light of a desperate situation was one thing, but she could not stop herself from grimacing.

Sam climbed up into the bus, his dog Winston clambering after him and trotting up to Joseph, pale and sickly. The dog treated the boy to a lick. Sam glanced at Joseph, stopped in his tracks and bent down and felt his brow.

'Ice cold. Malaria.'

'We haven't got any quinine.'

'Havildar Singh!' The giant Sikh clambered on to the bus, and had to crouch to make sure that his turban wasn't knocked off by the roof.

'Quinine for this lad. What's his name?'

The Havildar took a knapsack from his back and delved in it, taking out a bottle of pills. To her horror, she saw that the Havildar had only a couple of fingers on one hand and only half a finger on the other. Deftly, he used his most crippled hand to flick the pill bottle into the air, catch it and unscrew it.

'Joseph,' said Grace. 'He's ten, but he looks younger because of his condition. They call him a Mongol.'

'Hmm. I'm an elephant doctor. Don't do people. But I know what Little Joe needs. Whack him full of quinine.'

The Havildar sat down next to Joseph and, gently, shifted him upright.

'Miss,' said Molly in a whisper that could have been heard back in Rangoon, 'he's missing lots of fingers. What happened to his fingers?'

The Havildar turned to Molly and stared at her, saying nothing. She blushed bright red and looked down.

'Got any chocolate, Havildar?' asked Sam. 'These pills are so bloody bitter he's going to vomit them back up again straightaway, unless we give him something to take away the taste.'

At the mention of the word chocolate the girls turned their heads from the elephants and watched the Havildar pluck out a bar of Cadbury's, misshapen and squishy in the heat, from his knapsack. A gooey mess, but a luxury, for them, in Upper Burma in the spring of 1942, no words can convey. He scraped off a sludge of chocolate, pressed in a yellow pill, and said to Joseph, 'Come on, eat,' and popped it in his mouth. The boy munched quietly and the Havildar gave him a sip of water.

Ruby whispered to Emily: 'I'm going to pretend I've got malaria, too.'

Sam addressed the bus: 'Lucky you. You're all going for a ride on an elephant. In fact, you are all now officially members of the Number One Elephant Company of the Royal Indian Engineers of the Fourteenth Army. That means you're under orders, under my command. And the number one order of the Number One Elephant Company is… don't frighten the elephants. No shouting, no running near the elephants, no going under their legs. They can kill. Any breaking of those orders and Havildar Singh will come and chop your head off.'

A mistake. Most of Sam's audience were around twelve years old, some even younger, and they were all wide-eyed. They had noted that some of the Havildar's fingers were missing. Fearing that they were all going to start crying, Sam gabbled quickly.

'Actually, Havildar Singh is a bit of a lambkin. He doesn't go round chopping people's heads off. To be honest, he hands out chocolate. If you're good. But do obey him and the elephant men – they're called the oozies. Now, which one do you think is the most dangerous of all these elephants?'

Ruby's hand shot up. 'That big one, over there.' She was pointing to the tusker who woke up Grace.

'Rungdot. He's killed two men when he was in musht, that's on heat...oh, never mind, but as far you chaps are concerned he's not the most dangerous elephant by a long chalk. Any other suggestions?'

Molly shouted out: 'The little one, the one that soaked you.'

'Exactly right. That little one there.'

'What's his name?' asked Molly.

'Well, his oozie calls him "Oomy" which means Fat One. He's the sweetest little calf, but here's the problem. You're not daft enough to play around with Rungdot. But if you get in between Oomy and his mother– the name's pretty unpronounceable but it means Jewelled One – and he gets scared, he blows his trumpet and his mum will come charging and trample you to death without turning a hair. So, children, watch it with the little ones. Don't get between them and their mothers. Watch it with the big ones, too. Be wary of the elephants at all times.'

He studied them, hoping that some of his words were sinking in.

'Now you're going to ride in the baskets on top of the elephants' backs as they swim across the river. They may squirt you with water, just as little Oomy did to me and the Havildar. They may even swim underwater for a bit. Just hold on tight and pretend you're riding on a submarine. The wettest children on the wettest elephant will win a prize, once we get to the other side. After that, you're going to have to walk. All day, every day, for two weeks, maybe longer. So you're going to have to dump everything that's silly. You must only take stuff you need and which you can carry on your back. I'm sorry about that, but that's the way it is. We're going to split you up into six groups of ten each – Grace can you do that presently – and you've got to look after each other, even the ones you don't like. Especially the ones you don't like. You're going to hold on with one hand, hold hands with the next child with the other, and not let go. There are sixty-two bloody children here – and there will be sixty-two of you bloody buggers on the other side of the bank.'

Grace imagined the consternation if Miss Furroughs had been around to hear such language.

'Any questions?'

'Will the elephants eat us?' asked Molly.

'No, you're not tasty enough. Let's go. Last bugger across is the dirty rascal.'

The children started dumping their possessions brought with them all the way from Rangoon. Silk dresses, cheap bracelets, poetry books, Shakespeare's plays, magazines telling the latest gossip from Hollywood, hair brushes, bangles, boxes, shoes, even a fur stole, a gift from a father, long-gone, were dumped. Grace, too, threw all her precious possessions away, apart from one change of clothes, a book of Tennyson's poems given to her by Miss Furroughs, her copy of *Moonfleet*, the photograph of her mother, her bee in amber around her neck and the Masonic dagger, her one gift from the Jemadar. She crammed them all in the Jem's satchel, next to a large buff envelope.

Stepping down from the front step of Hants & Dorset for the last time, she remembered the naked traffic policeman on the day they fled Rangoon, Miss Furroughs snarling at the fat man as he pushed in front of the children at the docks – 'you horrible little man' – the Jemadar stamp-stamping the chit for petrol with such intensity that the pompous clerk gave in, and Allu, desperately trying to start the engine as the Zeroes came in over the treetops. Bowing her head, she said her farewell to the bus and all who had gone before and hurried off towards the line of elephants standing parallel to the river.

In baskets shaped like coracles the elephant men stacked guns, ammunition, paraffin oil, food rations, medicine chests. The coracles were to be paddled across first by a platoon of the Chin, not by elephant power, lest one of the great beasts panic and fling the precious valuables into the river.

Grace split up the children into small groups and appointed a leader for each one. Gathering together her own charges - Joseph, Michael, Emily, Ruby and Molly – she went towards the elephant with the long unpronounceable name, who was keeping an eye on her baby, Oomy, now cropping at a knot of elephant grass underfoot with her trunk. She waved at the oozie perched on top of a flattish natural seat immediately behind the elephant's forehead, his brown legs tucked behind the ears, and he waved back, grinning shyly, pointed to himself and said 'Po Net'. It was clear that he didn't speak a word of English but his gentle, amused patience meant something special to them. The goal? A great cane wicker pannier sat crossways on the elephant's back, more than ten feet above the ground, high-backed at both ends, the shape of a monster Victorian bath-tub.

'Looks safe enough,' said Grace.

'But it's so high up, Miss,' said Molly.

Aware that she would often have to look after the other children, Grace told them that she had to appoint a leader for this group too. Ruby was confident enough, but something made her call out another name.

'Emily? Would you mind leading this group? That means going up top first, I'm afraid.'

Po Net motioned for Emily to step closer to the elephant's head. The oozie pressed his right knee firmly against the back of the elephant's right ear and the beast rotated slowly to the left. Once they were in the correct position, he cried out, 'Hmit!' Immediately, the elephant bowed her head and bent her knees, withers still high in the air. 'Hmit' was elephant-speak for 'sit'. The basket was now at a crazy angle, front down, end up, but the nearest edge a mere six feet or so above the ground, yet still too high for Emily to step into. The elephant coiled her trunk so that the tip provided a low step, just a foot off the ground.

The girl hesitated. 'Go on,' said Ruby.

'Go on, Em,' said Molly.

'It looks as tall as a house, Miss.' Emily stepped up on to the trunk and slowly, a magician performing a trick, the elephant lifted her high up so that she was now within arm's reach of Po Net. He held out his hand and she grasped it and she leapt across the gap between trunk and on to the elephant's back and with her other hand grabbed the wicker basket which slipped half an inch towards her, then held – and she was in. Peeking from over the lip of the basket, she waved down at the rest of the girls: 'Miss, that was amazing' and Emily wore a smile that could have cut her face in two.

The game was on and they were all desperate to go next. The Havildar sauntered up to help and picked up Michael and almost catapulted the little boy into the basket. He landed in a heap of giggles next to Emily. The Sikh passed up Joseph's blanket first to Po Net, then stood on tiptoe and passed the boy up to the oozie who gently took him by the armpits and placed him in the basket on the other side of Emily. She started arranging Joseph's stuff and chatting to him, as if they were on the bus. Throughout, the elephant stood absolutely still. Grace, anxious that something could have gone wrong, studied the scene. The elephant seemed to perfectly understand their anxieties about Joseph and be as calm as possible. That required an intelligence, or an empathy, that astonished her.

Joseph peeped his head over the basket. 'I'm on the elfunt,' he said, matter-of-factly, as if he was on a train, and everybody laughed.

Ruby was hoisted up and then it was Molly's turn. She stepped on the elephant's trunk and planted a big kiss on her corrugated grey face. The elephant slowly lifted her trunk and Molly ascended to the level of the basket as if she was riding in a lift.

'What's her name again?' asked Molly.

Po Net, craning his neck round at them, made sense of her question and said something Molly judged ridiculously unpronounceable.

'What did he say her name was?' whispered Grace.

'Mother Engine, Miss.'

Grace pulled a face – 'that can't be right, Molly' – but Mother Engine, shortened to just Mother, was the name that stuck. The teacher went up last, heart fluttering because it felt very precarious. She stowed the Jemadar's satchel in a small wooden box, fixed to the basket. A squash, but all six of them were just getting comfortable in the basket, making cushions of their spare clothes, when a dreadful rumble came from the elephant's nether end.

'What's that pong?' asked Molly, mock-innocently.

'I am afraid that our elephant may have broken wind,' Grace replied and Joseph scrunched up his face in an ecstasy of disgust: 'Mother Engine has done a poo,' and everyone fell about.

Po Net kicked his feet into the fold of skins behind Mother's ears and cried out: 'Htah!' – 'Get up!' – and suddenly the elephant jerked off its fore-knees and the children looked terrified as, inside the basket, they toppled forwards and tottered backwards, and then they were sitting more than twelve feet off the ground.

'Woo,' Joseph cried out, 'wobbly elfunt.'

Mother began to plod towards the river, the basket yawing and lurching with every footfall.

'Oh, my word, I'm getting seasick, Miss,' said Emily as they rose and plunged, plunged and rose.

'Emily, we've got two hundred miles to go. I'm afraid you'd better get used to it.'

Mother shuffled to a halt. Oomy, preoccupied with his breakfast, had almost been forgotten. He lifted his head, made a little toot-toot noise with his trunk, and ran towards his mother. Only when Oomy was by the heels of Mother did she turn her great head and give his back a little pat with her trunk, making him wriggle with pleasure.

Ahead, a long traffic jam of elephants, waiting patiently in line for the order to cross the river. Ruby stood up in the basket, one palm stopping one line of imaginary traffic, the other waving fantasy vehicles on – the naked traffic policeman. Grace wagged a finger at Ruby, who sat down to hoots and catcalls.

Sam, riding on the very last animal at the back of the herd, raised his hand and, at the very front, Rungdot, the biggest, oldest bull, bearing a Siamese wicker basket, loaded with chains, food and other necessities of the elephant camp, led the way down to the river. An oozie rode on his neck, but two more elephant men accompanied his every step on shore, one on either side, carrying bamboo staves, tipped with a sharp iron hook. No one was taking any chances, lest he run amok. Rungdot's oozie dug in his heels, the two other elephant men climbed up into his basket and the great bull slid down the muddy bank, his forelegs sinking deep into the mud. He struggled, lurching unsteadily, for a second or two and then his legs found bottom and he surged forward into the stream. For the first one hundred yards or so he was tall enough to walk, breasting the current, but soon the river became deeper, the current faster, and he paddled strongly off towards the other bank, more than one thousand yards away.

For every yard the elephants crossed the river, they were pulled two downstream by the current. Their target, selected by Sam, was an eighty-foot-high tree on the far bank, bursting with orange, white and flame-red blossom, as bright as fireworks a mile or more downstream. Directly behind the old tusker came twelve cows carrying the children in their high baskets.

As Mother got out of her depth and started swimming, water lapped over their toes in the bottom of the basket, soon swilling dangerously close to their bottoms. Anxiously, Grace examined her gang – the two boys and the three girls - who beamed back at her, at the rolling mist, at the grey monster underneath their feet. They were enraptured.

Halfway across, with another five hundred yards to go, Grace was gazing at Oomy swimming his little heart out, keeping up with his mother, when a bank of mist rolled in, as thick as sea-fret, blanketing them. Sounding through the grey murk, a girl's voice, piping loud and strong:

'Thick jewell'd shone the saddle leather,
The helmet and the helmet-feather
Burn'd like one burning flame together,
As he rode down to Camelot.'

It was Emily, and the whole school sang out:

'"Tirra lira" by the river
Sang Sir Lancelot.'

The otherness of war.

'Bloody shut up! The bloody Japs might be listening,' shouted an angry voice through the mist. That could only be Sam.

Silence, broken only by the rippling of river water and the huffing and puffing of the swimming elephants. The sun scoured a hole in the mist, which widened into a tunnel, then, as suddenly as it had come, the mist was lifting fast and both banks of the great river and the green hills rising above them were visible.

Close to the west bank, the strength of the current picked up and wavelets lapped against the baskets, soaking everyone. Oomy started to mew anxiously, but within a few seconds Rungdot hit hard ground and walked up the bank, wiggling himself dry of water.

As Mother, the last of the elephants carrying children, and Oomy struggled against the current to step on to firm ground, fireworks from where they had just come from, the eastern bank, crackled and popped. Tiny figures scurried towards the river, spurting orange flame, and behind them were ten large brown-grey shapes.

The reason the Japanese had caught up so fast? They, too, had found that the fastest way of travelling across a land without roads is on the back of an elephant.

CHAPTER SIX

Mud sucked against Mother's legs as she laboured up the bank, the children in the basket craning their necks to watch the commotion on the eastern bank, Oomy bleating, struggling not to get left behind. Mother would wait patiently for her baby, to make sure she, too, made it to solid ground. Once there, ignorant of war, they started on a pre-luncheon snack of elephant grass. The river was so massively wide the threat from the Japanese seemed distant. Although chided by Po Net, mother and baby plodded slowly from the riverbank, stopping at a fresh clump of elephant grass and settled in for a late breakfast.

Thump, thump! Air pressure pummelled eardrums; overhead, a branch of a tree, sliced clean through, fell to the ground, silver-green light shivering off the tumbling leaves. Another great clap of air-pressure, ending in a soft pock! as something squelched into the mud, thirty feet from Mother. Another pock!, further off, sending up a riot of waterfowl.

'Mortars,' shouted Sam. 'Move!'

Mother's enormous ears cocked out, beating the air, her feet barely touching the ground, Po Net turning around, motioning to the children to get down, to flatten their bodies as much as they could and hold on, tight. They bounced about in the basket as Mother's legs scissored to and fro, a giant steeplechaser gaining speed before it took a monster fence, hands covering faces, stray lianas and elephant grass whipping at their arched backs with wicked force. Deep in thick forest, uphill and half a mile or more from the bank, Mother slowed to a trot.

'She was flying,' said Molly.

Grace ruffled Molly's hair. 'You know, it sounds mad, Molly, but you're right. When people say that elephants can't fly, they don't know what they are talking about. But we know. It's our secret. Elephants can fly.'

Mother turned around 360 degrees and raised her trunk like a periscope, sniffing the air. The hiss and clatter of the jungle's sounds gave way to the mother elephant breathing out a long, querulous sob.

'What's the matter with her?' asked Molly.

'Sssh,' said Emily.

Oomy was nowhere to be seen.

'It's the baby, Molly, he's got lost,' whispered Grace.

Another sob from Mother, a low, deep-throated sound full of melancholy and ache. The mother elephant was facing back towards the river, her ears wide out, cocked to hear the slightest sound.

The children, Grace and Po Net remained chapel-quiet, trying to pick out the baby elephant's answering cry above the general hubbub of the jungle.

A disturbance in the greenery to the left, the tops of the elephant grass waving this way and that. Hidden by the body of the grass, something was moving slowly, delicately, towards them. Molly yelped out, 'He's coming!'

'Sssh,' whispered Grace.

They tracked the swaying of the grass from their vantage point on the elephant's back. Soon Oomy would emerge from cover. Not a squeak from the children. The grass at the edge of the clearing rippled and a small brown deer peeked out at them, twitched its ears, scarpered across the open ground and vanished into the jungle.

The mother elephant lifted her trunk and gave out another sobbing trump. No reply. No sign of Oomy.

Without hurry but with determination Mother began to plod back down the path she'd just made through the elephant grass, back towards the Chindwin, towards the Japanese. Po Net turned his head to the basket and shook his head, grim-faced. He said nothing, but Grace understood the look to mean that if a mother elephant has lost her calf, there is no power on earth that can stop her from trying to track him down.

Again the mother elephant sobbed, a long quivering note, as if from a cello, of unbearable sadness. Suddenly, a high-pitched 'toot-toot', like the horn on a toy car, sounded nearby and Oomy crashed through the undergrowth and ran straight to Mother.

'Aah,' said Joseph. 'Baby come back.'

The calf was rewarded with a great thwack of mother's trunk on his backside. The trouble-maker trotted away a slight distance, a few steps, not far, coiled his trunk into his mouth and began sucking it, an action exactly like a small boy, having been scolded, sucking his thumb. Mother's trunk sidled over to him and trunk entwined with trunk, they nuzzled together. Mother throbbed with a new sound, a gargling burble of pleasure.

'She's purring, Miss,' said Emily.

'Yes, Em, I do believe you're right,' replied Grace.

Po Net turned round and gave one of his shy grins, as if he had understood every word.

With a few orders from Po Net, mother and calf found the rest of the party through call and counter-call, coming to rest in a cave of foliage roofed by a jungle canopy so high it hurt their necks to look up at it. Grace marvelled at the intelligence of the elephants. They'd picked this spot, the perfect place to take stock, hide from any Japanese planes, before moving on.

Rungdot, the monster, trumpeted his might and a few wild elephants, miles away, answered back, the sound re-echoing around the bowl of hills. As the elephants chomped peacefully at the grass underfoot, the mortar fire from the Japanese seemed a bizarre memory.

Po Net dug his heels into the elephant's hide and Mother buckled her hind-legs, jerking the pannier down earthwards. They scrambled out, Joseph, assisted by Grace, taking a little longer.

'All well?' asked Sam. His stern growl seemed a little softer, as if Bishop Strachan's School had passed some kind of Elephant Man test.

'Yes, no injuries,' said Grace. 'But when the baby got lost, Mother's distress... They're just like us,' she said.

'No,' said Sam. 'They're better. They don't make war,' and he made his strange, muted elephant trump noise. 'There are no refugees here, so you'll walk along with us till nightfall.' He headed off into the bush, but just before he did, he turned back. 'By the way, no more bloody *Lady of Shalott*.'

Emily blushed.

'No wonder the Japs found us.'

'But you and the Havildar had your noisy row by the riverbank,' replied Grace. 'That was much louder. Besides, Tennyson was *Poet Laureate*.' Cheekily, she over-emphasised the last two words, as if Sam was a little on the slow side.

He made his funny noise again, half-raspberry, half-bull-elephant snort. Had he spent so long in the jungle he spoke better Elephantese than English?

'The Japs have got their own elephants so best not hang about. The fit children, I'm afraid to say, you're walking.'

Sam's way of talking to the children was alarmingly frank but, nevertheless, it seemed to work. Not everyone could walk all day, of course: Joseph was judged too ill, and Michael too little, although that decision was partly to keep Joseph company. Another of the girls, suffering from a poor tummy, joined them on the back of Mother, the 'hospital elephant'. As the Havildar lofted Michael up into the sky, his school cap, which he had insisted on wearing all the way from Rangoon, a talisman, fell to the ground, whereupon Mother scooped it up with her trunk and popped it into her mouth.

'The elephant's eating my cap,' cried Michael.

Po Net gabbled something in Burmese to Sam, who roared with laughter, telling a distraught Michael: 'Don't worry, old chap. Po Net will look out for you and in a few days' time you'll get your cap back.'

'But it will be covered in elephant poo!' squeaked Michael, his eyes beginning to fill.

'Now listen here, old chap,' said Sam, resting on his haunches to look Michael in the eye. 'If having your cap gobbled up by a lady elephant is the worst thing that happens to you this year, then lucky you!'

The Havildar, glowering the whole time, produced a packet of biscuits from his knapsack and with his maimed hands passed them round the children. As they watched him walk on, Grace felt Molly pulling at the sleeve of her frock.

'Miss, what happened to his fingers?'

'Sssh, Molly, that's a rude question.' But the schoolteacher was dying to know the answer herself.

The old school crocodile formed up as it had done countless times before. They followed the curiously narrow trail of flattened jungle made by the elephants ahead. Within seconds, the elephants began to vanish. High up in the trees a monkey screeched, insects hissed and whispered to each other, but ahead she could make out nothing but a curtain of green. The ease with which the elephants disappeared into the jungle gave her comfort that it might just be possible for them to play hide and seek with the Japanese.

Sam marched ahead with his spaniel to pick the spot for camp that night.

On they trudged, unfit by the lack of exercise after being cooped up in the bus. The rain held off and the path was not atrociously steep or the track too difficult. Yet it was never easy. The heat, suffocating and damp, sapped Grace's strength as she stumbled through the green tunnel, the occasional pat of elephant dung the only clue to the creatures that had gone ahead.

At midday, they stopped for lunch. 'Usual muck for lunch, eh?' said Ruby mutinously.

'Hush, Ruby. Miss can't help it. Don't be so critical.' It was Emily, coming to the defence of Grace, who mouthed a silent 'thank you'.

But the elephant men did come up with lots of new things to eat: slices of mango, tiny wild bananas, more sour than sweet, and even a pudding of sorts, made of cold rice in bamboo leaf and one teaspoon of cocoa powder.

'Yuck!' cried Molly.

'Sssh, it's yummy,' said Ruby, 'like a chocolatey rice pudding. If you don't want it, I'll have your share.' Molly fell silent and tucked in.

Grace tracked down the Havildar, deep in conversation with Po Toke.

'Havildar, I have to say I am worried about our lunch. There's almost too much to eat.'

'Sam's orders. The more we eat, the lighter the load for the elephants, the faster we can go. This applies to the first few days, while the Japanese are so closely behind. We eat now, starve later.'

'Have they crossed the river?'

Smiling at Grace, Po Toke shook his head. 'Not yet, Miss.'

After a short rest, the children were on their feet again. They made much poorer progress in the afternoon, struggling up a steep ravine, maybe 1,500 feet high, then over its spine and down the other side, crossing a chaung or stream at the bottom. Some chaungs were dry, but this one was a roaring torrent, bursting with snow-melt from the Himalayas. The elephant men loaded up the children and they were soon across. Instead of dismounting, the children stared at the oozies with imploring eyes. They rode on, exhilarated.

Ruby, fit and old enough to have to walk, started to hum a tune, hopelessly incongruous in the jungle, but soon the marching army of children and oozies were joining in the hum as her smoky voice rang out:

'Any time you're Lambeth way,
Any evening, any day,

You'll find us all
Doin' the Lambeth Walk. Oi!'

Grace could have sworn that the elephants were taking two step forwards, one step back, in tune.

Before long the elephant grass swung back to reveal Sam, Winston at his heels, beside himself with fury.

'Shut up!' he barked. 'Shut up! No bloody singing. Or we will all be doing the Lambeth Walk in a Japanese prison camp.'

'Aaah,' said Ruby playfully.

'No, Miss, it isn't funny. We're on the run from the Imperial Japanese Army. If they catch us, they may kill some and put the rest of us in the bag. They plan to steal the elephants so that they can invade India. And you are doing your level best to make life easy for them. Do you understand?'

Ruby, one of nature's troublemakers, looked down. It was perhaps the very first time that Grace had seen her in any way submissive.

Sam's eyes drilled into Grace. 'Miss Collins, I beg you to keep these children under control. If I hear another squeak from them, I will hold you personally responsible. Now stay quiet. The sooner we find the main track, the sooner we can say goodbye,' he hissed, and disappeared back up the way he had come.

'Miss, why is he so bad-tempered?' asked Molly.

'I don't rightly know, Molly.'

'Perhaps he prefers the cha-cha-cha,' whispered Ruby, but not so quietly that Grace couldn't hear every word.

'Sssh,' said Grace, 'he's got a lot on his plate. You've got to remember that sometimes people with a bad temper may be right, after all.'

'Hmph.' A perfect imitation of Sam's signature elephantine grunt. Grace knew damn well it came from Ruby, she elected not to hear it.

'What will happen when we join up with the rest of the refugees, Miss?' asked Emily.

'The colonel would prefer it if we carried on to India on our own.'

'But we'd miss the elephants,' said Emily.

The last leg of the march was a slip-sliding miserable business, over low, swampy ground, thick with mosquitoes. The walkers looked up with envy at the lucky ones riding on their elephants. At six o'clock, another furious chaung, 100 yards across, blocked their path, the snow-melt raging against the rocks. For the strongest adult, it would be a suicidal risk to swim across. The elephants stepped across, the older ladies making sure their little ones were tucked in by their sides, sheltered from the force of the current. Grace bit her lip. This journey, without the help of the elephant men, would be impossible.

On the far bank, the children dismounted from their elephants, exhausted. In the golden half-hour before sundown the yellow-green glare filtering through the jungle canopy changed to ochre and saffron. Down at the water's edge Grace washed her hands, then lay full-length face down by the bank and plunged her head into the running water. It was bitingly cold but thrillingly refreshing. Her ears rang with the current, but she became aware of another sound – a weird bubbling. Lifting her dripping head out of the water, she saw an elephant's trunk two feet away. Like a boy bubbling up a strawberry milk-shake through his straw, Oomy was blowing air down his trunk into the water's muddy bottom. A few feet away Mother looked on, making a wholly different sound, that low, gravelly gurgle of old-fashioned plumbing, the elephant purr of motherly love.

Elephants weren't truly grey at all, Grace realised. It was mud and dust that turned them so. Washed clean in the stream Mother's skin was far darker than her calf's, almost blue-black for most of her body, but speckled black-on-pink like a trout behind her ears and across her trunk as it tapered into her head. Where her tummy met her legs the skin sagged in multiple folds, deeply corrugated and as comfortable as Grandad's corduroy trousers. The mother's eye, one only visible from side on, was tiny, set in the vast frame of her head, not pig-like because of the effect of a series of rings of skin rippling concentrically from it, as if the eye was a stone lobbed into a black pond. Whereas the eye remained locked on her calf, all but motionless, her trunk barely stayed still for a second, grubbing on the ground or raised up to sniff the wind. Entranced, Grace gazed on as Mother watched over her baby playing in the water.

Oomy was absorbed in his game of blowing bubbles, black eyelashes as beautiful as a girl's, shading a liquid brown eye. Mother tilted her head every now and then, this way and that, making sure that there was no threat to her son. A few yards further off upstream, two aunties were drinking the water, but also keeping the baby in full view. The two aunties formed two sides of a loose triangle, with Mother at the base, and the calf, playing in the water, in the middle: what looked a casual arrangement was in fact a fortress of flesh and trunk and bone, virtually impregnable. In the baby's playfulness and the subtle watchfulness of mother and aunties, Grace found the elephants more like humans than she had ever thought possible.

Stopping his game, Oomy's eye fixed on Grace. He gave her a wicked wink and showered her with a blast of mucky water.

'He got you, Miss!' shouted Molly.

'Baby,' said Joseph, pointing at Oomy. 'Aaah.'

Grace gave him a squeeze. 'Yes, Joseph, Oomy is Mother's baby.' The anti-malaria pills seemed to have done some good, to have slowed down his fever. He didn't look at all well, but he managed a feeble smile. Looking at Oomy, his eyes sparkling with glee, he repeated: 'Baby, aaah.'

Po Net used bark he had cut from a tree by the bank to create a kind of soap, and soon Mother's back was lathered with a scummy blancmange. Fearlessly, he crouched underneath her belly and washed where the ropes attaching the basket had chafed against her. He ordered her to lift each foot, which he checked laboriously for thorns and wear and tear. One stamp from the elephant would crush the oozie stone dead, and the children marvelled at how much man and beast trusted each other. Inspecting Oomy's feet was more problematic. He made such a fuss, squeaking and squirting Po Net whenever he got near the baby, that Mother had to give him a hefty thwack on his bottom before he settled down and let the oozie do his job.

Before dinner, Sam called a pow-wow of the adults. Recalling Sam's irritation with the singing of the Lambeth Walk, Grace put on her apologetic face. Her reward was a brief nod, and a grunt, in elephantese.

Addressing the Havildar, Po Net and Grace, he said: 'I'm still calculating that the main body of the Japs are intent on pressing north after our army. So long as we head due west, we'll be well out of harm's way. At least,' Sam continued, 'I think they won't press hard in this direction. But it remains a gamble. And the bad news is that they've got elephants, ten of them by the looks of things, and almost certainly my bloody elephants. We had to leave four hundred behind, thanks to the incompetence of some useless types in the British Army. The Japs have obviously found ten.

'No fires – and that means no hot meals, no boiling water, no tea tonight - because Japanese scouts will almost certainly have crossed the river on their elephant. They may confuse our party with a strong force of British soldiers, and that would not be good. Sentry pickets are to be placed on all four corners of the camp and five miles back down our track, less for fear of enemy attack than tigers, pythons and the like.'

Winston, Sam's spaniel, licked the Havildar's bare knee. He cursed the dog lavishly in Urdu and the animal yapped back at him and suddenly the two men were quarrelling, until Grace put a finger to her lips and cried: 'Sssh! You're setting a terrible example.'

A long, grisly silence, broken by a deep growly burbling. The Havildar was laughing. Everyone joined in, apart from Sam who glared at her. Grace had had enough of being demure and returned his gaze. After a beat, Sam studied his boots, the right-hand corner of his mouth wrinkling slightly.

The children were fed and watered, and the sick – Joseph and three girls with diarrhoea – were put up in the first aid tent. Word had got out that if you had the shakes you would get quinine and that meant chocolate to kill the taste, so Grace had to spend quite a bit of time suppressing a fake epidemic of malaria.

The fearsomeness of the Havildar helped. The children half-jumped every time he looked at them. At the end of the meal, Grace found she was standing next to him, as he gathered up the empty sardine tins.

'I hope you don't think I'm rude, Havdilar, but the children keep on asking: what happened to your hands?'

The Havildar stood up, towering over her, and smoothed his moustache down with the half-finger of his right hand. 'Dinner was late one night.' His voice was very deep. He paused. 'I was hungry.' Another pause, longer than before. 'So, I ate my fingers,' and, yelling at a Chin who had dared to start lighting a fire, he marched off.

The children were to sleep in the elephant baskets or placed two to a hammock, so that every one of them slept off the ground. No one was allowed a kerosene lamp in the open, but the stream, close by, gave off a faint phosphorescence which somehow grew more vivid the blacker the night became.

Sam had a moment to himself, reached into his pocket and produced a hip-flask, draining it deeply, and then he became aware of Grace standing close by.

'My weakness, I'm afraid. Home-made firewater. My own recipe. Do you want a sip?'

'Have you any to spare?'

'Not much, but I'm going to run out in the next few days so one sip won't make much of a difference. Go on. It will do you good. Sam's Own Peculiar.'

It was quite the most vile drink she had ever drunk, a slurry of rancid coconut milk, swamp juice and cough mixture with, she was sure, more than a hint of elephant excrement.

'Eeeyuckthankarrghyou,' her eyes watering at the strength of it. 'What's it made of?'

'Ah. That would be telling. After the war, I'm going to market it and become a rich man. Another?'

'No. Good luck with that,' she said so drily, and with such little sign of enthusiasm, that his right lip crinkled again.

'When we join the rest of the refugees, what will you do Sam?'

'The best track – correction, the only proper track – is due north. The problem is, it's bunged up with what's left of the army and thousands of refugees. Poor company for elephants and besides, the general staff have banned me from trying it, lest my elephants get in the way of their filing cabinets. So we're going due west, finding our own path. It's not easy without a proper map.'

'Gosh, no.'

'Hit the wrong ridge, and we add an extra week to the journey. And time is a luxury we don't have. Our destination is a tea estate the size of Yorkshire so we shouldn't miss it.'

'Do you know the people there?'

'Hell, no. They're in India, after all. I'm imagining a fine old bungalow, a vast, Victorian bath-tub, full of hot water, plenty of bars of soap with gleaming white towels and an unending line of gin and tonics – fine anti-malarial prophylactics. And in the morning bacon and eggs, white toast, Seville marmalade, nice chinwag with the planter, he'll be very old, and he'll have a charming young wife. And a fine bitch for Winston.'

The dog looked up, expectantly, and panted his approval.

'Sorry, that came out a bit wrong. Not used to company. Not used to female company, excepting elephant cow.'

'Excepting elephant cow,' she agreed, laughing. He wasn't sure but he suspected that because of the whiteness of her teeth in the gloom she was beaming at him.

'On behalf of the children I would like to say thank you very, very much for rescuing us, Sam.'

'Thank the elephants.'

'I'm thanking you.'

'I'm sorry I was pompous when we first met. How was Rangoon when you left it?'

'Stinking. Chaos, naked lunatics running around, looters. The Indians afraid of revenge from the Burmese. Thousands running away, walking, dying by the road.'

'We...' he hesitated '...let our people down. Badly. Both the Burmese and the Indians. Too many whites have just buggered off or flown out of Burma without a bloody care in the world. But the lesson I've taken from that is that you must not promise protection if you can't deliver it. Had I known that you'd spout bloody poetry in the middle of the Chindwin...'

'You would have abandoned us?'

'"Tirra-lirra said Sir Lancelot." Bloody disgrace,' and he gave his elephant snort.

'But you didn't abandon us. The children are loving it. They can't wait for morning. Yesterday was the worst day of my life but today may have been, somehow, the best. I thought we'd never, ever make it across the river.'

Another snort.

Moonrise. Shafts of silvery light tunnelled through the forest canopy high above and splashed down onto the jungle floor.

A commotion and three Chin guards – the rearguard – came, carrying a fourth man hanging in a sling from a bamboo pole.

The Chin lowered their burden in a puddle of moonlight, resting the man's bloodied head against a thick liana, his slumped form casting a shadow, eerie and forlorn. The Chin explained in Burmese that they had found him by the Chindwin.

The faint light illuminated the man, unconscious, blood on his head, dried almost black against his blond hair.

'That's *him*,' said Grace. The undergrowth murmured, twitching with a breath of air, the rhythm of the crickets rising and falling. 'That's the man who shot the Jemadar. That's the murderer.'

The last word detonated like an assassin's shot.

Sam motioned the Chin to carry the wounded man into his tent.

'Murderer or not, let's have a look at that head.' Inside, she glimpsed a wide hammock, a canvas chair and a small table, on it an unlit kerosene lamp.

The Chins sat the man, all but comatose, on the chair. Sam closed the tent flap after Grace, lit the kerosene lamp with a match and unlocked a small medical chest. He dabbed the head wound with alcohol spirit, wiping away the dried blood, and wrapped a clean white bandage around it, tying it off neatly.

By the lamplight she noticed something she hadn't seen before in the gloom: a framed picture of a dark-haired woman in her thirties, laughing at someone else's joke. In Burmese, Sam asked a Chin to find a hammock for the wounded man, telling him to get one of the sentries to check his breathing every hour and, if there was any change in his condition, to wake Sam up. They carried him away, gently, his head lolling onto the shoulder of the man supporting him.

'Nasty cut – shrapnel, of some sort, bit of concussion, but the skull isn't fractured. He'll live. Pretty bloody amazing for him to swim the Chindwin after that bash to his head. Luck of the devil.'

Stone-faced under the moonlight, Grace said: 'He's a killer.'

Sam extinguished the kerosene lamp, leaving his face all but invisible in the gloom of the tent. He made no reply.

She repeated what she had just said.

'He's no threat. He can barely breathe.'

'He shot the Jemadar in cold blood.'

'I'm not a judge, still less a hanging one.'

The reluctance to take her side riled Grace. 'I saw him shoot the Jemadar with my own eyes. I was but fifty feet away when it happened.'

'If you really think the army will be over the moon about the idea of prosecuting a British sergeant in the middle of a war, one we appear to be losing extremely badly, by the way, after one Indian officer has been killed, probably by a stray bullet, then you have another think coming.' Tiredness – no, worse than that, a grimy, exasperated fatigue – edged Sam's voice as he went: 'Are there any other witnesses? Oh, not the children. No court-martial will entertain a bunch of half-caste bastards.'

'The children didn't see anything. I was the only witness.'

'Well, I fear they will look at you and dismiss you as just a girl who knows next to nothing about war or soldiery or what stray bullets can do. The very last thing they will want to do is rake up the mud between an Indian officer and a British soldier, what with all this talk of Jiffs and everything. That will be a disaster for them. So, if you insist on calling this chap a murderer, you'd better be right, but it's going to be the word of a girl against a sergeant, one who has been injured in the line of duty. Nothing's going to happen to him until, or rather *if*, we all reach India. And if you think that's going to be easy, then, on that subject, too, you are horribly mistaken.'

'Mr Metcalf,' Grace started.

'It's either Sam or Colonel Metcalf, actually.'

'Colonel, then. Murder is murder. That man killed our Jemadar in cold blood because he couldn't abide waiting five minutes to help a busload of orphans flee the Japanese. He was not injured in the line of duty but in the act of making a very selfish escape from the enemy. He murdered an officer who was trying to maintain discipline and help us. What I think you are saying is that because the perpetrator is a white Englishman and the victim is of a coloured race, an Indian, no one will mind at all. I may be just a girl, in your view, in charge of sixty half-caste bastards, as you put it so disgracefully, but let me tell you this, Colonel, that to suggest he was killed by a stray bullet, sir, is a filthy lie. I saw what happened and I mind very much indeed, and when I am free of your travelling circus and get to civilisation, I shall say so, loud and clear. Good night to you, sir.'

'Grace, I didn't mean to...'

But she was gone.

CHAPTER SEVEN

The luck of the devil? Bugger that. Easing himself out of the hammock, he got to his feet puffing and blowing like an old man of ninety. The mist drifted in, a grey fuzz that confused the lines and shapes of everything ten feet beyond him. Groggily, he rolled up his hammock and passed it to one of the oozies who stowed it in a basket on the back of a pack elephant. After a pantomime of slapping down his shorts and shirt for a smoke, the oozie smiled and lobbed him a cheroot. Filthy things, but better than nothing. The Burmese produced a match, he lit his cheroot and inhaled deeply, saluting the oozie for the smoke and leant back against a tree, watching the elephant camp wake up.

Fingering his head wound through the bandage, it felt sore and gooey. Would it heal in the wet heat? Hmm. Still, not dead yet.

The mist winnowed, revealing the big bastard – Rungdot, they called him – emerging from a clump of bamboo, chomping away, riderless. They had chained one foreleg to a hind-leg so he could not wander far, but the oozies watching over him seemed on edge, looking askance, keeping an eye on him, angling their bodies, ready to run. That was stupid. You had to show who was boss. Funny thing was, they were watching him the same way, too.

Slowly, deliberately, he walked towards the monster. The oozies were occupied with a harness, further off, faffing about, but someone coughed and they began to take notice as the blond Englishman with the bandage on his head became dangerously close to Rungdot. Eddie Gregory came to a stop within touching distance of the elephant's tusks, blowing a cloud of cheroot smoke at the creature's face. The elephant raised his head and eyed the sergeant murderously. On the far side of the clearing Sam came out of his tent and his attention was immediately gripped by the scene beneath him. Looking on, Sam watched aghast as the sergeant puffed out another smoke cloud directly at Rungdot. The head of the great elephant dropped a fraction, held, then he swung his tusks away and hobbled off towards the edge of the clearing.

Gregory had stood his ground, had stared down the Man-Killer. The oozies looked at him, more than a little afraid. Sam shook his head, worried.

No luck in it at all.

A coiled fossil. Muddle-headed by sleep, she studied the coil, like an Ammonite from the Jurassic, at its dead centre a pretty brown eye. Fossils don't blink. This one did. Like a dripping wet dog getting out of a duck pond, her mind shook itself awake. If it blinked, it couldn't be a fossil. Not three feet from her hammock, Grace registered the presence of a baby elephant, his trunk tightly rolled up in on itself. Beyond the trunk was a grey convexity, his stomach. She stared intently at Oomy's trunk as it tentatively clawed at passing drifts of mist. The trunk made a fifth limb, which could pick up a pencil or, when he was older, roll a three-ton teak log uphill. Even now as a baby, one stomp from his clumping great feet could do her real harm and yet this was a species which would hardly ever abuse its great strength. The war, the wretchedness of the refugees dying by the wayside, the blitzing of Mandalay, the murder of the Jem, all of this was grim beyond the saying of it. But the few hours they had spent with the elephants… while not a consolation, since nothing could have made up for all those unnecessary deaths, had nevertheless been a time of wonderment and joy. To wake up, and the very first thing you see is the tucked-up trunk of a baby elephant, and then him blinking…

The day's march started, a steep climb through thick forest, Sam far ahead at the front, the Havildar next, in charge of the pack elephants, the children, led by Emily and Ruby and then Grace as 'sheepdogs', in the centre party, and the Chin guards bringing up the rear. The killer with the bandaged head? No sign of him. High above, they heard the odd grumble of thunder from the mountains, and every now and then a patter of light showers fell. The heavy rains threatened but didn't come.

Prickly wet heat crawled under skin. Bodies raw with salt, their clothes glued to them with sweat. Itches demanded to be scratched, but the more you scratched, the worse the itch became. It was depressing, too, not being able to see ahead for more than ten feet, not having a goal on the horizon, but just being locked inside an unchanging bubble – jungle with no end and no beginning, just foot after foot, yard after yard, mile after mile of foliage. Barred from seeing the open sky by the halo of forest canopy, the surroundings suffused by an eerie green light, it felt like being trapped inside an enormous fish tank.

The path – to glorify it with that description seemed absurd – was paved with a slime of dead leaves, rotting branches, puddles of dark liquid, a mulch of fungus. Under the pressure of the lightest footfall, the ground gave way. A first step ended in a squelch, the second a crumbling, the third a sharp snap. Waxy ferns which had been around in the time of the dinosaurs whacked into their faces. Above, the vegetable sky was pierced, every now and then, by beams of sunshine that managed to tunnel through. Lianas, as thick as ship's cables, fell diagonally across their path. Grace stopped to draw breath, a tingling in her left foot. Numberless black ants carved a new path across her toes. She swept them off and carried on.

Downwards, they staggered and slipped. A stinking blackwater bog, a clear stream, icy cold, then more bog until their path tilted uphill. Ceaselessly uphill they walked until they hit a ridge and then, down, slipping and sliding, clawing at roots and palms and rotten sticks to break their descent. Up, down, up down, hour after hour of it. Above all, it was a passage through an alien land, of hostile, never-ending, indecipherable noise. Long ago, in the ignorance of her gilded upbringing, Grace had assumed that the jungle would be a quiet place, so quiet that you could perhaps hear a snake slither by or make out individual birdsong. This jungle was as noisy as a train station. Nearby – but invisible – a stream roared and shouted its way down from the Himalayas, sometimes above them, sometimes below, the thunder of water against old stones creating a deep murmur of sound. Overlaying that, a nonsense wild-track of grunts and buzzes and clicks and bleeps and croaks from the things that creep and crawl. And, from high above in the forest canopy, whoops and squeaks and chirrups and trills and long, piercing screams. Monkeys, insects, bats, frogs, gibbons, lizards, birds. The noise pulled a freight train of anxiety in tow. That roar just then – a waterfall a hundred yards away, or behind that fern, a tiger? That creaking sound, so soft you could barely hear it? A liana brindled by sunlight, or a black and yellow Burmese krait, its venom a dozen times more deadly than cobra?

'Miss, listen.' Molly identified it first.

A shudder of unease passed through the group.

'Miss, I'm scared.'

'There's nothing to be afraid of, Molly,' said Grace, knowing the opposite was more honest.

The crackle-crackle grew more violent, purposeful. Ahead, Grace made out two grey blurs at the end of the tunnel of green. Mother elephant was ripping out thick clumps of bamboo from the ground with her trunk and popping them into Baby's mouth. Po Net, down on the ground, fussing over the leather ties and ropes which held the great cane basket in place, smiled at the arrival of the others, remounted and dug his heels in.

Mother started to march, her great backside rolling and yawing like a ship at sea, and the school party fell in behind. Instantly, their spirits lifted: it was so much easier walking in the immediate footsteps of elephants than through near-virgin jungle. Mother and baby crushed grass and ferns and palms flat, making footfalls which must have scared off every creepy spider or hungry tiger for miles and miles around. There was something wonderfully comical and yet keenly affecting about the baby following in the footsteps of a three-ton mass. A great gasp from Mother's bottom and out popped balls of semi-digested stodge in which Grace could make out blades of grass and shoots of bamboo and, half-buried in the last one, something that had been returned from the netherworld.

'Michael!' squeaked Grace, delighted, and Po Net, grinning hugely, turned Mother to one side so they all could see the results of the elephant's digestion. The old lady's trunk coiled forward and picked up the school cap and washed it in a deep puddle, to and fro, with the fastidiousness of a washerwoman. Up in their basket, the children, Michael too, were beside themselves with glee. Now soaked but still reeking of elephant dung, Mother swished the cap around in the puddle one last time and scooped it up with her trunk and raised it aloft to Po Net, who stood up on Mother's neck and turned round and bowed very low, before handing the cap to Michael. The po-faced five year old of a few days ago had become a hardened jungle traveller. Returning Po Net's bow, royally, he accepted the cap, dripping wet, smelly and speckled with gobbets of poo, and placed it on his head as if it were a top hat. Everyone cheered, but softly, in case Sam heard.

They trudged on, rising and falling, the march for those on foot made less grim by the squeals and giggles coming from within the pannier on the elephant's back. An orchid entranced Grace's eye – a golden orgy of tubes and stamens and scent – but Mother had chosen that instant to stop dead in her tracks and hoist her trunk to snack on a particularly juicy knot of mossy food. Colliding with the elephant's bottom, she skidded on a wide leaf as slippery as an icy puddle, lost her footing and fell with a thump to the ground.

'Oh, Miss, are you all right?' called out Ruby, marching arm-in-arm with Lucy, a perilously thin ten year old.

'I'm fine, Ruby, thank you, but I am bit worried about Mother.' As if she had heard every word, the mother elephant turned her enormous head and treated Grace to a look of mild irritation and shrugged in a very bored kind of way. Close by, Oomy chirrupped happily. Unlike some human beings, these animals, Grace thought, do not live to kill.

They halted for lunch. Po Net opened the tins with his jungle knife and Grace was sharing out the portions as fairly as she could when Molly started to moan: 'I'm sick of pilchards and biscuits. It's so boring.'

'Molly, come on,' said Ruby, 'it's better than nothing.'

'No, nothing *is* better than this dog food. You eat it, Rover.'

'Hush, Molly!'

'Miss!' cried Emily.

'Listen, you two, we've got to behave.'

'He's eating all the jam, Miss, the baby.'

Oomy tipped over the jam tin in his haste; it was virtually empty.

'Stop it, thief!' Grace yelled. He eyed her shiftily, head down, sulkily apologetic, and trotted off, docking at the far side of Mother, to peek his head out from underneath her legs, checking to see whether Grace was still angry with him. It was so utterly like the reaction of a naughty boy caught red-handed that she found it impossible to be cross.

'He's so cute,' cried Molly. The little girl watched Oomy's trunk hesitate over a hedge of grasses, like a fat boy hovering over a buffet before plumping for a clump of what looked like dark green shamrock and wolfing it. Molly stood up, walked to the far end of the hedgerow and tugged up a fresh clump of the favoured grass. She held it out to Oomy at arm's length; he paused, eye-ing the gift warily, before plucking it from her outstretched hand and tucking it into his mouth. He rewarded her with a dry touch, not slobbery at all, of his trunk on her hand and trotted off to hide behind his mother once more.

The lunch-break ended all too quickly and they were back inside the green tunnel again, up and down, monotonous, exhausting.

How long could the children keep this up? Three days? Another week, mused Grace, perhaps, but by that time the elephant men would have gone their own way and the children would have to walk along with the thousands of refugees on the main track. But what if the monsoon came early and they were stuck in the jungle for three weeks, even a month? Already the weaker ones were wilting, and it was only the first full day.

In the afternoon trek she had hoped to get her party to pick up its pace, intent on catching up with Sam to press home her fears about the sergeant. But as the hours passed, more and more of the girls tripped on hidden branches or just gave up the ghost, collapsing onto the ground to nurse minor scratches. The group lagged far behind and any hope of catching up with the front of the party before nightfall faded.

Around four o'clock the path grew crazily steeper, their progress pitifully slow. A sudden crash-crash and the head of the Chin rearguard emerged, followed by a dozen or so of the last group of elephants. Grace tried to maintain the order to march, but it was too late in the day and too many of the girls were done in. Only she, Emily and Ruby were walking alongside the elephants, pretty much the opposite of Sam's orders, when they arrived at the night's camp, in a glade of high trees, close by, a ravine carved by a jungle stream. There was plenty of water and fodder for the elephants but neither sign nor sound of the Japanese, nor of the other refugees, nor of Sam, nor of the sergeant.

She had planned to have it out with Sam there and then, but first she had to organise the children's camp for the night – where to tie their hammocks, then ensure they had been fed. By the time she had finished, night had come, and she could feel exhaustion creep into her bones. Grace resolved to find Sam once she had five minutes' rest in her hammock. She closed her eyes, only to feel the sun shining into her face, and her hammock rocking to and fro, to and fro.

A demented giant was swinging her awake. Eyes wide open, sleep banished, the stout bamboo tree supporting the foot of her hammock was being gobbled up. In a frenzy of alarm, she dived out of the hammock, scrambling to wrap her blanket around her half-naked body, and put a safe distance from her and the monster eating her bedroom for breakfast.

Greed for the fresh, juiciest young bamboo shoots was the root of the problem. Standing on hind legs and extending his trunk, the elephant, a young powerful tusker, could just reach the shoots of the bamboo high above but one hind leg had been tied to a foreleg, sabotaging his natural agility. Hobbled, he was bound to fail, and just as Grace dived to safety he overbalanced, front legs crashing down the side of the bamboo tree, smashing through branches and shredding Grace's hammock. The culprit shrugged off his fall, trumpeted irritably and staggered away in search of a less challenging meal.

La Mah, the deputy head elephant man, and another oozie emerged from behind a thicket of bamboo, displaying a glee that Grace found indecent – and she realised that was a fair description of her state of dress, too. Was there something a little forced about their humour? Had they deliberately led the elephant towards the bamboo her hammock was tied to? Perhaps. But the comedy of the moment broke in, relief that no real harm had been done, too, and she joined in their laughter. The two elephant men picked up the torn hammock with an apologetic air. From their faces, if not their words, she could tell that they would prefer it if she did not share this story of elephant chaos with Sam. Giving them a deep smile, she tried to convey that what had happened was not the end of the world but a small misfortune.

And then she saw her dress, originally pale cream, a Parisian design, decorated with red and yellow roses and, now planted on the bosom, a very large muddy footprint of an elephant. Lost in the jungle with a circus, and nothing to wear! Her shoulders shook, and she half-wept, half-exploded with the ridiculousness of it all, and set off for the stream a couple of hundred yards away, wrapped in her blanket.

The logic of the elephant camp came alive with the half-light of early morning. Men and animals were used to the routine, of pitching camp one night and upping sticks at dawn, all part of the nomadic life of harvesting the teak forests, and moving on when the work was done in that part of the woods. Elephant men, bent double, were returning from the bush, carrying great sheaves of bamboo on their backs.

Rice from a black pot, a spoonful of jam, washed down by foul-tasting chlorinated water. Back at the school in Rangoon in the old days, the children would have rioted at this breakfast, but out here, in the jungle, it was a banquet.

The Havildar stood over it all, looking as though he might chop off someone's head at a moment's notice, or strangle them with his two and a half fingers. The ferocious appearance was just a foil, she realised, the children sensing that he was not a man they should fear, that his fiery gaze and grisly hands were some sort of comic trick, like a gun that fired a little flag bearing the word: 'bang!'

Looking at the food fast disappearing into the mouths of the children, she sensed something of the scale of the logistical nightmare that her orphans presented to Sam and the elephant men. They didn't have enough food for a week, let alone a month, he'd told her the day before.

She called over to the Havildar: 'Where's Sam?'

'He got up very early this morning, Miss. He's gone ahead with Po Toke to scout the trail ahead. We'll catch up with him later.'

'When?'

'I don't know.' He stabbed his kirpan knife into a tin of sardines, opened it with the thumb and half-finger of his right hand and gave it to a ten-year-old girl with the sternest of frowns.

Grace stared at his maimed fingers and her curiosity got the better of her manners. 'Forgive me, what did happen to your hands, Havildar?'

'A tiger ate them.'

Thinking that the Havildar would never be good company at breakfast, she headed down to the stream, walking a good way on from the camp, upstream, past a clump of high elephant grass, to gain some sense of seclusion from prying eyes. At the water's edge, she unwrapped the blanket, laid it out on a bush, knelt down in her underwear and began to wash her frock, soaking it and rubbing soap into the elephant footprint. As she did so, her mind went over the elephant men's route out. Very few Europeans had ever been due west out of Upper Burma into Bengal, over the mountains, and certainly not a party of fifty-three elephants. The tusker that had stamped his footprint on her dress had been enjoying a breakfast of an enormous amount of bamboo. With no clear idea of what they would find when they pitched camp of an evening, they would have to take a huge cargo of bamboo with them, in case there wasn't enough food for the elephants later in the day. And the humans needed feeding too. That was why Sam was so keen to see the back of them.

Examining her dress critically, she saw that her washerwoman's work had broadened the mud-smudge, not removed it. It would have to do. A bird squawked derisively, suggesting to her a sound Miss Furroughs used to make when scolding her: 'I hope you haven't come all this way to take part in a fashion parade, Miss Grace. Rangoon is not Paris.'

Smiling at the memory of her vanity – it belonged to a different time - she decided to have a quick dip. The stream was deep, quickly flowing and clear down to the stony bottom. No monsters, only a feather of minnows darting in and out of the current. A gorgeous yellow butterfly skimmed the water and fluttered off into the jungle. But still she hesitated.

'Grace Collins,' she said out loud, 'you have been torpedoed. You are not afraid of a little water, are you?' And with that she plunged in, squealing at the shock of the cold. Not having had a proper wash for weeks, this was the first time when complete responsibility for the children had been lifted from her by the elephant men. It felt wonderful to get some of the grime off. She ducked down and held her breath for as long as possible. Bubbles of air passed between her lips and floated up but still she stayed below the surface, exhilarating in the sense of weightlessness, savouring the clear green-blue light, before she paddled up, gasping for air.

A bowl of mist had descended on the pool, walling it off from the rest of the world by a curtain of grey fog. She moved towards the rock where she had left her frock to see, standing by it, a man with a bandaged head.

'We haven't been introduced. Sergeant Edgar Gregory. You can call me Eddie.'

Not like this. Not half-naked, shoulder-deep, shivering in a jungle stream.

'Cat got your tongue?' His voice edged with mockery.

'You shot the Jemadar.'

The surprise on his face was genuine.

'What?' Cautious now: 'What are you talking about?'

Perhaps he hadn't seen her standing on the bluff.

'You shot the Jemadar. By the ferry. I saw the whole thing.'

A gibbon hooted its weird call, like a motor-car horn, close by, to be answered by a mate from further off.

'It was the Japanese. A sniper. I didn't shoot him. Cross my heart and hope to die. These things happen in war, don't they, Miss? You can't be sure, can you? You've got to have doubts.'

Doubts? Immobile, caught between going down to the ferry and Emily – oh why did it have to be Emily? – shouting at her that Joseph was having a fit, that she must come. The sergeant calling the Jemadar 'a black bastard'. The rifle trained on him halfway across the plank. 'Nigger, goodbye.'

One shot.

His neck spouts blood. Falling into the great river. Floating off, no different from a log.

'You shot the Jemadar. I have no doubts at all.'

Something implacable about the way she stared at him made him uncomfortable. Even, and this was a strange experience for him, a little afraid.

'I fancy hanging around here,' he said, 'for as long as I please. And who's going to make me move? You? And whose army?'

The mist began to lift.

'Miss.' Molly materialised from the undergrowth. 'The Havildar says we mustn't dilly-dally. He told me to find you, "Jaldi, Jaldi!" That means "hurry, hurry" in Urdu, Miss.' The girl paused her language lesson and took in the extraordinary scene: her teacher, half-naked, shivering in the river, the sergeant with the bandage on his head, taunting her from the bank. Molly took a tiny step back.

'Molly, I beg you to run back to the Havildar straight away and tell him to come here this instant.'

'No, you don't, you little Minx. You stay where you are,' Gregory's voice rasped. The sergeant walked towards her, saying 'Come on, love...' but he hadn't covered a yard before Molly spun on a sixpence and vanished into the jungle, scurrying back towards the camp.

The sergeant savoured Grace with one last stare, and disappeared.

Shivering in the smudged frock, Grace stumbled back towards the camp. Molly greeted her bearing a chapatti smeared with jam. 'I couldn't find the Havildar but I saved you breakfast, Miss.' The girl made it sound as grand as Eggs Benedict at Claridges.

Then:

'Miss, who was that man?'

'A Sergeant Gregory, Molly.'

'How did he hurt his head, Miss?'

'I don't know, Molly.'

Wolfing the chapatti and two sardines, she caught a glimpse of Gregory, sauntering through the trees up a hill towards Rungdot and the front section of the march.

Nearby, the Havildar was loading up Michael, Joseph and three girls with tummy problems onto one elephant.

'Havildar.'

He turned to lift a girl high up to an elephant, leaving her addressing his massive shoulder. 'I have a serious complaint to make,' she went on.

'Not now, Miss. I've got to make sure we get started. We're half an hour behindhand as it is, and Colonel Sam will have my guts if we're not out of here as soon as possible.'

'Sergeant Gregory threatened me.'

'Sam's gone ahead, Miss. Let's talk about it when we're on our way.' The big Sikh gestured and, in the distance, far ahead, she just caught a glimpse of a white bandage disappearing into the high bamboo, accompanying the first of the pack elephants.

Her suspicion grew that, faced with the charge of murdering the Jemadar, the sergeant would know how to lie about what had happened. If they ever got to India, there might be question marks raised about Gregory, but she worried that her word against his alone would never be enough to see him hang. And that would mean that Gregory would get away with the murder of the only man she had ever loved.

Emily and Ruby came down from the direction where Grace had last seen the sergeant, giggling to each other.

'That man, Emily, Ruby. Don't go anywhere near him,' said Grace.

Their laughter dried up. 'Why?' asked Emily. The challenge was direct and unfriendly.

'Because I said so.' It was the very worst thing an adult could say to a teenager, but Grace could think of no other way of putting it, short of telling the girls that she had witnessed him shooting the Jemadar in cold blood.

Emily stared back at her teacher, haughtily. Grace looked to Ruby for support, but the other girl kept her eyes locked on the ground and – was she mistaken? – seemed to be blushing.

CHAPTER EIGHT

Sick of it, he was, sick of the sodding endless green, sick of the heat, sick of the bloody place throbbing with noise the whole time. Sick of the endless walking. A right bellyful of it, he'd had. They let him ride on an elephant the first couple of days, because he was still poorly, but now they'd realised that he was fit they insisted he walked. Monkeys shrieking away in the trees, all manner of creepy crawlies underfoot, nasty insects making all sorts of weird clicks.

He should have stayed in the nick. Things would have been so different for him, if only he hadn't got caught in the first place. That Jewish bitch. He should have sorted her out, good and proper, when he had had the chance.

Sure, the jungle would be far worse if it weren't for the elephant men. They'd given him food, clothes, cheroots and even his very own dah, a thick broad knife with a square end. Handy at slicing through bamboo. He was getting on well with them, especially the three lads who looked after the big tusker, Rungdot. They'd seen him puff smoke in the old monster's mush – that had shown them. And they liked a laugh. He didn't speak their lingo but he could still make them smile with a gesture or look.

That teacher bitch, beautiful as she was, was pure poison. He'd had no idea there'd been a witness on the bank. Well, he'd have to do something about that. But the schoolgirls were all right. Most of them were just kids, but there were one or two he had his eye on. 'Miss – could you help me with my bandage?' That could do the trick. The thin one, about eighteen he was guessing, didn't know her name. She was a real beauty. He was playing it long with her, but he'd caught her looking at him out of the corner of her eyes. He'd see what he could do with her...

It was the end of another long day's march, in that precious half an hour before sundown when the jungle seemed to burn with flame. Taking a long drag on his cheroot, he thought back on how he had ended up here, surrounded by elephants and schoolgirls, on the run from the Japanese. And the others.

The strange thing was, he'd ended up doing pretty well in the army. That was the thing about the nick. It trained you to cope with the bullshit.

The old order, an England run by wretched fuddy duddies, was finished, useless when it came to a real fight. He'd always known he had it in him – the ability to command, the guts to take the tough decisions – but, of course, with his eel-pie accent and, the trouble he'd got into when he was a teenager, they'd never have let him be an officer. It was the war that had given him his chance. Gregory had come out East in a troopship, a private straight out of the nick, so low in the pecking order, his bunk so dark and tiny he declared to the others he missed the light and space of his 'rooms' back in the Scrubs. And the cuisine in the slammer had been so much better, too: toad-in-the-hole, consommé, rarebit – he had them all in stitches when he cracked that one. The ship his regiment had embarked on had just missed the disaster of Singapore and, at the very last minute, had been re-routed up the Bay of Bengal, to Rangoon.

Gregory didn't believe in fate. That was rubbish. But even so, he didn't like it when 100 miles out to sea the ocean turned blood-red. The sailors said it was just the muck from the Irrawaddy. Still, it looked like an omen, or something. The switch to Burma had only meant a delay in being smashed up by the Japanese war machine. The ship hadn't even docked when the Jap bombers came over, sunk five ships, machine-gunned the coolies, set fire to warehouses, cloaking the sky with smoke, so thick and black you could barely see your hand in front of your face. Most of the coolies had run away – afraid of the Japanese, or, just as likely, willing the end of the British Empire – leaving the wharves a ghost land. No cranes lifted, no tugs moved, nothing was working. The colonel hadn't even got out of his fancy cabin, let alone off the boat, before he had a heart attack and died. So there they were, anchored in the harbour, a sitting duck for the next wave of bombers, with all the majors and captains running around. Posh twits, clueless. It was Private Gregory, whose first job as a kid had been down the docks, who suggested he could drive a crane, that he could organise the unloading of the lorries, guns, ammo, gelignite and get the regiment off the boat. They made him a lance bombardier for that – on the spot – and sergeant the very next day when the Japanese airmen came back and he stayed in his crane, unloading the gelignite for the demolition of British Burma, doing his duty for King and Emperor, as the bombs rained down.

But for what? They hadn't even left the ship before all the government nobs, fancy pants and senior officers were bursting up the gangplank, desperate to flee. And behind them a sea of faces, Indians, men, women, children, cattle too, all mooing in terror that they might be left behind.

Once on land, they fought so that the lords and masters could run. When he and the other blokes worked out what the game was really about, they started running too. Back home, the papers had said that the Japanese were 'yellow men' with silly stick-out teeth and pebble thick glasses. Well, that was not how he'd seen it. It was the British who were yellow, who ran away, who were unfit for the struggle, who didn't want to fight. To Sergeant Gregory, the whole thing was a dirty, degrading sham. The British Empire was there to protect the 'lesser breeds without the law' – that's how one of the arty-farty officers on board ship had put it. Tell that to the thousands and thousands of Indians refugees he'd seen with his own eyes, walking, crawling along in the dust, hundreds of miles, getting thinner and sicker all the time, stick-limbed, as the brigadiers flashed by in their staff cars, racing past in a cloud of dust, running away from the Japanese. None of the officers stopped, not once. He'd seen the rich Europeans on the road too, big American cars, followed by lorries loaded with snooker tables and fancy furniture, while the poor bloody Indians had to walk. When the weaker ones could no longer be carried – babies, the old ones, the sick, shitting everywhere – some would be nursed hopelessly, and some would be dumped. They would lie there, in the full heat of the day, covered in flies, stinking to high heaven, for days. It was a strange bloody pong, too: sick, but somehow sugary. It lingered on your clothes.

The moment you saw the great black birds circle in the sky, you knew what you would find below. Tough as he was, Gregory started to gag just at the sight of the vultures in the distance. The crunch they made when their beaks bit into bones, that was the ugliest sound he'd ever heard.

Another eye-opener was the hatred race had for race. Back in the Smoke, you could feel the hate the boys had for Ikey Mo, the Jewish brethren. Gregory had known all about that. It was, after all, why he had ended up in the nick in the first place. The real shocker was the way the Burmese had it in for the Indians. One of the blokes said it was the British who had brought in the Indians to do all the dirty work in Rangoon, cleaning up the filth and all, and the smart ones had become landlords and the Burmese despised them. Now their British protectors were running away, and the Japanese were heading this way, it was time for revenge. You could see the Burmese line up by the side of the road as the Indian refugees passed through their villages, swinging their jungle knives, waiting for the dusk, waiting for the British Army to move on, so they could have their way. You could see the results of their handiwork after sunrise.

One boiling hot morning they had loaded up, lorries trailing the guns, and left camp. Sure enough the vultures were circling above a bend in the road, just before a bridge. Down the embankment of a dried-up paddy field, he had found this Indian woman and her kid. She had been a looker, a big-boned woman, not fat, but curvy, dressed up like a gipsy in a red skirt. Finchy said the gipsies came from India in the first place, but he didn't know about that. Still, no one would fancy her now. They'd cut her throat from ear to ear. Her blood, still warm, had spurted out and pooled up, congealing in her long black hair. One hand was across her face, protecting her, her top had been pulled down and the bastard that had killed her had left his knife stuck between her breasts. He'd hiked up her skirt, too, above her fanny. The kid was close by. They'd smashed his head in, and gooey grey stuff was dribbling out into the muck. Finchy shouted, pointing to some Burmese men running off in the distance, lifting the skirts they wore – sarongs they called them – so that they could leg it. Gregory had fired a few rounds off but the figures were too fuzzy in the heatwave, and they were gone.

Point was, of course, that they all hated each other. Why stick around? Why get killed by the Japanese if the bloody 'awficers' in charge were legging it as fast as their staff cars could go? They were all the same. Apart from that daft captain in charge of them with his la-de-dah public school accent and posh manners. Brave enough – nah, far too brave, acting as though it was the proper thing to get them all killed. He had ended up with a hole in his face. Well, to be strictly accurate, a hole in the back of his head that came out of his face, but that was the captain's look-out for leading from the front just once too often.

The Japanese had overtaken them, sure enough, and they had cut the only half-decent track out to India. You could fight and die, or think of getting out another way. Well, dying was a mistake that he was not going to make. He'd seen enough of death to know that King and Country wasn't worth risking your life for.

Dealing with that stupid teacher tart wasn't going to be easy, as easy as he had hoped. Whenever he looked out for her, she'd catch him watching her, alert, on edge whenever he came within 100 yards of her, and if it wasn't the bloody school marm then it was that little brat, Molly, they called her, keeping a look-out, staring at him from behind a tree or looking down at him from the top of a bloody elephant. He didn't think Grace had told the kids who'd shot the nigger – that would be too upsetting for the little darlings – but he couldn't be entirely sure. The way Molly looked at him made him feel uneasy.

And that Havildar had eyes in the back of his head. You had to watch it with cripples. Of course, the Havildar wasn't a proper cripple, but you don't lose that many fingers and not let it get to you.

As soon as they joined the refugee track, they were going their separate ways. He wouldn't do anything while they were with the elephant men. Once they split up, then he wouldn't hang about. Creep up on her in the middle of the night and slice her throat, double quick, the old one-two. But perhaps that would be too risky. The children would suspect him straight away. No one else wanted to hurt a hair on her head. The kids would talk and he would be hard placed to wheedle his way out of it. An accident could be arranged, a slip down a ravine or, if the worst came to the worst, a simple disappearance. Much better. They'd wake up, her hammock would be lying empty. No corpse, no proof that he had had anything to do with it. Teacher had got caught short in the dark, lost her way back to the camp in the thick of the jungle. Such a tragedy...

The thing about killing is that once you've started, you get a taste for it.

That bloody Jewess. She'd almost done for him.

The funny thing was, he'd almost ended up a Red. When he'd left school at fourteen, there were no jobs to be had in the whole of London docks. The great port of the Empire was just ticking over, the Labour Exchanges packed. You would have to queue for three hours to be told by some toffee-nosed old trout that there were no jobs but put your name down and they would see if anything came up.

'Next!'

And outside he'd met a Yid who gave him a leaflet about Communism and ending the Depression by sorting out the rich, by putting a boot in the face of the boss class. This bloke could talk the hind legs off a donkey. He was passionate and funny and almost demented about it. Up until then, all that Eddie had cared about was feeling up the girls, if they'd let him, wolfing down good grub and dodging Uncle Stan – though the old bastard was getting very breathless and he fancied his chances at giving Stan one on his jaw. But this Yid, Eli Finkelstein his name was, he could talk, stuff about the playwright George Bernard Shaw going to Russia and all, saying how wonderful it all was. So he took the leaflet and read it and went along to the meeting. They all sat there, quiet as mice, underneath these posters of a Yid with a big beard and some slit-eyed bald bastard and another creepy bloke with a moustache. They listened to old Eli the Yid go on about the science behind Communism and how capitalism was dying naturally, that it was all doomed. He went on for hours and hours. It was hard to concentrate on all of it, but he wasn't bored. It was interesting being part of something bigger than yourself. Towards the end, the Yid, Eli, started talking about the fascists and how they, too, should be smashed. That sounded all right by Eddie. So, at the end of it, he signed up and they made him a candidate member of the Communist Party and he promised to come along to the next meeting. It was free and he didn't have any money and after all, he was a member of the working class. No doubt about that. Well, he would have been if there were any jobs going. So he was a Red.

That bloody evening he was hanging around with his mates outside the Bucket of Blood when out popped Sydney, who was going out with his older sister, Beth. A hard man Syd, but a foreman down the docks and he knew people and was doing well for himself. Eddie looked up to him.

'I'm a Red now. Smash the ruling class,' he'd told Syd.

'You don't want to end up with them Commies, you idiot. You want to be a Fascist, son. The Black Shirts. They're the ones who know what to do. They're the ones who are going to take on the Yids. Britain for the British, and Ikey Mo can fuck off.'

'Ikey Mo?'

'Isaac Moses, you idiot. The reason why everybody is out of work is the fault of the Jews. You come to one of our meetings. Then you'll realise what's really going on.'

It was electrifying, the packed hall, the Leader arriving, surrounded by his biff boys, a gang of toughs, all wearing black shirts and trousers and a black belt with a wide square buckle and a little lightning flash on their lapels, hair slicked down with oil, the whole crowd rising to their feet and roaring out applause. The Leader talked about the Depression, about good people being out of work because of the crisis in international capitalism, why the British must look after their own. A smell in the air, like a boxing match when the big fighter is really hammering a loser, and everyone cheering him on and then

Old Mosley hit them with it: 'The slow soft days are behind us, perhaps forever. Hard days and nights lie ahead, no relaxing of the muscle or the mind...'

Gregory looked around at the others, their shirts swelling with pride and anger. Then Mosley read out a list of Red bastards, people who had beaten up British Fascists: 'John Feigenbaum, Hyman Goldstein, Barnett Bercow, Michael Goldberg' – they all laughed at that – and then he had a go at the Little Men in the House of Commons 'hysterically seeking to protect the negroid savage of Abyssinia... who lisp of China and Timbuctoo, on the rare occasions when their mouths are not stuffed with high living at the luxurious tables of the oppressors of the British people.'

On and on he went, his tone getting darker and more powerful with every word: 'I am going to tell you who your masters are. Who backs the Conservative Party? Who but international financiers? They are the people who put razor gangs on the streets. Who finances the Labour Party? The Little Jews in Whitechapel who sweat you in the sweat shops.'

He hadn't finished: 'Let us bring down our righteous anger against the festering scum who by their cowardice and sloth have reduced the British Empire to a moribund thing, in peril of annihilation.'

How they roared their hate!

Afterwards, when Mosley and his gang had marched off, Syd introduced him to another man, a bantam cock, his face carved by a razor-slash, chain-smoking, wearing a scruffy mac, thin, intense. He had a funny voice, posh, educated but peculiar– high-pitched it was, very nasal. But he was very sure of himself. He would stare at you, mocking like, stern and cruel then he'd flash a sudden smile at you. His whole face would light up. Eddie was only a kid, but even then he found William impressive. They always called him William – not Billy. No one called him Billy. William told him that they knew someone down the docks who would put in a good word for him about getting a job as an assistant on the cranes. 'But fair's fair,' he said. 'We expect you to do something for us by way of return.'

So that's how he became a runner for the Black Shirts. The Yids and the Commies were on to him pretty soon. They had people hanging out on the street, outside the offices of the British Union of Fascists, watching who went in and who went out. They clocked him fast. So pretty soon he started carrying a knife with a switchblade seven inches long. He showed it off to Syd and William and the others, and they all went 'woo' and acted unimpressed.

But he'd had the last laugh.

Syd gave him a pot of red paint and the two of them went out to the Yid areas of the East End, and started painting *Perish Judah* on the alley walls. Then this group of about five Yids came for them and they were in real trouble and Syd was about to run for it when Eddie, cool as mustard, flicked his knife out and started slashing the air and all the Yids ran for it, pell-mell. So, pretty soon, Eddie, young as he was, started to get a reputation. Some of the others were afraid of trouble, would run away. But not him.

One night, a lock-in down the Bucket of Blood, they brought in a piglet, squealing its head off it was, and fast as lightning. They blocked off all the exits and then they taunted him to see whether he could use his fancy knife to kill it, taking bets.

He'd never forget it. The boozy atmosphere and the cigarette smoke and the men in their black shirts all shouting and screaming at him and the piglet. They let the piglet go and the men started shouting: 'Kill Judah, kill Judah,' and he missed it oh, a dozen times, slashing the air – and then finally he cornered the shrieking pig and he feinted his left fist and the pig ran to the right and he jabbed and sliced a line across the animal's neck like a knife through bleeding butter. The sawdust on the floor of the pub thickened blood-red. What he liked the most about it was the speed of it, the ease with which he could deny life. Here was this thing, alive and screeching its runty head off, and one slash and the noise stopped and everything went dead quiet. It was – what's the word? – satisfying. After that the others treated him more like an adult, as if you wouldn't want to get on the wrong side of him. He liked that.

A few days later they were in the Bucket when Syd and William called him over to their table. He was doing well down the docks, not just fetching tea and screwdrivers, but watching how they operated the cranes – he was always a fast learner - and making more money than that bastard Uncle Stan, and he was quite the little mascot of the Black Shirts; even old Mosley would smile at him and he hardly smiled at anyone, being the Leader and all. So the two of them showed him a photograph of a man in a newspaper. It was the same Yid who had spoken at the Communist meeting, the funny one with the gob on him. Eli Finkelstein. They looked at the picture and old Syd grinned and said: 'You don't fancy doing what you did to that pig to this pig, do ya?'

'What's in it for me?' Because that was how the world worked. Syd smiled and said, 'Because you effing love your country.'

So then he started watching out for Eli, but taking pains to do it right. Eddie's blond hair and his youth made him stand out in the crowd, so he got it cut short and took to wearing a cap and an old man's overcoat. In the cold weather, you'd have to look twice to recognise him. They'd given him a leaflet advertising the next Commie meeting, place, date, time. Nothing to it really. Long before it started he just hung around on street corners, doing nothing, just watching. A good watcher, young Eddie, that's what they said about him. It looked as though not that many would turn up, but shortly before the meeting was due to start loads of them arrived, all sorts, Jews, English, posh types with glasses, even a few blackies and Indians. He hung back. There were far too many around to do anything.

Yack, yack, yackety yack. God, they talked. All talk and no action, the Commies. Snowflakes began to fall, not much, but enough. The bitter weather made him want to pack it in, just duck into the Bucket and forget all about it. His hands were gnarled, frozen with the cold. But he knew he couldn't. He knew that if he didn't do this for them, there would be trouble; they wouldn't let him forget it. After hours of it, the meeting finally broke up and they started to dribble out into the fresh air.

There! Eli Rosenthal, walking home. Tall guy, thin, his hair half bald, brain-box he was. He didn't have far to walk, just a few streets away from the meeting in Poplar, down an alley, underneath the railway arches. Gregory had hung back so much he almost missed Eli going into his house. Number thirteen. This Jewess opened the door. Black dress, hair piled up, gorgeous she was, beautiful body. Meaty. Lucky bloody Eli, but not lucky for long, my son, not lucky for long.

A week later, the same routine, the same meeting. Long before it was over, Gregory ducked away from the place where he could keep watch on the meeting and went to the railway arches. He'd picked his spot very carefully, creeping through a hole in a wire fence, a good 100 yards from the nearest house, sheltered from the weather by the railway above, dark in the shadow of the arch.

But this time Eli came home with his bloody Jewess, didn't he? He couldn't do it with a woman around. He just stayed in the shadows, feeling a bit of a sap. But what could he do? If he tried anything, she would have screamed the place down.

William and Syd had a real go at him about it. When he told them that he couldn't have done it because of the Jewess, Syd looked angry and disappointed, but William seemed to ignore him. It was that coldness that got him down. He liked being useful, he liked being needed.

The following week, as chance would have it, there was no bloody meeting. He took to hanging out underneath the arches, in his favourite shadow spot, waiting for Eli to come home. He had a really loud click-clack footstep. Unmistakeable it was – and that would mean the end of him. But when it came to it, everything went wrong.

Clickety-clack, clickety-clack. It was Eli all right. He held still, intent, listening for another's footsteps. No, just Eli, no one else.

Eli turned the corner and was now walking under the railway arches. Three, two, one. The Jew passed him hiding in the dark and he began to move but a bloody cat, as black as coal, chose that very moment to wriggle out under his feet and trip him up and he half-fell, half-stumbled and the sound caused Eli to look round to see him come towards him, knife in hand. So Eli started to run. But Gregory was fast, dead fast, so he got a slash in, side on, ripping a slice across the man's face and eye, blood spurting everywhere, but with that bloody great voice of Eli's, he started booming, 'Rebecca, help!'

It was enough to wake the dead. Doors started flying open up the street, light spilling out to the pavement. Eddie raced after him with the knife but Eli was running for his life, running like he'd never run before, still screaming, 'Rebecca, help, help!' It was more like a squeal, like that bloody pig. The noise wrong-footed him. He didn't know whether to go after him and finish the job, or leg it. On reflection – oh, and he had plenty of time for that, later – he should have legged it. But he didn't. He started running after him but he'd waited far too long and Eli had a good twenty yards on him. Still, he was faster and he made good ground. Eli got to his house and the door opened and he half-fell in the doorway and Gregory stabbed him hard in the back of the neck and curved the knife round his throat.

And then, blackness.

He should have killed her when he had had the chance. She only brained him with a candlestick, one of them funny Jewish ones with seven candles, didn't she? As heavy as a cosh it was, knocked him clean out. Came to in the police cell, staring at the Old Bill, and they didn't like the look of him one little bit.

William and Syd had done all right by him. Or they let him think they had, which was not quite the same thing. They got him a la-de-da brief, which was good, but in return they asked for their names to be left out of it. The trial was comical, really. He never mentioned William or Syd, but spoke about some Jewish brethren who had promised him £250 to kill Eli because they wanted him dead. The brethren had fallen out over some gold ring with diamonds on it. No one fell for it. The Jewess did for him. She got up in the witness box and said she had recognised him, hanging around their street. When she had mentioned seeing him to Eli, he had told her: 'Oh, that's the little blond Fascist. They like blond boys, the Fascists. The Aryan ideal. Funny thing is, he came to one of our meetings and he seemed very attentive. But next time I saw him he was wearing a black shirt and running errands for William Joyce.' When the Crown's brief asked her about the death of Eli, she sobbed and sobbed and the women on the jury cried too and he knew he was a goner. Would he get off? Would he bollocks.

The jury took about five minutes before they came back. 'Guilty.' The judge looked as though he would have loved to put the black cap on, but he talked about a new law that had been passed, preventing anyone under the age of eighteen from being sentenced to hanging. So Eddie got life instead, at His Majesty's Pleasure. The Jewess was crying her eyes out the whole time. Silly bitch. If he had killed her too, then he wouldn't have been in this mess. When he went down, he started whistling his tune, 'Oranges and lemons say the bells of St Clements'. To show them he didn't care.

William and Syd visited him in the nick. He'd worked it out by then. They started talking on in their way, but he cut them short: 'I know why you picked me. It was a set-up. Because I was so young, you knew they couldn't hang me, and that meant a lot less trouble for you lot. You got rid of Eli, the best Commie speaker in the whole of the East End, and you didn't get that much bother because it was only a mad kid that did it.'

Syd tried to deny it, to shake his head, but William smiled to himself, sheepish like, as if he had been smoked out. He got up and left. William never came to see him, after that.

Being inside wasn't as bad as they said it was. He missed the river and the sunshine and the girls. Your skin went grey inside. The rest of it wasn't too grim. Better than listening to Uncle Stan doing his mum at night. The others kept pretty much away from him. They knew what he'd done and some of them were scared of him.

The Scrubs wasn't so bad. But you had to look after yourself. They put a fat Yid bastard into his landing, who was gobby and knew that he'd been a fascist who'd knifed old Eli. So this Fat Yid goes yackety-yack about him. Eddie got hold of a fork and he broke off two of the prongs leaving just the one, and cornered him and told him any more from him and he'd be blind in both eyes. Then he shoved the prong in the Fat Yid's right eye. Fatty howled the bloody nick down. The screws came to take Fatty to hospital, screaming his head off he was, and Eddie just whistled 'Oranges and Lemons' and they all knew who'd done it but nobody said a bloody word to the screws.

After that, he overheard one of the screws say that he, Edgar Gregory, was the coldest bastard villain he'd ever met. He liked that. No relaxing of the muscle or the mind.

And then came the war. He was just the right age and he wanted to fight, anything to get out of the nick, and eventually they let him out again, to kill for King and Country. The ship out East was a holiday after the Scrubs. They had a wireless and they tuned into Radio Berlin and there, large as life, was old William, saying, 'Jairmany calling, Jairmany calling,' and he told all his shipmates that he'd used to be a painter for Lord Bloody Haw-Haw, touching up the woodwork in the East End. He didn't tell them the whole story about what he actually painted– *Perish Judah* and that, and how it all ended up, mind. That would have been stupid.

Even here, in this jungle, they hadn't found him out. That was the thing about killing. Once you'd done one, there was no point in stopping. Besides, he liked it.

Just before nightfall, a stroke of luck. Not that it felt like it at the time. The sun had gone inside the green bubble of jungle, and he'd put up his hammock and was having a quick snooze, getting in a few moments of shut-eye before dinner. That was when he felt something slide over his ankle, heavy, silken on his skin, and slowly wander up his thigh. Eh up, he thought, but it wasn't right, didn't feel like a woman, too slithery or whatever.

Slash.

Something was writhing on top of him, and he took a tumble out of the hammock and hit the ground - and came face to face with the severed head of a Burmese python. A few feet away, on the ground, was the rest of the snake, at its widest as barrel-chested as a small pig, marked with a deep brown zig-zag, longer than a fireman's hosepipe, it's tail still moving.

Terror choked him, but only for half a second, and then he smelt a rat. For a start, one of the oozies, standing about ten yards away, was giggling fit to bust. You don't have a laugh when a man is about to be killed by a snake. Second, the snake stank, of rotting flesh. Thirdly, the blood at the end of its severed neck had dried hard and brown. Fourthly, the neck end had its own thick halo of flies, buzzing this way and that. The flies in the jungle were fast, but not that fast. You had to be dead at least a couple of minutes before they started to feast. Finally, he'd just glimpsed one of his oozie mates hiding behind a bush, jiggling the carcase by its tail to give the impression of a snake still thrashing in its death throes. Dead snakes don't bite.

Po-faced, when one of the oozies shoved the python's head towards his mush a second later, impaled on a dah, he didn't budge an inch.

'Ha bloody ha. Pull the other one mate. This one's been dead as long as my Aunt Fanny.' The oozie didn't understand English, but the flatness in Eddie's voice needed no translation.

Later, giggling, the oozies mimed to him they'd found the python as they had set up camp, writhing around a tree trunk, and had hacked off its head there and then. The joke was guaranteed to make a man scream – some victims had, in the past, soiled themselves – so Gregory's stone-dead lack of reaction was even more remarkable. The incident confirmed his reputation among the elephant men as a man without fear.

No relaxing of the muscle or the mind. That was how he'd made it this far, that was how he was going to make it all the way to India and back to Blighty, and that was how that bitch poppet would end up a rotting carcase in the jungle.

Thing is, he could do something with the oozies' snake trick, he could use it for his own purposes. 'I'll be keeping that head for a bit,' he said, and levered it off the oozie's dah with his own knife, 'as a trophy.'

And he lit up a cheroot and worked up a plan while the oozies gathered fodder for the elephants and cooked dinner, giving the cold-blooded sergeant the widest of berths. The same trick, he thought, could work with one of the schoolgirls, that leggy one. Yeah, he'd plant the head in her hammock, swish it out – and then he'd be her hero for life. No, that wouldn't work. They kept too tight a watch on where the girls slept. It would have to be when she was going to the toilet in the bush. Yeah, they were all very sheepish about it, their bodily functions, that would be the moment. And no better time to strike than now.

Wrapping the snake's head in his blanket, he took his dah and sidled into the jungle. They'd stopped in the usual sort of place, heavy jungle overhead, hiding them from prying Japanese eyes in the sky, but with a stream, twenty foot wide, close by, so that the elephants could wash and scrub at the end of their long day's walk. As usual, he had been at the very head of the main party, with the girls and the schoolmarm some way back, and the Chin at the tail, guarding the entrance to the track they'd beaten through the jungle, such as it was.

He walked about fifty yards into the jungle and then cut and slashed his way downhill, roughly parallel to where the girls would be sleeping, and waited, his eyes adjusting to the growing gloom. If they weren't snappy, he'd miss dinner. Still, look at it this way, going a bit hungry for one night was better than a hanging.

Sure enough, there she was, wearing a frock that had become muddy brown with jungle dirt, a tear in it giving him a lovely glimpse of thigh, walking towards him into a small glade of trees, on which a little of the dying light to the west cast a red glow.

As she hoisted her dress and bent down to do her business, he curved around the glade, cutting off her retreat to the camp. He unwrapped the snake's head from the blanket and jammed his dah up through the mouth into the gullet.

A crackle underfoot. Damn his clumsiness. She looked up, uneasy, the very picture of startled innocence. He held still, motionless. Wiping herself with a fern, she stood up and started towards him.

Slash, slash, slash!

The snake's head, speared by his dah, landed a few feet in front of her. He came blundering out from behind a spread of bamboo and there she was, white-faced, frozen, goggle-eyes at the snake's head.

'Sssh,' said Gregory, 'it's all right now. Mr Snakey won't be causing you or anyone else any trouble, ever again.' He picked up the handle of his dah, swept the python past her face and lobbed the head into the undergrowth before she could work out the trick he had played on her.

'Oh sweet Jesus!' she whispered.

'It's all right, love. What's your name?'

'Emily.'

He could have her right now... But that would be bloody stupid and besides, play it long, and he could enjoy her night after night.

'I'm Eddie,' he said. 'Pleased to meet you.'

'Thank you ever so much. That snake, it could have...'

'Listen, Emily love, I'd rather you didn't tell anyone about this. I mean, they might think I'm a Peeping Tom, or somethink, hanging around the girls' camp.'

'No, no, you saved my life.'

'That's a lovely thing to say, love, thank you very much. You should go back now, lest they start to worry about you. But tomorrow night, love, do you fancy a chat or somethink? This time, just after dinner?'

'Yes.'

'Promise?'

'Yes.'

'Step out into the jungle, towards the west, where the sun sets, and I'll find you. And don't mention this to anyone. Not a soul, just a secret between you and me.'

'A secret. Yes,' and she smiled at him, and turned, and walked back towards the camp.

Emily would come to him the following night. And, if she stayed too long, then old Missy Grace would not be too far behind.

Luck of the devil, eh?

Whittling a piece of bamboo with his knife, he whistled his tune: 'Oranges and Lemons...'

CHAPTER NINE

A warm whoosh of air, tangy and moist, blew softly against her cheek-bones. Grace stirred from her midday snooze, her eyes opened, and she looked up into a dark, bristly tube. The tip of Mother's trunk patted her gently on her forehead and swung away from her face. As wake-up calls go, it was not as bad as the jangle of an alarm clock, but not to be recommended. She had only meant to have five minutes' rest from the heat and torpor of the day's march, but realised that she and the children by her must have dozed for much longer. Putting on her best schoolmarm voice, she roused the day-dreamers, got them on to their feet and they continued on their long slog to India.

The novelty of living cheek by jowl with the elephants was wearing off for Bishop Strachan's. A week ago, if someone had told Grace that she would get so accustomed to being woken by elephants that it would be only mildly irritating, she would have thought them quite mad.

And yet the sight of little Oomy scrabbling uphill to keep up with his mother, gently plodding along, could not but make her smile. Ahead of her was a rise in the ground, which Molly reached first.

'Look, Miss! Oh, that's gorgeous!'

Far below them, the forest floor was carpeted with butterflies, tens of thousands of fluttering wings, saffron, blue, orange, indigo, scarlet and black.

Emily, a girl who normally showed restraint, screamed with joy. 'Oh, Miss, that's the most beautiful thing!'

The butterflies lifted as one, a quivering rainbow of light that fluttered up towards them. Then the cloud disintegrated and a few seconds later it re-formed, a living kaleidoscope.

Screwing her eyes against the harsh sunlight, Grace saw that the butterflies were rising to make way for long lines of brown ants, all trudging westwards. No, not ants, but refugees, scurrying as best they could to India.

This was the end. This was where they would say goodbye to the elephant men. They'd come a long way, thanks to their help. She could not but feel cast down at the imminent split. Try as she might, she couldn't see how the children would cope, on their own. Men, elephants and the school party descended the slope to join the much broader path taken by the refugees. When they got to the path and walked through the clouds of butterflies, the creatures rose up, revealing a sight less beautiful, a landscape spattered with puddles of bile-yellow diarrhoea. By a tree in the shade, Grace saw something grinning at her. A half-rotted skull. Everywhere she looked, blankets of butterflies lifted to reveal the rotting carcases of the freshly dead. Butterflies rested on a skeleton adult hugging a skeleton child; butterflies on skin dragged over bone; butterflies on corpses flat on the jungle floor; butterflies on bodies kneeling upright, as if at prayer. Fluttering butterflies and the stink of the dead.

The worst, the most heart-breaking sight of all, was the families who were not yet dead, still walking, still managing to put one step after the other, but for how much longer? A father carried a toddler with stick limbs and a bloated belly on his back, a mother in mud-bespattered yellow sari prodding two young boys up the path. Behind them, Grandmother, every step causing her to grimace. Grace took out a banana leaf of stodgy rice she had been saving for a break from her bag and walked over to the emaciated grandmother. The old lady accepted it with a quick bow of the head, but said something in Bengali to her grandsons who scampered downhill and wolfed the rice in seconds. Granny would not make it to India, but her grandsons might, just.

Soon, the elephant men would carve their own track through the jungle and Grace and the children would be left, on this road of butterflies and bones.

Ahead, she saw at the edge of the track two shapes standing in the dark blue shade, hard to distinguish from where she was, half-blinded by the sun's glassy stare. Masking her eyes with the flat of her hand she made out Sam huddled with the Havildar. Sick to the bottom of her stomach, she trudged towards the two men. One of the Chin guides was pointing to a turning off the track, almost vertically straight uphill, running south-west, away from the north-west path taken by the body of refugees. The elephant men had halted, children on foot and in the baskets, hushed, pale-faced, wondering what was going on, what was going to happen next.

'So, is this goodbye?' she asked.

The Havildar was as stern as ever, his face impassive, unreadable. Sam was poker-faced too, staring down at his boots.

A vulture flapped its wings and barely managed to become airborne, heavy with a full meal.

When Sam lifted his face towards her she could see the right side of his lips crinkling, and his eyes had a rare twinkle in them.

'Change of plan. You chaps are coming with us. It would be boring without you.'

'Thank you, thank you so very much.'

'For God's sake, we can't promise safe passage. The Japanese...'

'Anything is better than this.' She looked back, down the track, at the dead and the dead to come.

'Yes.'

'Is there anything we can do to help them?'

'I'm ashamed to say, no. When we get to India we can tell Delhi what we've seen, what a bloody shambles the whole damn thing is. They probably won't believe us. I've given up counting the dead. It's a bloody disgrace. I am ashamed to be British.'

'Me too.'

Sam stared at the earth, lost in thought.

'Let's go,' barked the Havildar, and the whole caravan began to move on.

The elephant men's route – there was no track to speak of – led almost straight up, up a precipitous ridge that seemed to have no end. Mother turned her head away from the ridge in dismay. Prodded by Po Net, she gazed at the thick jungle growth and picked out a slightly less forbidding ascent, plopping one foot down, resting her weight, bringing up the next. Slow, laborious, tireless. Oomy was almost too weak for the climb. Three Chin guards, the Havildar and Sam pushed and shoved the little elephant up the last hill, one hundred feet, a cruel and unbearable slog at the end of an unforgiving day.

They gained the ridge, Oomy giving out a snort of irritation and running to Mother. Looking back at the riot of butterflies, Grace remembered Mr Peach's haiku from another life, the one about a pale butterfly, and knew she would not be unhappy if she never saw a butterfly again.

At camp that night they snacked on sardines and jam, again, sitting on a grassy bank and watching the elephants playing in the stream. None of the children spoke about what they had just seen. It was a dark secret, never to be mentioned again.

The elephants seemed ignorant of the black mood of the humans, enjoying play-fighting in the small stream that ran through the heart of the camp, clambering on each other's backs, squirting water and mud at each other.

Further off, a bull hooted his might, but the females snorted back their derision, as if to say 'pull the other one, Big Boy'. The babies played more gently, molly-coddled and secure, the grown-up ladies seeming to chat and chirrup to each other like next-door neighbours over the garden fence.

Faced with this display, the children, sitting on the bank of the stream, seemed to pick up a little. Soon, they were grinning, alert, and played a game of giving individual elephants nicknames. Rungdot, the biggest of them all, became Henry VIII. You would not want to mess with him. The whiskery tusker with a hollowed-out face and wobbly ears was Nebuchadnezzar, the oldest of them all. Four inseparable tuskers, Matthew, Mark, Luke and John. The youngest tusker, the one who had stamped on Grace's dress, was Ragamuffin and the last tusker to be named, who had a rather miserable face, was Clive, sometimes Boring Clive. Aside from Oomy, the other calves were named after the Seven Dwarves, Dopey, Sneezy and so on. The other mothers suffered the strangest of nicknames, flowing from imagined features which Grace could not at all fathom: Custard, Splot, Haberdashery, Shrubbery, Mrs Griffiths, Mrs Miggins, Lady Macbeth and Ophelia. But after that the children's invention trickled into sand, and calveless females were called, simply, Twenty-Nine or Forty-Three. Remembering their names and counting them was an endless game for the children. They tracked the fortunes of their favourite elephants with the same rapt attention as they used to follow their favourite Hollywood stars at the cinema in Rangoon.

The movies. The night she had gone to see *The Road to Zanzibar* with Mr Peach, had hurdled over the seats leaving him tangled up, all that seemed so long ago. The old, stodgy colonial life, the tired rituals of bridge and tea and cucumber sandwiches and adultery, Miss Furroughs reading the Brontes, the girls singing hymns, Colonel Handscombe and Mrs Peckham laughing in their black saloon. A lost world, peopled with numberless ghosts.

The clatter of a motorbike, rumbling back along the hillside road. Green eyes, peering across the abyss. Frozen in fear, the school bus dangling over the edge: 'Good morning, Miss Collins. Did you sleep well?'

Memory, a jagged edge. Helplessly, she began to sob out loud.

Molly stared at the teacher, made to say something but Emily shook her head and stared at the grass beneath her. Ruby frowned, unsure what to do. They had never seen her like this, not once, and none of them knew how to handle it.

A small boy's hand reached out and held Grace's: 'Baby, aaah.' Opening her eyes, she saw Joseph swinging his arm, miming Oomy's trunk. She lifted him to her, and held him close.

'Oh, Joseph, when we get to India I'll buy you the biggest cream bun you ever did see.'

Reflection was so painful – how much death she had seen, how much she had lost – that it was a good thing, she mused, that she hardly ever had a moment to herself. The last of the light was dedicated to sorting out the children's hammocks and panniers, making sure everyone was safe.

As darkness fell, it would have been the easiest thing in the world to have dropped into her hammock. Dog-tired, stunned by the sickening vision of the butterflies feasting on the dead, she made herself seek out Sam.

His tent had been erected in a shade of trees, on a rise looking down over the rest of the camp. In the gloom she could just make out that he was sitting in a canvas chair, a glass in his hand.

'Can I get you a drink?' From his voice, he did not sound especially happy to see her.

'It's not that stuff you gave me before, is it?'

'No. That's all gone. Gin and tonic.'

This brought out the Puritan in her. Frowning, she reflected that the children were struggling to survive on near-starvation rations, and here was Sam lording it over everyone, downing gin and tonics.

'There's no lemon, no ice, no tonic and no gin. I just drink water and imagine the rest.'

'Ah,' said Grace, declining the offer of the not-so gin and tonic.

'I just want to say once again, on behalf of the children, thank you so very...'

'Please, don't go about it.'

'No, I know what you're doing. I was torpedoed in the Atlantic, and we ended up in a lifeboat. There were many sailors in the ocean and a destroyer went by, and it didn't stop and rescue them, because if it stopped the U-boats would target it. By rescuing us, you run the risk of the Japanese capturing all of us. I know the huge risk you are running to save us, and I want to say thank you.'

'Let's hope the weather holds good tomorrow.'

'Don't change the subject.'

He was impossible. She was doing her absolute best to give him the credit for all that he was doing for them, and yet he made her sound like a bickering wife who no longer liked the look of the wallpaper in the lounge.

His quietness was a kind of rebuke. For a man who had pretty much forgotten how to speak English, he knew the value of silence.

'I'm sorry I snapped,' Grace said finally. 'Look, there's something else I need to talk to you about.'

'Sergeant Gregory?'

'Yes.'

He sighed.

'What are you going to do with him?' she wanted to know.

'The Havildar told me there was some unpleasantness between Gregory and you. He interrupted your bathing. Is that right?'

'He threatened me, but that's not the problem. He's a murderer. What are you going to do with him, Sam?'

'Do we have to have this conversation?'

'Yes.'

'Well, what the bloody hell do you want me to do?' Sam's exasperation flared again. 'Lock him up? Tie him to a tree and leave him to be eaten by ants? Hand him over to the Naga head-shrinkers? Listen Grace, I appreciate your feelings about him...'

Anger flashed through her mind. Feelings? She did not have 'feelings' about Gregory. He was a killer. Once again, Sam was softening the wrong, making life easy for the murderer.

A dark shadow came near. By its bulk, Grace recognised the Havildar. He coughed, diplomatically. Private business – a signal, she suspected, of bad news.

'What is it, Havildar?'

The Sikh coughed again.

'Go ahead,' said Sam. 'We're all in this together.'

'The Chin rearguard have just heard from the look-out who stayed behind to watch the Chindwin. The Japanese crossed by elephant and raft yesterday afternoon. Sir, there's hundreds of them, he reckoned. And they're coming this way, directly following our path.'

Sam made no reply.

'He said they're going very fast, sir, and they've got dogs.'

'How far behind us?'

'Two days, if that. Scouts might be much, much closer.'

'I'm not going to end my time in a bloody Japanese prisoner-of-war camp. We rise at four, everybody. I go ahead, to scout the route out to India. Havildar, you'll be in charge of the main elephant party. Tomorrow, we start moving. No more fannying about.'

'I'm sorry, Sam, but what about Sergeant Gregory?'

'You don't stop, do you? Listen, I will order him to keep away from you and the girls at all times and stay in the very front of the main column. The Havildar will watch him like a hawk. For now, that's the very best that we can do.'

And with that, he turned his back on her and started muttering to the Havildar.

CHAPTER TEN

The sight of Emily walking towards him was, something to savour for the rest of his days. Muscle and mind, see?

It hadn't taken him long to find somewhere – a fissure in the rock, a good two hundred yards from the camp, well out of the way, protected, leading down to a drop in the jungle floor, covered with a spongy moss that wasn't so bad to lie on. He'd cut some ferns to make it nice and comfy. No one would find them.

She was a real looker all right, the sweetness of her face shining through the muck, as she came towards him, keeping to the edge of the little clearing the elephant men had managed to hack out of the jungle. A whisper, 'Emily,' and she took a step into the greenery and she was in his arms, trembling. Soothing her, he ran his index finger down the side of an arm, saying: 'Don't worry, darling, I'm not going to hurt you. Just want a little natter, that's all,' and he took her hand and led the way to his new hiding place.

Once inside, they both had to kneel. He put a finger to her lips and said, 'I've got a little treat for you, Emily,' and produced from his knapsack half a bar of chocolate, stolen from the one of the boxes carried by the pack elephants. Chocolate was as precious as gold, reserved for the sick. To steal it, a crime. Unwrapping the silver foil for her, he placed the chocolate just in front of her mouth, steadying himself by resting a hand lightly on the side of her ribcage, his fingers brushing her left breast. She'd had no proper meal since leaving Rangoon. The bar smelt delicious. Tilting forward, she bit into the chocolate and nibbled.

'Nice?'

'Mmmm.'

He suppressed a grimace.

'Are you all right?'

'It's nothing.' He pulled out a cheroot from the packet in his shorts, lit it with a match, sucked in the smoke and exhaled.

Dying sunlight slashed through the trees, falling on her face.

'It's hard work keeping clean.' He started to speak.

'If you don't mind my asking.' But so did she.

Laughing, he invited her to go ahead.

'The bandage. How did you...?'

'Someone hit me with a frying pan.'

'No!'

He paused for perhaps a beat too long, then started to laugh. 'No, I'm pulling your leg. It was the Japanese.'

'Tell me what happened.'

'It's a long story.'

'There's not much competition, is there? I mean, I can hardly go to the movies tonight, can I?'

'Fair enough.'

His mind went back to what had happened before the ferry left. Better not tell Toots here about that.

'We'd been shot up pretty badly by the Japanese. The captain, God bless him, had bought it, a bullet in the face. With him dead, that meant I was in charge. We found the ferry crossing, but we had to dump the guns, and our dead. We did our best, saying prayers and marking their graves, but we couldn't hang about for long. Then we hopped on the ferry. Half-way across, along came the Zeroes. The first strafing run shot up two men.'

The others were fussing over the injured, uselessly, panicking, but he wasn't going to nurse dead meat. Gregory ignored the commotion and had his ears wide open, staring downriver, his eyes trained on where the Zeroes had gone to, and where they would come back from.

'I was patching up the injured best as I could manage, when the Zeroes returned.'

No relaxing of the muscle or the mind – the Leader was spot on about that. He'd realised what those Zeroes were up to, the military logic was clear. Knocking out one of the last ferries left working on the Chindwin was a must for the Japs. If they missed the ferry first time, they'd be back to finish the job.

The chop-axe of aero-engines came towards them, fast.

'I didn't give it much thought. Just heard the engines and dived in and swam for it. I don't want to sound boastful, but I've always been a good swimmer. For a bet, once, I swam the Thames just below the Tower. Have you been to London?'

'No,' said Emily. 'But I've read all about it. "I will fill my pockets with change for a sovereign in half-pence and drown myself in the Thames... I will become a damned, damp, moist, unpleasant body!'

'Come again?'

'*Nicholas Nickleby*. Dickens. It's a book.'

'Books, eh? Haven't read that much, myself. I was only a kid when I did it. The tide was on the way out and moving fast so I got worried I'd end up half the way to France. But I got stuck in and swam like I'd never swum before and I managed to stagger ashore at Shadwell. Bloody cold, excuse me, Emily. Still, I won the fiver. Luck of the devil, see?'

'You're not a devil. You saved me from that snake.'

'I'm no angel, sweet.'

'Go on. I love hearing your stories.'

'You're making me feel like an old war hero, now. Anyway, as the Zeroes came in, they hit the explosives we had on board, and the ferry blew up. I'd held my breath and dived deep, until my lungs were fit to burst and my ears were popping. And still I stayed down, until I could no longer bear it. When I came up, gasping for air, the water was blood-red. I'd got a nasty nick in the back of the head somehow. That was scary because I didn't know what kind of creatures were in the river, crocodiles or snakes or whatever. But the cold of the water kept me conscious and I carried on swimming and my feet touched bottom on a sandbank, some five hundred yards, maybe more, from the west bank, from safety.'

Muscle *and mind*. Yes, that was the true test of a man. The mind to survive, the mind to win. It would have been the easiest thing in the world just to have given up the ghost, lain down on that sandbank and gone to sleep. God knows, there hadn't been enough of that. He hadn't had a good night's sleep since they had been on that old rust bucket troopship chugging across the Indian Ocean.

'But I fought the temptation to have a kip, and I crawled across the sandbank – it was blazing hot and I burnt my hands and feet - and I forced myself to get back into the water. I swam to the far bank and climbed out onto a bit of grass, and only then did I allow myself to close my eyes. And the next thing I knew, I was being woken up by the elephant men. Bloody marvellous, it was.'

'Emily! Emily!' She could hear Ruby's voice, calling out for her.

'I'd better go,' she said. 'I'm just so pleased you managed to survive. So that you saved me from the snake.'

'Stay.'

'I can't.'

'Stay.' He needed her badly.

'No. I've got...'

'Go and tell her you've got the shits, and that you want to steer clear of the others, lest it's catching, and you will be back shortly. Then come back here.'

She hurried off, and he didn't really know whether she'd come back. He hadn't had a tart for a very long time. Not that Emily was like the other women he'd slept with.

The sun had dropped below a ridge to the west, but a rock face above them was still lit a brilliant ochre. He puffed on the last of his cheroot, thinking back to that day. The la-de-dah captain had been asking for it. If he hadn't dealt with him, well... And that cheeky black bastard by the ferry? He had had no choice but to shoot him. Military necessity. They had no time to wait and besides, there were plenty more from where he'd come from. Blacks don't tell whites what to do. He had it coming.

Come to think of it, it was a good job none of his mates had survived the attack on the ferry. That fat bastard gunner, he smelt a rat when Gregory told them all that their officer had been shot in the face. The cheeky sod had turned the officer's body over with his boot and checked out the back of his head and, blow me, the hole was tiny, the size of a bullet going in, like it was the true entry hole, like he'd been shot from behind, not by the Japanese. Fatty hadn't said anything, but he'd looked at the tiny hole in the back of the head and the great gob-stopper mess where the officer's mouth and nose had been and he looked up at Gregory and he knew Fatty was trouble too. And they'd seen what had happened to the Indian, the Jemadar. Fatty would have sung, had he had the chance. Some of the others too. Dead men can't sing.

But that teacher, she knew what he'd done all right. She'd warned the girls against him, said Emily. The way Teacher had looked at him when he caught her bathing, the deadness in her voice when she said: 'You shot the Jemadar.'

Not much doubt about it, there was real hatred in her. He wasn't scared of much – not after what he'd been through – but he knew he could never rest easy with her around.

Still, that was a problem that could easily be fixed.

The ferns parted and there she stood, a dark silhouette.

'We've got to move at four tomorrow. The Japanese are getting closer. I'd better go now.'

He winced, feigning pain.

'Are you all right?' Her voice was soft.

'When I got shot up by the Japanese, I hurt my back somehow.'

'Let me see.'

Unbuttoning his shirt, he lifted it above his head and rolled on to his stomach. Fingers kneaded his shoulder muscles, knotted and tense, the pressure easing as the feather-light pads of her fingertips trickled down his spine, a caress of astonishing gentleness. A lifting, a pause, then it started again, down by his ankles, her fingers idly stroking, inching towards his thighs, whirling patterns on skin.

He rolled over onto his back and she knelt between his legs and pulled her frock over her head. Inside the hide the light was a deep green, becoming gloomier by the minute, as she bent down and kissed his tummy button with her lips and her fingers undid his fly, button by button by button.

'I've never done this before,' she whispered, blushing.

'Makes it all the sweeter for me, love...'

Sated with pleasure, he lay on his back and lit a cheroot. No one would ever see the smoke, and besides, he no longer cared whether they found him or not.

Kneeling beside him, her fingers stroked his hair, soothing him.

'This lump on your head? How did you get it?'

'Someone tried to kill me.'

'What happened?'

'I don't want to talk about it. I was framed for a murder I didn't commit, and went to prison.'

'No!'

'I'm innocent, love. But no one believed me.'

She half-reared, cupping his head with her hands and arcing her back so that her left breast brushed against his face, his lips finding the nipple.

'You're in trouble. I've heard Miss complain about you to Colonel Sam, that you're a killer. Is that true?'

His eyes widened. 'I'm no killer.'

Emily was a whole woman now. She'd made love to a man and that emboldened her to tell her secret.

'Listen...'

She began with the story of the school's exodus from Rangoon, the naked lunatic, the disappearance of the old headmistress, 'a lovely woman, worn out by war' is how she described Miss Furroughs, and the arrival of the Jemadar, their saviour.

Blushing, she told him of her unrequited love for the Jemadar and her growing resentment for her rival. That night, when the Jem and Grace had thought the whole party was fast asleep, she had followed them, hiding in the bushes when they almost fell on top of her, writhing, coupling a few feet from the undiscovered listener. She had laid down, closed her eyes and listened to every judder of lust, every gasp of pleasure and every word that they exchanged.

'Quite the little spy, aren't you, Emily? Eh?' teased Gregory.

She smacked his hand with a mockery of force. But her mind was lost in that time, the night before they crossed the Chindwin, when the Jem's voice had lost its natural gentleness and the schoolgirl consumed with jealousy listened to the man she adored spit out his secret to his lover...

'What if I became a Jiff not because I was a traitor but because I had been jailed by the British, jailed for trying to do my job, jailed for fighting for the very Empire that has imprisoned my grandfather? In Malaya, before the fall of Singapore, an officer, British, gave the order to retreat, yet again. I challenged him, saying that we should stay and fight, at least to protect the wounded. If we fell back, our wounded would end up in Japanese hands. He hit me. I hit him back. For this, I was sent back to Singapore under arrest and locked up in Changi prison, pending my court martial. I protested my innocence, banged on the cell door. No one came. We could see nothing, only a shaft of light coming through a high window. But we could hear, hear the drone of the bombers coming, high in the sky. We could hear the whistle of the bombs as they fell, the explosions, the screams, the barking of dogs. It was hard to bear.'

He fell silent for a time. Then: 'My first visitor? The cell door opened and

I was looking at a Japanese captain. He spoke beautiful English, he'd read my Special Branch file, he was solicitous, clever. The Japanese gave me back my liberty. So what kind of traitor am I? How can I be a traitor if I never surrendered? It was the British who surrendered me.'

'Is that all of it?'

'No.'

'Go on, Jiff, the whole story.'

'I was disgusted by the surrender at Singapore, at the disdain of the British towards their loyal Indian officers like me, the patronising contempt. But there is something more.'

'Ouch, you're hurting me, Jiff. Please, let me go...'

The Jem released Grace, and the silent listener heard her gasp with relief as he released his grip on her arm.

'If I don't carry out my task, they will kill me. If I do, I would rather be dead. So it is no trivial question. Can I trust you, Grace? Can I tell you the truth, and you promise to me that you will never reveal it to a living soul?'

A long pause. When she spoke, her voice was very quiet, barely audible. 'Yes. Even though I have no idea who you really are. You can trust me.'

'My satchel...'

'Yes, I've wondered why you hold on to it all the time.'

'I am carrying secret messages from the Netaji to his men in India, the signal for a new mutiny.'

'From Bose? Hitler's Indian?'

'Yes, Bose himself. If these men do the Netaji's bidding, at his command there will be an uprising across all India. The Raj will be finished, and Hitler's soldiers and the Japanese will be shaking hands in Delhi or Baghdad.'

'That is treason.'

'Not treason, not to me. If these letters are delivered to the right people, the Axis may win the war. So this is no small thing.'

'But why are you telling me this?'

'What if I was jailed by the British, come from a family of Jiffs, or at least people who want the British out of India, but then see with my own eyes what the new conquerors are truly like? Exactly how our liberators from Nippon deal with people once they have fallen into their hands. What if I was a Jiff who started to have doubts about the Japanese? And then I fell in love with an Englishwoman, as proud and arrogant as she was beautiful? What then? If I don't carry on with my mission I betray my fellow Indians and, what's more, my father, who expects me to do my duty to the Netaji. But if I do, I betray the trust of the woman I love. So, what to do?'

'Who are you? I have no idea of who you really are.'

'First, I am exactly who I said I was. I did not lie to you but I did not tell you the whole story. My name really is Ahmed Rehman. I am the grandson of a Maharajah, the Lord of Swat. We are Pathans, Muslims who live in a beautiful valley, close to the line in the map the British drew, dividing Afghanistan and India. It snows where we live from November through to April, May. This place,' he eyed the sweltering jungle with disgust, 'is so far from what my home is like.

'So, we have money, land, peacocks. At the age of three I had my own butler. At seven, my own Rolls, even though I was too small to sit in the driving seat, let alone drive it. At ten, my own little zoo. Monkeys, a snake, but the best were the wallabies. They used to hop in the snow... it was the most amazing sight, better than the butler or the Rolls by a million times. We are wealthy but my family is a madhouse. Throughout India, my grandfather is famous, the rebel Maharajah, a prince on the side of the paupers, a lord for Congress. He is a very old man now, but still dangerous to the British. They have locked him up in prison, without trial, under their wartime emergency powers. They do not realise the mistake they are making. He is their true friend. Throughout his life he has been a great supporter of the Mahatma, and, also of the rule of law. In '31 he accompanied Gandhi to London, to listen to the British terms for the transfer of power. But it proved to be an empty trick, the British still playing games, playing divide and rule against us. India was insulted.'

The Jiff sighed. 'On the long series of hops flying home, Gandhi and my grandfather stopped off at Rome and, to play the British at their own game, it was decided that they would meet the Duce. My grandfather described Mussolini's office, an enormous gilded ballroom, empty of people, apart from this strutting ninny sitting at the very far end behind a very large desk. My grandfather was unimpressed with the Duce. His talk, he said, was full of violence, "blood, smoke, lava, destruction, and battles of all sorts, battles for the lira, battles for wheat, battles for births, battles against sparrows, battles against mice, battles for or against houseflies, he forgot which". After ten minutes of the Duce, the old man said, he longed to be back with the British, their tea, cakes and hypocrisy. My grandfather knows the British put him in jail from time to time, but if Mussolini ruled India, then he suspects he might have been shot. Hitler? Worse. And what did the Mahatma ask of the Great Duce? He called very meekly for a glass of castor oil.'

At the memory of this, the Jem smiled, explaining: 'The fascists make their enemies drink castor oil so they soil themselves, a bespoke humiliation. My grandfather said the translator didn't dare translate the request. When they brought tea instead, the Mahatma looked at the cup quizzically. He'd made his point. Mussolini understood it well enough. So Congress is wary of the men who march in step, fascists and Communists both.

'This is not India's way,' the Jemadar had continued. 'But as the thirties wore on, the British still would not leave. People became frustrated, frustrated with the British hanging on, frustrated, too, with the non-violence of the Mahatma. My father was one of them. He fell out with my grandfather, and became attracted to Bose, who said: "If someone strikes you, strike him back, twice".'

'That's why you ended up in Changi.'

'I am a soldier, not a pacifist. The independence movement in India had always been democratic, but Bose models himself on Hitler, Mussolini, Hirohito, dreaming of a strong, authoritarian state by the Ganges, directed by himself, the Leader, the Netaji. Bose came to Swat many times, a funny man, clever, educated – at least, they must do something at Cambridge - cynical, aware of what the Big Men he admires are capable of, but so enthused with the lust for power he didn't care. My father supports Bose, believes in him as India's only hope. When the war started, the British arrested my grandfather, not my father. They took the wrong man.

'Partly to get away from the madhouse, I joined up. It is a strange thing to be told that you are fighting for democracy, knowing that your grandfather, who because he is fighting for that very thing in his own country, is in jail. But, also that your father has become so frustrated by the denial of democracy, he ends up in league with its enemies. I tell you Grace, sometimes our family arguments made my head spin. But throughout all of it, I remembered what my grandfather told me about taking tea with Mussolini – that the Axis are far, far worse than the British.

'My time in the British Indian army made me question my grandfather's wisdom. It is an army of so-called equals. That, I am afraid to say, is a lie. The Indian Other Ranks must salute a British officer, but the British enlisted men do not have to salute an Indian officer. Soldiers are proud men. It is degrading. We are paid half the rate of the British officers, too. But that is less shaming than not being treated equally. In the first two years of the war I fought in North Africa, against the Italians. They ran away, they surrendered, they hardly ever fought. The Japanese are the opposite. But when you spoke to the Italian prisoners, you could understand why. They didn't believe in Mussolini, they didn't believe in his war for an Italian Empire in Africa and the British tried to deal with their prisoners correctly. We would make jokes about the Italians, but as prisoners they were *respected*. Again, the Japanese are the opposite.

'During the battle of Sidi Barani my platoon took control of a very large sand dune. We didn't know at the time but on the other side were thousands and thousands of Italians. They surrendered to me, a lowly Indian officer. The British gave me a medal, hurrah! But much better, the whole regiment was posted back to India and I was given leave – the British know how to treat the grandson of a Maharajah – and I spent some time at home in Swat. In the very middle of the night, there was a commotion, a visitor.

'I had been fast asleep but my mother woke me up so that I could be presented to the mystery visitor. I threw on my uniform, sleep-walked down the stairs and shook hands with the guest before I realised what I was doing, who he was. Bose, on the run from the British. He'd turned up at our house, having slipped out from house arrest while the Special Branch were snoozing. Had my grandfather been at home, he would have asked him to leave but my father was the man of the house, and Bose was an honoured guest, and we Pathans have a tradition of hospitality.'

'I remember Mr Peach...'

'Oh yes, the tall one, your lover.'

'He's not my lover.'

'The one who just happens to delay blowing up the biggest bridge in Burma, just for your ladyship's convenience...'

Grace interrupted him: 'He was as drunk as a lord, on that terrible day we evacuated from Rangoon. He told me that the British had lost track of Bose, that they had no idea where he was.'

'Well, he was in our house. I shook his hand and all I said was: "good luck, old man". Bose laughed like a drain, the idea of a British Indian officer, in uniform, wishing him well. He remembered it, and I think he mistook my courtesy in the middle of the night – the man was a guest, after all – for a sign that I was a devotee, that I would be happy to become his willing emissary. By rights, as an officer in the army, I should have reported Bose's presence straightaway, but that would have meant them arresting my father and taking him away too. My mother would not have liked that. So I said nothing to anyone and when I returned to my regiment, we were posted to Singapore.

'The British and the Indians fighting together in North Africa against the Italians were magnificent. In Singapore, a disgrace. The difference? I don't know. The generals, perhaps. Or in Africa we were fighting against the fascists. In Singapore we were fighting for the British Empire. Then came my little disagreement. The officer was planning to abandon the wounded when our position could still be defended. I challenged him and ended up in prison.'

'What was prison like for the grandson of a Maharajah?' Mischief edged her question.

'The champagne was rather flat.' He laughed without mirth. 'I am a soldier. You get used to everything. But this was a bad time to be locked behind bars. During the bombing, the prison wardens ran away. When a bomb falls, you cannot hide, you cannot run. You listen to the whistle as it falls and you pray. Allah looked over me.'

'Are you religious?'

'No. But more than I thought. The other prisoners... screams, weeping, fists pounding against the bars. So *helpless*. It frays the nerves. The wardens ran away for good. Two days and nights. No food, no water.

'And then the door of my cell swung open. As I said, I was freed by the Japs, an unusual experience for an officer of the King.'

'So you became a Jiff.'

'Yes. We, they, they call it the Indian National Army, the INA. The Japanese became, how shall I put this? Excited when they realised who I was, who my father and grandfather were. They had me march at the very front of the Jiffs, which is when that mechanic must have recognised me. How he escaped and ended up here in Upper Burma, I do not know. The Jiff high command trusted me because of my family name, without me saying a word. And I was sick of the British. I had been fighting their wars for them, and they had locked me up. So I was happy, at first, to turn a blind eye to what the Japanese were getting up to.'

The Jiff looked Grace in the eyes.

'You must understand, once the Jiff officers and the Japanese realised my family connection, that I'd actually met Bose, shook his hand, wished him "Good luck, old man" I was treated like a lord. Six of us Jiffs were invited to dinner at Raffles with the Kempeitai, their SS. Champagne, oysters, women smiling at us – most Chinese, a few Russian Jewesses - sitting on chairs in the background, but we knew they were, available, while our old colonial masters were shuffling around in the very prison I had been locked up in. One of us Jiffs told the Kempeitai general that we did not want to become a puppet army. Their general said: "We do not want you to be puppets. But if we do, what is the harm in being puppets? Why is *puppet* bad?"

'They drank whiskey until it came out of their ears, singing victory songs. My friend who spoke Japanese whispered the words the Japs were singing: "my grandfather catching fish in the Ganges..."

'After dinner, we left Raffles and went on to an officers' club the Japanese had taken over from the British. 'Then, while we ate and drank, they brought in...'

Suddenly, he was crying. Shocking for Grace, the sound of this man, utterly calm, sobbing.

She tried to soothe him with kisses.

'Nothing, there was nothing I could do. Just watch in silence.'

'What? They did what? What happened?'

'The Kempeitai brought in a British officer from some dungeon. We never found out his name. He had taunted them somehow, sworn at them. They had heard him say "Jesus". So, for them, a big joke,' he laughed, again joylessly, 'so childish and so brutal. In the club, surrounded by oil paintings and stuffed heads and golf trophies, while we drank fine wines served by waiters in immaculate turbans and cummerbunds, and the comfort women poured champagne over their breasts and invited us to lick their blouses, they brought in this poor chap and they nailed him to two wooden planks, gave him a crown of barbed wire. Drink, sing, fuck – they were fucking the comfort women – and, over there, just on the wall, a human being, nailed to a cross, in agony, eyes squirming, beseeching us, blood trickling down his face, holes in his hands and feet. What was this? *Entertainment?*

'They grew bored with him, screaming. They stuffed his mouth with a towel soaked in whisky. He would not shut up. He was a very, very brave man, and even through the gag you could hear him call them names. "Fuck, fuck you," something like this. A while later, the pain become too much for him, and he started to moan softly. A terrible sound. Finally, a good Japanese, a young officer, daring, stood up, bowed at the Englishman, and shot him dead through the eyes. A mercy. After the shot, silence. This *banquet*, I will never forget.'

The red moon vanished behind a wall of cloud.

'The next day, I was called in to the Kempeitai offices. I tell you Grace, I am no coward, but when I walked through that door, I was shaking inside. All smiles for the Indian officer who'd actually met the Netaji. "Here, take this satchel, a special mission for the Netaji. Take it to India. In this satchel are letters to the most important Jiffs in India, all officials or soldiers, all keeping their true sympathies from the British. Take these letters to them, hand-deliver each one, and soon India will fall."

'Crossing through to the British lines, just one more Indian officer on a motorbike, was pitifully easy. A few checkpoints, nothing. But things had changed. Or maybe I had. The British Army before it had been defeated at Singapore, was arrogant and rigid. In retreat, running for their lives, they showed some grace, some humanity, more than I had ever witnessed in Singapore. Now that I was a traitor to the British, I saw individual acts of bravery from British soldiers, doing their best to save the lives of others, Burmese, Chinese, Indian, too. One corporal told me: "If it was down to me, lad, if it was between keeping the British Empire or me being back home, I'd rather be watching Tranmere." He said it with a smile, but I knew it to be true. It made me suspect that the old soldiers of the British Army, the one I had my fight with over the fate of the wounded, were dinosaurs, from another time, and that there was a new Britain in the making, something different. Well, maybe I am wrong.

'And then in Mandalay I saw your headmistress walk down the hill and into the flames. Mad, but also extraordinarily brave. To be honest with you, Grace, helping Bishop Strachan's, leading the children out of Burma, was perfect cover. No one would suspect a Jiff spy escorting a busload of orphans. But about this, I became more and more ashamed – ashamed too, when I saw how the ordinary soldiers, British and African and Indian too, did their best to help the children. Were the men who held up the demolition of the last great bridge in Burma, saluting a bus full of half-castes, our racial masters? Your lover, the tall, silly one, Mr Daddy-long-legs.'

She shook her head, denying it.

'Is he an oppressor? Or just a man, trying to be decent in the worst of times? I watched how the soldiers at the bridge saluted the children. I remembered what the Japanese had done to that poor wretch of a British officer on his cross...'

Passing his satchel to her, he said: 'This needs safekeeping. Guard it with your life. When you get to India, give it to someone in British Intelligence. But, first, tell them this.' He whispered the secret of where Bose had gone to.

'But Jem, the Netaji's men, if they find out you have betrayed them...'

'...they will kill me. So. If they do, it's just one life. But knowing this changes everything,' he said. 'It changes the balance of the argument between the British who want to keep India at all costs and those who know that if they give up India, they might just be able to win the war. Tell them I told you, but tell them I was an Indian patriot, that I would like it very much if the British would please leave India as soon as the war is over.'

'Why are you telling me this? Why risk your life?'

'I have already made my decision, Grace. I made it when I rode back to the bus. It should have been easy for me to forget you all, you, the girls, the two boys. I could have slipped in to India – to hide in the chaos of war - but there is something about this bloody singing bus that never quite dies, that keeps on bringing me back. The children, too. And, then, to cap it all, you. I fell in love with you. And you call me a traitor? Yes, Grace, I am a traitor, twice over, once to the British, once to the Netaji and his men. But I will not betray the children. And I will not betray you. I have had enough of betrayal.'

Gregory listened with intense pleasure. The Jemadar, all holier-than-thou, had been a sodding Jiff. Surrendered at Singapore and the bloody Japs had recruited him, hadn't they?

'Em, what was this big secret that the Jem knew, about the big important Jiff geezer, about knowing where *he* is, whoever *he* is?'

'I couldn't hear everything. I don't know...'

Pleased as punch, was old Eddie-boy. He'd never get strung up for killing a sodding Jiff. There'd be witnesses, too, other Indians who'd seen the Jemadar go over to the Nips back in Singapore.

'So he was a traitor, the Jem.'

'No, that's not like it was,' said Emily. 'He'd gone over to the Japanese, but the way they treated the British prisoner repulsed him.'

'Once a Jiff, always a Jiff.'

'No, that's not right. That's why he gave the letters to Grace. If he was a traitor, he wouldn't have done that.'

'Letters?' Something about the edge to Gregory's voice frightened her, made her regret what she had just said.

'What letters?' he repeated.

'Nothing. I don't know.'

He struck her hard, brutally. Stung – she'd never been beaten by a man in her entire life – she held her hand to her face, not quite believing that this was happening to her.

'What letters?' He made to raise his hand again.

'I...I think...'

He hit her again. She gasped, more in astonishment than pain, and the words tumbled out.

'It was hard to tell. They were whispering, and everything, but I think he gave her something. I think they were letters, letters to people in India who are against the British.'

'Where are they now?'

'I... don't hit me. Please. In the basket, on Mother's back, there's a wooden box for precious stuff. She's got something locked away in it. Every time she opens it, she puts her body in front of it, so we can't see.'

'Nick 'em.'

'No, I can't.'

'Look kid, this isn't a stupid game. This is for real. This is proof that could save me from swinging.'

'What?' She had a look on her that he didn't like one bit.

'Nick 'em. And bring them to me. Do it. Do it tomorrow.'

Stunned by the abrupt change that had come over Gregory, Emily drew her knees up to her chin, at a loss to fathom what was going on behind those angelic eyes.

'You'd better go. Don't want to get you into trouble.'

She tried to argue, but he'd had enough of her. That was always the way with women. Too clingy, they needed too much of you.

He relit his cheroot as the shadows swallowed her up.

Getting his hands on these letters, proof that the Jem had been a Jiff, would be perfect. Point is, even if he didn't, he now knew enough to throw sand in their eyes. Sammy-boy, stuck-up elephant ponce that he was, wouldn't do anything to him once he knew he'd shot a Jiff. But he had to watch it. Grace was the real danger.

If that poisonous bitch got out, all the way to India and started blabbing and pointing the bloody finger and saying he killed the Indian bastard in cold blood, then it wouldn't take the Old Bill, thick as they were, too long to connect Sergeant Gregory, suspected of murdering an Indian Jemadar, Jiff or no Jiff, with Edgar Gregory, released on parole to serve in His Majesty's armed forces. If the Military Police made the connection between the teacher's story and his previous spot of bother...

Murder was murder, even if he got nicked at the tender age of fifteen. If he didn't watch his back, he might even end up swinging for the Indian bastard.

So there was only one witness left, between him and the prison cell, perhaps even the rope itself.

Well, here they were, surrounded by jungle, hundreds of miles from bleeding civilisation, surrounded by tigers and snakes and crazy elephants, the Japs breathing down their necks.

All sorts of terrible things could happen to a teacher and no one would ever know different. But it wasn't going to be easy. No bloody way. He'd have to play it careful, play it slow. Get to know the oozies better, keep thick with them, become their friend. Make himself useful, like he did with the Black Shirts. And the army. Help out where he could. And then, when he'd been accepted...

Real shame, wasn't it. The teacher was bloody gorgeous, a real beauty with a body like a pin-up, like Bette bloody Davis. He'd have his pleasure and then a quick slice of the old knife across the throat. He'd dump her in the jungle and no one would ever know. She'd just be one of the thousands who never made it out of Burma, missing, presumed dead. There was no other way round it. The same thing with the Yid's tart. Had he taken his moment and sorted out the Jewess, then he would never have been in this trouble in the first place. He'd made the mistake of being soft when it came to dealing with a woman. But once bitten, twice shy.

If the schoolmarm went missing, they would have to give him the benefit of the doubt. There'd be no evidence of anything untoward. No body, see? Just a lot of weeping kids wondering where the hell she'd got to. He'd even volunteer to lead the search-party for her. Lost in the jungle – what a terrible way to die.

Ooh, Miss Goody Two-Shoes Grace wouldn't be blabbing to any policeman all right – he'd make damn sure of that.

After he'd had his pleasure, mind. What was he going to do with her before the end? Well, that was something to think about.

And he began to whistle, 'Oranges and Lemons...'

CHAPTER ELEVEN

They rose at four, long before sunrise. The elephant men worked frantically, carrying children, still half-asleep, directly from their hammocks up into the elephant panniers. They didn't stop until every child was either walking or being carried on an elephant's back, and they were on the move in record time.

At the first light of day came the rain. The word does not describe the stair-rods of wetness crashing through the canopy, splattering drops as big as ha'pennies on the jungle floor, turning the ground into a stinking pancake of mud and goo. What had been relatively good going became, within minutes, a seeping swamp. Would the rain stop the insects? Fat chance. They became more obnoxious, fizzing up your nose or squatting on your ears or creeping along the edge of your eye-lashes, needling you. And the leeches, too. You'd slip underfoot, crash down into the muck, get up and ten minutes later feel something on the back of your leg. And there you'd find a big fat black slug, puffed full of your blood. The best way to get rid of them was to light up a cheroot and burn the leech off, but in the downpour it was nigh impossible to strike a match. So you would have to pull the creature off with your fingers. It would go all squishy and burst, covering your fingers with blood, but somehow its suckers would remain dug into your skin, and you'd have to rip the thing off you, taking with it a lump of skin. And the next time you fell down into the mud, the broken skin and the fresh bleeding would attract a new batch of leeches, and within minutes you'd get the same tingling feeling. Disgusting wasn't a powerful enough word for it.

Then as if someone had pulled a switch, the rain stopped. In muffled sunlight, they walked on, the jungle dripping, a brown-green stew of wet leaves, flies, heat, leeches. Abruptly, the trees thinned out. Ahead, Grace glimpsed blue sky above, Sam standing on the edge of a ravine and beyond him, a yawning gap, more than a hundred feet wide, and far below a furious stream tumbling through rocks.

Precious little space was to be had on the narrow mossy edge overlooking the drop as the elephant party backed up, a traffic jam with trunks. Sam hurried past Mother, moving uphill, away from the ravine, Winston, the Havildar and a dozen oozies in tow, carrying ropes and long doubled-ended saws. Grace called out to him from the basket: 'What's happening?'

'Bloody map. The ravine wasn't marked. Officially, it's not there. Not good.'

'What are you doing to do?'

'Write a letter to the *Daily Telegraph*,' and he vanished into the jungle, pursued by a posse of elephant men.

Po Net gave a command and Mother buckled underneath them. The children piled out, as accustomed to exiting the pannier as they had been to leaving the school bus, and the whole group followed the path Sam's party had made through the jungle. At the base of an enormously tall teak tree, two teams of oozies were sawing through a top and bottom bite of the trunk furiously, their arm muscles pumping, sweat dripping off their faces. But the trunk was so fat that Grace feared it would take them all day to chop it down. After ten minutes, their places were taken by four fresh oozies, who carried on the work in a sweet rhythm. By now Grace could see a stain of sap where the saws were eating into the teak. The bite in the trunk had become a dark grin.

Behind them, they heard chains being dragged along the jungle floor. The jungle parted and Henry VIII, ridden by one oozie, with two Burmese holding spikes on either side of his head, marched up, in harness, pulling a long ribbon of chains. The elephant grunted, bent his head and concentrated on feasting on a clump of bamboo.

The saw's bite had become yet deeper, another two feet into the trunk. Two new teams took over, losing barely a second, the teeth of the saws hissing against the trunk, the cut almost a third of the way across.

Grace's ears pricked. Over the hiss and clatter of the jungle, she could hear a metallic barking. The chatter of a sub-machine gun, never to be mistaken, echoed around the hills. It was hard to tell the distance, but she guessed, the noise came from less than five miles away. The elephant party only carried rifles. A machine-gun meant the Japanese, attacking someone. The rearguard? No idea. All she had to do was look at Sam's face to realise that the shooting was far too close.

'Havildar! Get these bloody children out of the way.'

The Sikh led Bishop Strachan's to the far side of the teak, away from the ravine. They stumbled through the undergrowth, climbing onto a slight hillock which provided a ring-side seat of the great tree and beyond it, the fearful drop and the gap it had to bridge.

'What are they chopping the tree down for, Miss? We're not going to walk across on the tree, are we?' asked Ruby, her voice hushed with awe.

Grace said nothing.

'We're not, are we?'

'Sssh, Ruby. I don't want to frighten the little ones,' whispered Grace. 'Or me.'

Guns pock-pocked, more sporadic, not a machine-gun, but closer, much closer.

The elephants, too, were led to the safety of the far side of the teak, Oomy squashing underneath Mother's belly. The mother elephant raised her trunk into the air, as if tasting the wind. Having seen the elephants easy and relaxed, there was no doubting their anxiety: a communal twitching of tails, ear flaps wide, trunks swishing agitatedly, this way and that. They might not know exactly what the threat was, thought Grace, but the idea that they were just dumb beasts was ignorant indeed.

The children started eating lunch, but the sense of foreboding dimmed appetites, and Grace had to cluck at the children for offering their scanty rations to the elephant calves.

Yells in Burmese, and then Sam's voice called out: 'Timber!' A slow splintering of wood built through a crescendo of ripping and snapping to a Niagara of sound, a great thundering roar as the teak shivered and fell across the ravine. Through the soles of their feet they felt a great shudder; overhead, monkeys, birds and insects screeched out against this new affront to the natural order of things.

'Miss, look!' cried out Molly. From their vantage point overlooking the ravine the children watched, enthralled, as a man with a dirty bandage on his head clambered up the side of the great teak, stood on top, and then sauntered along the trunk across the ravine as if he was walking down a pavement on

Oxford Street. He crossed to the far side and turned back to the watchers, bowed theatrically, and blew a kiss.

Sam called out to the children: 'Your turn next, ladies and gentlemen.'

'But the elephants?' asked Grace. The thought of crossing the ravine was making her feel nauseous.

'No. Children first.'

'Why?'

'Because the children are not heavy. The elephants might be too heavy, and we can't take any chances. Getting you across is the easy bit.'

There was a mumble of unease from the children, which Grace determined to nip in the bud. She hated heights, but she hated the sergeant more, and she was damned if she was going to be out-braved by him.

'Come along, children.' She gathered together the school crocodile and led it towards the trunk. 'Our turn now. Let's sing a song. Ruby?'

'Sam will be angry.'

'He's made more than enough noise already. Besides, it will be fun.'

'London Bridge is falling down, falling down...'

'Couldn't you think of a more appropriate one, Ruby?'

'No.'

They walked down to the trunk in silence. By the time they had got to the edge of the ravine, the elephant men had got a rope across, a handrail. Sam walked across the tree-bridge, Winston pattering along behind him, followed by the Havildar, carrying Joseph on his shoulders and holding Michael's hand. Most of the girls, all of them older than the boys, didn't want to look foolish and followed on. Grace occupied herself helping them get a leg-up the smooth side of the trunk, a good few feet taller than her. When it came to Emily's turn, the girl managed to scrabble up on her own.

Molly refused to cross, point-blank. Grace implored her. She shook her head, her pudding bowl haircut swishing this way and that. She was such a determined child that Grace did not know what to do. The Havildar strolled back across the trunk, slipped down the side, bent down, and whispered into Molly's ear. The little girl nodded, briefly, and soon the two of them were crossing the ravine, hand in hand.

How on earth did he do that? Grace wondered.

When the last of the girls were up and making the crossing, it was Grace's turn. Po Net helped her up. Lunging for the rope hand-rail, she steadied herself and started walking. After all the hours in the dim green gloom under the forest canopy, the white glare of the wide open sky played harshly on her eyes. She dared not look down, but the distant sound of the stream bubbling furiously below gave her a chilling idea of just how far she would fall if she lost her balance.

Gunfire, not so far away. A racket of birds of paradise, trailing bright violet tails, lifted up from the bottom of the ravine and came barrelling up towards the tree-bridge. She made to duck but a disembodied voice broke through: 'Head up, chest out, back straight'. Her father's advice. Where was he now? What was he doing? She'd last written to him a day before they fled from Rangoon, but she was pretty certain her letter would never have left the city. Had the Whitehall warrior any idea that his plan, that Burma would be safe for his daughter, might not have worked out quite as he had hoped? The absurdity of that thought, terrified as she was, gripping on to the rope hand-rail, 200 feet from a rocky death below, lost in the middle of the jungle in High Burma, with the Japanese Imperial Army within gunshot-sound, all but her made her skip across. Squinting in the sunlight, she focused on a figure in the shimmering heat helping the girls ahead of her down the side of the trunk on the far bank of the ravine: the man with the bandaged head.

Something about the elaborateness of his gallantry sickened her, made her entirely forget where she was. She all but ran the last ten yards along the trunk, and yelled at him: 'What the bloody hell do you think you are doing?'

'Lending a hand,' said Gregory, affecting hurt.

'Leave the children alone.' Her voice bore a querulous indignation which she didn't like but could not help.

'For God's sake, Grace, he's only helping.' It was Sam. 'There's no law against that.'

'No, I'm not putting up with this. I've asked you to keep this man,' only now did Grace become aware that almost the whole school was staring at her, unkindly, as if she was some kind of madwoman barking out at dangers no else saw, 'under control.'

'As I said, he was only helping. I'd ask you to keep a civil tongue in your head for everybody in this party, and that includes Sergeant Gregory.' The rebuke was all the more telling because of the unusual gentleness, the pity in Sam's voice, as if he was becoming concerned whether Grace was losing her grip.

She had to suffer her rebuke in silence as the men worked to prepare for the elephants crossing. It was one thing to get a party of orphans across a tree-bridge. Quite different, to get fifty-three elephants across.

Po Toke climbed onto the teak trunk and withdrew from his rucksack a length of sugar beet. Henry VIII's trunk wafted the airwaves, picked up the scent of the sugar, stood on a side branch and was atop the trunk with all the agility of a circus elephant. Po Toke had to skip across the tree-bridge as nimbly as he could because Henry VIII almost trotted along, heedless of the drop below. Once the lord of the elephants had made the crossing, the oozies seemed more relaxed. Matthew, Mark, Luke and John trundled across, unconcerned. Ragamuffin seemed to dance, Clive crossed dully and Nebuchadnezzar took an age. Each elephant was different. Some would cross with no fuss. Others had to be cajoled, encouraged with commands or bribed with sugar beet or a handful of salt. They were working as fast as they could, but getting fifty-three across, one at a time, was going to take them the best part of an hour. The work occupied the oozies led by Po Toke. Sam and the Havildar could only watch and fret.

'Havildar!' squeaked Molly. 'You promised you would tell me. If I walked across.'

'Ah, yes.'

'What did he promise?' asked Grace.

'That if I walked across the tree-trunk,' said Molly, 'he'd tell me the story of how he lost his fingers.'

The children, sitting in the shade on the far, western side of the ravine, listened, ears agog.

He caressed his moustache with the back of his fist, and started: 'I was born in the Punjab – this means The Land of Five Rivers – to a family that had fought with the British since the mutiny, back in 1857. I was a boy soldier at sixteen. In the summer of 1917 we sailed from India all the way to Italy. The ship wobbled and I was sick.'

The children laughed, enraptured.

He'd loathed every second of the voyage, staring at the rocking deep blue, fearing torpedo strike or shipwreck at the sight of white caps as the wind freshened to a breeze. The docks at Naples – not normally associated with goodliness – were, to him, nirvana. The moment he crossed the gang-plank, he fell to his knees, kissed the earth and prayed, thanking God for a safe passage.

Once the floor beneath his feet didn't rock, he became his own man again, enchanting his friends in the regiment, the 13th Baluchi Rifles, with a selection of Hindi love songs, sung in a rich piping voice, as the troop train clickerty-clacked up Italy on their way to the Great War.

'Winter was coming and I was a boy from the plains of the Punjab. I had never seen such snow, so deep, icicles hanging from the little wooden eaves of the railway halts, almost burying the houses as we pulled north. One morning the Havildar of our regiment, an ancient Baluchi, banged open the doors to our carriages and we looked up to see crags, black silhouettes against the rising sun, the Dolomites.

'It was so cold we slept with the horses. At day break, when the silver-grey night mists still hung in the valleys beneath, we would uncap our big guns, point the muzzles at the mountain tops on the other side of the valley and blast away at the Austrians. They would fire back, sending up plumes of snow into the air, occasionally killing my friends. But this was not the worst thing for us.

'We did not have proper winter clothing for the cold we faced. One night I felt a pain in my little toe, as if it was on fire. In the morning, coal-black, it snapped off in my fingers like a twig. The following night, the middle finger of my right hand started to burn. Our colonel, an Englishman from Todmorden in Lancashire called Malone, telephoned the Adjutant-General at staff headquarters thirty miles back from the front and demanded proper winter clothes for us. Nothing happened. Our colonel sent telegram after telegram. Still nothing. Then he went down to staff headquarters, saw the Adjutant-General, and asked him to visit the front line. Again, nothing happened. Our colonel returned to staff headquarters, found the Adjutant-General in a restaurant drinking prosecco with two women. He drew his revolver, kidnapped him, drove him back to the foot of the mountains, tied him to a mule, backwards, facing its tail, and brought him all the way up to the snows, the ice-line. In front of all of us, at gun-point, the colonel forced the Adjutant-General to strip off his warm British officer winter clothes until he was all but naked and then the colonel gave them to me, as I was the youngest of them all. The Adjutant-General put on my clothes. He started to shiver, uncontrollably. Then he asked to make a telephone call. We heard him order two hundred British winter uniforms, wool-lined boots, leather gauntlets up from the stores to the ice-line that very day. By this time I had one thumb and two fingers on this left hand and a thumb and half a finger on my right. So that's how I lost my fingers.'

'What happened to your colonel?' asked Emily.

'The next day the Military Police, the Red Caps, came to take him away. He was to be court-martialled. We all stood up, and we saluted him. The Austrians sent a whizz-bang...'

'What's a whizz-bang?' asked Molly.

'A shell, like a bomb but from an artillery piece. They go whizz, and then bang. We could tell from the whizz that this one would fly harmlessly over our heads but the Red Caps didn't know that, and they all ducked. We Indian sepoys remained standing, saluting our brave colonel. He, too, was standing. He told us in Urdu: "There are a lot of idiots in the British Army, but sooner or later, someone stands up and does the proper thing. Remember that. Thank you, carry on." And then, in English: "Perhaps you might tell these chaps that they can get up now. They'll catch their death." Without this man, I would have no fingers at all, so I bless God because I am lucky.'

Grace had never seen the children so silent, so still, so enthralled.

He got up and started organising the elephant train, while Po Toke and the oozies set about getting the last of the calves and their mothers across. The calves' skittishness made it quite possible that they could tumble from the trunk. Their mothers lined up on the far side of the ravine, babies behind them, trunk hanging on to mother's tail, and all crossed sweetly, the last two being Mrs Griffiths leading Dopey and Mother leading her baby. As Oomy crossed over to the safety of the west side of the ravine, he appeared to give the watching children a bow.

Sam gave orders for Henry VIII and Matthew, Mark, Luke and John to be led up to the trunk and they hunkered head-down, to shove the great tree over the edge of the ravine. The elephant men were not going to give the Japanese the luxury of their home-made short cut. The hind legs of the five great beasts quivered with strain. It moved barely an inch, if that.

'What about the rearguard? The Chin?' Grace asked the Havildar but it was Sam who answered.

'Got to leave them on the other side. No choice. They know the jungle. They can disappear into it and the Japanese won't find them. Hopefully, they will find their way round the ravine and catch up with us. Or go home, and wait for us to return to Burma. But we can't wait, and we can't leave this bloody tree bridge here. That last burst of gunfire sounded too damn close. I hope these jumbos get a move on.'

A heavy branch, snagging the ground, was ripped free and the trunk began to shift more easily, testament to the immense power of the elephants.

On the far side of the ravine, about two hundred feet downhill from where they had just crossed, there was a rippling through the long elephant grass, higher than a man's head. A voice – panting, exhausted - shouted: 'Wait! Wait!'

'It's a trick,' yelled Sergeant Gregory. 'Everybody get down.' Grabbing a rifle from an oozie, he ducked prone on to the ground and aimed across the abyss, firing twice.

'Hold fire! Take cover,' yelled Sam. Children and adults scrambled to hide behind boulders and stout tree trunks, while the oozies working Henry and the Gospel elephants urged them to push harder, so that the trunk would be over the edge before the Japanese could get to the trunk.

'Don't shoot. We're British!' The elephant grass waved this way and that, still holding the secret of who was running towards the edge of the ravine.

'It's a Jap jitter party,' shouted Eddie Gregory, reloading.

A very tall British officer emerged from the grass, hands high in the air: 'Don't shoot.'

'Hold fire!' repeated Sam.

'It's a dirty trick,' roared Gregory, and with his rifle sight on the stranger's heart, he squeezed the trigger.

'Hold fire!'

Something kicked hard against Gregory's gun-arm and the bullet went zinging high into the jungle canopy.

'What the bloody hell do you think you're doing? Don't kick me, you silly bitch!' yelled Gregory, outraged.

'It's no trick.' Grace was not for repenting. 'I know that man. I'm sure you'll enjoy meeting him, Sergeant. He's a magistrate,' and gave him another kick, no more gentle than the first.

'Grace, it's you!' Hard to pack boyish delight and unbearable longing in a shout that could be heard from the far side of a ravine, but the tall soldier somehow managed it.

'Mr Peach!' Grace shouted back and began racing downhill to narrow the gap between them.

Absurd as it was, she found herself giggling, delight and happiness bubbling up inside her. That time they had first met, in the meeting room at Government House, she'd thought he was odd, almost freakish and not a little bit melancholic. No hint then of what she felt for him now. That ghastly time when he was drunk, lobbing billiard balls at the portraits of British Burma's great and good on the walls – *'no, Mr Peach, I think you're a damned fool.'*

But it was Mr Peach who had warned her to evacuate the children to India, Mr Peach who had halted the demolition of the great bridge across the Irrawaddy so that they could pass, and here he was, still a damned fool, but alive.

Alive? She winced. And the Jemadar? Was she so shallow a flibbertigibbet that she'd forgotten the one man she had truly loved so quickly? The Jemadar was dead, yes, but that was nothing to do with Mr Peach. As he staggered out of the elephant grass, she could see that he was grinning from ear to ear. A good man. No, better – rarer than that – a good man in a dark time, and his survival, through all the hardships of Burma at war, was worth smiling about.

Seven more wraiths followed Peach out of the elephant grass, pitifully thin, sun-blasted, trapped on the wrong side of the ravine, exhaustion written on their faces, the only clue that they were soldiers the rifles slung over their shoulders.

'Oh, Christ!' yelled Sam. 'We thought… we thought… you were the Japs.'

'Oh, no.'

Grace stopped in her tracks and swung around and stared and became horribly aware that a second awful mistake might be about to happen.

Sam ascended the slope to where Gregory was standing. 'Are you deaf?'

'I thought they were the Japs. So did you.'

'I told you to hold fire. Twice, three times.'

'Better safe than sorry.' Gregory gave Sam a cold eye.

'No, better obey orders than kill our chaps. From the state of some of those men they could be dead within a day or two. If they do die, that's because you were too bloody trigger-happy and opened fire before we could work out who the bloody hell they were. Give me that rifle.'

Truculently, Gregory gave Sam the weapon.

'Nobody opens fire unless I say so. When I say "hold fire" I mean it. Do you understand?'

Nothing from Gregory.

'Do you understand?' repeated Sam.

'Yes,' said Gregory, turning his back on Sam as he brushed himself down.

'I don't want to see you with a gun in your hands again.' He walked away from Gregory, down towards where Grace was stood across the ravine from Peach.

'Stop! Stop the elephants!' screamed Grace.

The oozies urging the big tuskers on to push the great tree over the cliff were higher up the valley and did not heed her shouts. Over the roar from the falling water below they could not possibly hear her. Gregory, closer to the oozies than Grace or Sam or the Havildar, waved them encouragement, to keep on with what they were doing.

'Stop! Stop the elephants!' Her shout ended in a sobbing whimper. 'Stop! For God's sake, stop!'

Their massive skulls pressed against the cylinder of teak, the elephants shoved again, spurts of dust rising from where their heels were grinding against the earth. What happened next took place with unconscionable slowness, like scenes from a movie shown by a faltering projector. The great tree began to tip over the edge of the ravine, inch by inch. The elephants gave one last burst of power, the balance of weight teetered and the tree accelerated into the ravine, great boughs breaking against the rock walls, generating a splintering roar which echoed around the hills as it crashed down to the rocks below and landed with a giant thud.

The absurdly tall Englishman walked up to the edge of the ravine, looked down at the bridge that was a bridge no longer and fell to his knees, burying his face in his hands. The watchers on the far bank looked on, aghast, silent but for one.

'Oh, Bertie,' cried Grace. 'I'm so sorry.'

Pulling himself up, he shook his head once with aching slowness, then fixed the grimmest of smiles on his face. He retrieved a book from his knapsack, tore out a blank page and wrote something on it in pencil. Turning his back on the watchers from the western side of the ravine, he did something with the paper.

He stood up and walked to the very edge of the ravine, in his hands a paper plane, and threw it towards Grace. The plane flew straight and true for some seconds, darted this way and that, and then started to fall down towards the torrent far below. But at the last moment it rose up, powered by some unseen uplift, and cleared the rock edge, landing in the grass at Grace's feet.

She picked up the plane and opened it out. On one side were a few lines of Japanese writing, indecipherable to her. Puzzled, she looked across at him. He motioned for her to look at the other side. And there, written in English, were these words:

'Though I go to you
ceaselessly along dream paths,
the sum of those trysts
is less than a single glimpse
of you in the waking world.'

Ono no Komachi, 9th century

Holding the paper plane to her lips, she kissed it.

On the far side of the ravine, a ninth man, Sergeant-Major Barr, had caught up with the others. 'We'd better move, sir. It's a bit fooking exposed here. Come on, let's hop it.'

But Peach stood stock-still, staring at Grace.

'We're sitting ducks here. We've got to fook off, sir.'

Gregory walked out of the shade. He was the best part of two hundred feet across from Peach, his features washed out by the acid brightness of the sun, but even so there was something about him that jolted Peach.

'Sir...' said the sergeant-major, anxiety giving an edge to his ordinarily flat tone.

A file lying open on Peach's desk back in Rangoon. A photograph, a striking, child-demon face and blond hair – and beneath it, typewritten, double-spaced, the details.

'Them Jap buggers are on our tails,' Barr fretted, 'and if we don't move sharpish, they'll have us.'

Peach had become pretty familiar with reports complaining about the poor quality of some of the troops sent out from Britain to this forgotten war, but even so, that particular file had offended his sense that the Empire's military necessity should not override every consideration. What was the name? Damn his memory. He'd forget where he'd left his nose next. Name of a bishop. No, a pope...Pius? No. Constantine. No. *Gregory*. That was the man's name. What had he done again? A custodial sentence, yes, but for what? It was lost, one line of detail in tens of thousands of typewritten files, blurred and fuzzy, a few months away in time, a world away, standing in this jungle, on the wrong side of hope.

'Oh, Christ!' The most beautiful woman in the whole world, separated from him by a bloody ravine, was in grave danger. So were they all.

Peach yelled: 'That man – he's a murderer!' but he was drowned out by a metallic roar. Overhead, a fat bough of a banyan tree trembled and fell to the ground, shredded by a mortar. A second mortar landed with a sharp clang against an outcrop of rock, a third whizzed into the greenery, sending a troup of macaque monkeys screaming and gibbering away across the tree-tops. On the far side of the ravine, the elephant men and the orphans were vanishing into the jungle.

'Murderer!' screamed Peach, but a fresh hail of mortar shells crashed in, rendering his warning fatuous.

'Stop fannying about, you idiot, you're going to get fooking killed,' roared the sergeant-major. 'Move, you daft bugger.'

He physically grabbed Peach and pushed him back into the elephant grass.

The elephant men harried the children and elephants to move as fast as they could until the immediate danger of the Japanese mortars was safely behind them. Once the pace had slowed down a little, Sam walked back down the line of elephants and found Grace.

'I'm going on ahead with ten men, no elephants, so that we don't have any more unpleasant surprises like the ravine,' he told hero. 'The Havildar will be in charge of the main party. I've told that idiot Gregory to leave you well alone. That's the best I can do for now. But, for your part, stop going on about him.'

Grace nodded, not trusting in her judgment to challenge him.

Sam's scouting party climbed up and up, ascending three, four thousand feet, the jungle thinning dramatically as they entered a new world of Alpine meadow, sparsely covered with brush, often treeless. Six thousand feet high, maybe more.

No man's-land, a void, where immense foothills higher than any mountain in Scotland ran down from the Himalayas and formed the backbone which split India from Burma. No one had ever built a road here, no one had bothered to cross it and certainly no one had ever bothered to map it. Marco Polo had crossed the Gobi Desert centuries ago and the Sahara was like Piccadilly

Circus compared to this. Well, Sam conceded that he might be over-egging the pud a bit. That was the trouble with spending too much time without company of your own kind. You started chattering on to yourself. Stop that talk, Sam, stop it now.

They marched on.

Until just before sundown, a full stop. Dead ahead lay a wall of rock, tinting red in the dying light, God knows how many miles long and impossibly high. After the Great War, he'd spent a month's leave in Rome. The Coliseum was just short of two hundred feet high. This rock was maybe two and a half times that, perhaps 500 feet. From what he could see through his binoculars, the rock was sheer. No man could climb it, certainly no animal. Making a tree-bridge across the ravine had bought them half a day – he was pretty sure that the Japanese didn't have the professional lumberjacks amongst their men that he had – but they weren't far behind the main party led by the Havildar. To the south, the Japanese. To the north, more Japanese, pressing on towards Imphal. They heard the artillery duels in the neighbouring valleys more clearly now they were high above them, making short, sharp bangs, more snappy than thunder. It was plain as a pikestaff to Sam that the war was catching up with them. Their only route was straight ahead, due west, but they weren't tunnel men.

And elephants can't fly.

He could be wrong, but it looked as though they were finished, that his dream of taking his jumbos out of Burma by a route that didn't exist was dead. It had been a good dream while it lasted, but soon it would turn into a bloody nightmare.

A thin chimney of smoke rose above the jungle a few hundred feet away. He ordered a halt, and complete silence, and took Po Toke with him, crawling through the undergrowth to discover a few huts in a clearing by a stream, abandoned. They got up and walked towards the smoke and found a pot of stew still bubbling over an open fire.

On the edge of the clearing, something moved, a blur, vanishing into the jungle. Sam called out to whoever it was in Burmese or Urdu, but he remembered that someone had once told him that up here, the Naga people spoke something quite different, half-Thibetan, half-Stone-Age-ish.

The elephant men were on edge. They didn't much like the idea of taking over someone else's village. None of them had been this far north in their lives.

Come to think of it, no one he knew had. They were uneasy about the Naga people, believing that they still hunted heads, despite the official line from the Governor in Rangoon – not that there was a Governor in Rangoon any more – that cannibalism was a thing of the past.

'No shrivelled heads here,' said Sam to Po Toke, the others listening in. The claim fell on silence. His elephant men weren't having any of it. The power of their traditions was not to be taken lightly, and out of respect for them, he slogged upstream another quarter of a mile, pitching camp not far from the base of the rock. It loomed over them, blocking out the stars of the western sky.

Sam hadn't shared his pessimism with Po Toke, still less the other Burmese, but it was obvious that the rock spelt trouble. His men hurried to pitch hammocks and make a camp before the light died.

As night fell, it grew shockingly cold. The chill got to the Chin and the oozies, bringing out malarial fevers in some of his chaps. Long ago they'd abandoned blankets and warm clothes, since it was ludicrously hot down in the jungle, but up here, you could almost smell the snow blowing in the wind from the north, from the Himalayas.

And now they had to climb a bloody mountain of rock and that looked impossible. Just before the light died to the west, he studied the rock with his binoculars, once again.

No way out.

Twenty-two years he'd spent in the jungle in Upper Burma, and it had taught him one thing above all: never take the jungle for granted. During the Great War he had served in the Camel Corps in the Transjordan, doing his utmost to keep the ill-tempered ships of the desert healthy in the service of the British as the Ottoman Empire crumbled to dust. Sam was a natural when dealing with animals. He'd find foot-rot in one camel missed by the vet, soothe a red-eyed beast famous for being obnoxious, dangerous even to any European master, disappear for days and then reappear with a score more semi-trained beasts he'd tracked down in the desert. Back at their base in East Jerusalem, he had spent hours with the Bedouin and a translator, soaking in their knowledge of how a thirsty camel can taste water on the wind, how many days a camel could go without food and water, what were their tolerances before they gave up the ghost. Soon, word got out that if you needed a camel train for a journey into the desert, there was no point in leaving until Sam Metcalf had checked out the beasts, adjusted their saddles, talked to the Bedouin, planned the route from well to well. But, best of all, you'd better take Sam with you.

At the end of the war, just as they were winding down the Camel Corps, news of a job came up in Upper Burma, handling elephants. Sam knew nothing about them, apart from the fact they had bigger ears, were occasionally more dangerous but on the whole wiser and more intelligent than camels. At least, they didn't spit. He got the job on the strength of his references from the Camel Corps and he sailed for Rangoon, and then took a stern-wheeler up the Irrawaddy into the jungle. At that time in the early twenties the Burma Teak Corporation pretty much owned all the teak in the country, as of right. All they had to do was to get it down to the sawmills of Mandalay and Rangoon, though that wasn't quite as easy as it sounded.

High up in the forests, the loggers would bring the teak crashing down, great monsters of trees. Using hand saws seven feet long, they would hack off branches, reducing the tree to a series of roughly smooth sections, twenty or thirty feet long. Enter the elephants. They would push, shove or drag the logs tumbling into dry riverbeds, pointing sweetly downstream, not blocking the flow. Come the monsoon, the rains would turn a sandy riverbed into a raging torrent in a few hours, violent with energy, lifting the great logs as if they were as light as lily-pads, and sending them floating down a series of bigger and bigger tributaries. Once they entered the larger rivers, the Corporation's flotilla of barges would capture the logs, lash them to each other to make enormous floating rafts, then nudge them downstream to the sawmills. From the moment a tree was felled to its floating to the sawmill in Rangoon could take a year. Or four. When you had the timber rights for the whole country, time didn't matter that much.

None of this could happen in the road-less wastes of jungle were it not for the elephants and their extraordinary relationship with man. Immense strength, tamed by guile and goodness. Sam had got to know his animals so well that a famous man-killer like Rungdot – Henry VIII was how the kids called him – in musht, trusted him enough to allow him to pierce an abscess the size of a football with a hammer and a knife. One powerful strike and the boil was burst, then wiped clean with disinfectant, all the while the elephant eyeing him attentively. Had Sam dithered or faltered, the beast could have knocked him over and stamped on his head in a flash of time. But Rungdot had trusted him. Soon the great tusker was back at work, nuzzling 20 ton monster logs of teak into line as if they were matchsticks.

Twenty-two years, the prime of his life. He'd married, had children – they were safe and sound in India, God bless them – but still he kept on going back, when a chap of his years could easily have got a desk job, running an inkwell and a typewriter in Simla or some damnfool place. But now his hubris had come to haunt him. How was he going to explain to the others, especially the children, that they were road-blocked by a lump of rock? That it was now very likely that they would never make it out to India.

He reflected on what High Burma had taught him.

That fear of a nat – a jungle spirit – could kill a man, as surely as a shot to the heart.

That elephants had real intelligence.

And that men were stupid and cruel to one another, and to creatures too. Which was why he'd spent so much of his time alone, apart from his dog and the Burmese oozies and the elephants, which wasn't alone at all, really.

But it turned out that he could still be surprised, surprised by the speed and ferocity of the Japanese attack, surprised by the chaos and, yes, the lack of the right stuff from the British forces, and lately surprised by a bloody Hants and Dorset bus arriving in the middle of his jungle, crammed full of kids and their schoolmarm to boot.

The jungle had played perhaps one last trick on him. A bloody great big lump of rock just where he hadn't been expecting it. An owl hooted somewhere close by, and Sam twitched. A real owl? Or a Japanese jitter party? His men were too few to put out pickets to guard their approaches. He relied on his jungle skills and the antennae of his men, but neither was infallible.

Once, a bull elephant that had already killed three men charged at him. Armed only with a one-chambered elephant gun, he'd taken aim, fired, but the round was dud. He'd broken the shot-gun, extracted the dud, rammed in a fresh round, taken aim and shot the bull. It slumbered to a slow fox-trot, swayed and collapsed a single yard from Sam. After that, word got round High Burma that Sam Metcalf had nerves of steel. If a hoot from an owl could turn him into a scared little bunny rabbit, his nerves were shot.

The reddening sky cast the rock into dark shadow. If the worst came to the worst and there was no way through, then he wondered how he would break it to the main party, travelling two days' march behind him now. They could try and sneak past the Japanese, but he feared the elephants would be shot up, and the children would be helpless if forced to make it to India on their own, having to carry what food they had left. Many of them, the little ones, and that little lad who was a bit simple, they would die.

Oh, Christ, perhaps they should never have tried it.

One of the chaps came to Sam to explain that they'd pretty much run out of food. Sam had an answer to that – and sod the Japanese. The echoes would fool them. A few hundred yards down from their camp ran a branch of the stream they had been climbing up, which filled out into a deep pool. Hurrying to catch the available light, he scampered down, fetched his knapsack off his back and took out a hand-grenade, pulled out the pin and lobbed the grenade into the still water.

Bang! A great whoosh of water, soaking him, enough noise to wake the dead in Thibet, the sound of the explosion echoing against the rock. As the water in the pool settled, a dozen perch, two or three a respectable size and one enormous, ugly thing, with long barbels extruding from its mouth, like the tendrils of a tramp's beard, floated belly-up, on the surface. Very satisfying. He gave permission for the men to light a fire. True, the Japs were out there in the jungle, somewhere. But there was another jeopardy, that his men, over-worked, exhausted, half of them coming down with malaria, under-nourished and cold to the marrow, wouldn't be able to push on, if they didn't have some fresh hot food and a warm fire through the night. He'd picked a heavily wooded spot in a cleft in the mountain for their camp, so the chances of anyone seeing the fire through the tree cover from far away was dim. But the bang had been loud enough. Still, lobbing the odd hand-grenade in a pond remained, to Sam, the finest way to fish. No messing about with trying to put a worm on a hook. Bugger that.

His Burmese seemed happy as Larry, roasting the fish on a hand-made spit, laughing and making a little too much noise. Once more, he weighed the risk of being caught napping by a Japanese scouting party. What were the odds? Hard to judge. They were on the very far edge of the Emperor of Japan's domain, taking a route which, it turned out, made no military sense whatsoever.

He loved his elephants, missed them more than it would appear proper to say. In the old days he'd hunted, killed elephants for game too, something he now regretted. These days, after all his time working with the great beasts, he put special store by the human-elephant relationship, but he wasn't a bloody

Buddhist. Jungle leeches? He'd exterminate them, quick as a flash.

Somebody had had to scout the route to India ahead and he had been best-placed to do so, to shoulder the responsibility. If someone had to make a decision and it ended up being a terrible mistake, then it was better him than anyone else. They had only one shot at it. A mistake like walking into a slab of rock 500 feet high. But he also knew that a little part of why he had elected to go on the scouting mission was his dislike of people, of getting tangled up in the lives of others.

Take Grace. A woman of stunning beauty, but half-crackers too, raving on about how that wounded sergeant had shot her Jemadar. Hmm – maybe there was something in it. He'd given orders to the Havildar to keep the sergeant out of her hair and to keep an eye on him at all times. But he was sceptical, suspected that she might have got the wrong end of the stick. The Jemadar could well have been felled by a stray bullet. Somebody else could sort that one out, when they got to India.

If they ever got there.

Po Toke approached with roast fish, a little black around the edges, wrapped in a shiny banana leaf.

'Fish, but no chips,' said Po Toke in his passable English and the two men laughed. Sam had explained the weird culinary pleasures of the British to the Burman long ago. Sam hadn't had fish and chips in a very long time. It was funny what you missed, what you had fantasies about. Not lobsters or oysters or a great salmon, but simple fish and chips wrapped up in yesterday's *Western Daily Post*, a bottle of beer and, as the sun dipped, the flash of the nearest lighthouse. No chance of that here.

He ate. The cooked fish was good, the first proper meal, not out of a tin, that he'd had in ages. He was more hungry than he'd realised, and when he'd eaten, he slumped into his hammock, cursing their luck. All this way, but no way out.

In the morning: ice-grime.

A coating of frost covered their bedding, their faces, their feet where they protruded out of their blankets. The Burmese had never seen anything like it, tiny crystals of coldness, which burnt the tongue. Sam told them about snow, so deep it could bury a man, and they looked at him as if he had turned idiot.

They shivered violently as they rolled up their hammocks and prepared for the day's work. Sam divided up the party into five groups of two, and set off to explore the rockface. The fittest, youngest ones were sent off to the furthest extremities, north and south, while Sam and Po Toke had given themselves the task of examining the rock immediately in front of them. To the north for two miles, nothing. They retraced their steps and found, almost immediately in front of the camp, a landslip tumbling down towards them, strewn with boulders and overgrown with lianas and bamboo.

He doubted whether he could get up the fifty feet of the landslip, let alone an elephant. Po Toke, who knew what elephants could do, better than any man alive, shook his head. But still, they had no choice but to explore it.

They spent two long hours hacking through the undergrowth to climb forty feet or so. The last ten feet were almost perpendicular, Sam having to jump from one stony outcrop to another, but eventually he hauled himself up onto a goat track, invisible from below, which slowly ascended, running to the south-west around the side of the rockface. Gingerly, Sam and Po Toke followed the path upwards. Much of the time, it was ten feet wide, maybe more, but they came to a narrow point, just twelve inches wide, curving around a bend in the rock, the path out of view, as if ending in the sky itself. Sam made himself go first, edging his way along, facing the wall of rock, eyes on the path ahead, not daring to look down to the drop below.

Four feet along and the path narrowed an inch or two. A spasm of fear gripped him. Going back now would be more dreadful. His legs froze, his arms extended, fingers scrabbling and flailing to gain some traction on the smooth-as-soap surface. Despite himself, he looked down the sheer wall beneath his feet to the jungle far below, as green as a bottle, welcoming, seductive, deadly.

They had no hope. The path was barely wide enough to allow one man, impossibly narrow for an elephant, let alone fifty-three. The smallest calf would be knocked off the goat-track by the fatness of his belly.

To the north, a mass of clouds piled up, punctured by the sun. The wind, cold and fresh from Thibet, soughed over the rocks. Hard – no, impossible – to judge the distances made by sounds. Was that the soft crump-crump of the big guns? And, not so far off, the fire-crackers of small-arms fire? Or thunder and lightning from fifty miles away?

Out loud, Sam heard himself say: 'Get a grip, old man,' and he straightened his back and started moving, imagining that he was about to plunge into the sea off Cornwall. Five, six, seven steps, a bend – and the path widened to a large space, covered by an overhang of rock, shading him from the sun, almost dark, as spacious and restful as a hay barn. Giddy with suppressed fear, he made for the ground furthest from the drop and pressed his back against the rock, luxuriating in its solidity.

Forcing himself back to the cliff edge, waiting for Po Toke, he tried to affect an air of nonchalance, but in his heart he had to deal with facts.

There was no way out.

They had lost. He'd have to shoot the elephants.

CHAPTER TWELVE

They trekked on and on, slow, sluggishly, looking over their shoulders at the impassive wall of green behind them, half-wanting the Japanese to be there to put an end to the relentless anxiety. The trudge through jungle came to a halt as they watched Henry VIII toboggan on his haunches down a muddy bank into a dried-up riverbed. The rest followed, finding themselves in a sandy gulley with both banks above them steep walls of rock. At the start, the dried-up bed was much, much easier-going than the jungle and they made good progress on sand and cracked mud, picking their way through boulders as big as houses and side-stepping deep pools of water.

They walked on, locked inside the funnel of rock, the banks getting steeper and more forbidding as the riverbed twisted and turned. Halfway through the afternoon, a long, drawn-out rumble sounded from the north.

Thunder.

To Eddie Gregory's ears practised, from his days with the gunners, it made a bigger noise than artillery, easily distinguished. The rain came, even harder than before, a relentless curtain of water falling, connecting up the deep pools by a thread, then a tracery, soon a blanket of water, until you'd take a step and plunge in down to your waist and struggle to hold upright. Thank God he'd parked all his kit, apart from his knife, in the big elephant's basket.

Whoever the bright spark was who'd thought of taking a short cut along the dried-up riverbed hadn't worked out what might happen if it started to rain, big-time. Because pretty soon the river wasn't dried up at all, but running freely, the water level rising and rising fast. One inch, two inches. A trickle turned into a sluggish flow. Five inches, six inches. The flow started to move little stones, bits of dead wood began to be carried away by the current.

The rain thrummed down through the trees that arced overhead, the job of sloshing uphill against the current becoming harder, with every step.

Sick of plunging out of his depth, Gregory studied the great elephant's progress. The animal never put a foot wrong. It must be something in the pads of the creature's feet. When unsure of himself, the animal had a way of testing a step, to make sure it would carry the burden of his great weight, before he would move. But the elephant was even smarter than that. For much of the time the beast ploughed on up the stream, making quite good going, keeping an eye out for signs that the bed of the stream was sound. He could work out, Gregory realised, when he could walk steadily and when he had to slow down and take soundings. The oozies knew this, and never pushed the tusker when he suddenly stopped, and started dipping his toe into the water and testing his weight rather than plodding robotically on. If he ever got out of here, and sorted out that bitch of a schoolmarm, then he would have some tales to tell about his time with the elephants.

How long would they stay in the riverbed? Gregory raised his eyes and studied the slabs towering above them. Sheer rock, sprouting a bit of jungle here and there, a good thirty feet on one side, maybe a hundred on the other. If the river kept on rising at the current rate – and the stream was being fed from the hills and mountains to the north, where the thunder was coming from – then pretty soon it would be a forceful torrent, down which dead trees would come, smashing everything in their wake, and then they'd have to look out.

Reading the faces of the oozies, he could tell that they didn't like it one bit. There was no panic, not yet, but a growing jitteriness amongst the Burmese. To prove the point, a biggish tree trunk idled past them, and then locked still for some seconds, a branch snagging on the bottom, before it spun free. As it passed Gregory, a high branch brushed against his face. He jerked his head away fast, but not fast enough, and the left side of his face bore a nasty tracery of scratches.

That set him thinking. The oozies by him were leading the most powerful elephant of the whole pack, walking with the fittest men, and they looked worried. Further down the march, the schoolgirls and the baby elephants, would be in trouble.

An opportunity, maybe, to settle things with the schoolmarm? No harm in taking a look, was there? Gregory made a thing of asking the lead oozie on the big one, using sign language, for his permission so that he could go back down the stream to see how the others were coping, whether they needed to quit the riverbed now. That was a bit academic, like, because they were trapped in the funnel of rock until it opened out. The oozie, high up on the tusker's neck, grasped Gregory's meaning, nodded, and the sergeant turned on his heel and began to saunter downstream. It was easy-going compared to slogging uphill, but every now and then something caught his feet underwater and he would stumble and stagger, working hard to keep upright. His boots filled with water but he didn't dare risk taking them off lest he tread on something sharp. Remembering where the elephant had hesitated, he managed to avoid the deep sumps of water, and came to a bend in the riverbed. Far to the side was a kind of cave, a shelter made by a misshapen roof of rock and a spread of thick waxy ferns. Underneath the ferns the ground, standing proud of the stream, was dry-ish and quite comfortable to sit down on. He could rest, hidden behind the greenery, and people and elephants could pass him a few feet away and have no idea that he was watching them.

Smart. And so he sat down and waited to see who would pass by.

The Havildar came first, almost running, scowling, looking anxious, followed by a troop of pack elephants, moving faster than normal. Not running exactly, but kind of trotting, if elephants could be said to trot, calves skipping after mothers, little trunks flapping this way and that. Nearly all of the children were being carried in panniers, which was against Sam's rules. By foot came a group of the older girls, Emily passing only a few feet from him, chatting to another girl, beak-nosed and lippy, a Jewess, and finally, there she was, the princess schoolmarm, rain plastering her blonde hair wet over her shoulders, her frock – once cream - a muddy brown and, to the delight of the secret watcher, all but see-through.

And what was bloody marvellous, she was alone.

Gregory checked upstream: all clear. The older girls had rounded a bend and had disappeared, out of sight.

Thirty feet away from him, blissfully unaware, she was walking towards him.

Now?

Hold the knife to her long, lovely throat, drag her under the ferns, make sure everybody had passed – it would not take that long, because they were all hurrying up the riverbed – wait until the last of them had gone. He'd wait five minutes, maybe ten, just to be sure.

Then he'd tie her up with a liana, her hands behind her back, cut away that old dress with his knife. Have her, nice and slow.

And then...

With a bit of luck, if the rain kept on pouring and the river level rising, her body would be flushed downstream so fast no one would ever find it. He'd have to do a bit of explaining about why he was so late, so far behind – he'd fallen down a sump, knocked his head, the old concussion. Strange no one had spotted him lying by the side of the bank, but that was hardly his fault, was it? They'd missed him in their panic to get out of the river before it became a torrent. Sam and the Havildar might suspect some funny business but, with no body, they wouldn't be able to pin anything on him. No evidence, see?

Better wait until she had passed him.

A few more steps.

So close to him he could reach out and stroke her hair, could see her shoulderblades sculpted through the sodden fabric of her frock.

In the dull green light, the blade of his knife not shining...

CHAPTER THIRTEEN

There was something awesome about the force of the melt-water powering down from the Himalayas, surging like great Atlantic breakers crashing against boulders as big as a house; something awesome about the finality of what it meant to the raggle-taggle army of last-ditchers.

The end of hope.

The men slumped against mossy-green rocks, enjoying the relief of the spray, cooling after the heat of the forced march. They had clattered down from the plateau above and were now at the very bottom of the ravine. The waters were hellishly strong.

'Cross that?' The sergeant-major gestured with the slightest twitch of his head. 'Fat chance.'

One man, tall, gaunt, paddled into the shallows, squinted across to the west bank, fuzzy in the cloud of mist.

'We've got to move.' Desperation in his voice.

'The lads need a break, sir. You're killing them at this pace. Besides, there's not a man among us who could cross that and live. That goes for you too. We can't swim that. We're fooked this time, sir.'

It was not much more than 100 yards to the far bank. In the old days, at school, he could have run that distance handsomely in a twinkling of an eye. Now, the force of the water would knock him flying in the first five feet and he would certainly drown – and he was probably the fittest, or, rather, the least poorly man, out of the nine of them. Some of the chaps could barely hobble.

He was angered by the sergeant-major's realism. They had been following the river downstream for hours and they had not seen a single place where they could get across. They had been moving fast, every one of them knowing that the Japanese had time on their side. If they could not ford the torrent, they were trapped and they knew that sooner or later, the Japs would hunt them down. Only nine of them were left, haggard, pitifully thin, all of them beyond exhaustion. Only the officer's mad insistence that they must catch up with the others, must at all costs reach them, drove them on. Had it not been for Peach, they would have dawdled to a halt hours ago.

'Sergeant-major, may I remind you that I am the officer in charge,' said Peach.

The sergeant-major was a good eighteen inches shorter than Peach, but his eyes flashed with contempt.

'Aye, and it's my job to tell you that the lads cannot keep this pace up. They fooking want to kill you, which would be a black spot on your career, wouldn't it, Lieutenant? Being dead and all?'

'Are you threatening me?' The two men stared at each other.

'No, sir, I'm not threatening you. I'm telling you that killing your men on some wild-goose chase to rescue some silly totty is conduct unbecoming of an officer. Sit down, lads – we're having a break.'

Peach almost hit him. His frustration, and fear, that Gregory was a real danger to Grace, was boiling up inside him. After a moment, he stormed off, running downstream a further two hundred yards, wading up to an islet in the torrent, thick with bamboo. The water was running fast even here, and he had to fight the current to find what he was looking for. On the west corner of the islet, impossible to see from the bank, was a sandy bluff, standing proud of the water. The bamboo – higher than a lamppost – shielded observation from the south, too. It was the perfect hiding place. He hurried back to the men, resting against the mossy rocks.

'We're moving, and that's an order.'

The sergeant-major stayed where he was; the others took their cue from him.

'This is a bad place to stop, Eric,' Peach said. 'The Japs will be able to see us from miles off. I've found a better resting place a few yards downstream. We've got to move. It's not far.'

The waters thundered on; the spray from the wet mist soaking everything.

'Fook off, you love-sick bastard.'

'Eric!' Peach was appalled.

'Only joking, sir. Attention!' The sergeant-major pulled himself up and motioned with his head for the men to move. With infinite weariness, five stood up and pulled up their packs onto their backs. But two men, furthest from the sergeant and the officer, refused to stir. Barr walked towards them. He kicked one in the leg, and bent over the other and whispered into his ear. Both men struggled up and began to walk.

Peach led the way, downstream, and stood in the water, waist–deep, ensuring that none of them lost their footing as they fought through the current to the safety of the islet.

With all of them safe and out of sight of the Japanese above, Peach allowed himself to collapse flat on his back on the sand.

'What did you say to him?'

'I threatened to stick a cricket bat up his arse, sir. He's a Methodist and doesn't like that sort of talk.'

'Very good, Sergeant-major.'

'I'm sorry...'

'No, don't. I'm sorry, too. I know the men are exhausted.' Peach shook his head.

They had grown so used to each other's thinking that speaking out loud was almost unnecessary.

'Shall we call it a day, Sergeant-major?'

'Surrender, sir?'

'What do you think?'

'Japs don't take prisoners, sir. They'll just kill us, and they'll take their time about doing it.'

'Yes. That's my thinking, too. And it seems a shame, having come all this way, just to give in when we're almost there.'

'Right.' Barr glanced uphill, towards the unseen enemy. 'They can't see us from up there. As awficers go, you're not all bad.'

'Eric?'

'Sir?'

'Why did you call me a love-sick bastard?'

'Oh, come on, sir.'

'What makes you say that, Sergeant-major?'

'It's bleedin' obvious, sir. Making out them orphans to be the bloody aristocracy. Not blowing up that bridge when you were ordered.'

'One word from you, and I would have blown the bridge then and there.'

'So it was all my fault, then, sir?'

'Yes, Sergeant-major, it was.'

'Fook off, sir.'

'If you carry on like that, Sergeant-major, I'll put you on a charge.'

Barr started to laugh, a high-pitched giggle, almost girlish.

'There is...' continued Peach.

'Sir?'

'There is one way, we might get across.'

'What's that, sir?'

'On an elephant.'

'We haven't got an elephant, sir.'

'Yes, I know that, Sergeant-major. I'm suggesting that we borrow one.'

'From who, sir?'

'Emperor Hirohito, Sergeant-major.'

'He might not like that, sir.'

'But what if we ask him nicely, Sergeant-major?'

'That should make all the difference, sir.'

'There's slightly more to my plan than that, Sergeant-major.'

'I'm all ears, sir.'

'I once met a man in a bar, Sergeant-major. He told me all about the training of an elephant, how they pair up a calf elephant with a teenage boy, of around fourteen or so, and with a bit of luck the two of them make a team for life. So not anyone can ride an elephant. Each animal must have its own dedicated oozie, a man he trusts. So, clever as the Japanese are, they're not that clever. The elephants we've seen them with, they must be ridden by Burmese oozies.'

'So?'

'Our best shot is that we try and meet one of the oozies working for the Japs at dead of night, and we offer them a fair passage to India, and gold at the other end of the rainbow, if they will run away from the Japs and give us a lift across this river. What about it, Sergeant-major?'

'You're the officer. You give the order and we do what you tell us to.'

'You know damn well it doesn't work like that, Eric. What do you really think?'

'You've gone crackers, sir.'

Another pause.

'Ever gone bonkers, sir? Lost your marbles, sir?'

'No, Sergeant-major. Or, at least, not yet. That time when I was a magistrate and I jailed an officer for crashing into those two Burmese women – that was difficult... War had just broken out and I had applied for a commission. I got a letter back, declining my offer, and someone had scrawled on the envelope, LMF.'

'Lacking Moral Fibre.'

'I was pretty cut up by it, back then. Grace was the first European woman to break the spell. She had no idea that I had been boycotted. She didn't like me very much, but she didn't like me because of who I was, which is fair enough, not because of what I had done to stand up for the rule of law.'

'Well, you're in the army, now, sir.'

'Very funny, Sergeant-major.' But Peach was aware that he might have been sounding rather pompous. 'She ran away from me once. We'd gone to the cinema, to see some damnfool show, Bob Hope and Bill Crosby. One of their road movies. At the end of the show, I tried to kiss her and she started hurdling over the cinema seats. I tried to chase after her but I fell over. I felt absolutely frustrated at the time. Everybody was laughing me. Humiliating. Looking back at it now, damn funny.'

'What did she look like, jumping across the seats?'

'Bit like Tipperary Tim winning the Grand National, Sergeant-major. She took those cinema seats like old Tim leaping Becher's Brook.'

'You're in love, sir.'

'I prefer it when you're saying that I'm bonkers.'

'I went bonkers, once.'

This, from the man he trusted most in the world, came as a shock.

'Raving, I was. Doo-lally.'

'Why?'

'Family stuff.'

'You've got a wife and kids.'

'Aye. I came out here in thirty-eight. Two kids and the missus, safe at home in Leeds. Then along comes the youngest. Born in 1940. Three kids. But I was out here.'

'Oh,' said Peach.

'Aye. When I calmed down, I wrote to her saying: "When I get back to Yorkshire, I'm going to throttle you with my own bare hands".'

'I see. Will you?'

'No, not now. Seen too many dead. It's only a bit of slap'n'tickle that went wrong. That's what she says. Any road, there's nowt I can do about it out here. He's a lad, and all. Name of Jake. I've only had the daughters before. Nowt wrong with girls, but...'

'Yes.'

'Thing is, sir...'

'Call me Bertie'

'Silly fooking name, Bertie. I'm calling you sir. Thing is...' Barr struggled to get the words out. 'If I fooking die out here, she'll think I died bitter an' all, and I'm not. I'm not fooking proud of her, but you can't go through a bloody war and not learn a thing or two about human weakness and all, so if I get killed...'

'Which you are absolutely not going to do.'

'If I do get killed, then will you go and see her, and tell her from me, that she's a silly whore, but I still love her with all my heart, and I love little Jakey too, and I'm sorry I wrote mean things to her. You'll do that, won't you, sir?'

'You're not going to die.'

'But?'

'Of course. What's her name?'

'Agnes.'

'Do the same for me, Sergeant-major. Tell Grace I forgive her for making me look like a complete idiot.'

'Aye, I will and all.'

They sat in silence, listening to the river's roar. After a while it was Peach who broke the spell.

'But if I have gone bonkers,' he said, 'then it's your duty to relieve me of my command. So if I really am mad, then you're in charge, Sergeant-major. What shall we do?'

'Fook that for a game of soldiers.'

'Well?'

'Fook it.' He turned away and raised his voice. 'Lads, pay attention. The officer says we're going to borrow an elephant.'

No moon that night. They'd left the rest of the men on the islet. On their return, the password would be 'Sheffield Wednesday', making a change from the usual 'Leeds United'.

In pitch dark, Peach and Barr waded across the shallows to the eastern bank, faces blackened with stinking river mud. Each man carried two grenades and one jungle knife. Their rifles would not be much use in the dark and they had precious little ammunition left between all of them. The whole point of this exercise was to 'borrow' an elephant or two without disturbing the Japanese.

The officer and the sergeant-major had had one of their semi-silent discussions about risking both their lives on this foolishness. If the Japanese caught them, the remaining seven last-ditchers would be leaderless. But the soldiers were pretty far gone. If this plan didn't work, well, that was pretty much it for all of them.

The two men were well accustomed to the sounds of the jungle at night by now: the sudden, unexplained mechanical bangs and crashes, subtle creaks and inhuman gibbering. But some new sound gripped Peach's attention. What was that...?

He sensed the sergeant-major freeze beside him and he flattened his stomach against the ground as best he could. Ear down, he could just make out a patter of soft footfalls, then silence. The silhouette of the sergeant-major remained immobile. Fighting in the jungle – or just staying alive – was as much a matter of patience as anything else.

The footfalls started again, diminishing with each step. They crawled forward on their bellies, as lightly as they could, until they found what they had been looking for: seven, eight, nine, ten elephants, standing, obelisk-still in a circle, and beyond them they could make out hammocks stretching between trees, a deeper black against the blackness of the night. One of the elephants stirred, shuffling his hobbled legs, uneasy. The beast chirruped, a strange high-pitched sound for such a big animal. Had they been smelt out?

Peach stiffened as he felt the light brush of a blade of grass against the back of his neck. No, he was wrong about that. This blade was made of steel.

CHAPTER FOURTEEN

A movement, downstream, something grey coming round the bend. Damn and blast and bloody hell. The luck of the bitch. Bloody elephant with its baby in tow, on its neck an oozie and on the back in the basket two boys, including the soft one, a couple of girls and that all-seeing brat Molly.

Schoolmarm was waiting for them to pass, waiting with a great smile on her lips. Bitch.

Keeping his breathing nice and shallow, putting the jungle knife down by his side. The whole sodding bunch of them had missed him, so he was pretty confident that he would remain hidden.

He'd have to wait a bit, then catch up and take his chance later. Just breathe quiet, be still...

Oh no, fucking hell, damn, damn, damn. Stone him, if the baby elephant didn't come right up to his hiding place, stick out its sodding trunk and shove the ferns and shrubbery aside, then start to eat his cover, showing him to all and sodding sundry. On seeing him the baby took fright, squeaked like a piglet and ran back to his fat mother, who gave Gregory a nasty look. That was nothing compared to Grace's reaction. When she saw Gregory revealed in his hiding place, her eyes grew as big as dinner-plates and she screamed – piercingly loud - and skittered over to the far side of the riverbed, placing the big elephant and baby between her and him.

'You!' Grace shouted at him, pointing her finger at him, hiding in the ferns.

The Burmese on the elephant's neck took it all in. Eddie fancied that he'd clocked his dah. Pretty soon, the oozie might have a word with the Havildar, and that could be tricky. The kids, too, especially that brat Molly, stared at him as if he was some bloody creep hiding in the bushes. The baby elephant trumpeted shrilly at him, and then the little bastard had the cheek to suck up a puddle of water through his trunk and squirt it at him. Bloody circus trick. The kids were all laughing at him. Not funny, not funny at all.

On the surface, the cold hatred that consumed him did not show. Smiling, as if he didn't have a care in the world, he stood up, bowed from the waist and sauntered off upstream, against the torrent.

That bastard baby elephant had saved the bitch's life. But old Eddie Gregory wasn't finished yet, not by a long chalk.

He would have to do the teacher, to save his neck. The way she'd pointed the finger at him, screaming 'You!' he knew there was no way he could smarm his way out of it. They'd suspect him, but tough. If she ever got to India, she'd start digging, she would be just the type, and then he'd be for it. A woman like Grace, she'd be certain to find out about old Eli and write letters to that bitch Jewess and the two of them would never shut up until he was dangling from a rope. Well, that wasn't going to happen. He'd have to sort her out that very night, once and for all.

But that wasn't the only score he wanted to settle. That little fat bastard Baby Elephant had humiliated him too, catching him in the bushes, squirting him, soaking him to the skin. And no one and nothing made a monkey out of Eddie Gregory. What would he do about it?

Come to think of it, if a tiger – yeah, that would do it nicely – if a tiger attacked the baby elephant in the night, that would make a nice little distraction. Everybody would fuss over the wounded little baby jumbo – he could already hear the children crying, how awful it was, the savage cruelty of the tiger – and while they were all worrying about it, no one would notice if schoolmarm went missing. At least, it would buy him some time. And if Sammy-boy started causing him trouble later, then he'd do him too, and that meant Sergeant Gregory would be the last white man standing, and no one would believe the word of a bunch of niggers and mud-coloured kids against a warrant officer of the British Army. The Havildar, though – he'd have to watch the sodding Sikh, old Cripple Fingers.

Slowing his pace, his thoughts turned to planning his revenge on the baby elephant.

Got it. Muscle and mind. When his darling elephant mama wasn't looking, he'd give Baby Elephant a lovely shoot of bamboo in one hand and he'd stab an eye out with the other. And if it dared squirt him again, he'd do the other eye too, and then he'd be a blind Baby Elephant and he wouldn't last five minutes in this shithole of a jungle. That'd teach him.

He would think of something. If he got the right opportunity he would make sure that the baby would rue the day he humiliated Eddie Gregory. And he began to whistle – 'Oranges and Lemons' – over and over again.

The Havildar's eyes – ribbed with blood, red-raw and gritted with worry – told their own story. The elephant men had fallen into a trap of their own making. The riverbed was no longer dry, but three foot deep at its shallowest, and when the two banks narrowed closer together, it turned into a furiously fast stream five feet deep against which men struggled and children had to scale the rocks to avoid. Worse, there seemed no end to it, no prospect of them finding a way of climbing out and up into the jungle; worst, a secret no one knew, he couldn't swim. The water scared him more than he could say.

What to do? Leave the river and they'd lose another day. But stay in the river, and he might lose a calf or a child. A less courageous man, given his terror of water, would have tried to get out of the river sooner, but the Havildar did not want his personal weakness to impede the operation to get the elephants and people as far away from the Japanese as fast as humanly possible.

Still, the river was getting deeper all the time. Soon, it might carry away a calf and then the rest of the elephants would panic and that could cause carnage. He clambered up the stony bank, his two and a half fingers scrabbling for handholds, to scan the rocks above him. Upstream, as far as he could see, there was nothing. Downstream on the bank he was standing on, again nothing, just smooth rock, maybe 50 feet high. But on the far bank, 100 yards back, he spotted a fissure in the rock wall, carpeted with vegetation– steep but perhaps just about manageable for the big elephants, leading up to who knew what.

Down below, a fresh surge of water bore down on the waiting elephants, causing a calf to lose his footing and be swept, squealing and trunk flailing, off his feet. His mother trumpeted a terrified alarm, the eyes of her oozie flashed anxiety. Instantly two aunties downstream angled their bodies so that the calf was swept towards the bank, where in the shallower water he regained his footing. Mother caught up with him and gave him a loving clout with her trunk, and the three adult elephants penned him in against the bank, so that he wouldn't go surfing again.

The Havildar shouted down to the oozies to halt while he slithered down the bank, splashed into the river and shot down the current until he got to the foot of the break and managed to stand up against the flow. His breathing was deep and uneven, fear of drowning an unspoken terror. Unsheathing his jungle knife, he clamped it into his teeth and climbed up, gripping a trailing liana as a rope with his maimed hands.

Molly, watching agog from the safety of their elephant basket, whispered to Ruby, 'He looks like a pirate king.'

The liana creaked and, cursing in Urdu, he scrabbled to find a firm handhold for his stumps, thinking back to the days when he had fingers. He heaved himself up the last few feet and was over the worst of it, sitting on a plateau of rock thirty feet above the riverbed, pressed in by thick jungle.

Ferns, bamboo, great lianas came crashing down as he slashed away with his dah until he came out to find himself on a ridge that dropped gently down to the west, to the next watershed. He'd no idea what lay beyond but they could camp here for the night.

As he turned back, his decision was made for him.

The whole green sky became an upturned bucket and the storm rain sluiced down, drenching everything and everyone. By the time he got back down to the riverbed, the water level had risen another two inches, reaching his waist and he was the tallest man of the whole march. If they didn't get out soon, they might all die.

The elephants had sensed the danger of staying in the riverbed and were climbing out of it willingly, the pads of their feet prospecting for the strongest footholds, tempering their weight, their agility a wonder to behold as three tons of animal floated up the sides of the near-vertical bank. The baby elephants found it the hardest, too little to scale the ledges of rock, too heavy for the mothers or their oozies to lift them easily. The rain made everything worse, turning the rocks slippery-smooth, the children fractious, the elephant men at the end of their tether.

Mother was to go up before Oomy, the last of all the elephants. Po Net struggled to untie the harness ropes that secured the basket, but did so and the empty basket was man-handled up the slope. The oozie dismounted from Mother's neck and held her gently by the ear, using his bamboo stick to point out the best route up, the elephant powering her heft up to the top with a nimbleness that belied her size. The moment Mother was up, she turned around on a sixpence and gazed down to see her baby follow. Coaxing, shoving, pushing didn't seem to work. The little fellow looked up at the 30-foot climb, flapped his ears, bleated, and wouldn't budge. Po Net found three strong lianas, cut them free, lashed them together and descended to the calf. He placed the middle of his cat's cradle behind the calf's bottom, and climbed back to the top with the two ends of the liana. At his signal, two tuskers tugged hard on their ends of the liana, while two more oozies and the Havildar worked to keep the cat's cradle in place around Oomy's fat bottom. At that moment, Eddie Gregory appeared at the top of the ridge, took in the scene and climbed down from the top, taking over from one of the exhausted oozies at Oomy's level. Slowly the calf was dragged up, piping and yelping, Mother looking on, quivering with anxiety: twenty feet away, fifteen, ten, five.

'Almost there, Oomy,' said Molly, willing the baby to safety. The rest of the school were clustered around the top of the bank, gawking at the drama.

The tip of Oomy's trunk touched the loose soil right at the top when, losing his footing on a slab of rock as smooth as a tombstone, Gregory's side of the cradle slipped, the calf in danger of crashing down 25 feet. The Havildar, directly beneath the animal, braced himself as the full weight of the baby pressed down on his chest, two fingers of his left hand locked on to a snag of rock, his face blood-red with the strain. From her standpoint on the ledge above, Grace watched Gregory right himself, his fingers tugging, working on the cradle: she couldn't quite see exactly what he was doing. Then Gregory gave a shout and the tuskers tugged on the lianas, taking the strain off the Havildar and the baby elephant began to rise again.

The liana that Gregory had been working on just a moment before snapped with a whip-crack and Oomy tumbled out of the sling, falling away from the Havildar, sliding and tripping down the bank, squealing horribly. The Havildar lunged out to catch him by the tail, but the baby elephant fell, splashing into the river like a great boulder. Mother bellowed, a ghastly, heart-piercing cry of anguish, and the watching children stared, mute in horror, as Oomy was picked up by the racing current and, bobbing up and down like a fat brown cork, vanished around the bend.

CHAPTER FIFTEEN

Pinned like a beetle in a museum drawer, the knife-blade pressing yet more firmly against his neck, Peach lay rigid, unmoving. Fingers tugged at his belt, removing his own knife and the grenades, knotting his hands behind his back. A man whispered, 'Shhh!' into his ear and he found himself dragged upright and led off into the jungle. Close by, he heard a scuffle and a dull thud but it was too dark to see how Eric was faring. He stumbled on a stray liana and went flying face down, cutting his face above his eye on a jagged edge of rock. The blood streamed down from the cut, half-blinding him in his right eye, and tasting sickly as it wet his lips. In the green-black darkness, he could only make out a blur of shapes picking him up, and dragging him, hurriedly, away from the Japanese elephant camp. Stumbling, half-falling, they led him staggering through the jungle until the sound of the river grew noisier and noisier, and they pushed him down on his knees.

Are they going to drown me? The thought of being thrown in the water with his hands tied behind his back made him feel as helpless as an infant. They shoved his head down into the freezing torrent – and he felt his courage drain from him.

Chaos, utter chaos. Mother stared transfixed at the river bend where her baby had vanished. Head down, trumpeting thunderously loud, she smashed into the thick undergrowth at the top of the bank, following the route high above the swollen river. Po Net and three other oozies ran after the mother elephant, thrashing at the jungle with their dahs to carve a way through it. The remaining mother elephants grizzled and moaned and formed a tight circle, keeping their young inside, tightly guarded, their ears-flaps wide out– a danger sign.

The sun was falling fast in the sky, a red tinge to the west. The smooth logic of the previous camps, the site carefully selected after the best scouts in High Burma had considered all the options, had gone to pot. There was no time to cut a proper clearing, carving room enough for elephants and people to have some space. Instead, they had to make do with a makeshift nest in the foliage – elephants, men and children next to other, cheek by jowl, the animals churning up the mud underfoot, the edge of the ravine and the closeness of the jungle cramping them in.

On a vast exotic fern by Grace, a spider's web shimmered in the crimson light, its lacework the colour of blood.

'Miss, Miss, look.'

Grace walked over and crouched down next to the little girl who was staring motionless at something in a patch of mud on the jungle floor. Marks in the mud, as if left by the hand of a giant, all thumbs, no fingers. The schoolteacher called Po Ling, one of the senior oozies, over, and he confirmed her worst fears: 'Tiger.'

The prints were deep and fresh, the mud not yet dry. Half an hour old, if that. Huge printmarks, too.

'Tiger, eh?' It was Sergeant Gregory. 'I'm buggered if I'm going to be dinner for Mister Stripes.' Coolly, he walked over to the pannier containing the elephant men's armoury.

He was about to help himself to a rifle when the Havildar called out: 'Don't touch that. Sam's orders.'

'Bugger that.'

The contempt for the Havildar's authority was clear. Gregory made to fetch the rifle, but his arm was gripped by the Havildar.

'Get your cripple fingers off me.'

'Leave that alone.'

'Listen, mate, I ain't done nothing wrong. I don't want to get eaten by a tiger, do I?'

'Leave that alone.' The Havildar towered over Gregory. For any other man, the message would have been absolutely clear.

'Listen, mate, you don't seem to be understanding the English bloody language. That's tiger prints over there. I have got a right to protect myself. So you're out of order. Right?'

'Leave that alone.'

The Englishman raised his eyes to the heavens. 'Like a bloody gramophone record that's got stuck, you are. I ain't done anything, so shut it. Stop telling me off for something I ain't done. Let me go. Get your crippled hands off me.'

The Havildar released him, but placed his bulk between him and the rifles.

'Just a big bag of wind, aren't you? A nigger and a coward, that's all.' Gregory turned his back on him and walked off.

The Havildar, breathing heavily, leant his back against a Y-shaped tree, watching the man with the bandaged head walk away, downhill, into the jungle.

'Havildar, you shouldn't have allowed him to talk to you like that,' said Grace, keeping her voice down so that none of the children or the oozies could hear her.

'Nobody has talked to me like that for a long time.' A silence followed, the Havildar studying the ground. Then: 'I've never spoken about this. After the Great War, I was at Amritsar. No warning was given. Just the shout of command, "Open fire!" A sepoy of the British Indian Army obeys orders.'

Through his gun-sight he had killed, killed without number.

'Three hundred and seventy-nine people were posted killed that day. It was more.'

How many times had he relived that moment, when sweat trickled down from his forehead and he blinked and he stopped firing to wipe his eye and he became aware that *his* finger was on the trigger of *his* rifle, that *he* was one of the soldiers making faces splatter red, making bodies jerk. He had wiped the sweat from his murderous eye and stopped firing. An officer spotted him and berated him for his cowardice, but he suffered the abuse in silence. From that day on, he had done his duty as bravely as he could, patrolling the north-west frontier, driving supply convoys through the Pathan-controlled wild country, surviving countless ambushes where several of his friends got killed. Promoted through the ranks until he became Havildar.

'Since that day in Amritsar,' he told Grace, 'I have never harmed a soul, never fired a bullet at anyone, never struck anyone. The more bad-tempered I have pretended to be, the more I showed off my crippled hands, offering no proper explanation, the less likely that anyone would find me out. Find out that on the very day of the terrible killing at Amritsar I made a vow to myself, never to take life again, ever. And I don't know how, but in some way he' – he gestured to Gregory's retreating figure – 'he knows that. He can smell my fear, my fear of killing.'

Calling out from a ridge above them, Molly had made a new find. Grace struggled uphill on all fours and when she got to the flat peak she stood up. They'd made it to the top of a spine of jungle, far higher than anything they'd climbed before, and before them was a great hole in the forest canopy, the trees thinning out, the undergrowth only a few feet high. Grace wondered to herself whether the ridge had been hit by lightning, and a fire had scoured out a clearing in the jungle. Whatever the cause, the consequence was spectacular. For the first time in what seemed like an eternity they could see all around them, as far as the eye could see. Behind them, to the east, ridges of green forest descended to a great plain and there, to the south-east, the Chindwin snaked its way through a gorge, molten silver, glittering in the late-afternoon sun. Ahead, to the west, a great drop, every inch covered by forest canopy, but then the next ridge was only spotted with trees and beyond that just grass, like a meadow in Scotland, rising, rising, until it reached the sky. They were close to the edge of the jungle. And to the north?

Above the jungle canopy, the day was dying but the air was clear, free of low cloud, and they could see an incredible distance. Far, far away, beyond the smudge of green, immense mountains papered the sky brilliant white.

'Look, Miss, is that snow?' asked Molly.

'Yes, Molly, they're the Himalayas, the highest mountains in the whole world. And that, unless I am very much mistaken, is Thibet.'

'Does anyone live there?'

'Why yes, people do live there. They are called Thibetans and their leader is a God-King. They call him the Dalai Lama and he is two thousand years old.'

Immediately below them was a flattish bluff of land, the earth in places bare, populated by wooden huts on spindly stilts. They looked out for strangers, for the hill villagers, but no one seemed to be around. The first sign of humanity Grace saw was a white bandage, bobbing up and down as its wearer walked away from them, hopping over a small stream.

Gregory knelt, scooped water over his face, then looked back at her, stared, and walked off into the bush.

'What is this place?' asked Ruby.

'It looks like a village that's been abandoned.'

'Like a ghost village, Miss?'

'No, dear, not like that all.' But even as she denied it, she could feel her flesh goose-pimple.

They made their beds out in the open, tying their hammocks to the stilts of the abandoned homes. Exhausted by the events of the day, fatigued by the endless questions – 'when will Oomy and Mother come back?' – she worked hard to ensure that the children were fed. The elephant men seemed tense. They dropped off the children's hammocks and elephant baskets and hurried back towards the riverside, some unspoken anxiety troubling them.

To the west, a memory of light. Strange, how the human animal craved the sun's glow, how just a blur of red in the sky warmed the heart. One day their ordeal would end, one day they could snuggle into real beds and wake up in the morning and not have to march another yard. And into this waking idyll entered a face, one that had seldom troubled her day-dreams before, that of Mr Peach.

Damn fool that he was, she knew that he would have seen through Gregory, that his very presence here now would have made her feel safe, secure. She cursed their misfortune, how the elephants had pushed the tree-bridge into the ravine just as they were about to unite. Peach was a silly thing. No, that wasn't right. Before, he had been silly – a damned fool – and melancholic and drunk and unpleasant. But she'd seen him grow, to become an officer with the balls to ignore a foolish order, one that would have caused great suffering to a busload of refugees, one who had the courage to run towards gunfire to try and save his men. She re-read the Japanese poem he had written out for her. Fool that he was, there was something about him, the romance of sending a love poem by paper plane, that made her heart lift.

'Good luck, Mr Peach,' she whispered into the dark.

He came up gasping for air, inhaling oxygen and the gift of life. Peach's brain worked feverishly. If they had meant to kill him, they could have done so far more easily by slitting his throat by the Japanese elephant camp, not go to the bother of dragging him through the countryside. If they meant to interrogate him, where were the Japanese officers? Something else was going on, but what?

Peach felt hands wipe the blood from his face, and a movement behind him in the dark.

By the dim phosphorescent glow from the torrent he saw a man approach him – then, all but lost in the gloom, the outlines of a face. Peach said, 'Hello' in Burmese, the national idiom as spoken in Rangoon, but the man shook his head and gabbled something utterly beyond his comprehension. Clearly, he spoke an impenetrable dialect from this part of High Burma.

No way through this, no way to communicate.

The man offered him a cigarette. One of Peach's many idiosyncrasies was that he couldn't abide smoking. He said, 'No, thank you' in English, then Burmese, then Urdu, and then, just for a laugh, in Japanese.

His captor snapped back in the same tongue: 'How does an Englishman speak Japanese?'

'Badly,' said Peach, and the man laughed.

Peach pressed home his advantage. 'I learnt from a book. And how may I ask, did a Burman learn Japanese?'

'From a whip.'

'Japanese is a beautiful language,' said Peach, 'but the ways of the Imperial Japanese Army are less so.'

'They treat us like slaves. They have been bad to us, and bad to the elephants,' said the Burman.

'You are the leader of the oozies? Yes?'

'No. I am not the leader. But many of us are unhappy with the Japanese. We want to run away.'

'How many are you?'

'Twenty men. Ten elephants.'

Peach did a quick calculation in his head. 'If you help us reach India, I will pay you one hundred thousand rupees for each elephant, one million rupees in total.'

It was a king's ransom. At that moment, Peach's belongings amounted to the clothes he was wearing and a pair of water-logged army boots.

'You promise?'

'On my life.'

'When do we leave?'

'Tonight.'

'Very well. But first we must kill our leader.'

Before the war, Peach would have been greatly troubled at the thought of taking any man's life without a fair trial. Now he did not give the fate of the pro-Japanese oozie a moment's thought.

'The rest of my men, they are hiding by the river,' he told the Burman.

'Yes, we know where they are. In the jungle, they make too much noise. They sound like a herd of love-sick cats.'

'Will the elephants be able to take us across the river at dawn?'

'The river is too strong. But we must. Otherwise, the Japanese will kill us all.'

In his excitement at making a deal with the rebel oozies, Peach had forgotten Eric. Cursing himself for his selfishness, he asked: 'Where is my friend, the other Englishman?'

'He fought too much. We had to knock him on the head. Maybe he is dead, maybe not.'

'Where is he?'

'We left him behind.'

'Bring him to me. Bring him to me now.'

He could sense the oozie hesitate, perhaps at Peach's imperious tone. He tried to think how the other man would react, how his request could make more sense.

'He is my friend. If I do not know for certain that he is dead, then his spirit will trouble me for the rest of my life.'

'We will try. But we need to do many things tonight. To kill our leader, to steal the elephants away from the Japanese.'

'Please...'

'We will try.'

The thought of abandoning Eric in the jungle made Peach sick at heart, but on this, like so much else, he had no choice but to trust the stranger.

A presence loomed in the gathering darkness, the Havildar.

'Miss Grace,' he said, 'the elephants won't move. They are still down by the river. We've tried everything but they won't go anywhere until we find the baby who fell back into the river and the mother who has chased after her calf.'

'What are you going to do?'

'I must take some men and go back, and help find them. Without the missing two, the rest of them will not move. They are like that – they are very loyal to each other. Do you mind staying here, looking after the children, while I find the missing elephants?'

Grace could read the anxiety on his face. He had been placed in charge, and everything had gone wrong. She said yes straightaway, adding: 'Havildar, without you and Sam, the children would have had nothing to eat days ago. Come back soon.'

The Havildar disappeared. She was about to fall into her hammock when, out of the corner of her eye, she sensed something not quite right about Mother's basket. In the darkness it was hard to tell. But she walked over to the basket and was able to make out that the lid of the box was not flat down, not securely fastened. It had been days since she had last peeped inside to check whether everything in the Jemadar's satchel was safe. Hesitantly, kneeling down by the box, she undid the half-locked hasp and opened the lid.

The Jemadar's satchel had gone.

CHAPTER SIXTEEN

Out in the jungle, something was creaking. It sounded metallic, like a rusty door-hinge, and had a bit of weight to it too, but that was wrong, there'd be nothing out there like that. He put out his cheroot and crept out of his den and stood up.

It was the hour before dawn. An astounding number of stars were shining, the jungle far less dense than down in the valleys, the canopy patched with holes, letting in chunks of the night sky. Down the ridge slope, in the opposite direction from the makeshift camp in the ghost village, he could just make out something, a great black cape, blocking out the starlight. That was where the creaking was coming from. Creepy, the sound of it. Not a monkey, not a bird. Could be some bloody insect. No, too loud. It did sound like metal, cracking.

A faint reddening of light to the east.

It was metal an' all. Bloody hell! Realising what he'd found, he stumbled a few feet towards it, but the lianas and stray roots underfoot tripped him. He steadied himself, and pressed on.

They called it The Hump. The Himalayan mountain chain, the roof of the world, an arch over the top of India and Burma to China, above which the transport planes must fly to supply the Chinese with everything, guns, big and little, bullets, shells, grenades, food, drink, medicine, to enable them to keep in the war, to keep the Nationalists fighting the Japanese. Many pilots, the vast majority American volunteers in the Flying Tigers, but some British, Indian and Chinese, perished because their aeroplanes were overloaded and crashed on take-off or iced-up over The Hump or were blown off-course by two hundred mph headwinds or flew head-on into hillsides, blinded by fogs, mist, monsoon rain, snow. There was no radar, no reliable radio, no navigation aids, no night-lights at aerodromes. The pilots were pretty much defenceless, too, against Japanese fighters if they were found by them. But enough planes got through to keep China in the war.

This one hadn't. Gregory recognised the tiger teeth on the nose of the plane from a photograph he'd seen in the papers months ago, and he knew a dead airman when he saw one: here were two. The transport plane had skimmed the jungle canopy rising from the ridge, its left wing torn off, the right wing bent, twisted into a cloak of silver silhouetting against the sky. That's what Gregory had seen against the starlight. The cockpit black with fire, the pilots charred skeletons sat in their seats, waiting for an encore that would never come.

The ridge fell precipitously here, the plane wreck suspended twenty feet above the ground by the nose. Getting into the plane to see what he could loot wasn't going to be easy. A fat liana, tumbling down from a giant teak tree, might be handy. Slashing at it where it met the ground, he hacked away until it came free, and dragged it towards the stump of the left wing and slowly climbed up. The moment he stepped on the wing itself, the whole wreck lurched two feet down, the stressed metal creaking and squeaking, an orchestra in a scrap-metal yard. Funny if he bought it here, inside a smashed plane, after all he'd been through.

In for a penny...

Swinging through an open hatch, perhaps at least one of the crew had managed to bail out, he was inside the fuselage, the metal creaking horribly. The air stank, that sickly, honeyish smell Gregory knew so well. Not much room, the cargo bay piled high with wooden crates, ammo mostly, the calibre of the bullets stencilled on the sides. He squeezed down the aisle, towards the tail. Ah, this was what he was looking for. Prising open a crate with his jungle knife: two Tommy guns, six drums of ammo. Perfect. Could fight a small war with that.

As he worked his way along the cargo bay the coming dawn streaming in through the tail-gunner's Perspex bubble illuminated the stencils on the crates more clearly, and on a stack Gregory read '*Strictly for the household of H.E. Chiang Kai-Shek*'. Opening the top one, he laughed, exhilarated, finding champagne, posh stuff from the label, tins of caviar, pickled gherkins, a jar of Gentleman's Relish. A second crate contained sugar, chocolate bars, tea, tins of pate, ham, salmon, a bottle of fine Scottish malt. Gregory opened the malt, put it to his lips, savouring the tang of smoked peat and pure water. Another swig, and a third, then he replaced the cork and put it back in the crate. If he got sloshed here, he'd never get back to his den.

Down at the very tail of the plane the stink clotted the air. The tail-gunner hadn't survived the landing, his neck jerked backwards at a sickening angle. The dead airman's flesh was a bluey dark green, not quite black, so dead about a month, the discoloured skin revoltingly bloated, as if it might burst at any second. Gregory slipped his hand into the airman's breast pocket, stirring a light fizz of flies, and, yes!, helped himself to a packet of Lucky Strikes and a box of matches.

The crates were too heavy for him to handle as he struggled down the liana, so he dropped them from the hatch. If they smashed open, who cared? The crates landed on the soggy mulch of the jungle floor, pretty much intact. The loot was heavy, and by the time he'd hefted it back to his den he was sweating profusely. Still, it was bloody good going: two tommy guns, six drums of ammo, caviar, pate, champagne, chocolate. The bubbly wouldn't be chilled, but you couldn't ask for everything.

Eyes cast down, submissive, miserable, Emily was waiting for him, kneeling, her weight on her haunches, her hands on her knees.

Sullen bitch. He wanted to slap her, hard, teach her a lesson she wouldn't forget. He was about to strike her, to shake her up a bit, when her eyes slid sideways and in the half-light of the den he made out a leather satchel. Good girl. He didn't care what they thought, so long as they did what he said. Old Mosley had once spoken about some Roman git, who'd said: 'Let them hate, so long as they fear'. Very true, that.

Lowering the crates to the ground, swinging the two tommy guns off his shoulder, he took off a lid, wiped his brow and said: 'I've brought you some caviar and champagne, courtesy of the USA, darling.' The 'darling' was a sneer but, pleased to see the satchel, he worked the cork out of the champagne bottle.

The pop, when it came, was such a surreal sound in the jungle, it made him half-smile. A swig, a belch, not so polite, and he handed her the bottle while he stabbed a tin of caviar with his knife and scooped out a handful of eggs. Salty and black, he couldn't quite see what all the fuss was about. He'd never tasted caviar before.

He passed the tin to Emily who, despite looking famished, only pecked at it, as if it was beneath her. Something about the way her body moved, her frock riding an inch up her thigh as she leant over to scoop up the caviar, aroused him. That, and the very fact of her sullenness, that she was behaving as though having given her body to him she had suddenly seen through his angel looks, that she loathed the very sight of him, that she didn't want to be near him. That aroused him too. Time enough for her, later.

Inside the satchel was a knife with funny designs on the blade, a couple of books – he tossed them to one side – a fading sepia tint of some old tart, not bad-looking, blow me, a medal, the Military Cross, and a thick buff envelope. Inside, he found a series of smaller, hand-addressed envelopes. He opened one and read the contents.

Began to whistle a cheap tune.

'What's that?' asked Emily.

'"Lili Marlene". A song old Jerry likes.'

Taking out one of the tail-gunner's Lucky Strikes, he offered one to Emily, but she declined with a slight shake of her head. He lit up, breathed in the smoke, and read on by the light of the coming dawn. Inhaling deeply, thinking, thinking hard.

These letters could be worth a bob or two, in the right hands. The British wouldn't give him much for them, just a pat on the back, if that.

Who'd have thought it, eh? No wonder the Jemadar and his tart the schoolmarm were whispering about it. What a snake in the grass the Jemadar had turned out to be, eh? He dismissed the stuff about him changing his mind and all, the crucifixion of the British officer, handing the satchel over to Grace. That wasn't going anywhere, that story. Nor was the bloody schoolmarm. She wasn't going to India, full bloody stop, he'd make damn sure of that.

Stroking the snout of the tommy gun, he considered the angles, this way and that. Did he owe His Majesty's Government any favours? No. They'd locked him up, thrown away the key, then sent him off to fight a war in a bloody jungle. It was only down to him that he'd survived. True enough, the old Jemadar's letters would be worth something to the British. But they might be worth much, much more in someone else's hands, and that was a fact. Once he got to India, he could make copies, stash them in a hotel, then get in touch with some of these posh Indians, suggest that if the right amount of money – nah, diamonds – came his way, then no one would hear any more about it. But if they didn't hand over the money, then the Old Bill would get to hear about their treachery and he'd have made copies. They swung for treason in India, same as they did in England. It was risky, but then what way of making money fast wasn't?

Slugging more champagne, he eyed Emily.

'What's happening at the camp?'

Silence.

Reproach, dressed up to try and make him feel sorry for her. He hated it. Why couldn't the bitch stand up for herself, say something. What had got into her?

'You heard me. What's happening back at the camp?'

More silence. He groped towards Emily, and he slapped her twice, hard, on the cheek, and grabbed the worn, dirty fabric of her frock, which tore easily in his hands, revealing her half-naked. Covering her nipples with her hands, she dared not look at him.

'So?'

'The Havildar, he...' Quiet, he could barely hear a word. '...he left last night, to try and find the missing elephants.'

'Who's in charge?'

Silence.

He slapped her again, with all his strength, so powerfully that she fell onto her side.

Piteously soft, the name came out.

He hadn't heard something that funny in years. Alone in charge of a bunch of schoolkids, bloody Grace.

Too bloody funny for words. Grabbing a fistful of Emily's long dark hair, he pulled her down towards him.

Muscle and mind, boys. Muscle and mind would always win through in the end. Right?

'Emily?'

Thunder, the scraping of heaven's chairs, crackled, heavy and low. You could cut the humidity with a knife. The monsoon would come any day now.

'Emily? Emily?' Grace, alone, out beyond the abandoned village, down the slope of the ridge, called for her missing pupil, not too loud, not wanting the whole camp to know the girl had gone missing. She wanted to find Emily herself before sounding the general alarm.

'Emily? Where are you?'

Holding a tommy gun in one hand and a bottle of champagne in the other,

Gregory emerged from behind a stand of teak. Hanging from his shoulder was the Jemadar's satchel. The black snout of the tommy gun motioned to Grace that she should come with him.

There was no point in screaming, she quickly saw. They were too far away from the camp and besides the thickness of the jungle obscured the two of them from the children. With Sam and the Havildar gone, there was little they could do, anyway. But if she went with him now...

Again, he motioned with the gun, for her to follow him.

She stood her ground.

Swigging the champagne – the bubbles left an acrid dryness in his throat, but hell, he hadn't had a drink in ages – he burped and weighed the satchel in his free hand, taunting her.

'That does not belong to you.'

His mouth creased into a grim smile. 'The nigger's, eh?'

She repeated what she had just said.

'Cheeky bitch. He was a traitor, your nigger.'

Silence.

'There's no argument about it.' His left hand scrabbled in the satchel and came out with a fistful of envelopes. 'Look at these. Carrying them, he was.' Reading, he listed some of the addressees, 'All Indians, all traitors. Officers, police chiefs, ooh, look, here's the Chief Prison Officer in Delhi.'

He opened that one, just for the hell of it. The paper was thick to the touch, creamy, expensive. Smoothing out the page, he took in the swastika at the head of the letter, underneath, in English, was written, *Office of the Netaji of a Free All-India.*

Gregory read out loud: '*The Netaji is calling on his trusted supporters, Indians in high positions in the Raj, to overthrow the British on September 3rd, the anniversary of the start of the war. As Chief Prison Officer, the Netaji instructs you to prepare for a mass prison break-out on the day, and in the chaos, to make sure that a list of twenty high security prisoners, all men who have sworn an oath of loyalty to the Netaji, can escape. The Netaji knows he can trust in the honour, blah blah bloody blah, to free India of its hated British oppressors, blah bloody blah.*'

A clap of thunder, softened by distance.

'Your boyfriend, it turns out, was carrying letters for the leader of the Jiffs, the Netaji. Your boyfriend, bitch, was a traitor.'

Silence.

'Do you know where the old Netaji is?'

Silence.

'Here's a clue.' A few bars of 'Lili Marlene', the haunting melody surreal in the baking sun of High Burma. 'Got it?'

Silence.

'Thirty-three Prinz-Albrecht Strasse, Berlin,' he read. 'Ber-lin. That proves it. The boyfriend, a traitor, right?'

Above their heads, a gap in the jungle canopy down which sunlight streamed, igniting motes of dust, spiralling diamonds suspended above the earth. Behind him, in the cave created by the darkness of the black-green shade, was… what? Something moving?

'Know what happens to traitors?' Gregory swayed slightly, and wetted his lips with the champagne.

Nothing, just a trick of the light, a fern rising and falling, ruffled by the light breeze.

'They hang.'

No, again, it moved. Something...

'I shot the traitor, so they'll give me a medal. They'll lock you up, for aiding and abetting the King's enemies.'

'You are quite wrong about that, Sergeant. The Jemadar was no traitor.' She needed, desperately, to keep on talking, to keep his attention, to stop him from turning around. 'He told me to tell the British that the Netaji was in Berlin. What's more, he told me how he got there in the spring of 1941, escaping from house arrest, through Peshawar and Swat, and on to Afghanistan, to Kabul where the Abwehr disguised him as an Italian count. This was when Russia was still on Hitler's side, when Stalin was sending millions of tons of wheat and oil to Germany. Stalin, back then, would do anything for Hitler. The Italian count went by limousine to the north of Afghanistan, across the Oxus by ferry, and on to Dushanbe in Soviet Russia. Then by Siberian Express across half of Russia to Moscow, where he was met by the German Ambassador. From Moscow, a Luftwaffe plane flew him directly to Berlin. He was very special, this Italian count. That's how the Jemadar put it.'

'Traitor.'

'Those letters are proof that the Jemadar was no such thing.'

His face darkened. 'Bitch. You've no idea what you're talking about.'

'Oh yes I have. When the Intelligence people read the letters, they will arrest all the recipients and the Jiff uprising will never happen, thanks to the Jem. But also, now that we know the leader of the Jiffs is in Berlin, we must promise India her independence. He gave those letters to me to give to the British. You stole them. The Jem was no traitor.'

'You would say that. You were fucking him. Traitor's bitch, ain't ya? Little bird told me all about it.'

Not the obscenity, but that *he* knew the truth of it shocked her, revolted her. That *he* should know that she had made love with the Jemadar, the most precious memory of her whole life, was to be defiled, utterly, unutterably.

Who had told him? How did he know? Who had betrayed her?

'Emily.'

It was he could read her mind.

'Little, sweet Emily told me all about it. She heard you and him, heard every last word. There's nothing I don't know about you and him.'

'Oh.'

Life – her life – depended on self-discipline, on keeping her mind level and focused, on keeping him talking for as long as possible. In boasting about Emily's betrayal of her and the Jemadar, she knew he was playing with her mind, she knew he wanted her to explode at him, and as she did so, she knew that she was falling into the trap with eyes wide open. But she could not bear to hold back, not bear to dissemble with him, for a second longer.

'You were not there.' She spat out each syllable, righteous anger in every word. 'You were not there. How dare you speak ill of the Jemadar? You, sir, are a common thief and a common murderer. You shot him in cold blood. You didn't know him. He was a better man than you will ever be. No traitor. He wasn't loyal to nations, to flags. He was loyal to people, loyal to the children, loyal, God help him, to me. He wasn't a traitor. You are.'

He waved the tommy gun at her.

'Don't give me cheek, traitor's bitch. Dance.'

She did not move.

The champagne bottle fell to the ground with a soft clunk, liquid slopping from its lip. Making a great show of cocking his finger, he placed it on the trigger of the tommy gun and pointed the snout directly at Grace.

'Dance.'

She did not move.

'Dance, bitch, or you're dead.'

She did not move.

'I'll count to three. One.'

She did not move.

'Two.'

She did not move.

In the sky above, circling a vulture.

'Thr...'

Exactly as Gregory's finger locked on to the trigger, the champagne bottle whacked him on the side of his head.

Emily's throw was weak. She stood in the grass, ten feet from him, half-dead with self-loathing. Groggy, Gregory rubbed his head with his free hand, recovered his balance, and aimed the tommy gun, first at Emily, then at Grace, back to Emily and hovered in between.

'Dance, bitch, or I'll kill her.'

'Miss, I'm so sorry. I didn't want to tell him. I'm so sorry.'

'Shut it, you tart.'

A simple killer, Grace realised, would have shot them both dead by now but there was something sick about Gregory, the way he found his pleasure in the tension suffered by the dead-to-be. He meant to kill them – of that she had absolutely no doubt – but all in his own time, after his enjoyment.

A slow waltz, the loneliest dance in the whole world, her bedraggled blonde hair, sweaty body and grimy frock, once cream, illuminated in the falling sunbeams. Ten seconds, twenty, an agony of humiliation.

'Take your clothes off.'

The snout of the gun pointed directly at her; behind his back, coming up the slope...

'No.'

'I'll shoot her.'

'You like killing, don't you?'

'Take your clothes off.'

'And prove what? That a man with a gun can terrify an unarmed girl?'

A shudder of bass, thunder.

'Does it excite you, two women at your mercy, helpless? You're going to kill us, aren't you? I can dance for you, make love to you, but still, the killing is the real pleasure for you, isn't it? You'll kill me, kill her, kill the rest of them, won't you? Just like you killed him.'

A school of monkeys chattered to one another, heedless.

'Shut it. Take your clothes off.'

'No.'

Closing her eyes, Grace waited for the inevitable.

A single shot from the tommy gun, and a ruby petal grew between the eyes of Gregory's victim. She sank to the ground, stone dead.

CHAPTER SEVENTEEN

War is all about waiting, thought Peach. Here he was, waiting by the river, waiting for the rebel oozies to return with ten elephants and Eric, alive or dead. Of course, they could betray him, sell him out to the Japanese. But one million rupees was an awful lot of money, far more than the Japanese would ever give them. Too much, thought Mr Peach. If they ever get to India, there will be a terrible argy-bargy with some revolting specimen sitting behind a desk. Well, what could they do? Sack him? Lock him up? Not hand over the money?

Ah, yes, they would do that, all right. But he would write out a receipt for the elephants and give it to the oozies, and keep a copy, and find them the best lawyer in the whole of Bengal to fight their case, and phone up the newspapermen to tell them all about it. On the bright side, he would have turned up with ten elephants and they were worth something, especially in this war. And if a million rupees was the cost of getting his chaps safely out to India, fair enough. And to get word to Grace, that she was in mortal danger. How was she doing? he wondered. She was probably in India already, draining a gin and tonic and relaxing in a cosy chair, flirting with some new victim.

Maybe not.

All he could do was wait.

It was amazing how quietly they could move, these great beasts, through the jungle, even though it was quite pitch-black. The first and second filed passed him, but the third one stopped and he found himself being lifted up high onto the animal's naked back, joining another man sitting behind the oozie.

'Ooh, look what the fucking cat's dragged home,' said a familiar voice.

'How is your head, Sergeant-major?'

'It hurts. Some bastard whacked me hard enough to send me to Kingdom Come. But here I am. Bloody hell, I don't know how long this is going on for, but it's bloody uncomfortable sitting here, legs akimbo.'

'Sssh, Sergeant-major, sssh.'

Peach hissed 'Sheffield United'.

Nothing moved.

Then a voice growled: 'It's Sheffield bloody Wednesday, yon idiot. I almost blew your head off.'

Their little group of nine men were reunited, but they had the river to cross, a ferocious boiling mass of water plummeting down from the mountains. The oozies had had to abandon all the elephant gear when they vanished from the Japanese camp so the animals could not be tethered together. However, they lined up the elephants, two-by-two, in five rows. Just before they were about to cross, one of the elephants whinnied in fear, and tried to pull away. Dawn was beginning to break, and everyone knew that the Japanese would very soon realise that something was wrong – and that the only direction the oozies would have taken was to the west. There was no time to lose. Desperately, the oozie urged the panicking elephant to calm down, whispering into his ear until finally the animal turned back and, an immense mass of bone and muscle, the ten elephants and their human cargo began to ford the river, the force of the current threatening to knock them sideways at every step. The light was brightening with every second – brighter out in mid-stream where the jungle canopy didn't over-hang - and Peach felt horribly exposed. The water leapt up the flanks of the elephant carrying him and the sergeant-major, soaking them, but still the great beast plodded on. Two thirds of the way across was another islet. Bamboo parted, and they heard a high-pitched squeak as a tiny baby elephant emerged.

The bigger elephants appeared to cluck and mother him. A she-elephant wrapped her trunk around the little one's head, and soon the whole caravan was swimming across the final third of the river. Here, the current was at its fastest and most treacherous but they made the bank, slogged up its steep side and were safe, for the time being. All they had to do now was keep one step ahead of the Japanese, and find Grace and the others before it was too late. From the direction of the sun, Peach reckoned they had saved maybe half a day's march on where he thought the rest of the party might be. But there was no hurrying the elephants. They ploughed through the jungle, steady and slow, the little one squeaking and parping, calling out to its lost mother.

Two hours' marching later on, there was a great crash and splintering of bamboo, and Mother burst through. The reunion of Mother and baby was one of the most touching things that Peach had ever seen, the old lady's trunk ruffling the red-brown fuzz of hair on his back, then entwining her trunk with his. Burbling with joy, baby plugged into her teat.

'Booger me, that's a story to tell the bairns,' said the sergeant-major, and Peach could not but agree.

Soon they met up with a great Sikh with crippled hands. He was delighted to see Mother and baby reunited, but his face darkened when Peach asked him the whereabouts of Grace and Gregory. The Sikh led the way, Peach by his shoulder, pounding through the jungle. Strangely, Mother and Oomy kept up, as if they too shared Peach's worst fears.

'No.' The sound came from the survivor, soft, almost beyond the edge of hearing. She dropped down and knelt, holding the lifeless head in her hands, uselessly.

'I told you, didn't I?' said Gregory plaintively.

'Oh, no,' she repeated, kissing the hair on top of the victim's head.

'Your decision, love.'

The good and the beautiful die, and the people left alive know only one thing for certain, that they do not deserve to breathe, that life is some absurd and cruel gift, granted by a malign idiot. Not that she would live long. Gregory had her in his power, and she knew that soon he would become bored and shoot her too. And there was nothing she could do to stop him. For him, killing was as simple and natural and necessary as breathing. Someday, the good people might catch up with him but so far Gregory's luck had proved stronger than justice. In front of him, human decency seemed to shrivel and die.

He raised the tommy gun straight at her chest and started to smile. An evil smile. Was this to be her last ever thought?

There was a grey blur, a thud, a sickening crack, the sound of a branch snapping in two. The jungle, for once still, the quiet broken by gargling from a blood-frothed throat; the mouth spurting bright red. She hated Gregory more than she had ever hated anyone or anything in her whole life, but she could not but wince.

Flies immediately settled on the blood-flecked mouth, black, green, iridescent; beyond them, fuzzy, out-of-focus, men, and then one man hurtling towards them, his absurdly long legs bounding through the jungle, other British soldiers following him, then more elephants, ridden by oozies she did not recognise at all.

Peach took in the scene, Grace nuzzling the schoolgirl with a bullet through her brain, surreally beautiful in death, the sergeant on the ground, face down, dead, gripping a tommy gun in one hand, a letter with a swastika on it close by, the paper rustling in the light morning breeze, spotted with blood. A few yards off, a baby elephant suckling his mother, the latter's eyes blinking in quiet ecstasy, a splash of red on one of her front feet.

'Grace!' There was something intense about the way he said her name.

She kissed the forehead of the dead girl.

'Christ, Grace, I'm so sorry.'

'He should have shot *me*. He had no reason to kill her.'

'Grace, it's not your fault.'

Kneeling, Peach held her, as she held the dead girl, locking together the living and the dead.

After a time Peach motioned to the killer on the jungle floor, his bloody mouth already black with flies.

'How?'

'Mother,' said Grace.

'What?'

'The mother elephant. She knocked him down and I heard the sound of his spine breaking.'

'Why?'

Grace explained 'We'd been climbing out of a riverbed. I believe Gregory deliberately cut the cradle they were using to haul the baby out of the river. He fell back into the water and disappeared. Mother got her own back.'

'No.' The story affronted Peach's sceptical intelligence.

Mother nuzzled her baby, as peaceably as any living thing.

'Is she capable of revenge?'

'Yes, Bertie, I do believe she is. Gregory did wrong by her baby. That's all.'

The elephant men started digging two graves, one for the killer, one for his sometime lover. They buried the two bodies far apart, Emily in a little dip, open to the sky, kissed by sunlight, with a view of the setting sun to the west; Gregory in a dank bog, the shallowest of graves, the big toe of his right foot, blue-grey, peeping through the soil. Two bits of wood tied together made a cross for Emily; nothing for Gregory.

Over Emily's grave, Peach said the Lord's Prayer in a dull, official's voice. As he did so, Grace wept soundlessly; Ruby sobbed Emily's name out loud again and again, shrieking, until the Havildar gently hugged her into silence. The other children stood mute.

Then they left.

They walked in silence for hours.

But eventually the rhythm of the journey took over, and besides, Peach had his duty to learn what the enemy was planning. In late afternoon they stumbled across a fossilised oyster-bed, a thousand miles from the sea.

They stared at the coils of rock while Peach summoned up the courage to raise the subject of the letter with the swastika on it.

'That letter. It was from Bose. Have you any more?'

'About a dozen.'

'Bloody hell. How on God's earth did you get hold of this stuff, here, in the middle of the Burmese jungle? It's from Berlin. Bose is in Berlin. Of all the places on earth, what's it doing here?'

'Long story.'

'Grace, I know you think I'm a bloody fool but I happen to be an Intelligence Officer and I can't just produce this and they ask, "Where did you get it?" and I say, "Long story". It just won't do.'

As they walked on, she told him all of it, her love affair with the Jem, how he had confessed to her that he had been a Jiff, his horror at discovering the true ambitions of the Japanese, giving her the letters, how Gregory had killed him at the ferry crossing on the Chindwin and how eventually Gregory had found out about them from Emily and stolen them.

'He called the Jem a traitor.'

'The Indian chap on the motorbike, escorting the bus? Crossed the Irrawaddy with you?'

'Yes, that's him.'

'I remember thinking... These letters, they are pure gold. I'll recommend the Jem for a medal. Posthumous, of course, so it won't make a damn bit of difference to him, but his family might appreciate it.'

'I'm not quite sure they will, Bertie.'

'Oh.'

'His grandfather is in jail.'

'One of ours?'

'Yes.'

'The Jem will get his medal. They can always throw it back at us. I probably would.'

Two scouts from Sam's party found them. With the help of the scouts, the elephant party arrived at the foot of the rock in the last hour before sunset.

Sam was struck dumb by their news, the murder of Emily, the killing of Gregory. He closed his eyes and held his head in his hands for a time.

'I let you down,' he told Grace.

'Sam, we would all of us be dead without you. It's no one's fault. Or rather, it's all of our faults.'

He was overjoyed to see that Peach had brought with him ten more elephants. But he had news of his own and it was grim.

'We can pass, but not the elephants. The track's not wide enough. We're going to have to abandon the elephants. Or risk losing them to the Japanese. Or shoot them.'

Grace asked to borrow his binoculars. The rock glowed a darkening pink with the dying of the light.

'Sandstone,' she said.

'So?'

Close by, an outcrop of rock punched through the green mattress of the jungle floor. Grace asked, 'May I borrow your knife?'

'Yes, but what are you doing?'

'This rock is sandstone. Watch.'

She took the heavy dah, raised it over her head and slashed down into the side of the rock. It didn't bounce off, as Sam expected, but bit into the rock, surprisingly deeply. She pulled the knife out, and slashed again, at a different angle. Three more cuts and a lump of rock fell away, leaving a rough bite out of the rock, like a quarter-moon.

'I didn't teach all that geography for nothing,' said Grace. 'You can carve sandstone.'

'Are you sure?'

'You can sculpt it, carve it, shape it. We can shape the rock so that the elephants can pass.'

'What a bloody marvellous example of the fair sex you are.'

'It will be as hard to work with as frozen butter.'

'You bloody marvel. You bloody marvellous girl. If I weren't so old, I'd kiss you. Havildar! Havildar! Where's that bloody Sikh? Havildar, get twenty men with dahs, now, and lights, torches. We'll work through the night.'

'Me too,' said Grace.

'But you're just a girl.' Sam regretted saying it as soon as he had opened his mouth. 'I thought you might be a little afraid.' She gave the elephant man such a look of scorn. 'Yes, of course you will. I don't know what I was thinking.'

'Miss Collins isn't afraid of a Bengal Tiger,' said the Havildar, wiggling his two-and-a-half fingers.

The moon rose behind them them as they clambered up the rock, framing a tusker against its silvery disc. 'Elephant Moon,' said Grace, and brushed her hand against Peach's.

They laboured as the wind hissed and whistled, carving the sandstone. When the moon sank, they carried on working by feel and touch, rather than seeing, occasionally lighting small fires which cast eerie shadows against the rock. To one side was a chasm, unseen, black, to the other, the rockface at its narrowest. They chipped away with jungle knives and sharp-edged rocks. As dawn broke, the grey light revealed their work.

'What do you think?' asked Grace.

'You might be able to squeeze a thinnish pig, the runt of the litter, along here,' said Peach. 'But there's not enough room for an elephant.'

After they were relieved by a fresh roster of elephant men, Sam sought out Peach.

'The rearguard.'

'Is there one?'

'No. We kind of mislaid it, back at that ravine.'

'We'll handle that,' said Peach.

'Get some rest for an hour or two. And then–'

'Five miles down the track?'

'Yes. Good luck.'

Grace and Peach began the descent back to the camp. When they reached the jungle floor they walked off the main path for a distance and came to sit on a mossy bank to catch their breath. Sunlight cast threads of golden light against the higher treetops, while rags of mist still drifted this way and that, drawing a curtain between them and the world. It was the first time they had been alone together since they had met at Government House in Rangoon, when he had been obnoxiously drunk.

'I feel so guilty,' said Grace, 'so guilty to be alive.'

'You shouldn't.'

'I didn't used to believe in evil. But I do now.'

'Yes. There doesn't seem to be another explanation. I still don't quite believe that an elephant deliberately killed a man. They seem such gentle creatures.'

'They're gentle, that's true, Bertie. But they're more like us than you think. They joke around, they get angry, they remember.'

He fell silent. Sunlight slid down the tree trunks, burning off the mist, igniting the light in her eyes, the oval beauty of her face framed against the dank green-blackness of the jungle behind her.

An awkwardness between them.

'Did you love him, the Jemadar, very much?'

'Yes.'

'Oh.'

He was soon to go back down the track, towards Burma, towards the Japanese. He might never come back, he might die like all the others, the hanged planter, the refugees by the roadside, Miss Furroughs, Allu, the Jemadar and Emily.

Part of her was utterly afraid, afraid that this love too would end with a bullet in the throat. Did she love Peach? Not as much as she should, as she had loved the Jem. But there was something pitiful about his 'oh' – so full of frustrated desire and unquenched lust and human need that touched her.

'Come here, you damned fool.' Her fingers lightly brushing his shoulders, running down his chest, undoing the buttons of his shirt. The touch of her fingers on his skin made him shudder, as if she had whipped him with an electric live wire, and the aching hunger of his desire was matched by her unfathomable lightness of spirit, masking the guilt rippling through her.

When they were done he rolled off her and lay on his back and started to laugh, a rich deep sound, like a big Atlantic wave crashing into a shingly beach.

'What?' She was a little taken back, a trifle angry.

'I've dreamt about this, about us making love, about you and me, a thousand times. Since that very first time.'

'There was a lizard on the wall. I had come to complain about a man reading *Mein Kampf*.'

'A Burmese in a suit. Wearing glasses. Great description.'

'You still haven't explained. Why laugh?'

'Well, after all that effort, chasing you around Rangoon and up the length of Burma, and all the people we've lost, I finally get to make love to you. This is the greatest moment in my entire life.'

'So why are you laughing?'

'Because I am lying in elephant dung.'

And when he put a hand underneath his bottom and it came out with a handful of tangy elephant muck she started to laugh too, lost in the pure absurdity of the moment. Right then, she began to believe that Peach could be her man.

An hour later she woke up to find him dressed and ready to go.

'Rearguard duty. No problem. I'm sure the Japanese have given up long ago.'

'The truth?'

'They don't give up very easily. But fingers crossed, they've gone.'

She kissed him hungrily, then they hurried down to the main elephant camp where the children and the oozies eyed them with comic knowingness. Peach and his Sergeant-major left to head back down their track, east, him turning to her and waving shyly just before he disappeared from view. For the first time in a long time she closed her eyes and made a prayer, to the God of Love, that, of all the thousands who had died on the road of this terrible journey, Bertie Peach would make it back, whole.

It was hard, exhausting work, sawing and chopping, levering out a few inches of rock at a time. But the elephant men knew what was at stake and they were relentless. At times, their jungle knives would snap in two, at others the wind, soughing down from the Himalayas, would gather force and they were compelled to lie flat and grip the rock lest they be blown over the side to a certain death hundreds of feet below.

The slenderest of eclipses grew and grew as the elephant men fought against the rock, wider and deeper, higher and bigger.

By the end of the day the Havildar came down from the rock, his beard coated in sandstone dust.

'Well?' asked Sam.

'It will still be a squeeze for the bigger elephants. '

'But possible?'

'So long as they breathe in. Yes.'

'Fingers crossed, eh, Havildar?' It was a joke that Sam risked only when he knew the Havildar was in a very good mood.

'When do we start?'

'The hour before dawn.'

To begin with, everything went beautifully to plan. Henry VIII, led by Po Toke gently holding his ear, ascended the land-slip in the half-light before sunrise, one footfall at a time, until they reached the flattish start to the goat-track. Sam, superstitious, decided to walk on ahead, to the other side of the narrow path sculpted by the Havildar and his men.

He waited an eternity of time – or so it felt like, to him – but eventually he caught sight of the magnificent tusker rounding the bend, his enormous belly scraping against the freshly sculpted rock wall, and hundreds of feet far below, an eagle spiralling on a thermal. Then came Po Toke, who gave Sam an enormous wink, and behind him, Matthew, Mark, Luke and John, Claude, Ragamuffin, Nebuchadnezzar, and all the other elephants following steadily, their oozies on foot. He stood and counted every single one go past him. Forty-five adults and eight calves, fifty-three in all, the last being little Oomy, trotting on behind Mother, her aching leg muscles shivering with fatigue.

After the elephants passed him, he heard a snatch of something on the wind. It died, and came again, stronger this time, all the stranger and more moving because it was sung here, far above an alien jungle, on one of the highest points on the India-Burma border south of Thibet itself, so utterly, eerily, out of place:

'Meadowsweet and lady smocks

Gentian, lupin and tall hollyhocks
Roses, foxgloves, snowdrops, forget-me-nots
In an English country garden.'

Bishop Strachan's filed past, Joseph in a litter hanging from bamboo poles carried by two oozies, Ruby with Molly and Michael, and last, Grace, and every single one of them grinned at Elephant Sam as he looked on, upon a peak in Burma. Not one child looked down at the appalling drop a few feet away. They were all too busy singing, singing their hearts out.

The chatter of machine-guns rang out across the mountain. The Japanese were on their tails, again. The children hurried on towards India, but going back down the track at a tremendous rate was the Havildar, carrying a rucksack heavy with grenades. The plan had been simple. Once the rearguard, made up of Peach's men, appeared and climbed past the narrow ledge of the goat-track, they were going to blow a bloody big hole in the mountain, making it impossible for any Japanese to follow in their footsteps.

More gunfire from below, from where they'd just come. The children quickened their pace. Sam took the rucksack from the Havildar and the two men started placing the grenades in the holes that had already been drilled, prior to demolishing the track. He looked up and scowled.

'Grace, you need to be with the children. We're going to blow the track.'

'Sam,' the Havildar grunted and vanished back down the narrow path.

'Grace, you must go. The children need you. We're going to blow the track.'

'Let me...'

'What now, for Christsakes?'

The Havildar returned, panting. 'No sign of Peach. Six, seven Japs, coming up the track. Behind them, another thirty, half a mile back, with dogs. Moving fast.'

'Well, let's blow the bloody thing to Kingdom Come. Grace, you must go.'

'You've got to wait for Peach,' said Grace flatly.

'Enough,' cut in Sam.

'Wait for him. You must!'

'Please don't fool around,' said Sam.

'Hold the demolition! Don't blow the track. You need to double-check.'

'I'll go and check,' said the Havildar.

'No, God help me, I will,' said Grace, and before they could stop her she was gone around the bend, towards the Japanese.

'That bloody woman!' cried Sam, taking the binoculars and following her around the ledge. The wind was freshening, and began to whistle sourly through the chiselled half-tunnel.

Down below they could see the Japanese, unmistakable in their uniforms of burnt ochre, climb up the land-slip.

'You see Grace, we've got no choice.'

There came a ragged burst of fire, and it was the turn of the Japanese to scatter. Five British soldiers emerged from cover at the very top of the land-slip and started to run uphill. None of them was especially tall.

'Once these chaps are through, we've got no choice.'

More gunfire, then a small barrel of a man appeared, giving a piggyback ride to a daddy-long-legs of a man, moving with unbearable slowness.

The first of the Yorkshiremen arrived at the neck of the narrow gap, gasping for air. He turned round, aimed his rifle at the Japanese, and started firing. Two, three, four, five men made it. The barrel-man and his gangly burden were still hobbling towards them.

The Havildar disappeared, rattling down the slope at an astonishing speed for such a big man. He reached the pair, shouldered the tall man and began racing up towards them, followed closely behind by the sergeant-major.

A bullet hiss-cracked overhead, a second slammed into the rock beneath them, sending shards of sandstone spinning down to the jungle floor below.

They ducked, backing into the shadow of the half-tunnel, and had barely come to rest when the giant Sikh appeared carrying Lieutenant Herbert Peach, his face a deathly green, his right calf a porridge of skin and blood and bone.

'Bertie!'

'They shot him up, Miss,' said the sergeant-major. 'Not sure he's going to make it.'

The wound to his leg was ugly. Sam looked grim, shook his head. 'Not good. May lose the leg. May lose him. There's some new medicine, pencillin they call it. Might fix it, but we need to get him to a hospital fast. Once we're in India.'

Peach groaned, opened his eyes, saw Grace, and said with limpid clarity: 'Grace, about that glass of champagne...'

And then he passed out. More bullets whined past their heads, chipping the rock.

'Everybody out of here, NOW!' shouted Sam.

They all ran through the half-tunnel to the far side. Sam had wired the grenades together, so that with one yank of the wire, the whole lot would go up. At least, that was the theory. He counted to thirty, giving the others enough time to climb further up, flattened his belly to the ground, pressed his head into the rock and pulled.

EPILOGUE

There was not that much to running a tea estate, really. The sun shone, the rain fell, the tea bushes did their trick. You had to keep an eye on the accounts, make sure the schoolteacher didn't brainwash everybody with talk of the Mahatma, look out that the chaps and the ladies were paid, fair and square, especially the tea-pickers for their back-breaking work, keep the cricket pitch flat – he'd managed to purloin a cast-iron roller, his pride and joy – and that was pretty much it. No, there was not much drama to running a tea estate, even one on the very far eastern edge of India. At least, that's what Mr McGregor thought until one afternoon in May 1942 at half-past four, just before the monsoon broke. He was enjoying a cuppa on his verandah when the biggest elephant he had ever seen came clumping up his drive, eating his hydrangeas on the run, on its back a pannier full of half-caste kids and a bloody white woman to boot.

Behind the monster came a whole long line of more elephants, dozens of them, snacking on his tea, trampling over his prized garden.

The monster stopped, half-buckled and the woman and the children tumbled out. She was blonde, needed a good wash from the look of her, and started yelling at him.

'I'm sorry to intrude, sir' – she spoke rather nicely, considering her attitude towards hygiene – 'but may I ask, have you a telephone?'

'Yes, of course,' shouted Mr McGregor. 'Would you care for some tea?' Of that, they had an elegant sufficiency.

The line was ghastly, a stew of hisses and crackles, but finally, she heard a clipped voice: 'Dugdale.'

No time for introductions, the line could die at any moment.

'Bose, he's in Berlin.'

'My word. What's your evidence?'

'Twelve letters to Jiff sympathisers from his address in Berlin, personally signed by Bose himself. To be hand-carried to the recipients by messenger, to launch an uprising against the British in September.'

'And have you got the letters?'

'Yes.'

'Who the hell are you?'

'Grace Collins, schoolteacher, formerly of Rangoon, only daughter of Alfred Collins, of HM Treasury. Sir, we have a British officer with us, he wrote a report on the Jiffs. He's dying, he was shot by the Japanese, he needs penicillin.'

'How did you get hold of these letters?'

'They were given to me,' Grace could scarcely bring herself to finish the sentence, 'by Bose's personal messenger, the courier. A Jiff who turned against the Japs.'

'Where is he?'

'Dead. Murdered. He wanted me to tell you.'

The line creaked and howled.

'What?'

'He wanted me to tell you that he wanted an independent India. With Bose in Berlin, we must promise independence.'

'That's for upstairs, Miss Collins.'

'Then you must tell upstairs. You must promise.'

'I promise I will. Where the hell are you?'

She told him the name of the tea estate.

'How did you get there from Burma?'

'By elephant.'

A weird knocking on the line, a fizz, then his voice, more clearly than before: 'What did you say?'

'E-L-E-P-H-A-N-T.'

'Is that bugger Sam Metcalf anything to do with this?'

'Yes, he's brought fifty-three elephants into India. He can't talk on the phone because he's still a little deaf. He blew up half a mountain to stop the Japanese from following us.'

'Typical. Officially, he's been dead for two months. Tell Sam we've got a new boss, name of Slim. He's good. And tell him we've stopped losing to the

Japs. What's the name of the injured officer, the one who wrote the report on the Jiffs?'

'Peach. Lieutenant Peach. Bertie Peach.'

'Ah, yes, Colonel Handscombe's told me all about him.'

'Good?'

'No, all bad.'

'Oh dear.'

'Don't worry. Handscombe's a moron. Can't wait to meet Peach. I'll get the penicillin. Need those letters from Bose. Where's the nearest airstrip?'

She asked McGregor, who told her the name of a town.

'How far is that?'

'One hundred miles away.'

She told Dugdale.

'That's too far. Make one.'

'What?' It was her turn to be incredulous.

'Ask the elephants nicely to roll around on their bottoms and you'll have an airstrip in no time. Three hundred yards long. No bumps. Got that? We'll land at nine o'clock tomorrow morning. I'll bring a quack with me, and a bucket of penicillin.'

'What if—'

'Winston wants to know where Bose is, has been driving everyone mad about it, always "Where's Bose?" No bumps. See you in the morning. Bye.'

They worked through the night, the estate lit by hurricane lights, Henry VIII, Matthew, Mark, Luke and John and the others expanding the cricket pitch, uprooting the tea bushes, the animals taking turns to flatten the ground with the roller. Oomy tried to help but really he just got in the way. By sunrise, the tea estate boasted the smoothest landing strip in the whole of Bengal.

Sam looked in on the patient lying in the McGregors' guest bedroom, with a view east, looking at the high country from which they had come. Grace was nursing him, dabbing his feverish skin with cold water, but the infection was gaining on him. The elephant man unpeeled the make-shift bandage, revealing the sorry mess of his right leg. The foot was beginning to go a pale green.

He shook his head. 'The leg has to be amputated, I'm afraid.'

'Can you do it?'

'I'd rather not. I do elephants, not humans.'

'Can it wait?'

'No. If the foot is going gangrenous, the blood poisoning could kill him in hours.'

'So?'

Sam sighed, closed his eyes. 'I'll do it.'

He took off Peach's right leg, below the knee. After he had finished making a tourniquet for the amputated stump, Grace glanced at Sam. He shrugged: 'That's the best I can do. He might pull through. We need that penicillin.'

She soothed Peach's brow with a damp rag, and kissed him on the lips and said: 'Stay with us, you damned fool.'

A murmur outside, and she raised her head to look out of the window to see the entire school watching, silent in sympathy.

At nine o'clock sharp, they heard the drone of an aeroplane engine, rising and falling. The pilot turned to his first officer, saying 'Looks like a bloody zoo down there' and tilted the wing, losing height with every second.

THE END

AUTHOR'S NOTE

This is a work of fiction, but the story of the elephant men rescuing refugees from Burma after the Fall of Rangoon in 1942 is true. Two men in particular stand out: J. H. Williams, author of *Elephant Bill*, a wonderful read, part natural history, part epic trek out of Burma, over the mountains, and Gyles Mackrell, whose film of his elephants braving raging waters to save desperate men has recently been put on YouTube by Cambridge University. The Jiffs failed. Burma was liberated from Japanese rule by the Fourteenth Army, but India, Pakistan and Burma got their independence from the British. Bose came to a sticky end, jumping from Japan to the Soviet Union at the end of the war, before being swallowed up in the Gulag lest he tell tales about the time when Stalin toasted the Nazis with champagne.

This book is dedicated to the memory of the refugees, including children very much like the ones imagined in this book, and to the bravery of the elephant men and their elephants, who did their best to save them.

John Sweeney, London, 2012